AXE COP

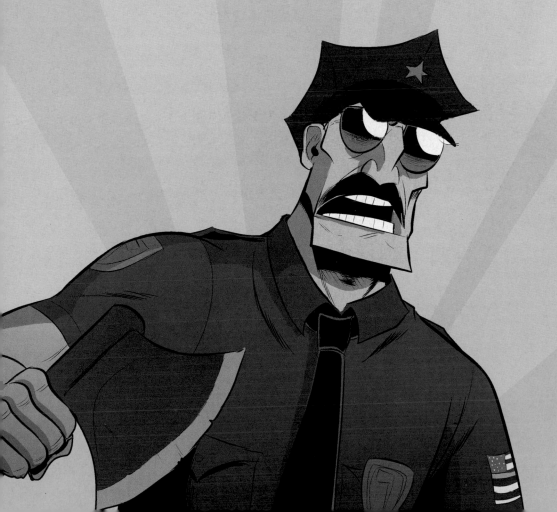

WRITTEN BY **MALACHAI NICOLLE (AGE 6)**
DRAWN BY **ETHAN NICOLLE (AGE 30)**
COLORS BY **DIRK ERIK SCHULZ (AGE 27)**
COVER PENCILLED BY **ETHAN NICOLLE**
COVER PAINTED BY **DAVE RAPOZA**

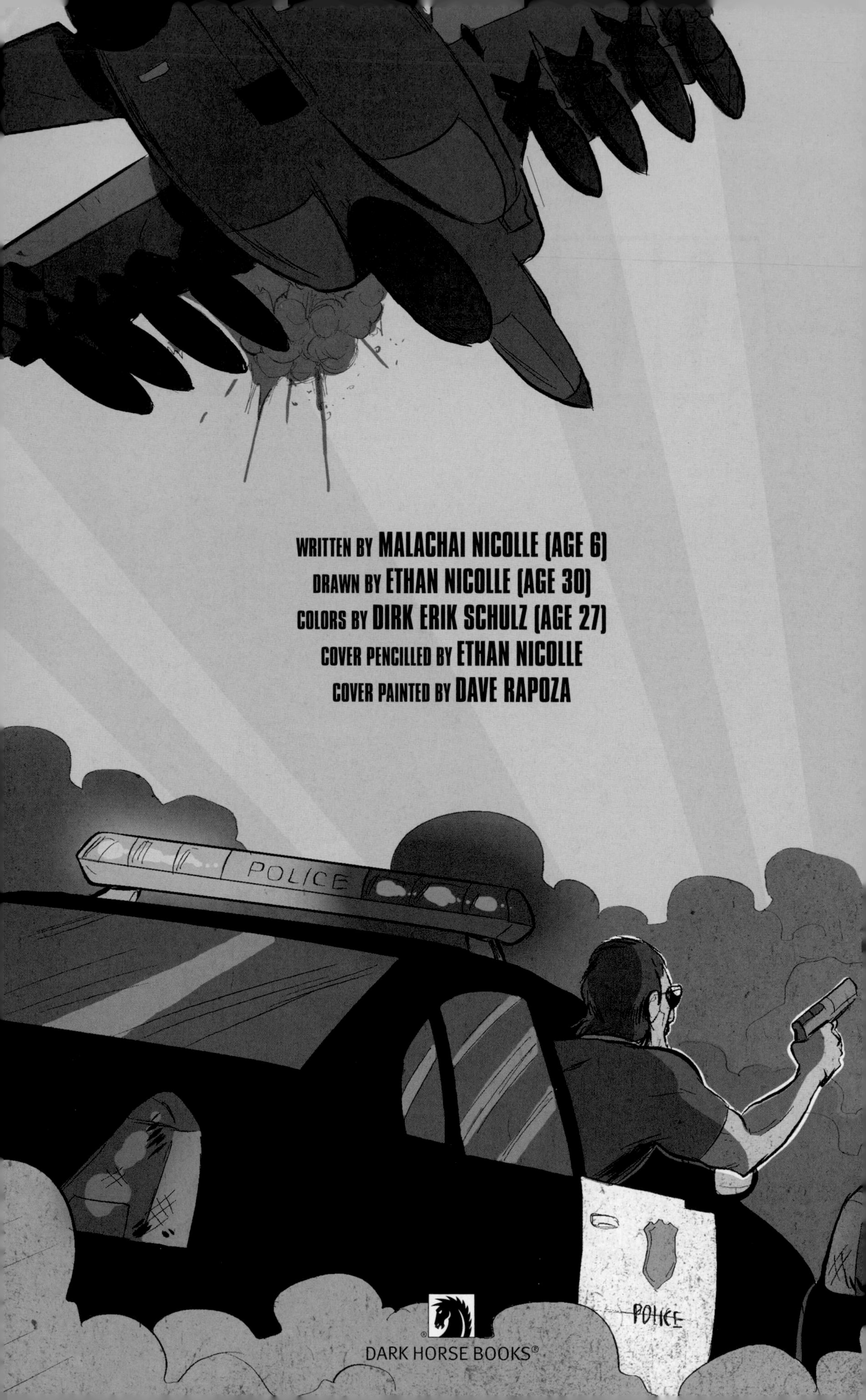
POLICE
POLICE

DARK HORSE BOOKS®

AXE COP™

BAD GUY EARTH

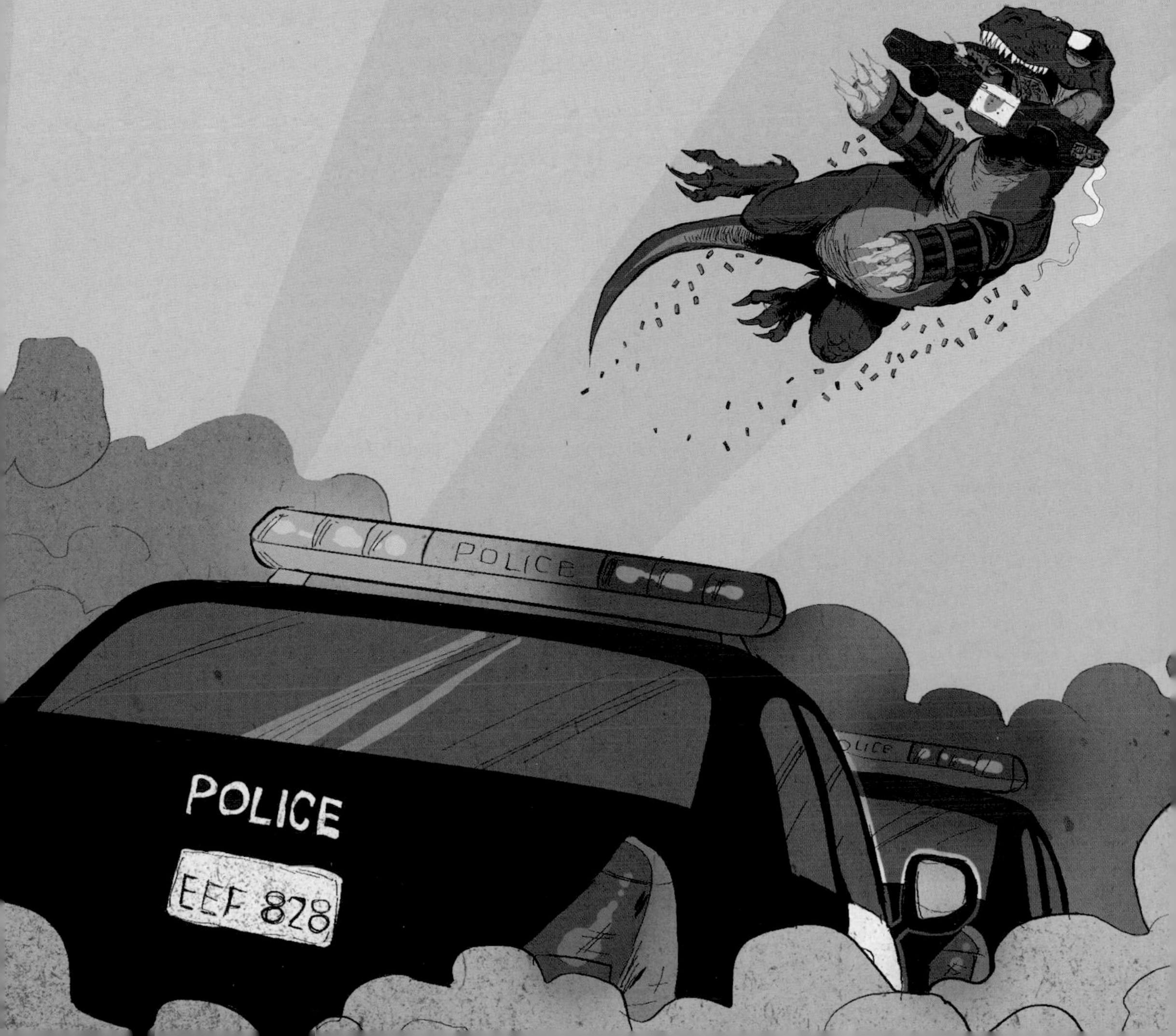
POLICE
POLICE
EEF 828

**MALACHAI AND ETHAN DEDICATE THIS BOOK TO
THEIR BEST FRIENDS, BRAYDEN AND DOUG.**

PRESIDENT AND PUBLISHER **MIKE RICHARDSON**
EDITOR **SHAWNA GORE**
ASSOCIATE EDITOR **RACHEL EDIDIN**
DESIGNER **KAT LARSON**

Published by Dark Horse Books
A division of Dark Horse Comics, Inc.
10956 SE Main Street
Milwaukie, OR 97222

DarkHorse.com   AxeCop.com

First edition: October 2011
ISBN 978-1-59582-825-5

3 5 7 9 10 8 6 4 2

Printed at Midas Printing International, Ltd., Huizhou, China

AXE COP VOLUME 2: BAD GUY EARTH

INTRODUCTION

The awesome and ridiculous adventure into which you're about to jump is the result of an experiment. And like a lot of experiments, this one was conducted with a combination of scientific curiosity and gut-level instincts about the elements involved. Here's what we knew going into the creation of Axe Cop: Bad Guy Earth: we had one hilarious six year-old with a ballistic imagination (Malachai Nicolle), one extremely talented older brother/ cartoonist (Ethan Nicolle), and the incredibly goofy cast of characters they created together while making the hit web comic Axe Cop.

This eclectic combination worked in spades with the weekly Axe Cop comic strips that Ethan began posting online in January 2010. Those earliest Axe Cop adventures were not only boundless in terms of the imaginative stories they told, they were also boundless in terms of . . . you know, boundaries. Physical and spatial ones. Like the kind of boundaries—and requirements—that come with creating comic stories for print.

When Ethan drew the first few Axe Cop comics, he had no expectation or intention that they would ever see print. He drew them for his family and friends based on Malachai's wonderfully silly idea for a make-believe game while they were spending family time together at Christmas. Malachai, who was six at the time, gave Ethan the choice of being "Axe Cop" and using a toy fireman axe for a weapon, or being "Flute Cop" and brandishing a little plastic music-class recorder against whatever nefarious bad guys might come marauding out of their combined imaginations.

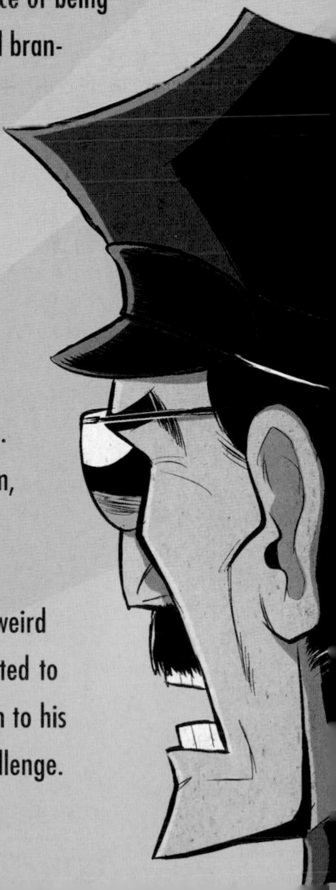

The resulting comics were as freeform as they were hysterically funny. The first "episode" was the equivalent of a single standard comic-book page, the second was a little longer, and each subsequent comic Ethan drew was however long it needed to be to depict the impossible scenarios the brothers concocted. This unpredictability is part of the charm of those early stories. Whenever the thousands of eager Axe Cop fans clicked back to AxeCop.com, there might be eight new panels of story posted . . . or forty.

But what worked so well for wooing readers online sounded like it might be a weird fit for a print comic-book series. Luckily for me and everyone else who wanted to see the series happen, Ethan—who already had one Eisner Award nomination to his name and the work ethic of a team of bionic Clydesdales—was up for the challenge.

Before committing to the series, we decided Ethan should spend enough time with Malachai to determine if there was enough fun and adventure left in the play world of Axe Cop to fuel a story that would span three issues. And if the potential adventures were there, along with the same gleeful enthusiasm that powered the creation of the original strips, Ethan knew he'd have what he'd need to fill a miniseries.

You're reading the introduction to this book right now, so obviously our little experiment worked. In fact, at the back of this book, you'll find a detailed look at the entire creative process that Ethan documented while working on Bad Guy Earth so you can see for yourself that the experimental part of getting so much amazing storytelling genius out of one wacky kid isn't as mysterious or unlikely as it might seem.

The unlikely part isn't that a sweet, hilarious, and bright kid with a maniacal imagination and a big heart is the creative force behind a hit comic-book series and web comic/media empire. What's truly unlikely and remarkable here is that this awesome kid has such an amazing older brother, one whose capacity to love and appreciate his littlest brother is possibly only transcended by his creative talents.

While Malachai's fantastic ingenuity is the source of the very genesis of Axe Cop, Dinosaur Soldier, Wexter, the Psychic Planet, the Bad Guy Machine, and every other wonderful thing there is to love about this book, Axe Cop the comic wouldn't exist for the rest of us if it weren't for Ethan. Cartoonists who are as astute as Ethan are rare, as are belly laughs like the ones you'll enjoy while reading this book. While funny, brilliant little kids aren't necessarily all that rare (I'm pretty sure most kids have some kind of magic-minded creative impulse), it's not every day we remember or acknowledge that fact. Indeed, it's unusual for most people to even really listen to children while we're puttering around doing our grown-up things. I'm overjoyed that there's one grown up—one phenomenally talented grown-up brother—who's listening.

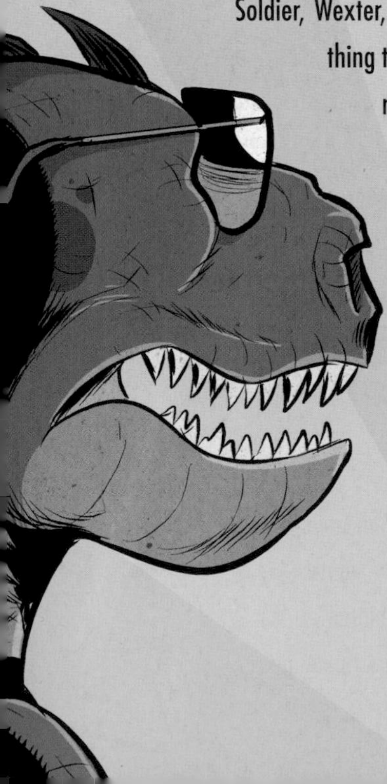

Shawna Gore
May 20, 2011

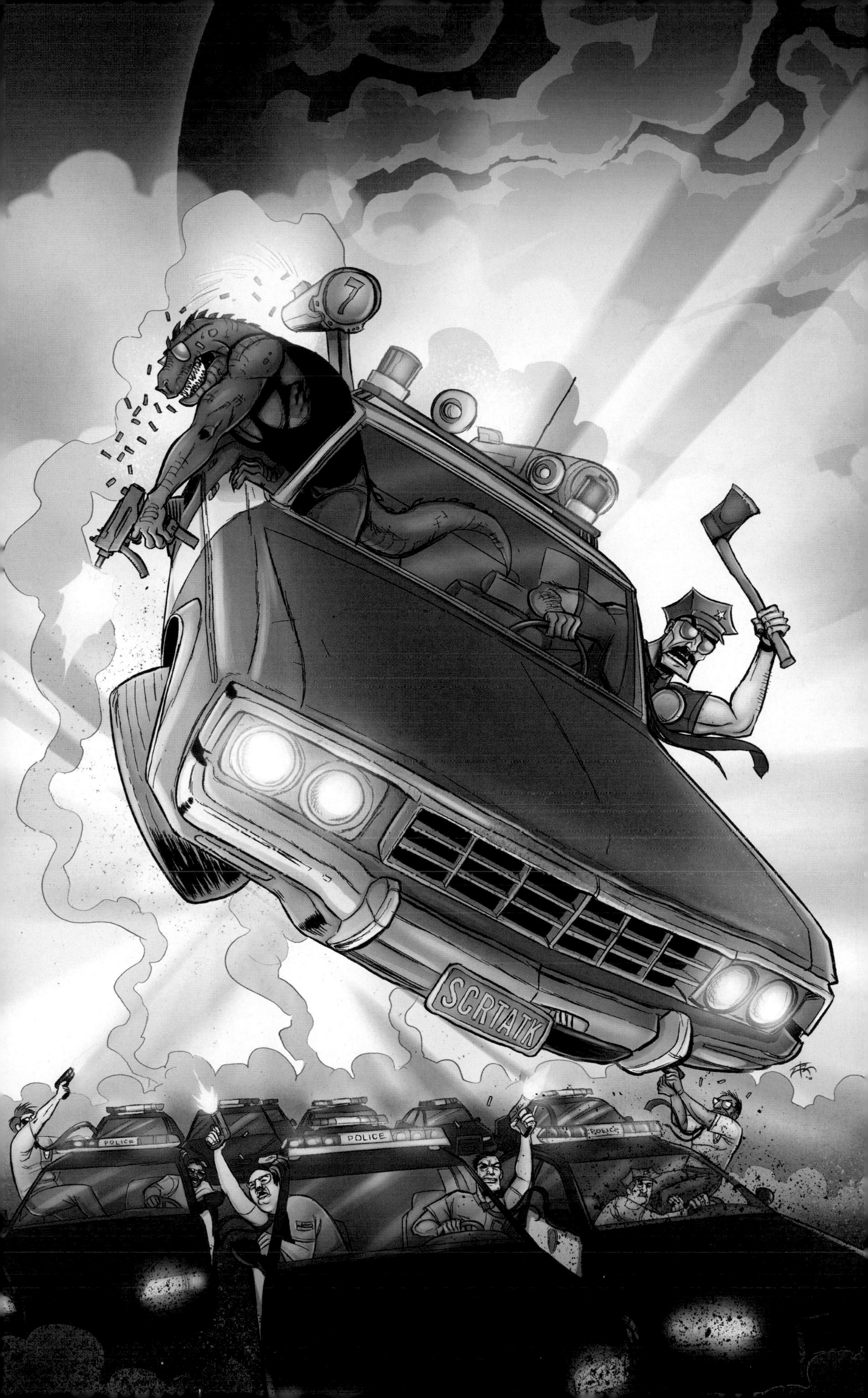
SCRTATK
POLICE
POLICE
POLICE

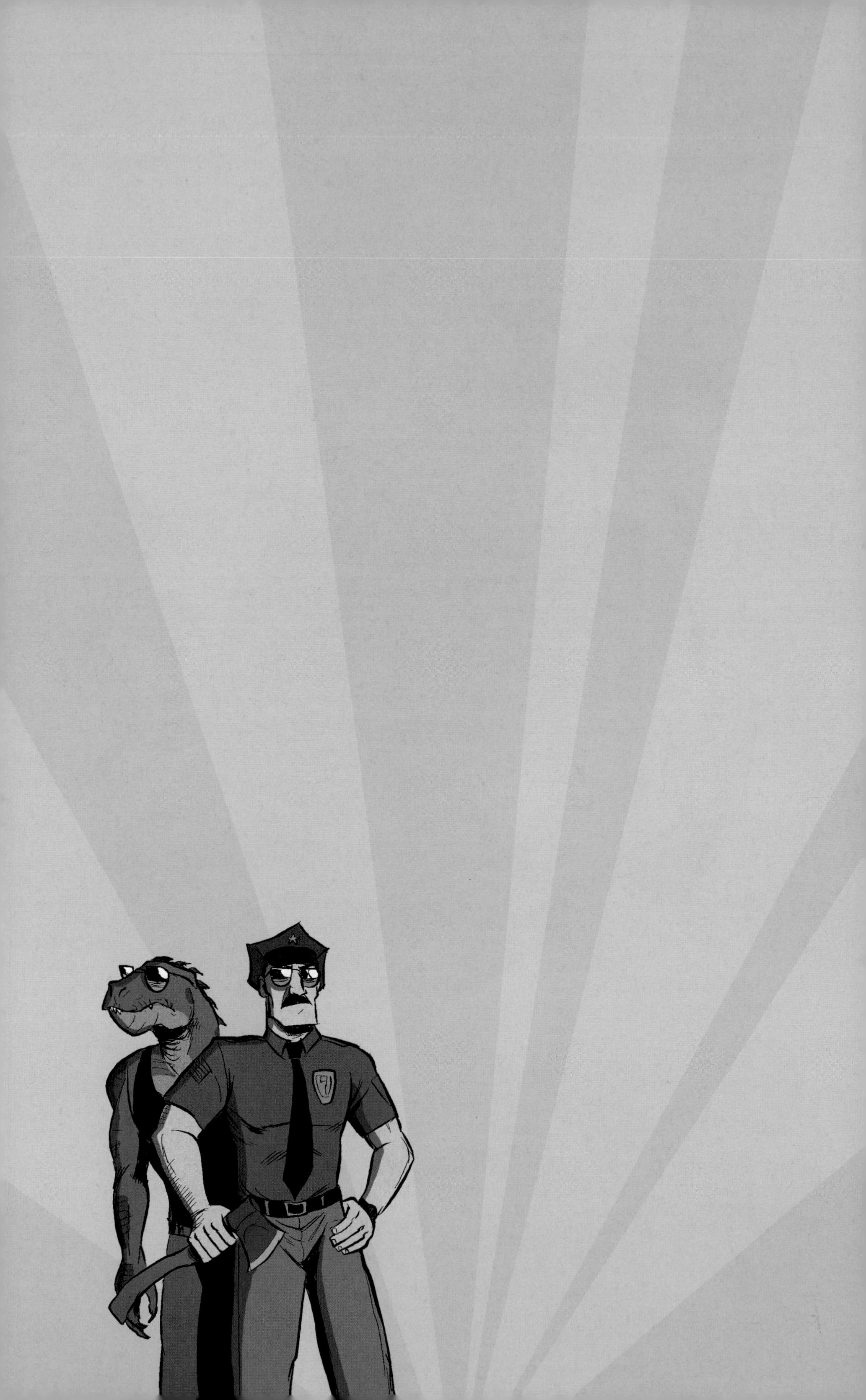

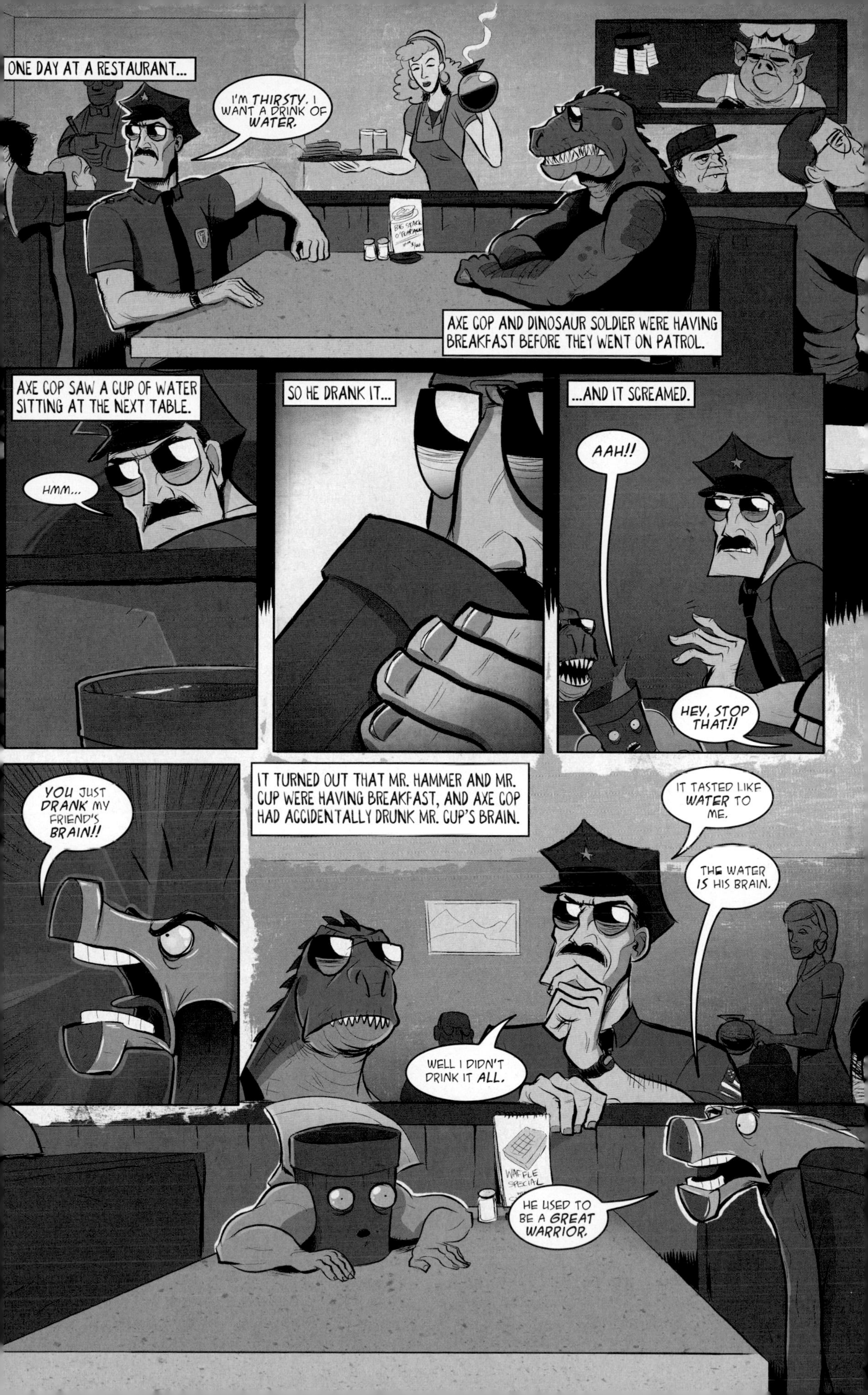
ONE DAY AT A RESTAURANT...
I'M THIRSTY. I WANT A DRINK OF WATER.
BIG STACK O' FLAPJACKS
AXE COP AND DINOSAUR SOLDIER WERE HAVING BREAKFAST BEFORE THEY WENT ON PATROL.
AXE COP SAW A CUP OF WATER SITTING AT THE NEXT TABLE.
HMM...
SO HE DRANK IT...
...AND IT SCREAMED.
AAH!!
HEY, STOP THAT!!
YOU JUST DRANK MY FRIEND'S BRAIN!!
IT TURNED OUT THAT MR. HAMMER AND MR. CUP WERE HAVING BREAKFAST, AND AXE COP HAD ACCIDENTALLY DRUNK MR. CUP'S BRAIN.
IT TASTED LIKE WATER TO ME.
THE WATER IS HIS BRAIN.
WELL I DIDN'T DRINK IT ALL.
WAFFLE SPECIAL
HE USED TO BE A GREAT WARRIOR.

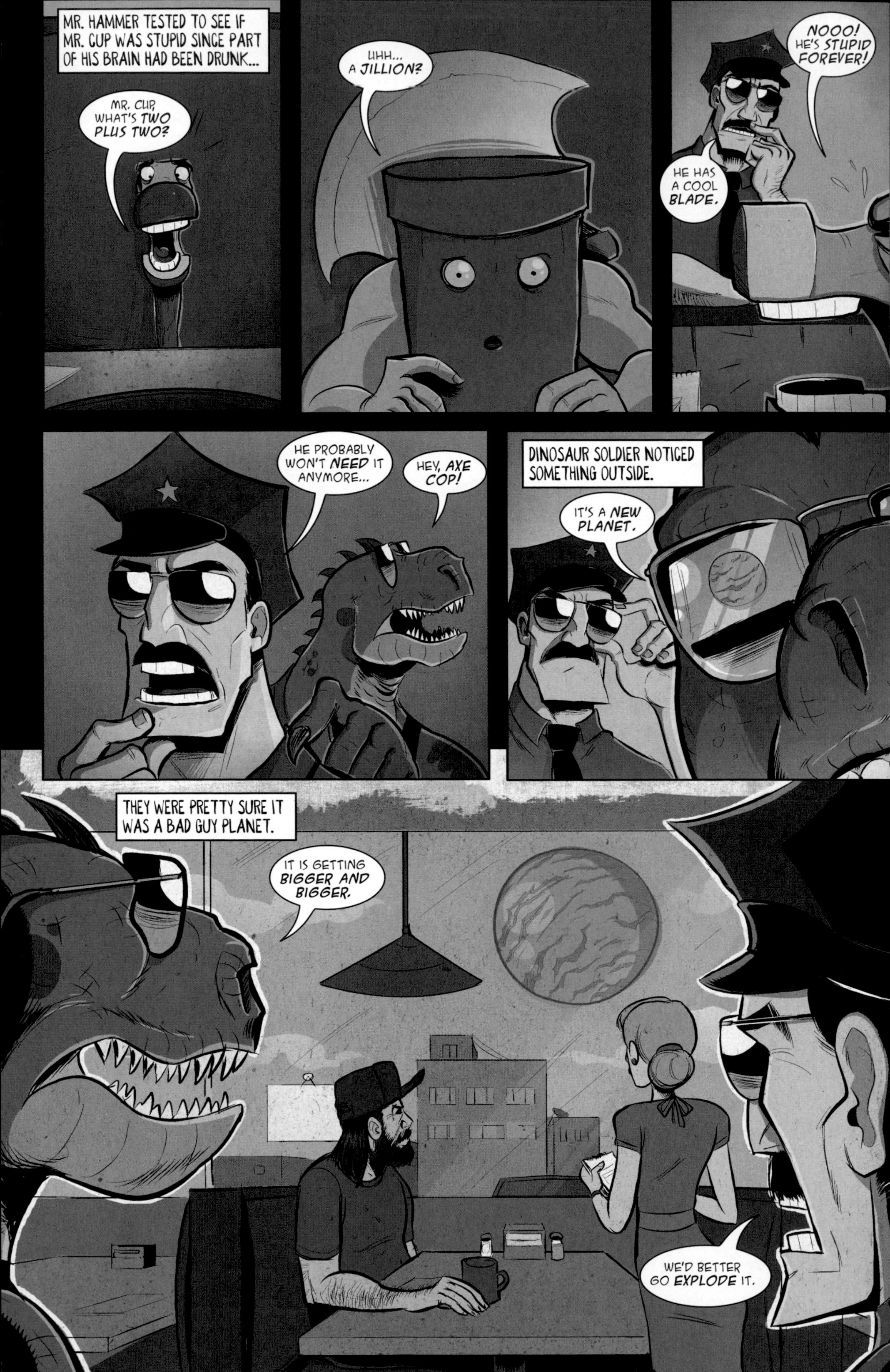
MR. HAMMER TESTED TO SEE IF MR. CUP WAS STUPID SINCE PART OF HIS BRAIN HAD BEEN DRUNK...
MR. CUP, WHAT'S TWO PLUS TWO?
UHH... A JILLION?
NOOO! HE'S STUPID FOREVER!
HE HAS A COOL BLADE.
HE PROBABLY WON'T NEED IT ANYMORE...
HEY, AXE COP!
DINOSAUR SOLDIER NOTICED SOMETHING OUTSIDE.
IT'S A NEW PLANET.
THEY WERE PRETTY SURE IT WAS A BAD GUY PLANET.
IT IS GETTING BIGGER AND BIGGER.
WE'D BETTER GO EXPLODE IT.

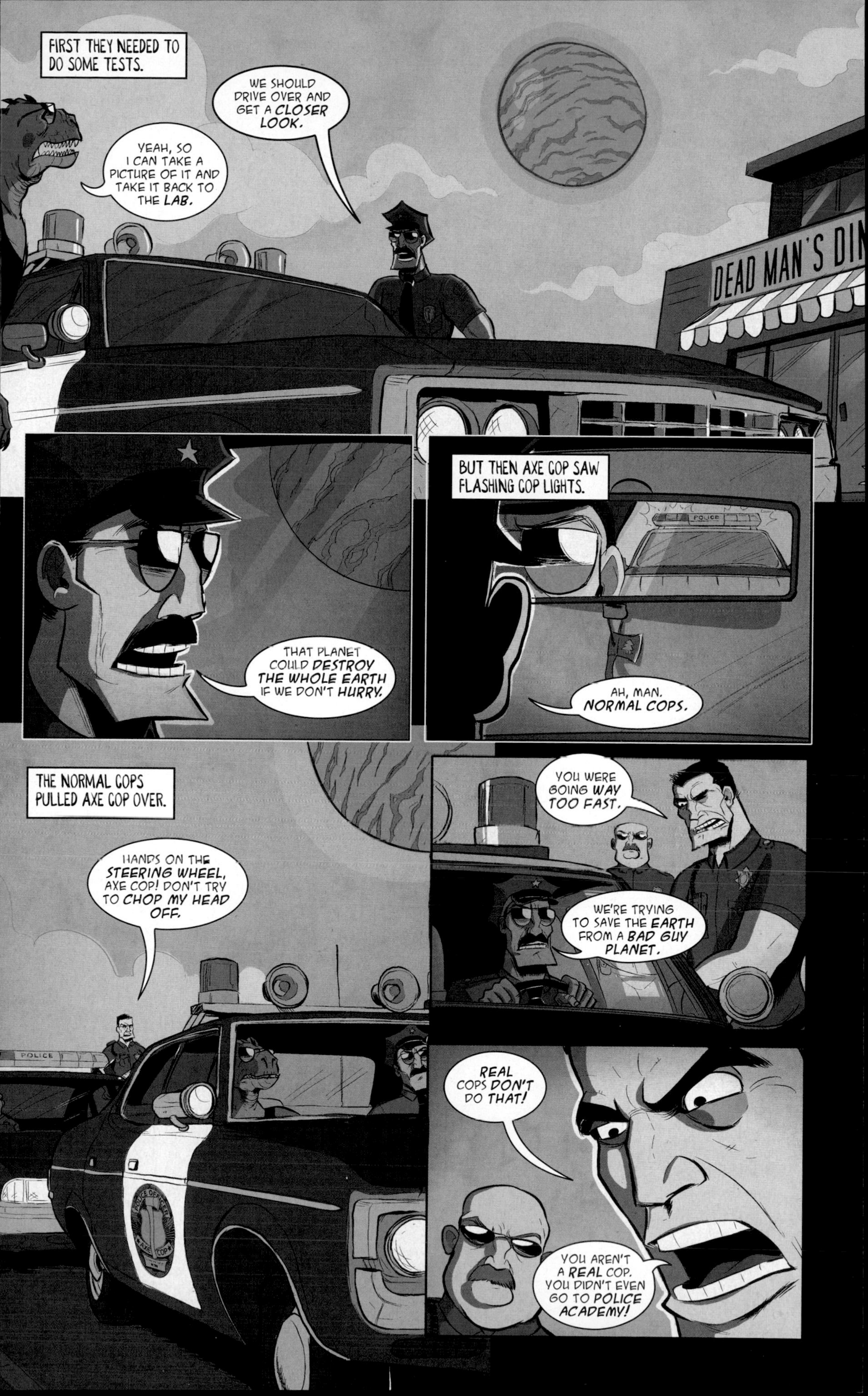
FIRST THEY NEEDED TO DO SOME TESTS.
WE SHOULD DRIVE OVER AND GET A CLOSER LOOK.
YEAH, SO I CAN TAKE A PICTURE OF IT AND TAKE IT BACK TO THE LAB.
DEAD MAN'S DI
THAT PLANET COULD DESTROY THE WHOLE EARTH IF WE DON'T HURRY.
BUT THEN AXE COP SAW FLASHING COP LIGHTS.
POLICE
AH, MAN. NORMAL COPS.
THE NORMAL COPS PULLED AXE COP OVER.
HANDS ON THE STEERING WHEEL, AXE COP! DON'T TRY TO CHOP MY HEAD OFF.
YOU WERE GOING WAY TOO FAST.
WE'RE TRYING TO SAVE THE EARTH FROM A BAD GUY PLANET.
POLICE
REAL COPS DON'T DO THAT!
YOU AREN'T A REAL COP. YOU DIDN'T EVEN GO TO POLICE ACADEMY!

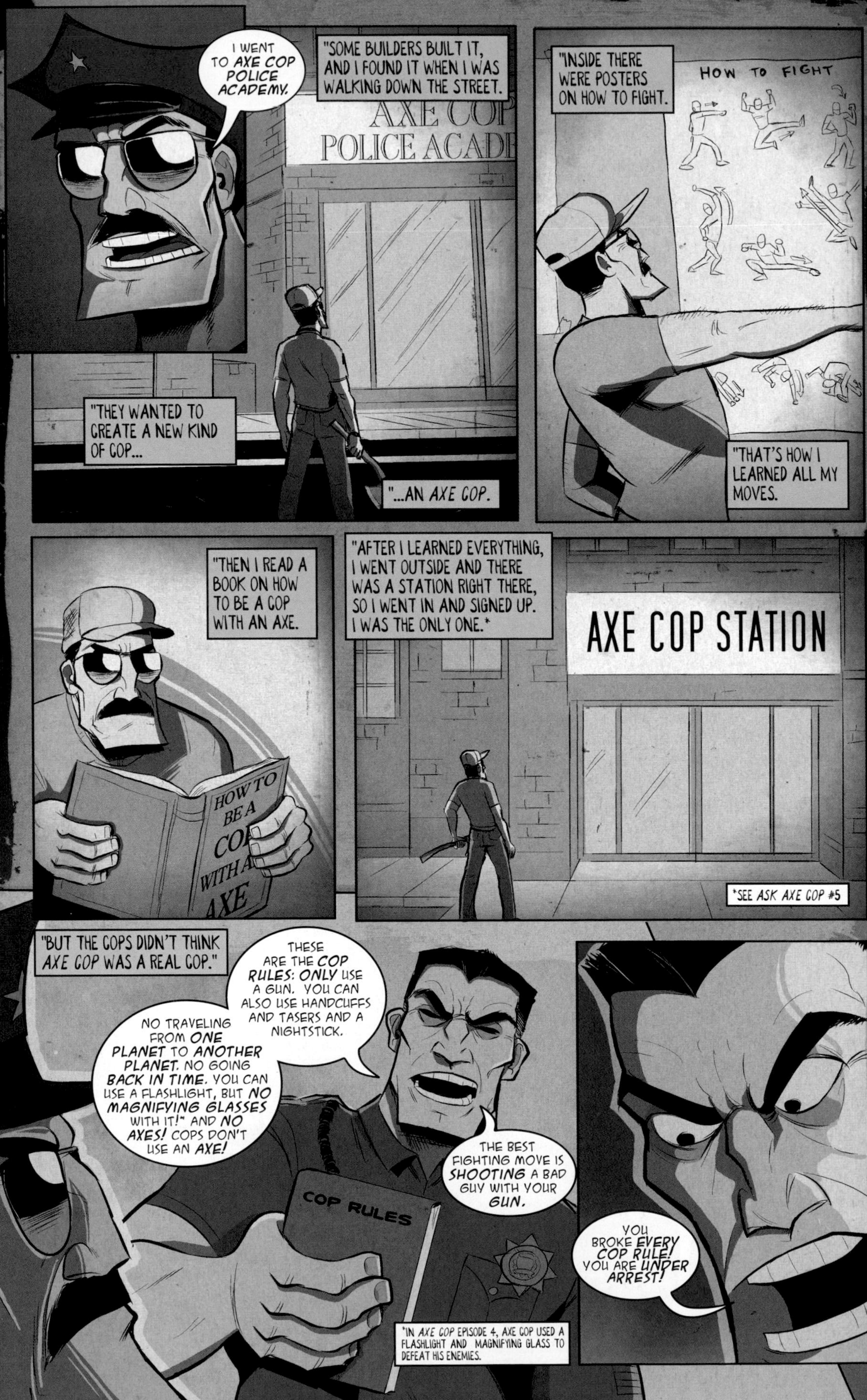
I WENT TO AXE COP POLICE ACADEMY.
"SOME BUILDERS BUILT IT, AND I FOUND IT WHEN I WAS WALKING DOWN THE STREET.
AXE COP POLICE ACAD
"THEY WANTED TO CREATE A NEW KIND OF COP...
"...AN AXE COP.
"INSIDE THERE WERE POSTERS ON HOW TO FIGHT.
HOW TO FIGHT
"THAT'S HOW I LEARNED ALL MY MOVES.
"THEN I READ A BOOK ON HOW TO BE A COP WITH AN AXE.
HOW TO BE A CO WITH A AXE
"AFTER I LEARNED EVERYTHING, I WENT OUTSIDE AND THERE WAS A STATION RIGHT THERE, SO I WENT IN AND SIGNED UP. I WAS THE ONLY ONE.*
AXE COP STATION
*SEE ASK AXE COP #5
"BUT THE COPS DIDN'T THINK AXE COP WAS A REAL COP."
THESE ARE THE COP RULES: ONLY USE A GUN. YOU CAN ALSO USE HANDCUFFS AND TASERS AND A NIGHTSTICK.
NO TRAVELING FROM ONE PLANET TO ANOTHER PLANET. NO GOING BACK IN TIME. YOU CAN USE A FLASHLIGHT, BUT NO MAGNIFYING GLASSES WITH IT!* AND NO AXES! COPS DON'T USE AN AXE!
THE BEST FIGHTING MOVE IS SHOOTING A BAD GUY WITH YOUR GUN.
COP RULES
*IN AXE COP EPISODE 4, AXE COP USED A FLASHLIGHT AND MAGNIFYING GLASS TO DEFEAT HIS ENEMIES.
YOU BROKE EVERY COP RULE! YOU ARE UNDER ARREST!

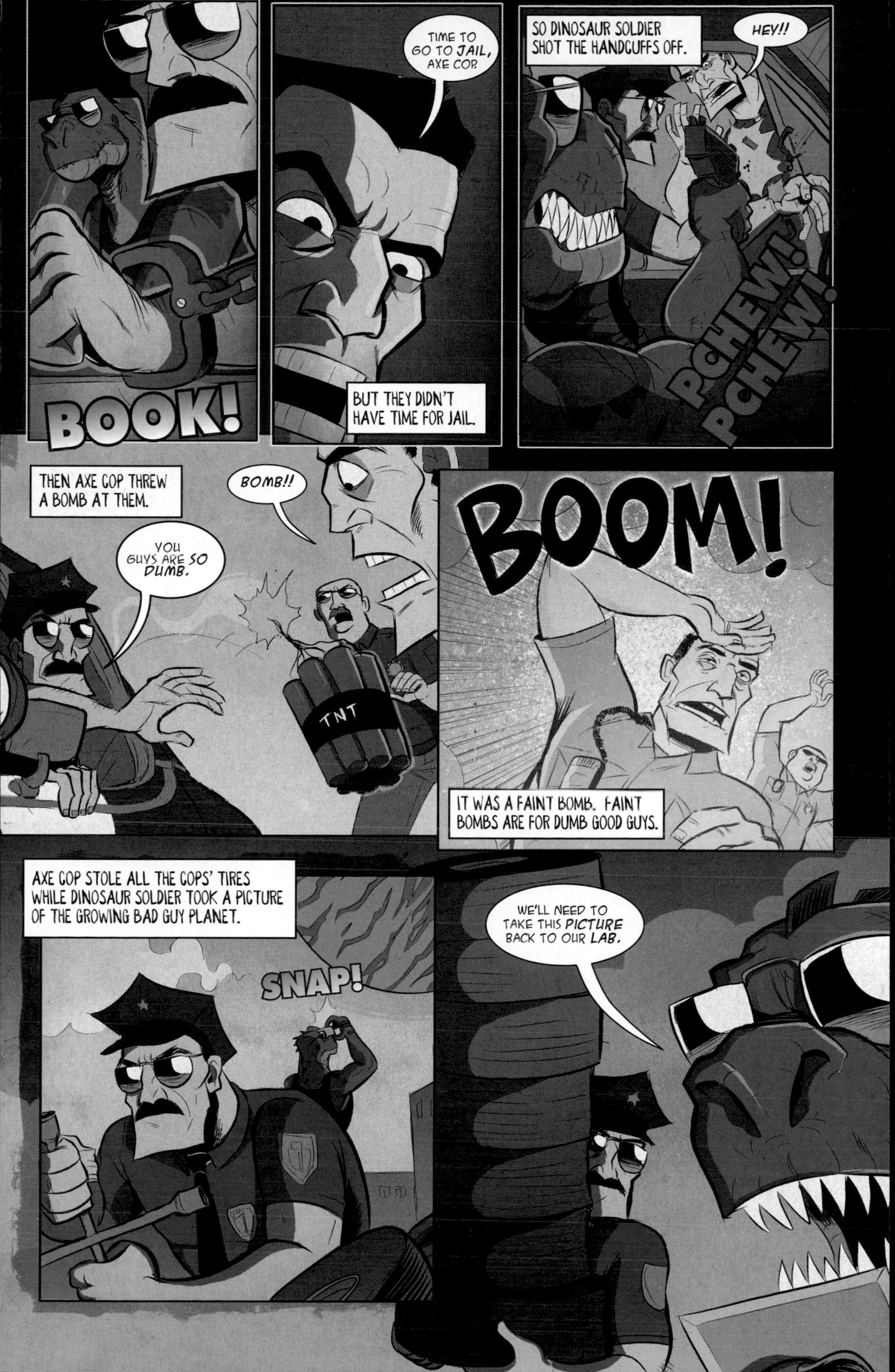
BOOK!
TIME TO GO TO JAIL, AXE COP.
BUT THEY DIDN'T HAVE TIME FOR JAIL.
SO DINOSAUR SOLDIER SHOT THE HANDCUFFS OFF.
HEY!!
PCHEW! PCHEW!
THEN AXE COP THREW A BOMB AT THEM.
BOMB!!
YOU GUYS ARE SO DUMB.
TNT
BOOM!
IT WAS A FAINT BOMB. FAINT BOMBS ARE FOR DUMB GOOD GUYS.
AXE COP STOLE ALL THE COPS' TIRES WHILE DINOSAUR SOLDIER TOOK A PICTURE OF THE GROWING BAD GUY PLANET.
SNAP!
WE'LL NEED TO TAKE THIS PICTURE BACK TO OUR LAB.

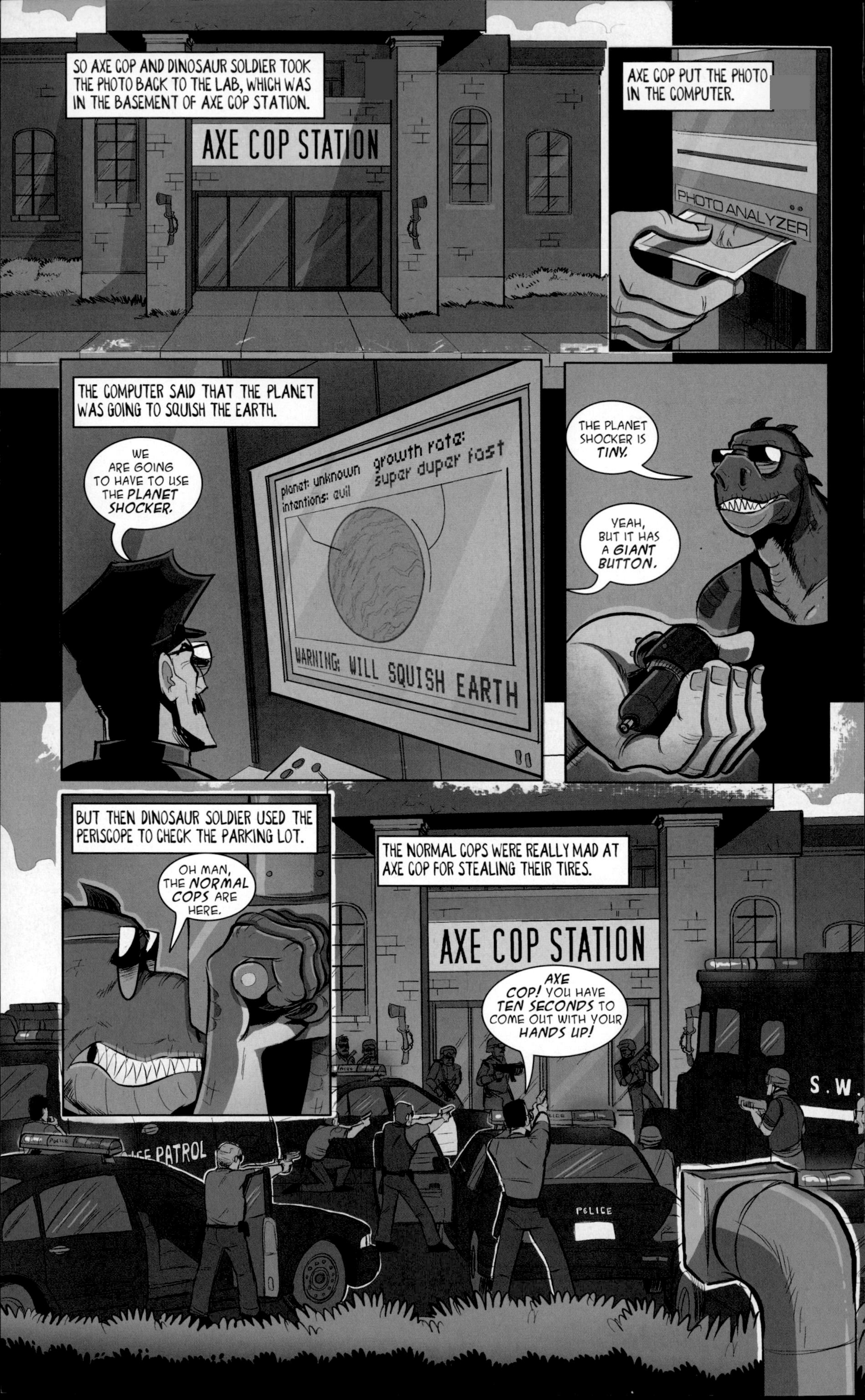

SO AXE COP AND DINOSAUR SOLDIER TOOK THE PHOTO BACK TO THE LAB, WHICH WAS IN THE BASEMENT OF AXE COP STATION.
AXE COP STATION
AXE COP PUT THE PHOTO IN THE COMPUTER.
PHOTO ANALYZER
THE COMPUTER SAID THAT THE PLANET WAS GOING TO SQUISH THE EARTH.
WE ARE GOING TO HAVE TO USE THE PLANET SHOCKER.
planet: unknown
intentions: evil
growth rate: super duper fast
WARNING: WILL SQUISH EARTH
THE PLANET SHOCKER IS TINY.
YEAH, BUT IT HAS A GIANT BUTTON.
BUT THEN DINOSAUR SOLDIER USED THE PERISCOPE TO CHECK THE PARKING LOT.
OH MAN, THE NORMAL COPS ARE HERE.
THE NORMAL COPS WERE REALLY MAD AT AXE COP FOR STEALING THEIR TIRES.
AXE COP STATION
AXE COP! YOU HAVE TEN SECONDS TO COME OUT WITH YOUR HANDS UP!
S.W.
PATROL
POLICE

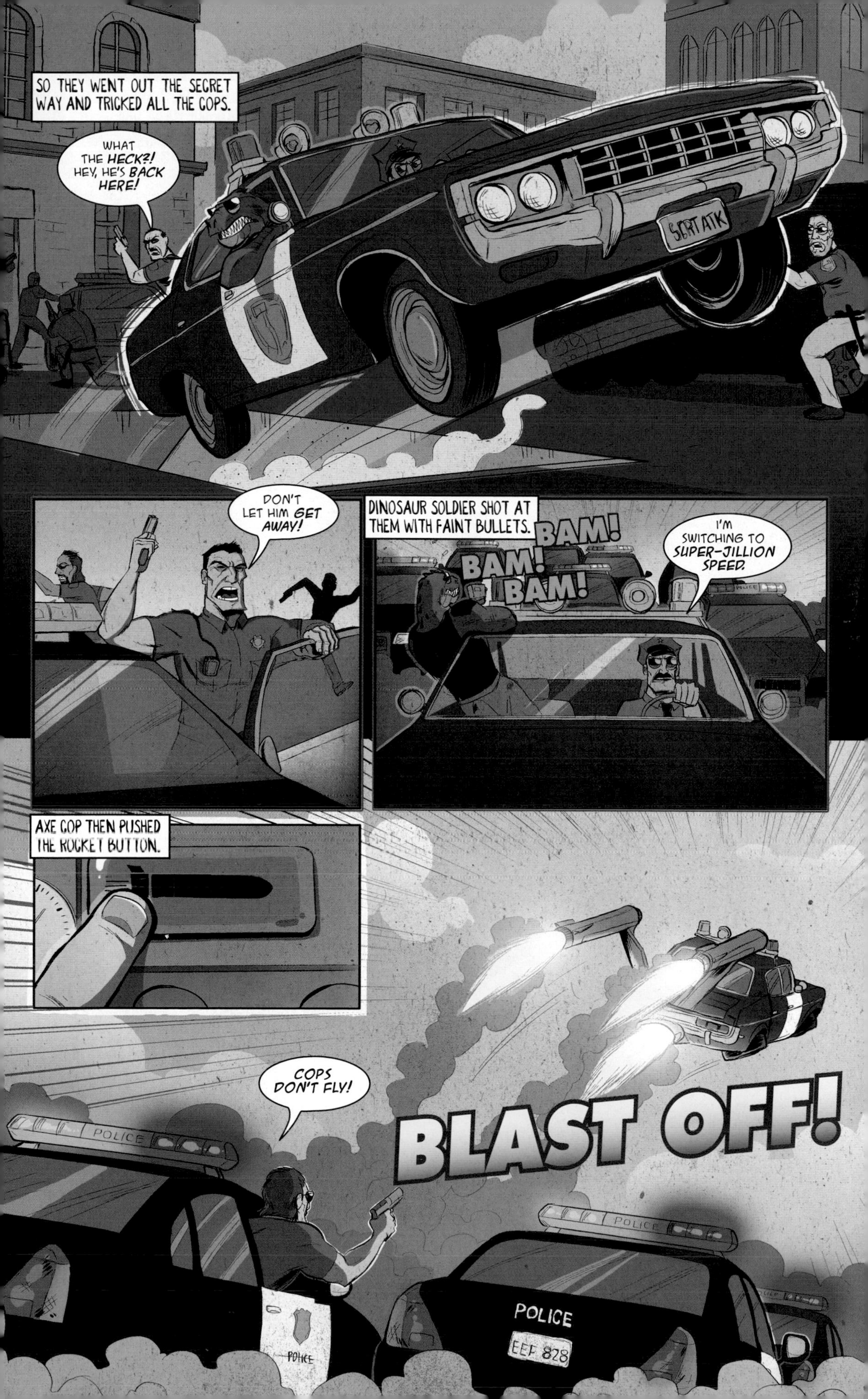
SO THEY WENT OUT THE SECRET WAY AND TRICKED ALL THE COPS.
WHAT THE HECK?! HEY, HE'S BACK HERE!
SGRT ATK
DON'T LET HIM GET AWAY!
DINOSAUR SOLDIER SHOT AT THEM WITH FAINT BULLETS.
BAM!
BAM!
BAM!
I'M SWITCHING TO SUPER-JILLION SPEED.
AXE COP THEN PUSHED THE ROCKET BUTTON.
COPS DON'T FLY!
BLAST OFF!
POLICE
POLICE
POLICE
EEF 828
POLICE

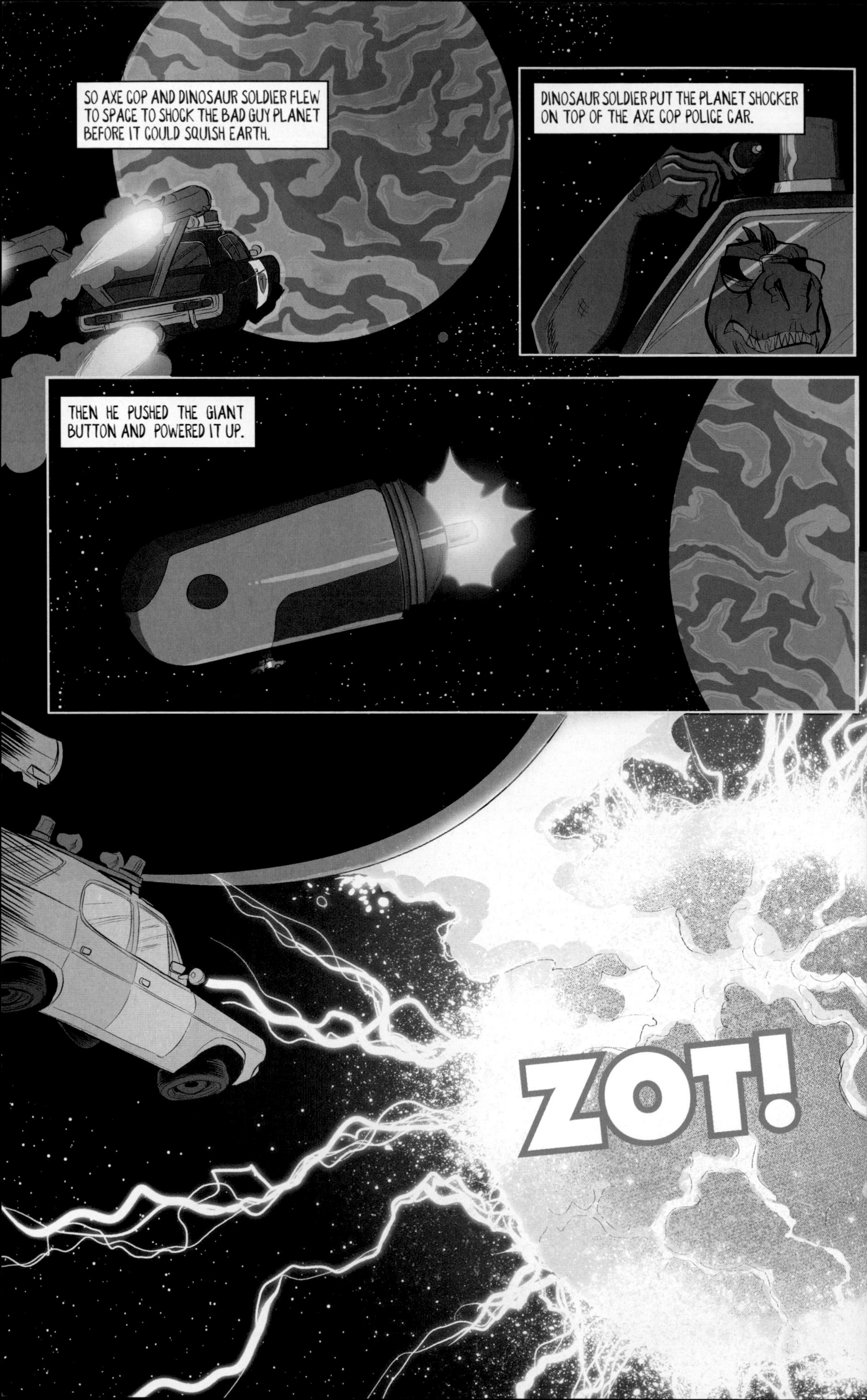
SO AXE COP AND DINOSAUR SOLDIER FLEW TO SPACE TO SHOCK THE BAD GUY PLANET BEFORE IT COULD SQUISH EARTH.
DINOSAUR SOLDIER PUT THE PLANET SHOCKER ON TOP OF THE AXE COP POLICE CAR.
THEN HE PUSHED THE GIANT BUTTON AND POWERED IT UP.
ZOT!

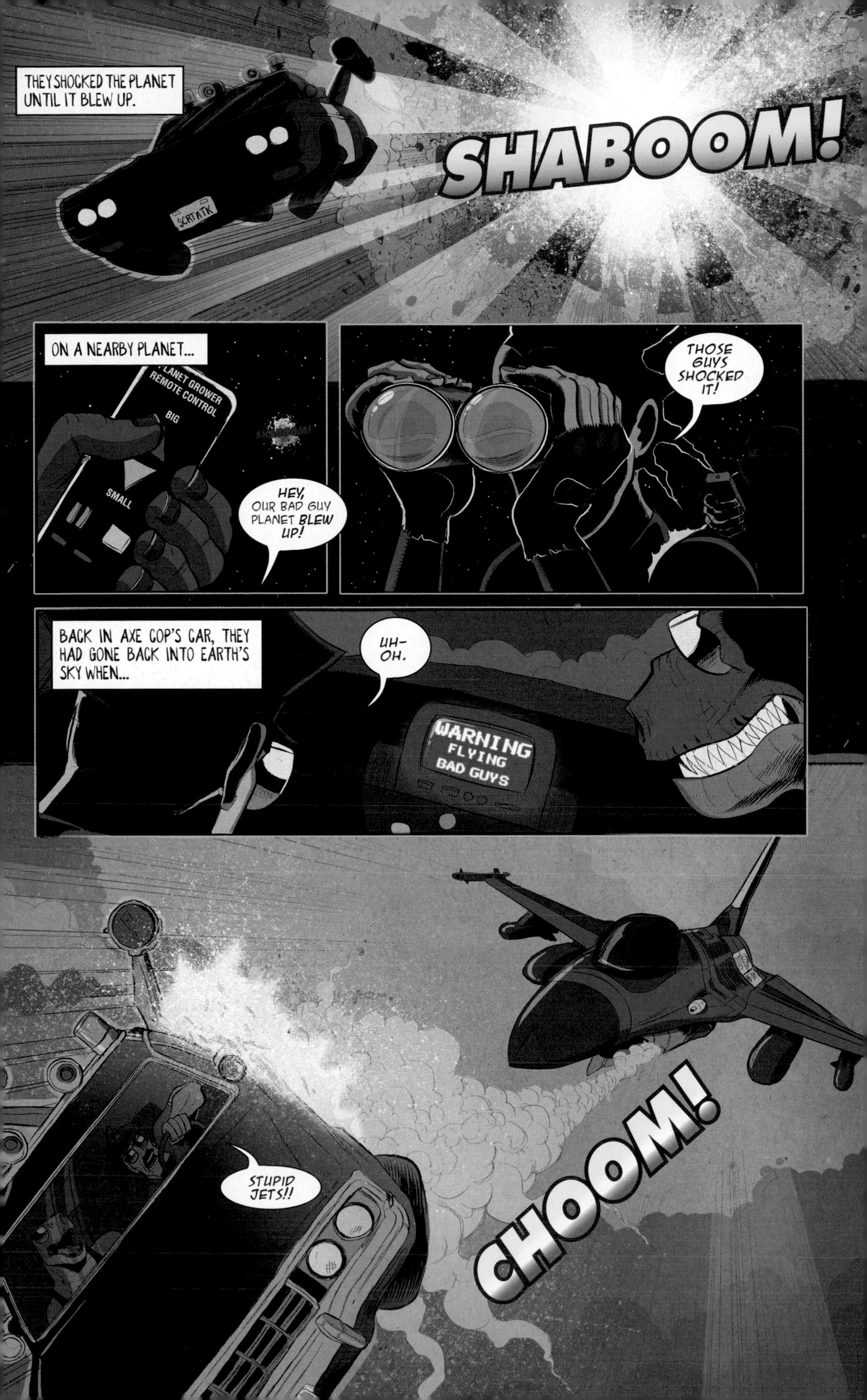
THEY SHOCKED THE PLANET UNTIL IT BLEW UP.
SCRTATK
SHABOOM!
ON A NEARBY PLANET...
PLANET GROWER REMOTE CONTROL
BIG
SMALL
HEY, OUR BAD GUY PLANET BLEW UP!
THOSE GUYS SHOCKED IT!
BACK IN AXE COP'S CAR, THEY HAD GONE BACK INTO EARTH'S SKY WHEN...
UH-OH.
WARNING FLYING BAD GUYS
STUPID JETS!!
CHOOM!

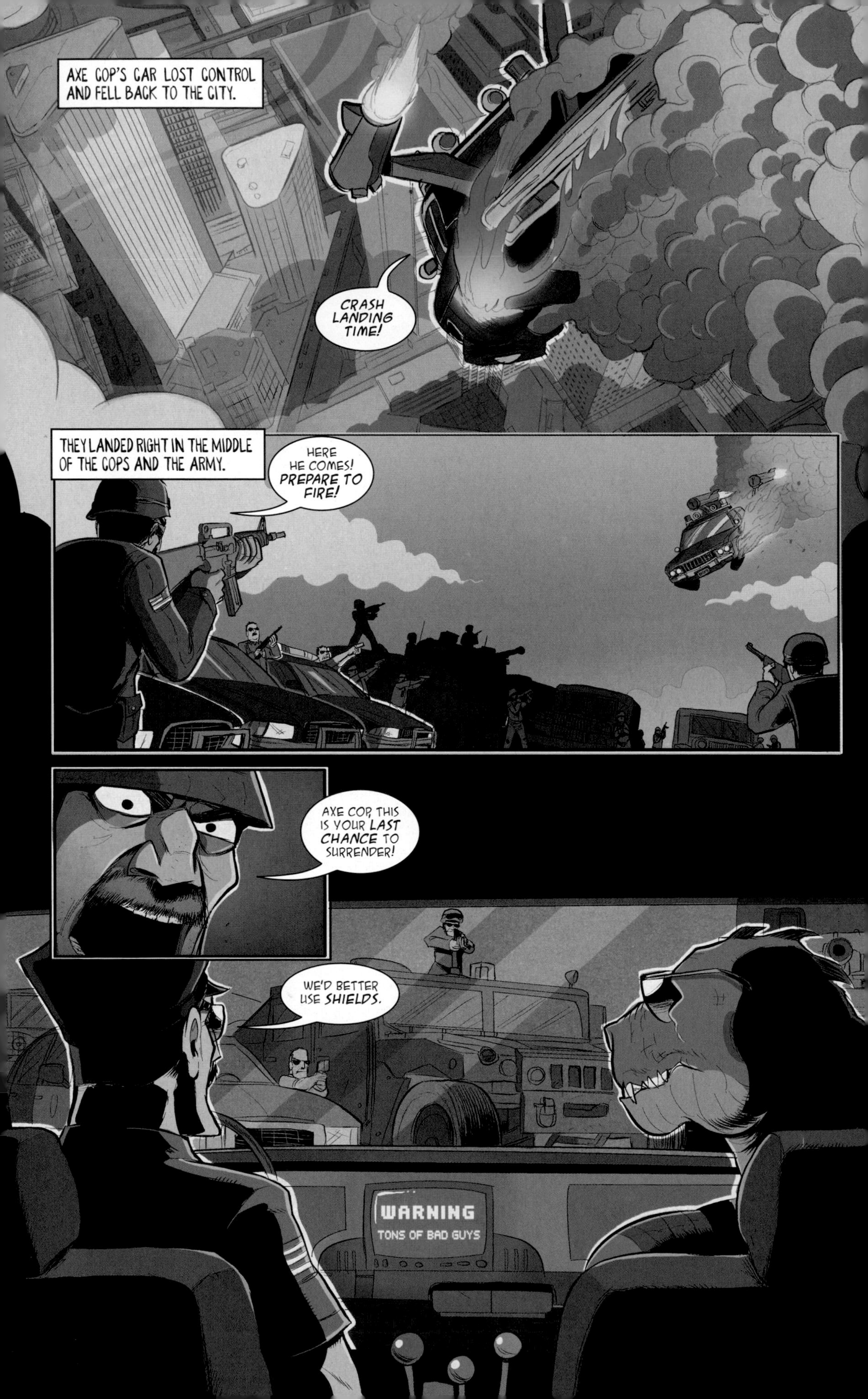
AXE COP'S CAR LOST CONTROL AND FELL BACK TO THE CITY.
CRASH LANDING TIME!
THEY LANDED RIGHT IN THE MIDDLE OF THE COPS AND THE ARMY.
HERE HE COMES! PREPARE TO FIRE!
AXE COP, THIS IS YOUR LAST CHANCE TO SURRENDER!
WE'D BETTER USE SHIELDS.
WARNING
TONS OF BAD GUYS

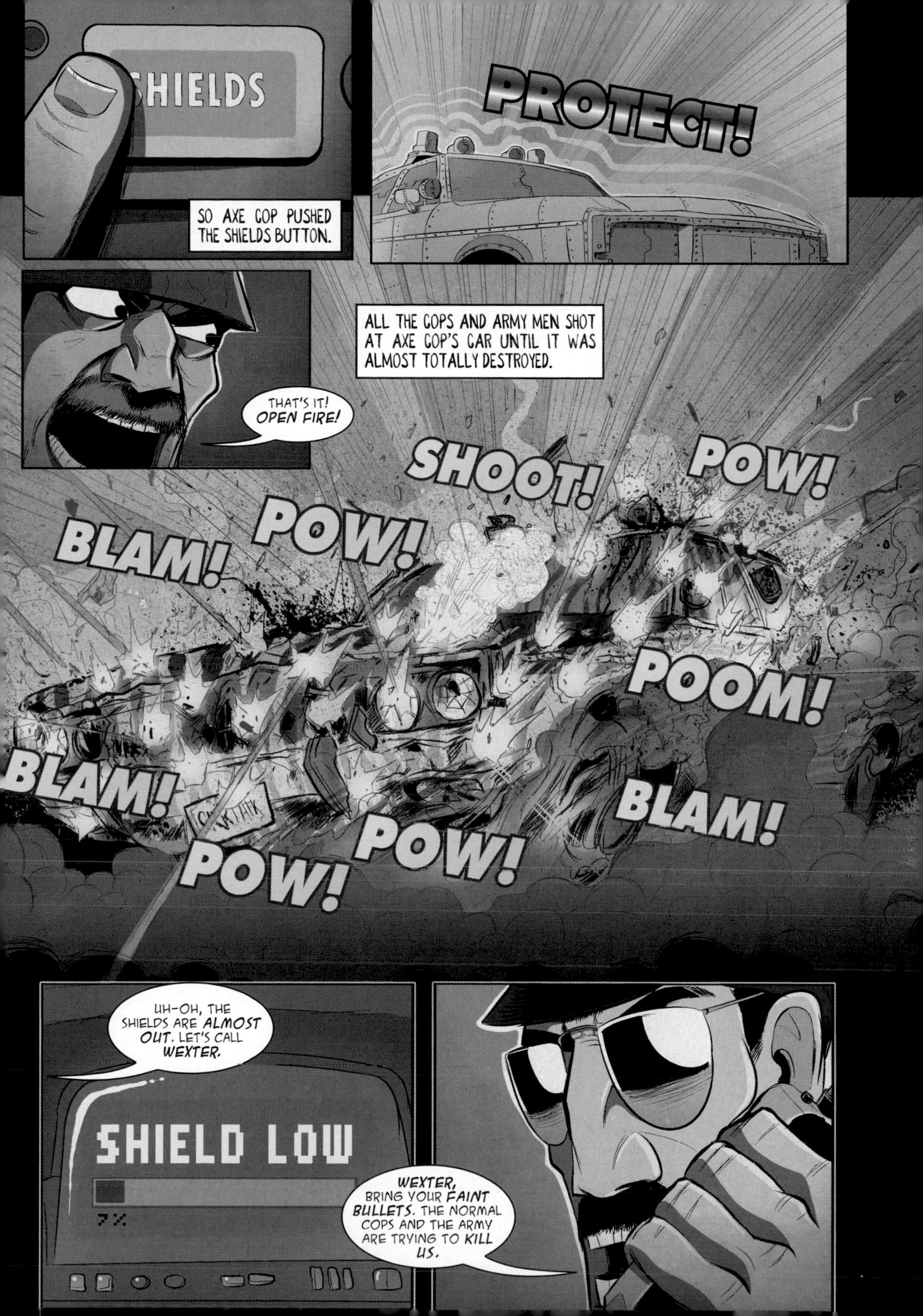
SHIELDS
SO AXE COP PUSHED THE SHIELDS BUTTON.
PROTECT!
ALL THE COPS AND ARMY MEN SHOT AT AXE COP'S CAR UNTIL IT WAS ALMOST TOTALLY DESTROYED.
THAT'S IT! OPEN FIRE!
SHOOT!
POW!
BLAM!
POW!
POOM!
BLAM!
BLAM!
POW!
POW!
UH-OH, THE SHIELDS ARE ALMOST OUT. LET'S CALL WEXTER.
SHIELD LOW
7%
WEXTER, BRING YOUR FAINT BULLETS. THE NORMAL COPS AND THE ARMY ARE TRYING TO KILL US.

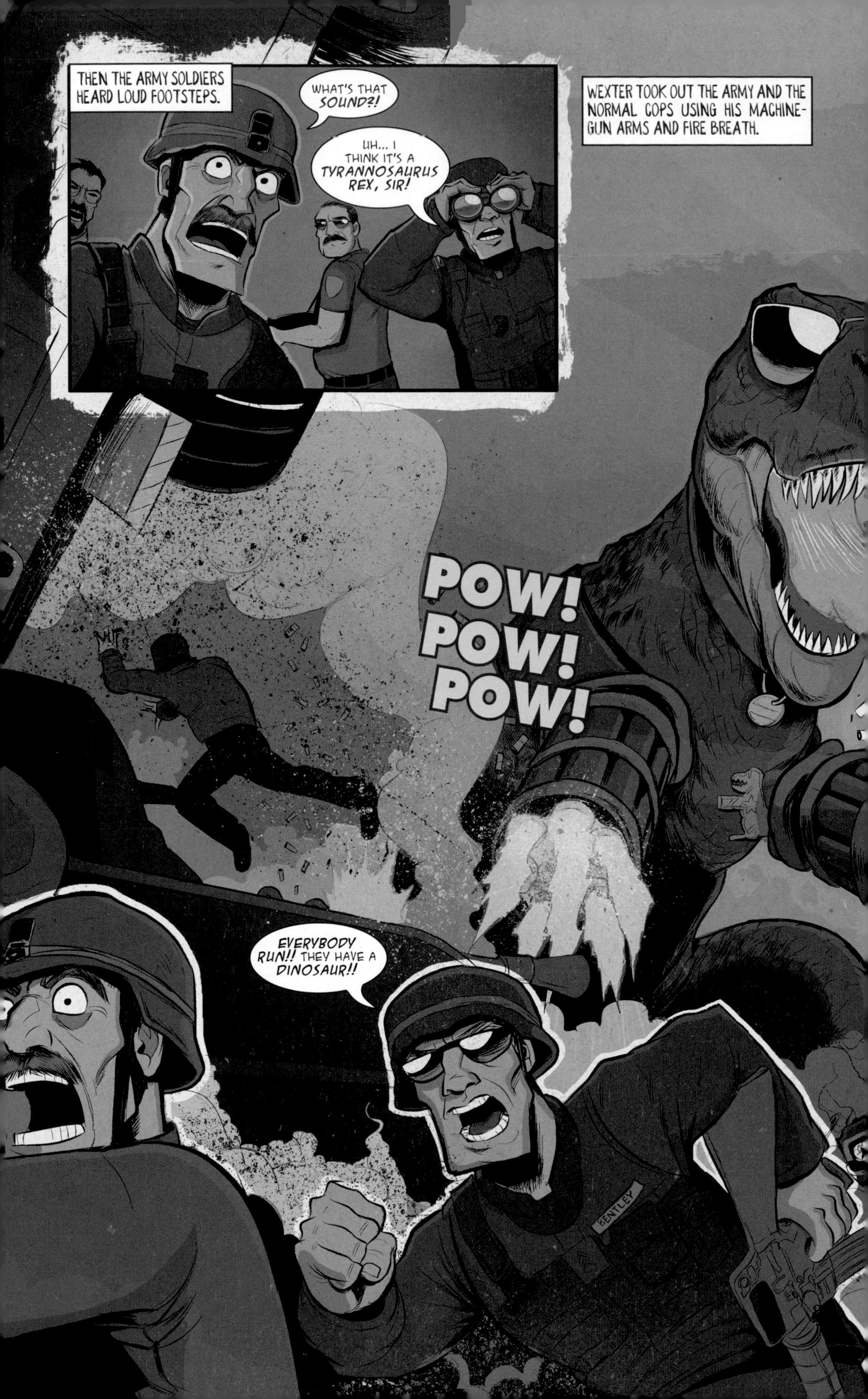
THEN THE ARMY SOLDIERS HEARD LOUD FOOTSTEPS.
WHAT'S THAT SOUND?!
UH... I THINK IT'S A TYRANNOSAURUS REX, SIR!
WEXTER TOOK OUT THE ARMY AND THE NORMAL COPS USING HIS MACHINE-GUN ARMS AND FIRE BREATH.
POW! POW! POW!
EVERYBODY RUN!! THEY HAVE A DINOSAUR!!
BENTLEY

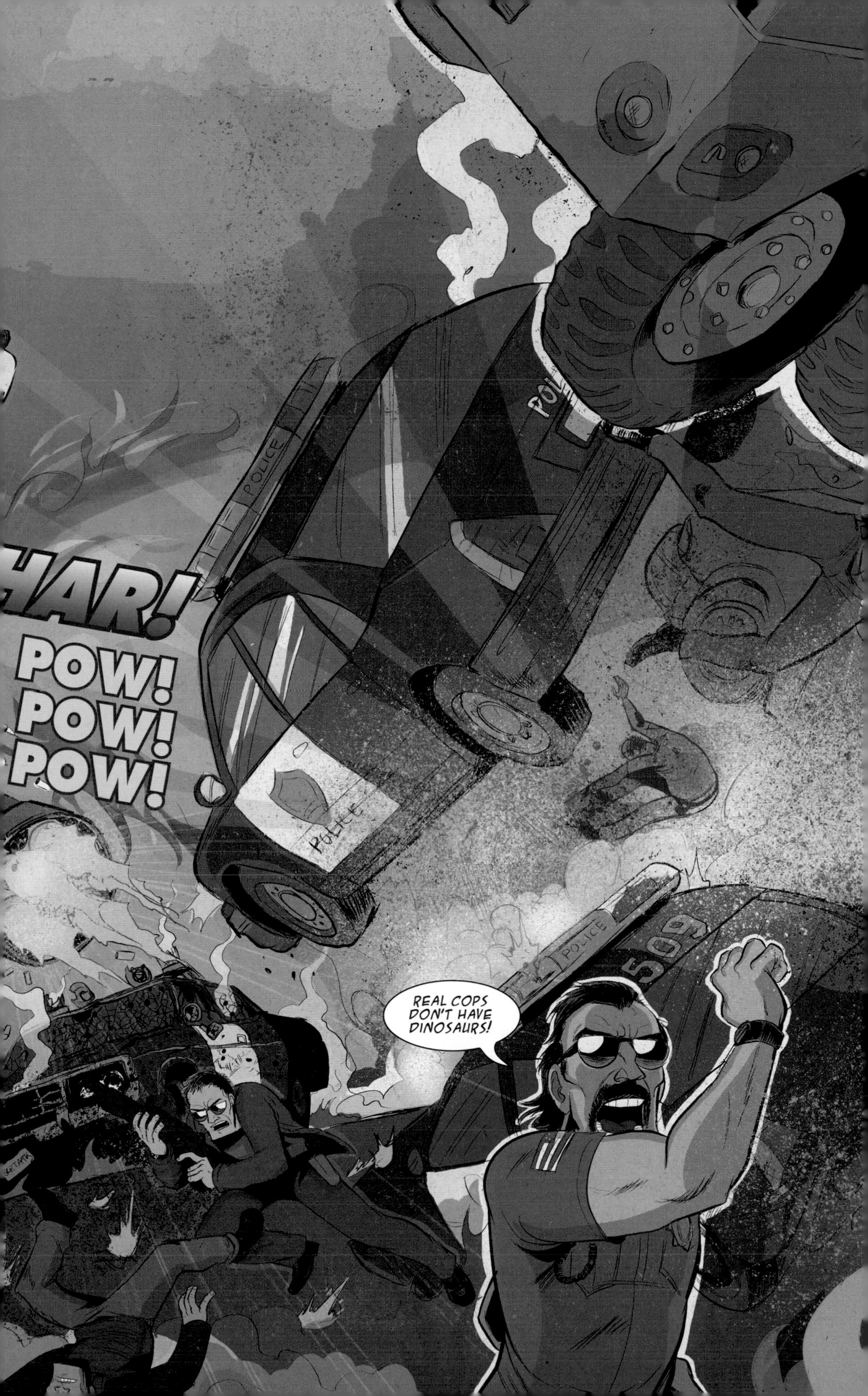
HAR!
POW! POW! POW!
REAL COPS DON'T HAVE DINOSAURS!

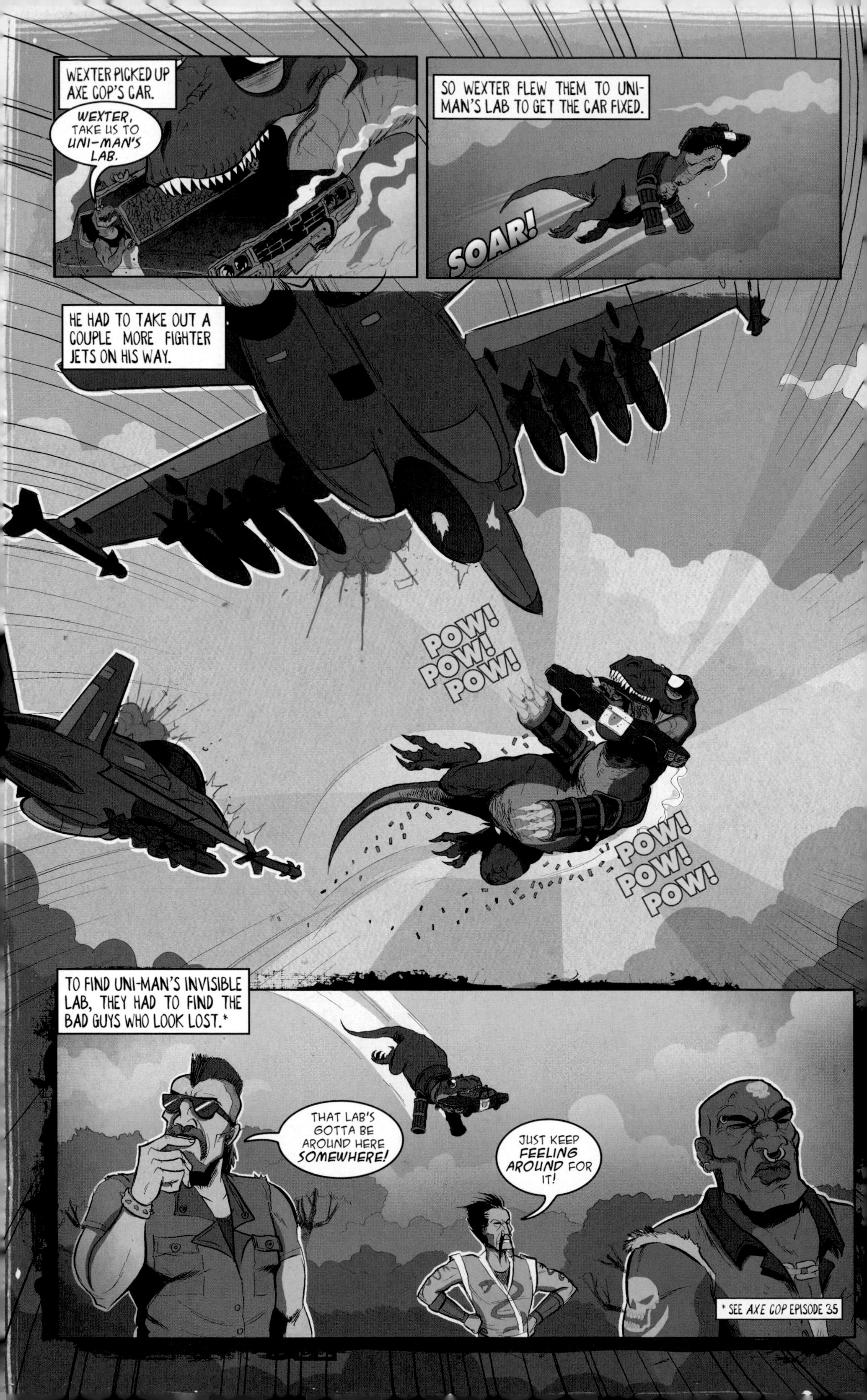
WEXTER PICKED UP AXE COP'S CAR.
WEXTER, TAKE US TO UNI-MAN'S LAB.
SO WEXTER FLEW THEM TO UNI-MAN'S LAB TO GET THE CAR FIXED.
SOAR!
HE HAD TO TAKE OUT A COUPLE MORE FIGHTER JETS ON HIS WAY.
POW! POW! POW!
POW! POW! POW!
TO FIND UNI-MAN'S INVISIBLE LAB, THEY HAD TO FIND THE BAD GUYS WHO LOOK LOST.*
THAT LAB'S GOTTA BE AROUND HERE SOMEWHERE!
JUST KEEP FEELING AROUND FOR IT!
* SEE AXE COP EPISODE 35

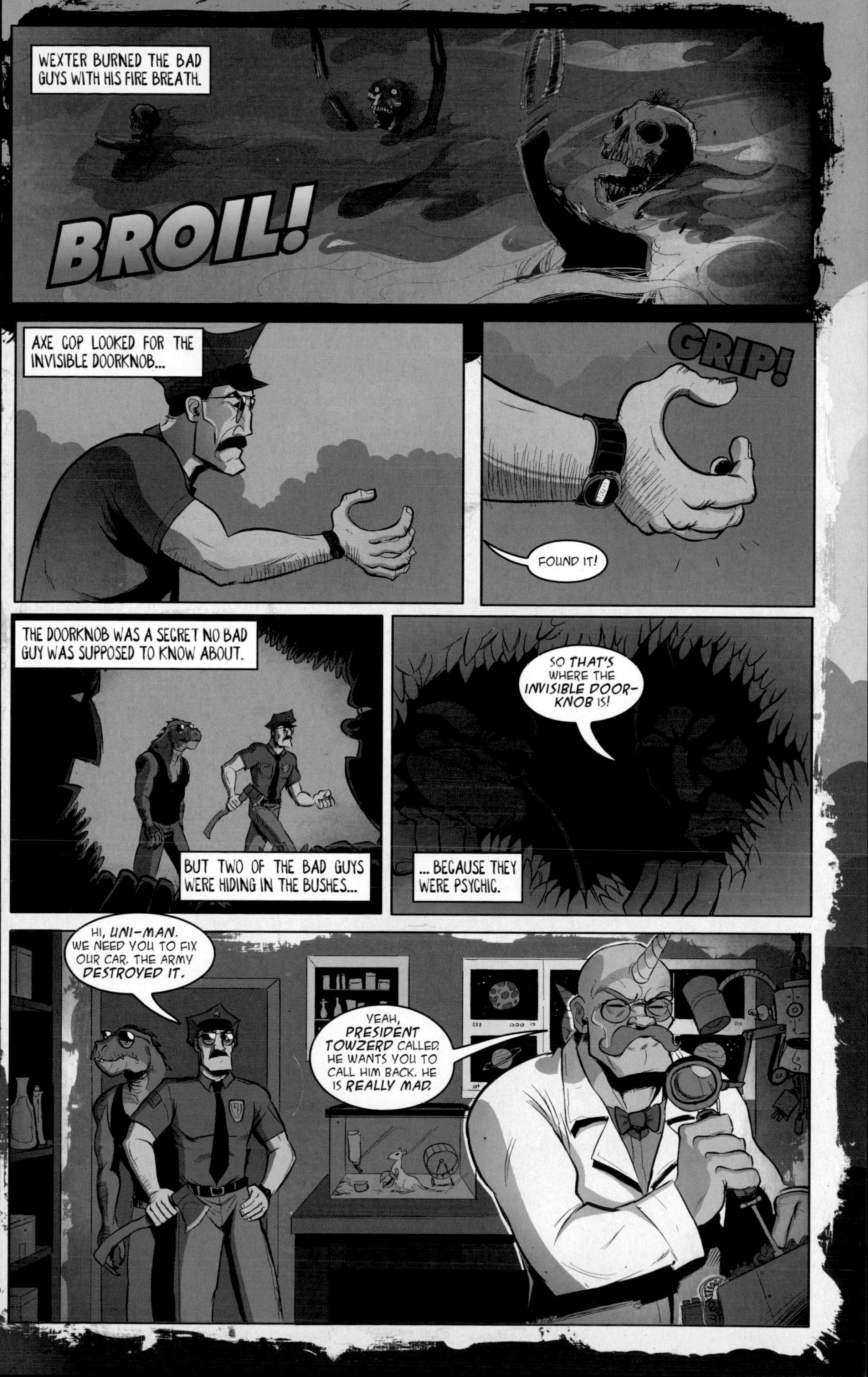
WEXTER BURNED THE BAD GUYS WITH HIS FIRE BREATH.
BROIL!
AXE COP LOOKED FOR THE INVISIBLE DOORKNOB...
GRIP!
FOUND IT!
THE DOORKNOB WAS A SECRET NO BAD GUY WAS SUPPOSED TO KNOW ABOUT.
BUT TWO OF THE BAD GUYS WERE HIDING IN THE BUSHES...
SO THAT'S WHERE THE INVISIBLE DOOR-KNOB IS!
... BECAUSE THEY WERE PSYCHIC.
HI, UNI-MAN. WE NEED YOU TO FIX OUR CAR. THE ARMY DESTROYED IT.
YEAH, PRESIDENT TOWZERD CALLED. HE WANTS YOU TO CALL HIM BACK. HE IS REALLY MAD.

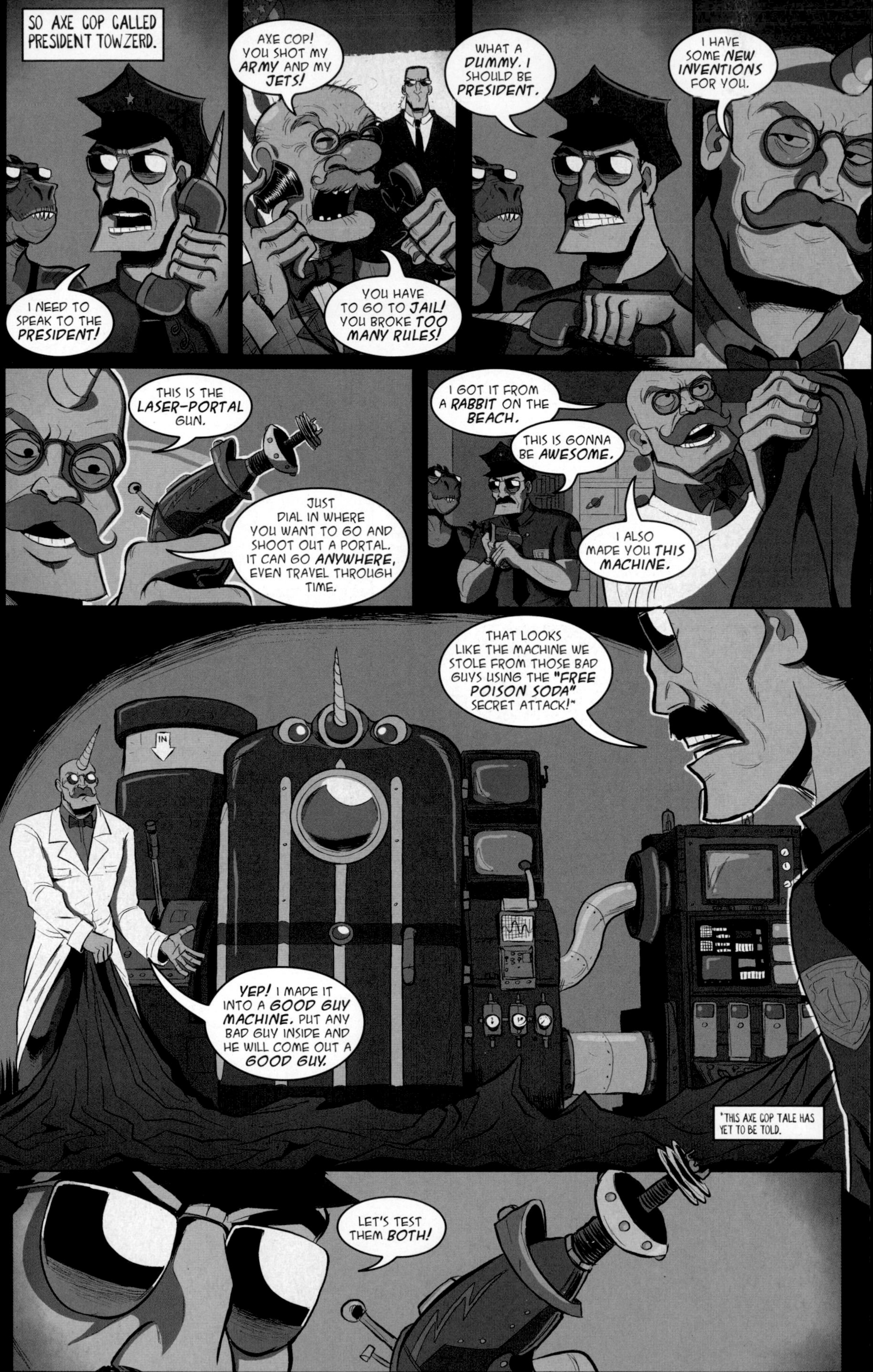

SO AXE COP CALLED PRESIDENT TOWZERD.
I NEED TO SPEAK TO THE PRESIDENT!
AXE COP! YOU SHOT MY ARMY AND MY JETS!
YOU HAVE TO GO TO JAIL! YOU BROKE TOO MANY RULES!
WHAT A DUMMY. I SHOULD BE PRESIDENT.
I HAVE SOME NEW INVENTIONS FOR YOU.
THIS IS THE LASER-PORTAL GUN.
JUST DIAL IN WHERE YOU WANT TO GO AND SHOOT OUT A PORTAL. IT CAN GO ANYWHERE, EVEN TRAVEL THROUGH TIME.
I GOT IT FROM A RABBIT ON THE BEACH.
THIS IS GONNA BE AWESOME.
I ALSO MADE YOU THIS MACHINE.
THAT LOOKS LIKE THE MACHINE WE STOLE FROM THOSE BAD GUYS USING THE "FREE POISON SODA" SECRET ATTACK!*
IN
YEP! I MADE IT INTO A GOOD GUY MACHINE. PUT ANY BAD GUY INSIDE AND HE WILL COME OUT A GOOD GUY.
*THIS AXE COP TALE HAS YET TO BE TOLD.
LET'S TEST THEM BOTH!

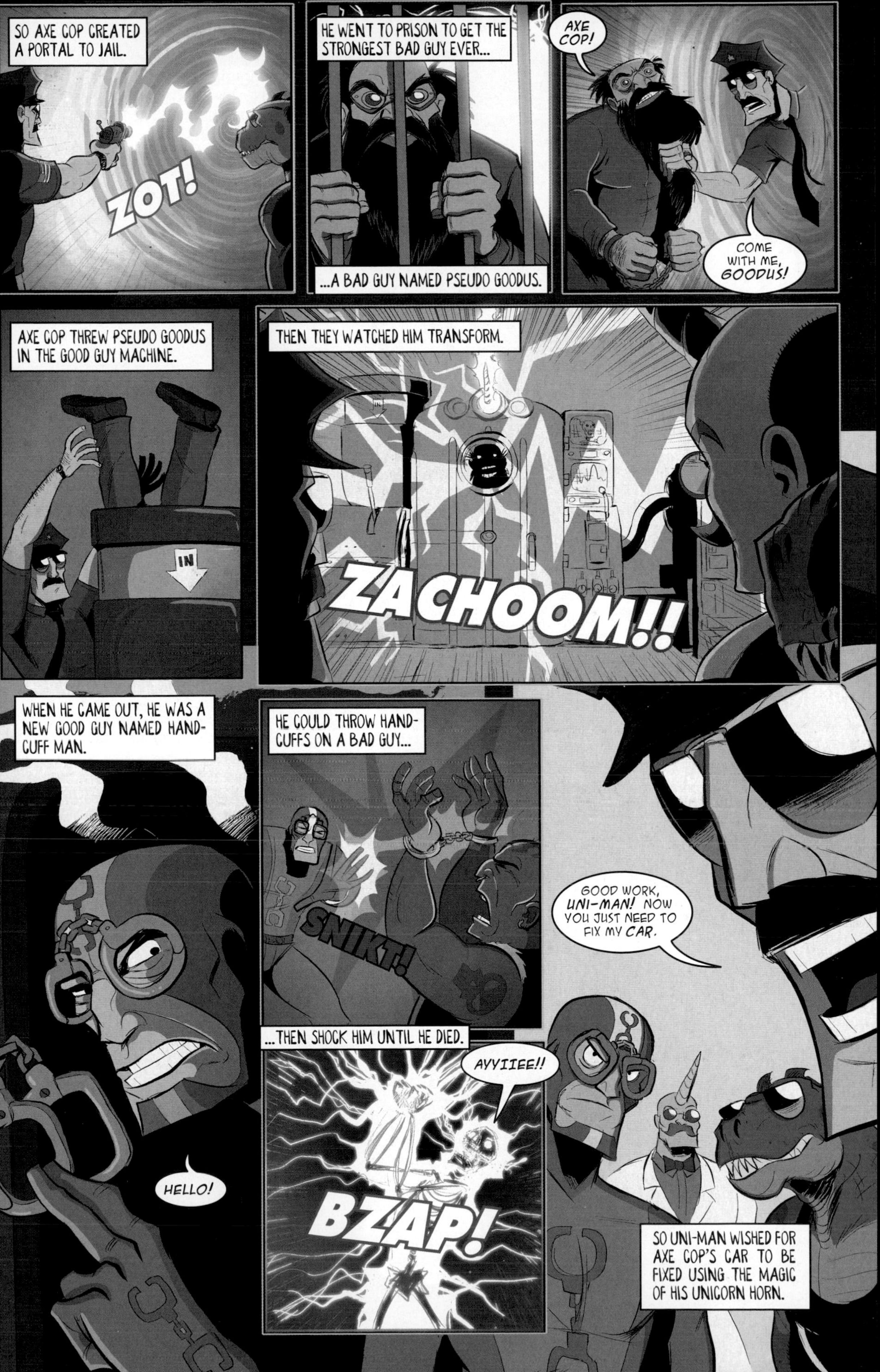
SO AXE COP CREATED A PORTAL TO JAIL.
ZOT!
HE WENT TO PRISON TO GET THE STRONGEST BAD GUY EVER...
...A BAD GUY NAMED PSEUDO GOODUS.
AXE COP!
COME WITH ME, GOODUS!
AXE COP THREW PSEUDO GOODUS IN THE GOOD GUY MACHINE.
IN
THEN THEY WATCHED HIM TRANSFORM.
IN
ZACHOOM!!
WHEN HE CAME OUT, HE WAS A NEW GOOD GUY NAMED HAND-CUFF MAN.
HELLO!
HE COULD THROW HAND-CUFFS ON A BAD GUY...
SNIKT!
...THEN SHOCK HIM UNTIL HE DIED.
AYYIIEE!!
BZAP!
GOOD WORK, UNI-MAN! NOW YOU JUST NEED TO FIX MY CAR.
SO UNI-MAN WISHED FOR AXE COP'S CAR TO BE FIXED USING THE MAGIC OF HIS UNICORN HORN.

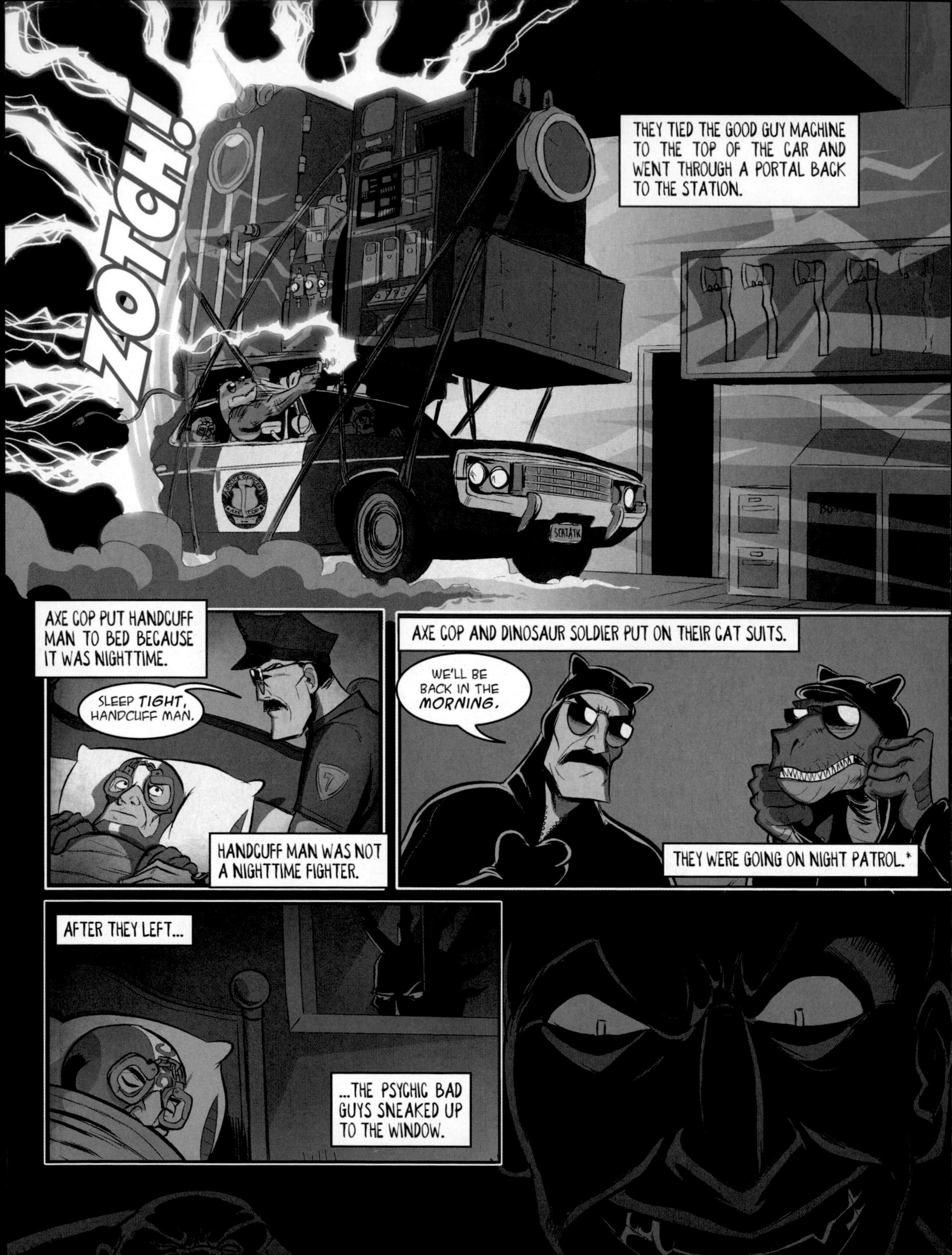
ZOTCH!
THEY TIED THE GOOD GUY MACHINE TO THE TOP OF THE CAR AND WENT THROUGH A PORTAL BACK TO THE STATION.
AXE COP PUT HANDCUFF MAN TO BED BECAUSE IT WAS NIGHTTIME.
SLEEP TIGHT, HANDCUFF MAN.
HANDCUFF MAN WAS NOT A NIGHTTIME FIGHTER.
AXE COP AND DINOSAUR SOLDIER PUT ON THEIR CAT SUITS.
WE'LL BE BACK IN THE MORNING.
THEY WERE GOING ON NIGHT PATROL.*
AFTER THEY LEFT...
...THE PSYCHIC BAD GUYS SNEAKED UP TO THE WINDOW.

WHEN THEY WENT IN, THEY DECIDED TO KILL HANDCUFF MAN.

WE NEED TO KILL THAT GUY.

I'LL TURN INTO A *SCORPION*.

SO THE BAD GUY TURNED INTO A SCORPION AND SNEAKED UP TO HANDCUFF MAN'S BED.

THEN HE KILLED HIM.

AAAGH!

THEY STOLE AXE COP'S EVERYTHING STICK... *

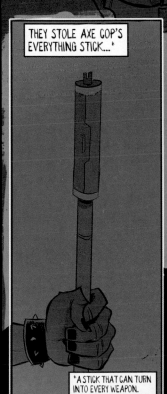

*A STICK THAT CAN TURN INTO EVERY WEAPON.

...ALL HIS POWER-UPS...

POWER-UP
POWER-UP
POWER-UP
POWER-UP
POWER-UP
POWER-UP
POWER-UP
POWER-UP
POWER-UP
WER-UP

...AND...

...LET'S STEAL THE *GOOD GUY MACHINE!*

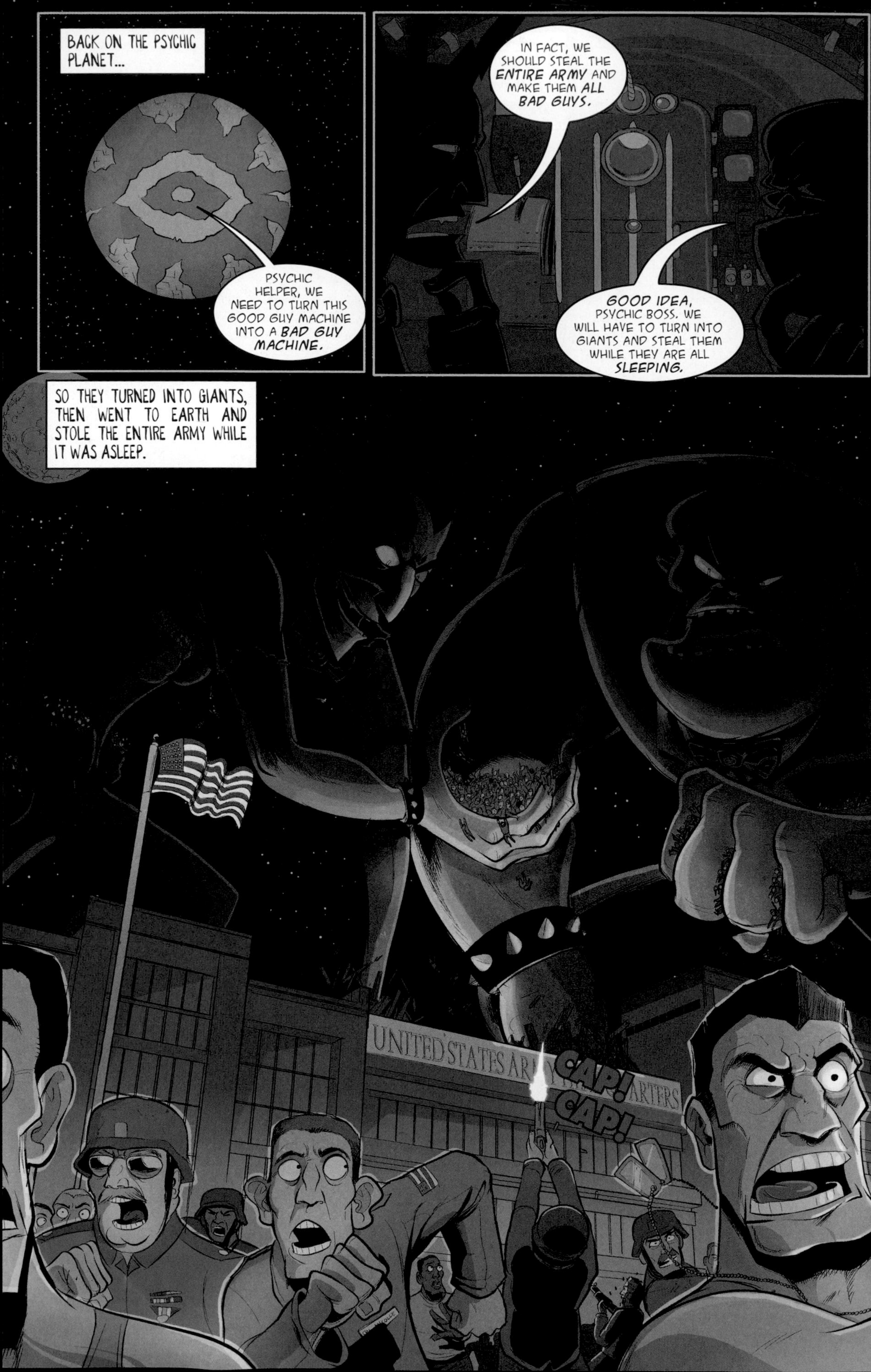
BACK ON THE PSYCHIC PLANET...
PSYCHIC HELPER, WE NEED TO TURN THIS GOOD GUY MACHINE INTO A *BAD GUY MACHINE.*
IN FACT, WE SHOULD STEAL THE *ENTIRE ARMY* AND MAKE THEM *ALL BAD GUYS.*
GOOD IDEA, PSYCHIC BOSS. WE WILL HAVE TO TURN INTO GIANTS AND STEAL THEM WHILE THEY ARE ALL *SLEEPING.*
SO THEY TURNED INTO GIANTS, THEN WENT TO EARTH AND STOLE THE ENTIRE ARMY WHILE IT WAS ASLEEP.
UNITED STATES ARMY
CAP! CAP!

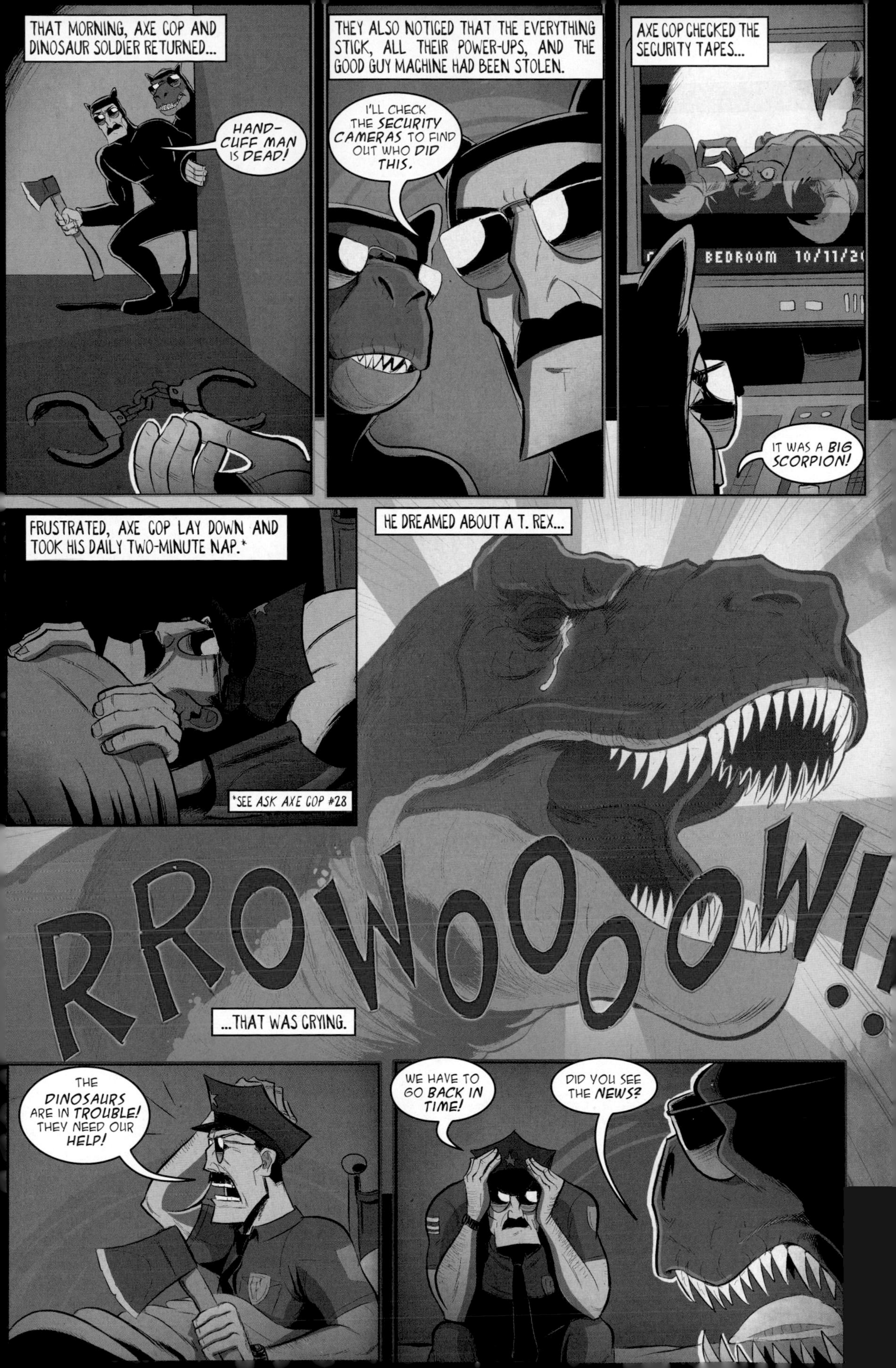
THAT MORNING, AXE COP AND DINOSAUR SOLDIER RETURNED...
HAND-CUFF MAN IS DEAD!
THEY ALSO NOTICED THAT THE EVERYTHING STICK, ALL THEIR POWER-UPS, AND THE GOOD GUY MACHINE HAD BEEN STOLEN.
I'LL CHECK THE SECURITY CAMERAS TO FIND OUT WHO DID THIS.
AXE COP CHECKED THE SECURITY TAPES...
BEDROOM 10/11/2
IT WAS A BIG SCORPION!
FRUSTRATED, AXE COP LAY DOWN AND TOOK HIS DAILY TWO-MINUTE NAP.*
*SEE ASK AXE COP #28
HE DREAMED ABOUT A T. REX...
RROWOOOOW!..
...THAT WAS CRYING.
THE DINOSAURS ARE IN TROUBLE! THEY NEED OUR HELP!
WE HAVE TO GO BACK IN TIME!
DID YOU SEE THE NEWS?

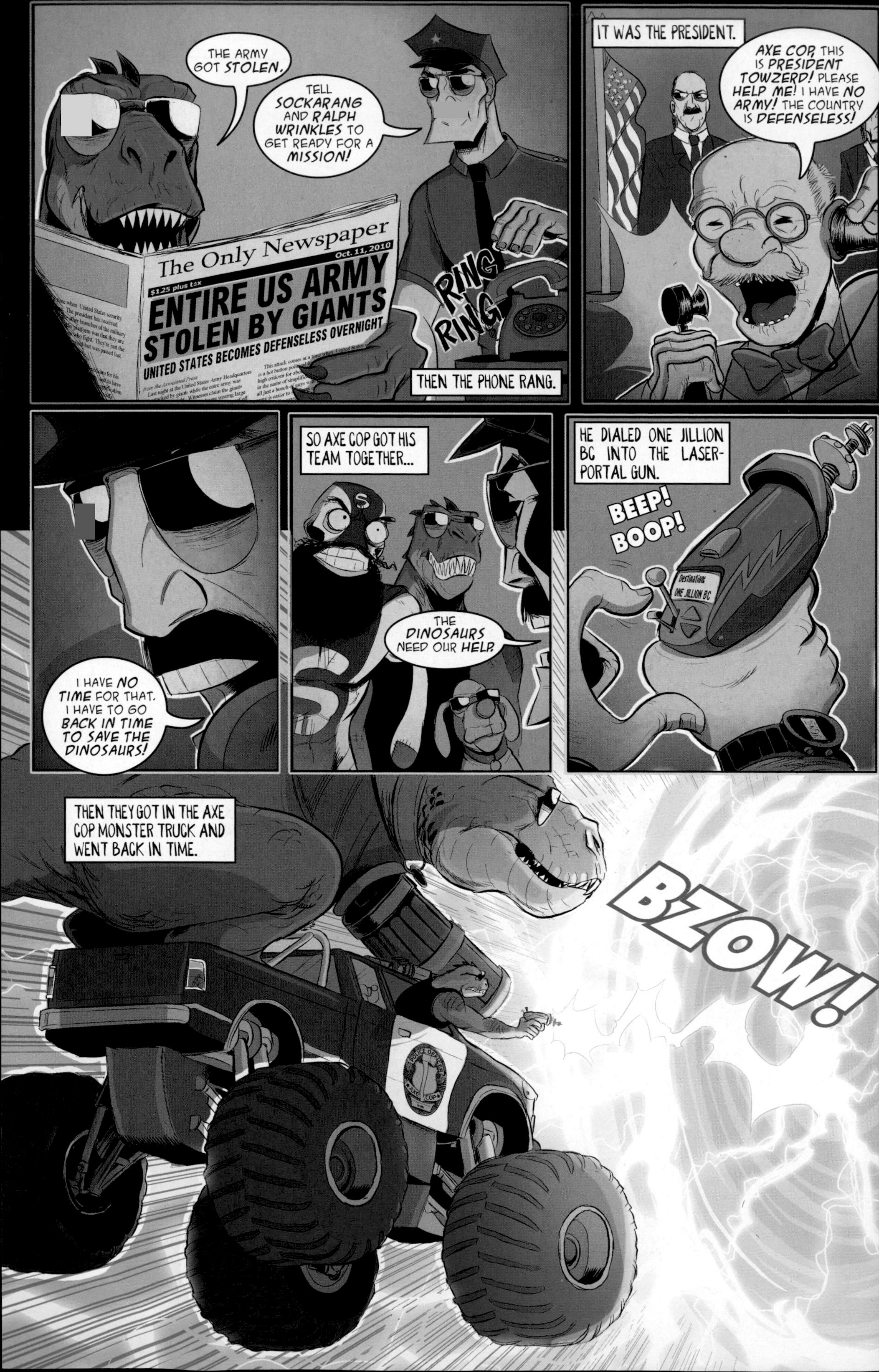
THE ARMY GOT STOLEN.
TELL SOCKARANG AND RALPH WRINKLES TO GET READY FOR A MISSION!
The Only Newspaper
Oct. 11, 2010
$1.25 plus tax
ENTIRE US ARMY STOLEN BY GIANTS
UNITED STATES BECOMES DEFENSELESS OVERNIGHT
RING RING
THEN THE PHONE RANG.
IT WAS THE PRESIDENT.
AXE COP, THIS IS PRESIDENT TOWZERD! PLEASE HELP ME! I HAVE NO ARMY! THE COUNTRY IS DEFENSELESS!
I HAVE NO TIME FOR THAT. I HAVE TO GO BACK IN TIME TO SAVE THE DINOSAURS!
SO AXE COP GOT HIS TEAM TOGETHER...
THE DINOSAURS NEED OUR HELP.
HE DIALED ONE JILLION BC INTO THE LASER-PORTAL GUN.
BEEP! BOOP!
Destination: ONE JILLION BC
THEN THEY GOT IN THE AXE COP MONSTER TRUCK AND WENT BACK IN TIME.
BZOW!

MEANWHILE, ON A CHICKEN FARM.

CLUCK!
CLUCK!
CLUCK!
BGAK!
CLUCK!
CLUCK!
CLUCK!
CLUCK!
CLUCK!
BERGAK!
CLUCK!
CLUCK!

ALL THE CHICKENS' BRAINS POPPED OUT.

POP!
POP!
POP!

THE BRAINS TURNED INTO BAD GUYS.

THEY HAD ROBOTIC BODY PARTS AND SWORDS.

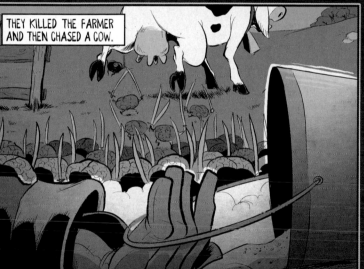

THEY KILLED THE FARMER AND THEN CHASED A COW.

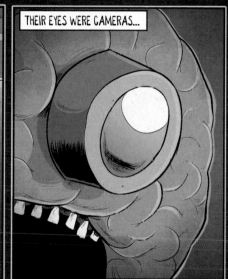

THEIR EYES WERE CAMERAS...

THE CHICKEN-BRAIN ROBOTS WORKED LIKE A CHARM, BROTHER. NOW THEY CAN GO AND STEAL THE WHITE DIAMOND!

CHICKEN-BRAIN CAMERA VIEWER

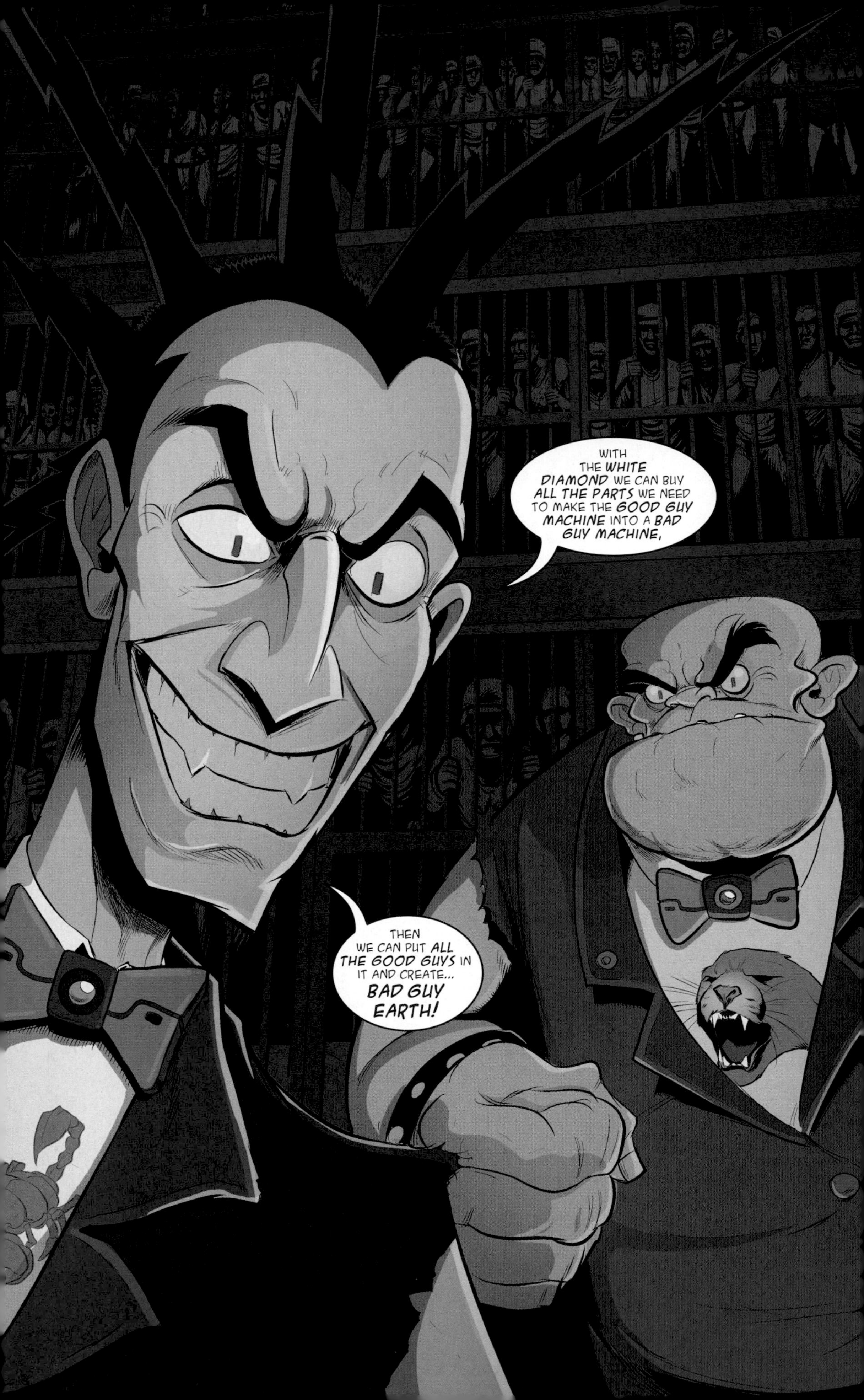
WITH THE WHITE DIAMOND WE CAN BUY ALL THE PARTS WE NEED TO MAKE THE GOOD GUY MACHINE INTO A BAD GUY MACHINE,
THEN WE CAN PUT ALL THE GOOD GUYS IN IT AND CREATE... BAD GUY EARTH!

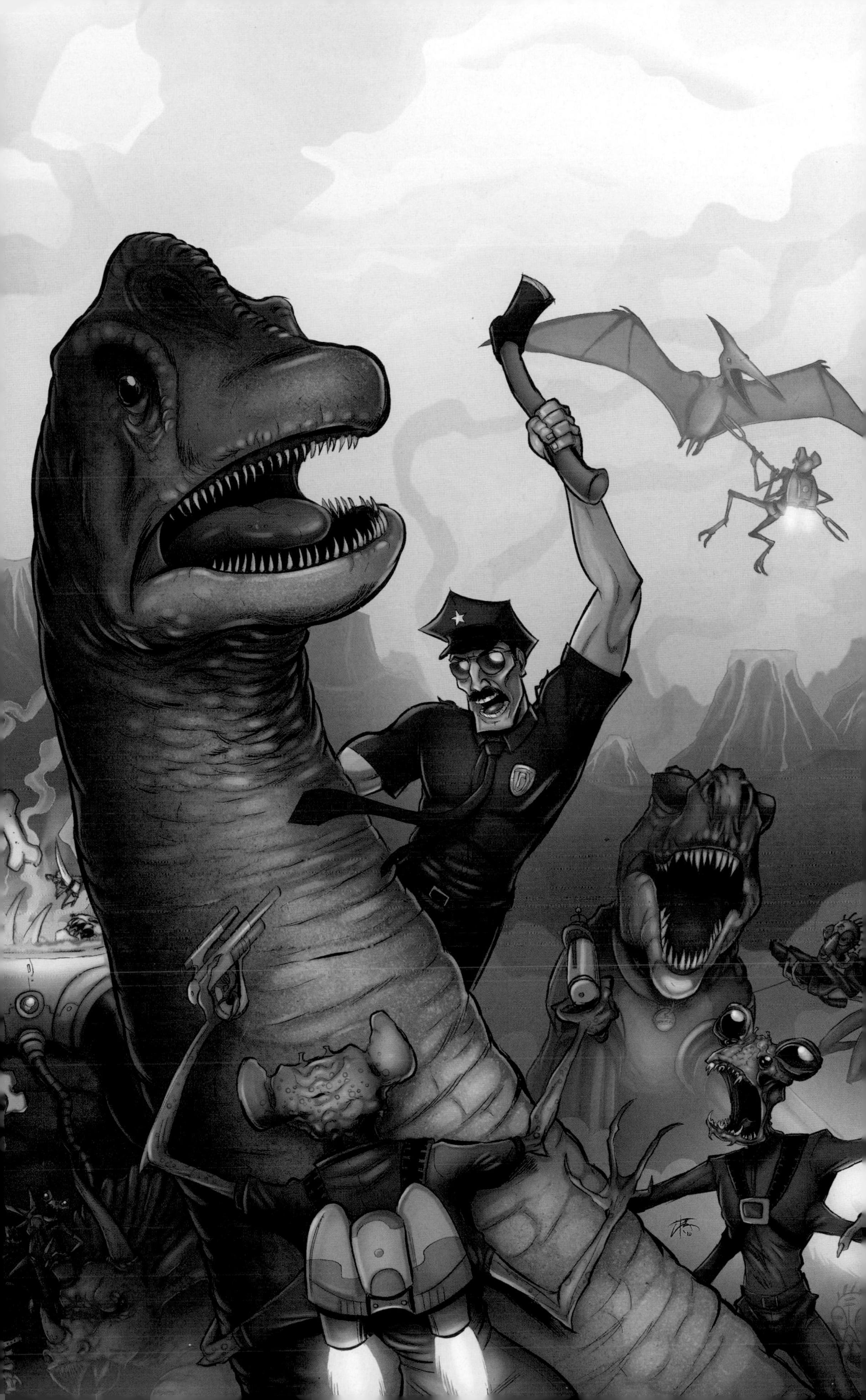

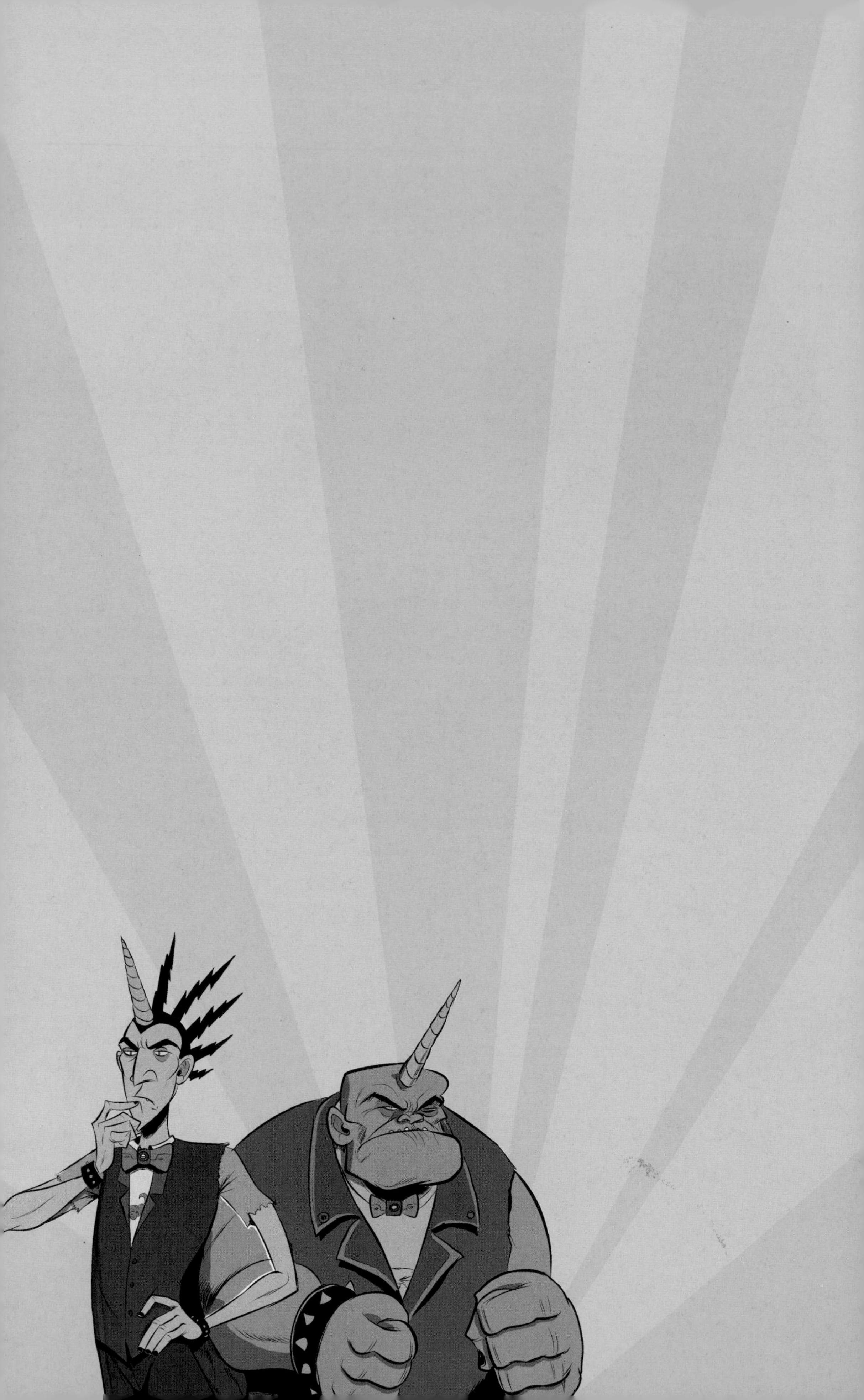

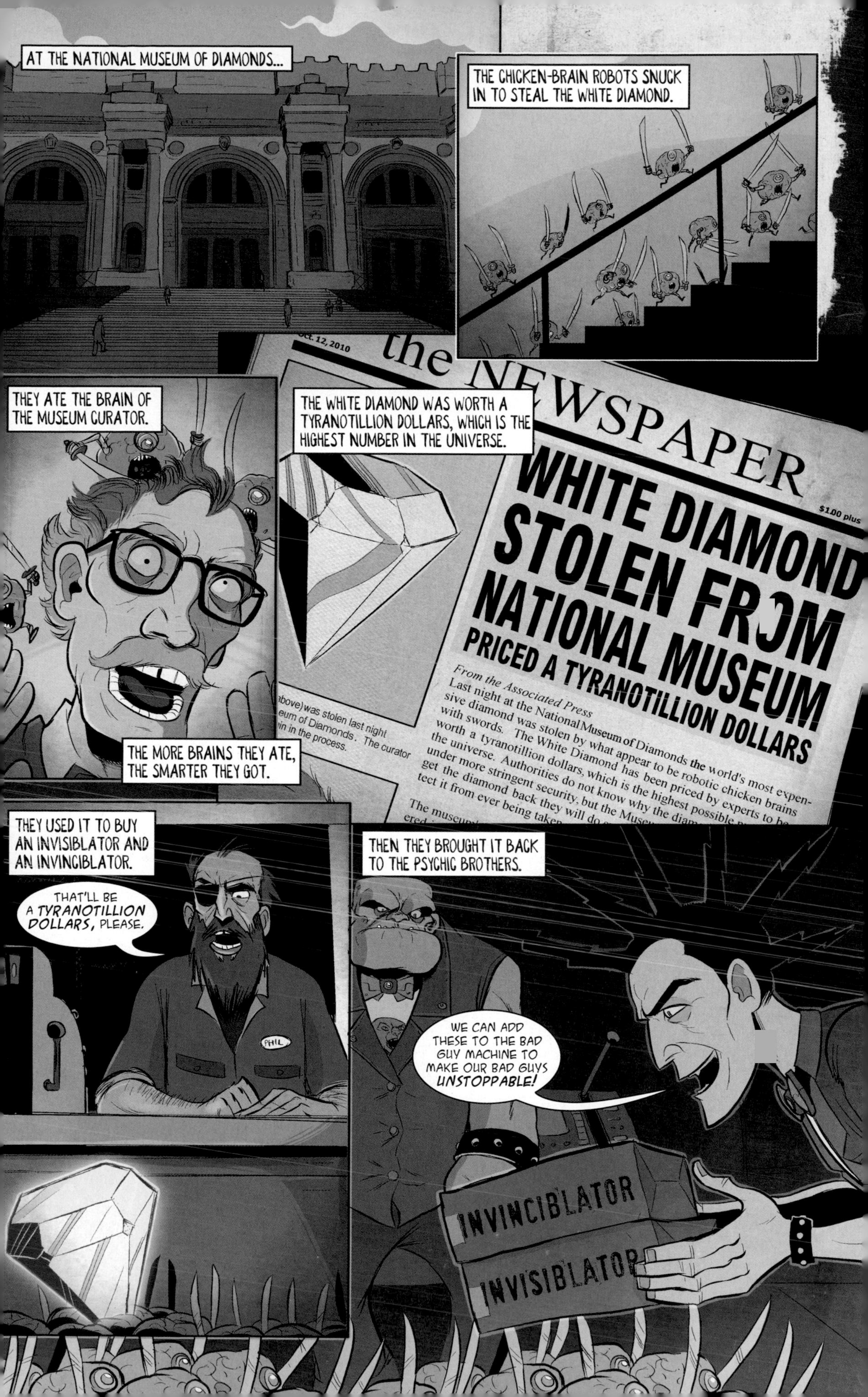
AT THE NATIONAL MUSEUM OF DIAMONDS...
THE CHICKEN-BRAIN ROBOTS SNUCK IN TO STEAL THE WHITE DIAMOND.
THEY ATE THE BRAIN OF THE MUSEUM CURATOR.
THE WHITE DIAMOND WAS WORTH A TYRANOTILLION DOLLARS, WHICH IS THE HIGHEST NUMBER IN THE UNIVERSE.
Oct. 12, 2010
the NEWSPAPER
$1.00 plus
WHITE DIAMOND STOLEN FROM NATIONAL MUSEUM
PRICED A TYRANOTILLION DOLLARS
From the Associated Press
Last night at the National Museum of Diamonds the world's most expen-
sive diamond was stolen by what appear to be robotic chicken brains
with swords. The White Diamond has been priced by experts to be
worth a tyranotillion dollars, which is the highest possible
the universe. Authorities do not know why the diam
under more stringent security, but the Museu
get the diamond back they will do s
tect it from ever being taken
above) was stolen last night
eum of Diamonds. The curator
in in the process.
THE MORE BRAINS THEY ATE, THE SMARTER THEY GOT.
THEY USED IT TO BUY AN INVISIBLATOR AND AN INVINCIBLATOR.
THAT'LL BE A *TYRANOTILLION DOLLARS*, PLEASE.
PHIL
THEN THEY BROUGHT IT BACK TO THE PSYCHIC BROTHERS.
WE CAN ADD THESE TO THE BAD GUY MACHINE TO MAKE OUR BAD GUYS *UNSTOPPABLE!*
INVINCIBLATOR
INVISIBLATOR

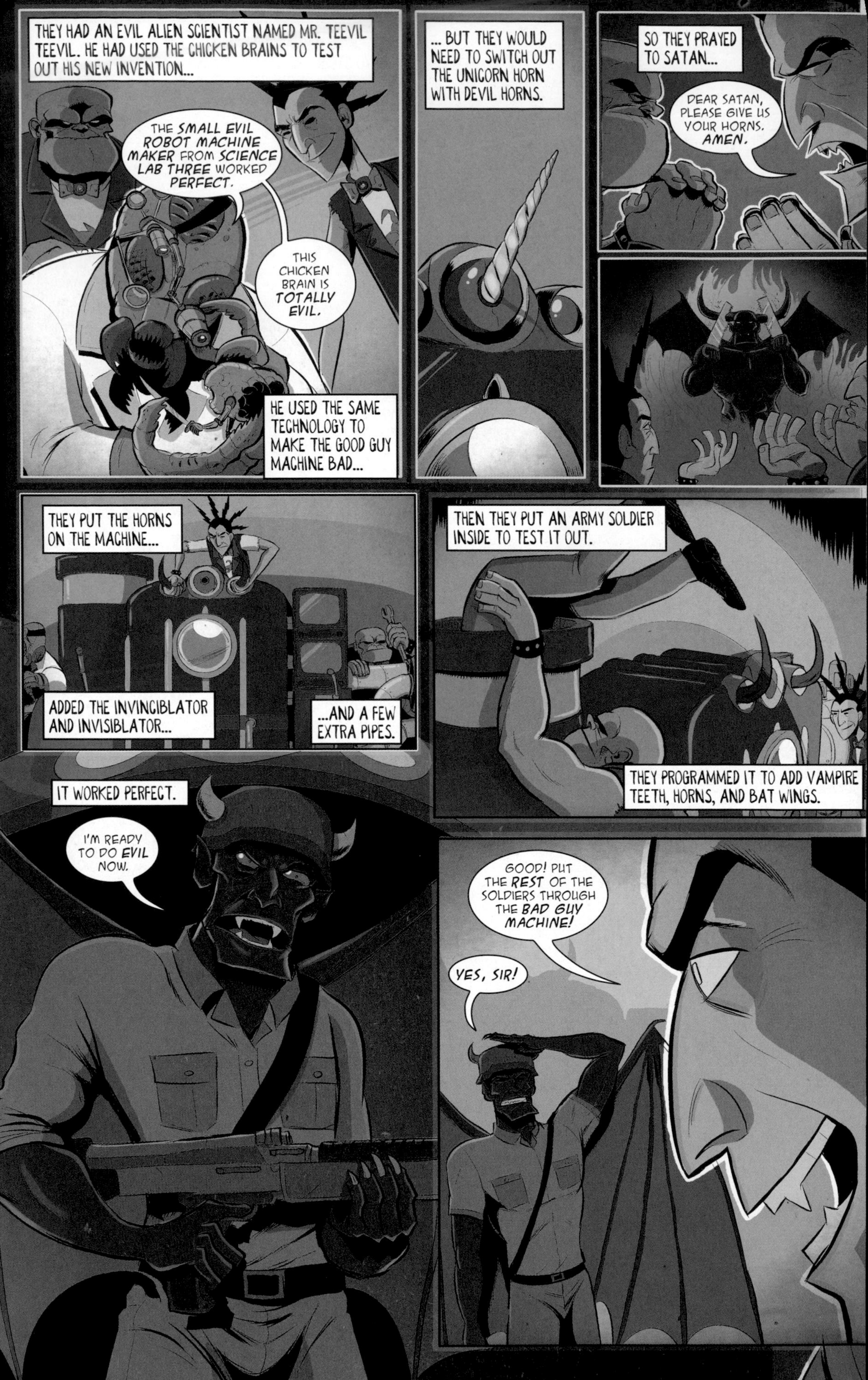
THEY HAD AN EVIL ALIEN SCIENTIST NAMED MR. TEEVIL TEEVIL. HE HAD USED THE CHICKEN BRAINS TO TEST OUT HIS NEW INVENTION...
THE SMALL EVIL ROBOT MACHINE MAKER FROM SCIENCE LAB THREE WORKED PERFECT.
THIS CHICKEN BRAIN IS TOTALLY EVIL.
HE USED THE SAME TECHNOLOGY TO MAKE THE GOOD GUY MACHINE BAD...
... BUT THEY WOULD NEED TO SWITCH OUT THE UNICORN HORN WITH DEVIL HORNS.
SO THEY PRAYED TO SATAN...
DEAR SATAN, PLEASE GIVE US YOUR HORNS. AMEN.
THEY PUT THE HORNS ON THE MACHINE...
ADDED THE INVINCIBLATOR AND INVISIBLATOR...
...AND A FEW EXTRA PIPES.
THEN THEY PUT AN ARMY SOLDIER INSIDE TO TEST IT OUT.
THEY PROGRAMMED IT TO ADD VAMPIRE TEETH, HORNS, AND BAT WINGS.
IT WORKED PERFECT.
I'M READY TO DO EVIL NOW.
GOOD! PUT THE REST OF THE SOLDIERS THROUGH THE BAD GUY MACHINE!
YES, SIR!

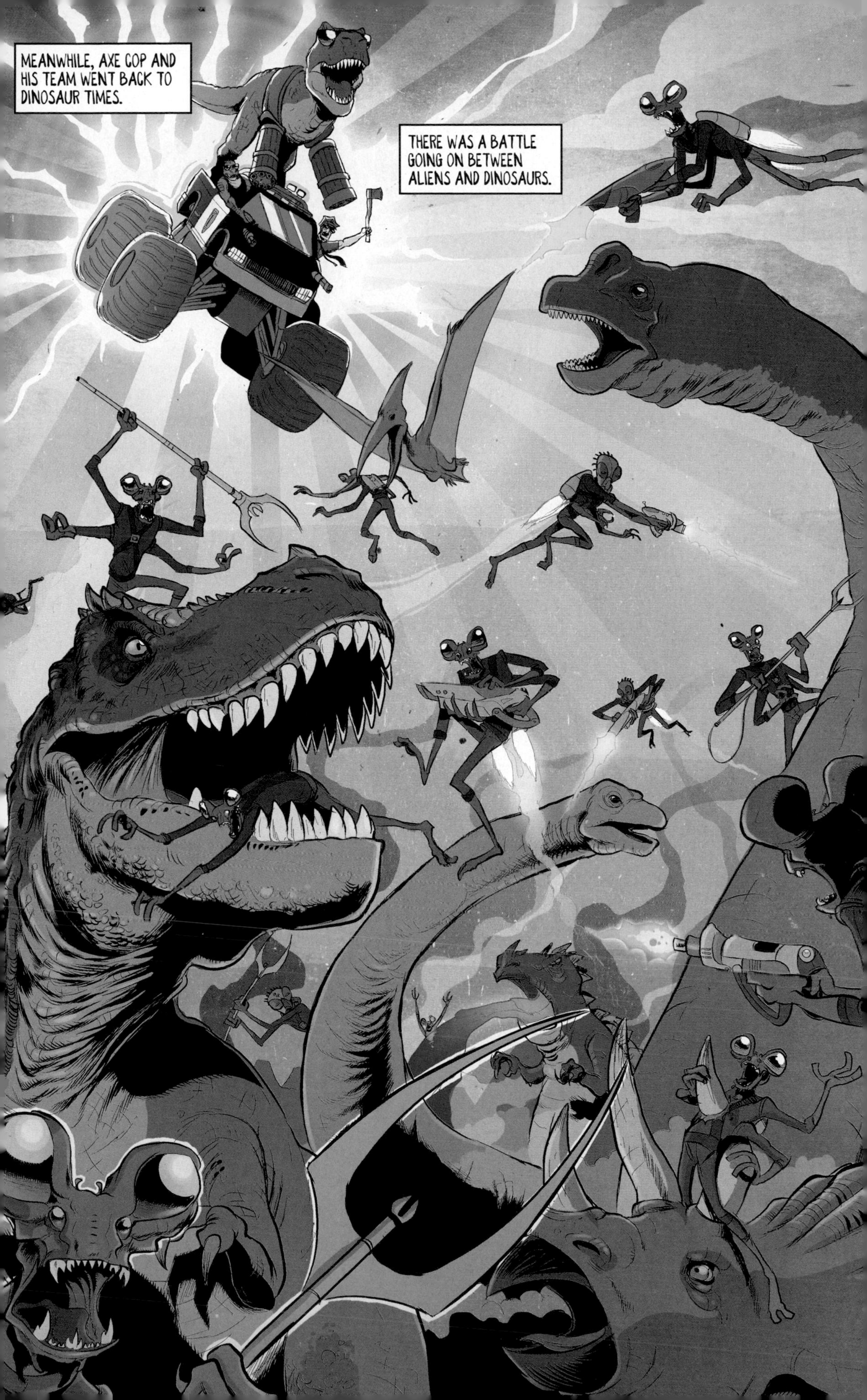
MEANWHILE, AXE COP AND HIS TEAM WENT BACK TO DINOSAUR TIMES.
THERE WAS A BATTLE GOING ON BETWEEN ALIENS AND DINOSAURS.

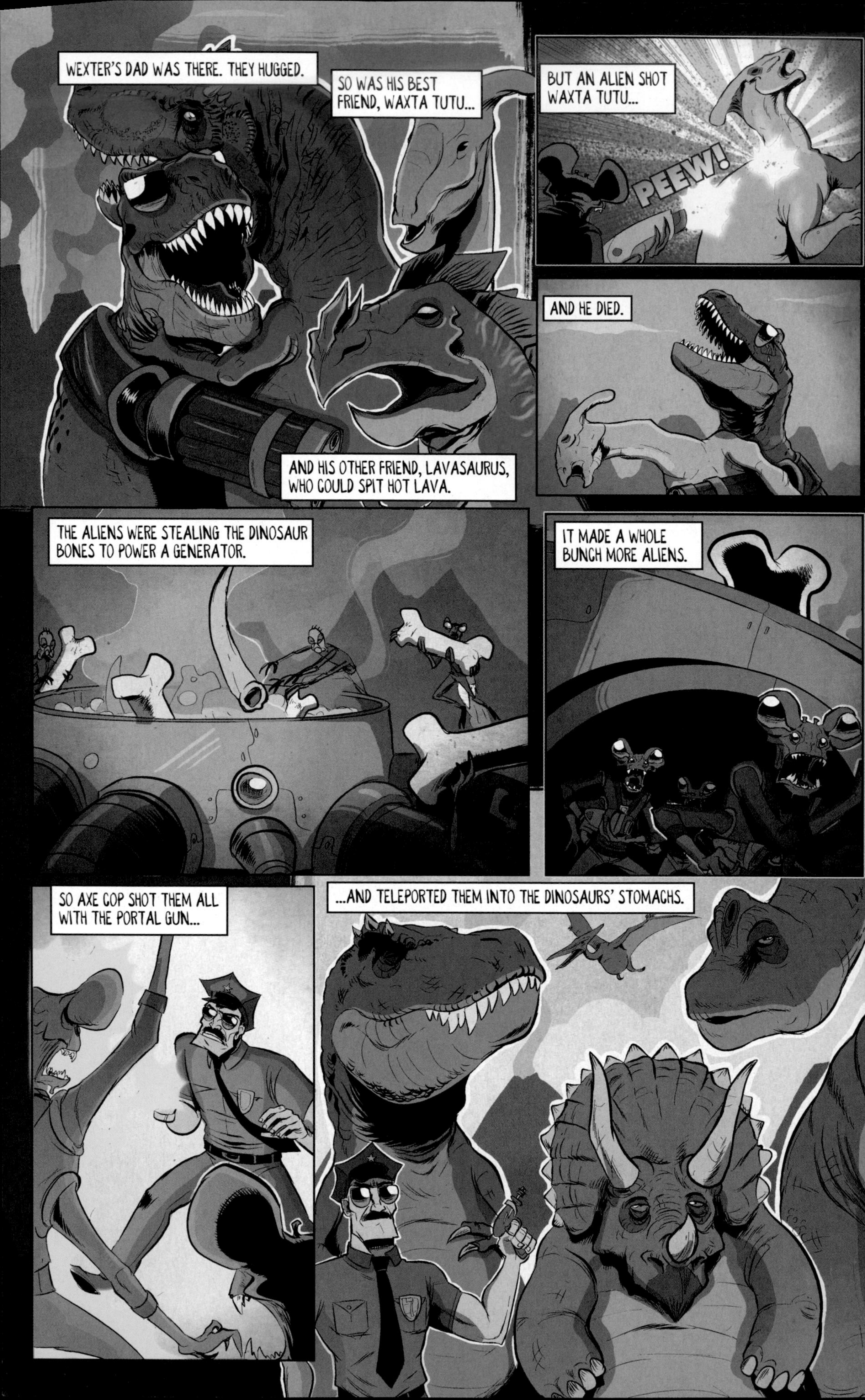
WEXTER'S DAD WAS THERE. THEY HUGGED.
SO WAS HIS BEST FRIEND, WAXTA TUTU...
AND HIS OTHER FRIEND, LAVASAURUS, WHO COULD SPIT HOT LAVA.
BUT AN ALIEN SHOT WAXTA TUTU...
PEEW!
AND HE DIED.
THE ALIENS WERE STEALING THE DINOSAUR BONES TO POWER A GENERATOR.
IT MADE A WHOLE BUNCH MORE ALIENS.
SO AXE COP SHOT THEM ALL WITH THE PORTAL GUN...
...AND TELEPORTED THEM INTO THE DINOSAURS' STOMACHS.

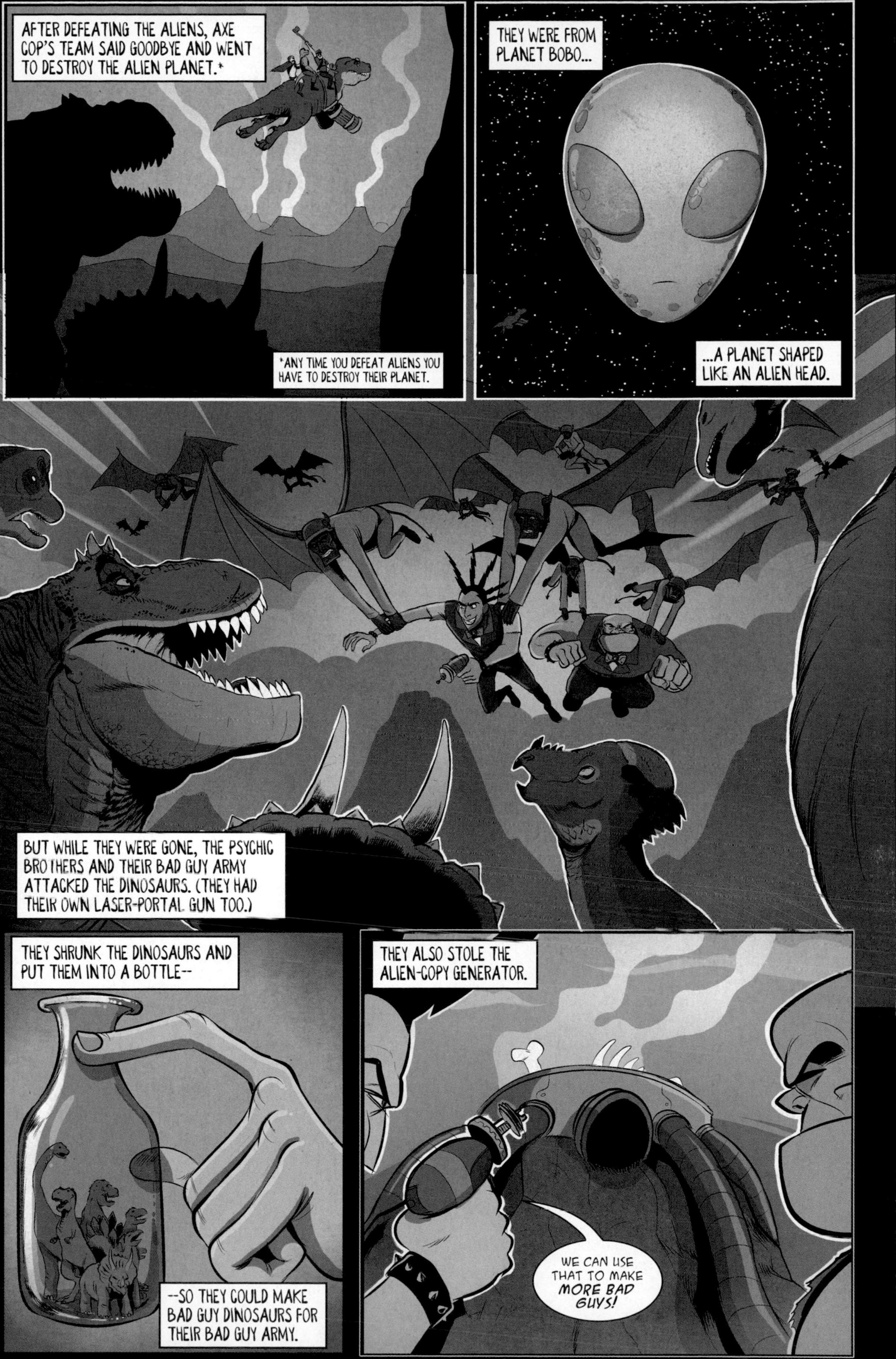
AFTER DEFEATING THE ALIENS, AXE COP'S TEAM SAID GOODBYE AND WENT TO DESTROY THE ALIEN PLANET.*
*ANY TIME YOU DEFEAT ALIENS YOU HAVE TO DESTROY THEIR PLANET.
THEY WERE FROM PLANET BOBO...
...A PLANET SHAPED LIKE AN ALIEN HEAD.
BUT WHILE THEY WERE GONE, THE PSYCHIC BROTHERS AND THEIR BAD GUY ARMY ATTACKED THE DINOSAURS. (THEY HAD THEIR OWN LASER-PORTAL GUN TOO.)
THEY SHRUNK THE DINOSAURS AND PUT THEM INTO A BOTTLE--
--SO THEY COULD MAKE BAD GUY DINOSAURS FOR THEIR BAD GUY ARMY.
THEY ALSO STOLE THE ALIEN-COPY GENERATOR.
WE CAN USE THAT TO MAKE *MORE BAD GUYS!*

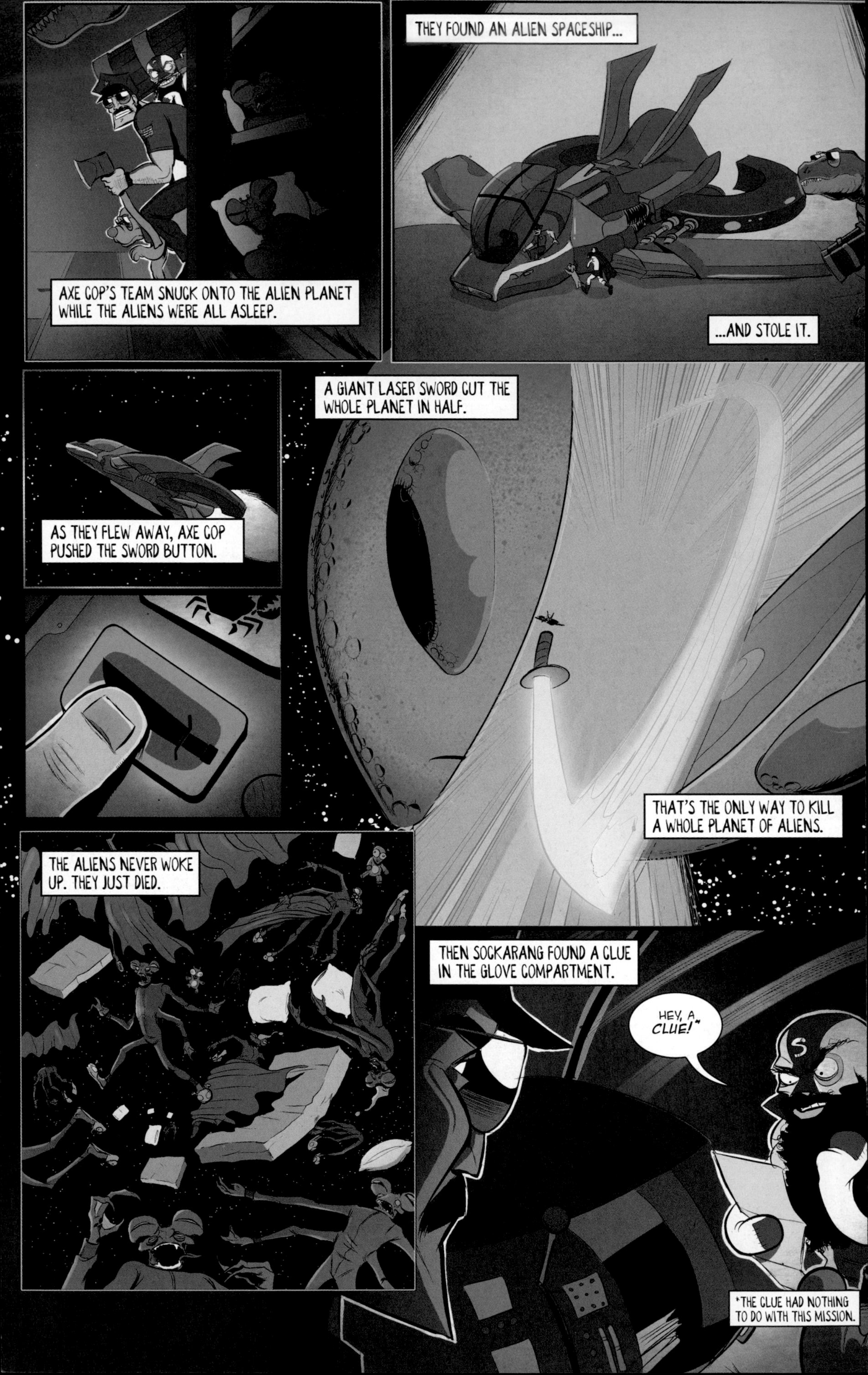
AXE COP'S TEAM SNUCK ONTO THE ALIEN PLANET WHILE THE ALIENS WERE ALL ASLEEP.
THEY FOUND AN ALIEN SPACESHIP...
...AND STOLE IT.
AS THEY FLEW AWAY, AXE COP PUSHED THE SWORD BUTTON.
A GIANT LASER SWORD CUT THE WHOLE PLANET IN HALF.
THAT'S THE ONLY WAY TO KILL A WHOLE PLANET OF ALIENS.
THE ALIENS NEVER WOKE UP. THEY JUST DIED.
THEN SOCKARANG FOUND A CLUE IN THE GLOVE COMPARTMENT.
HEY, A CLUE!*
*THE CLUE HAD NOTHING TO DO WITH THIS MISSION.

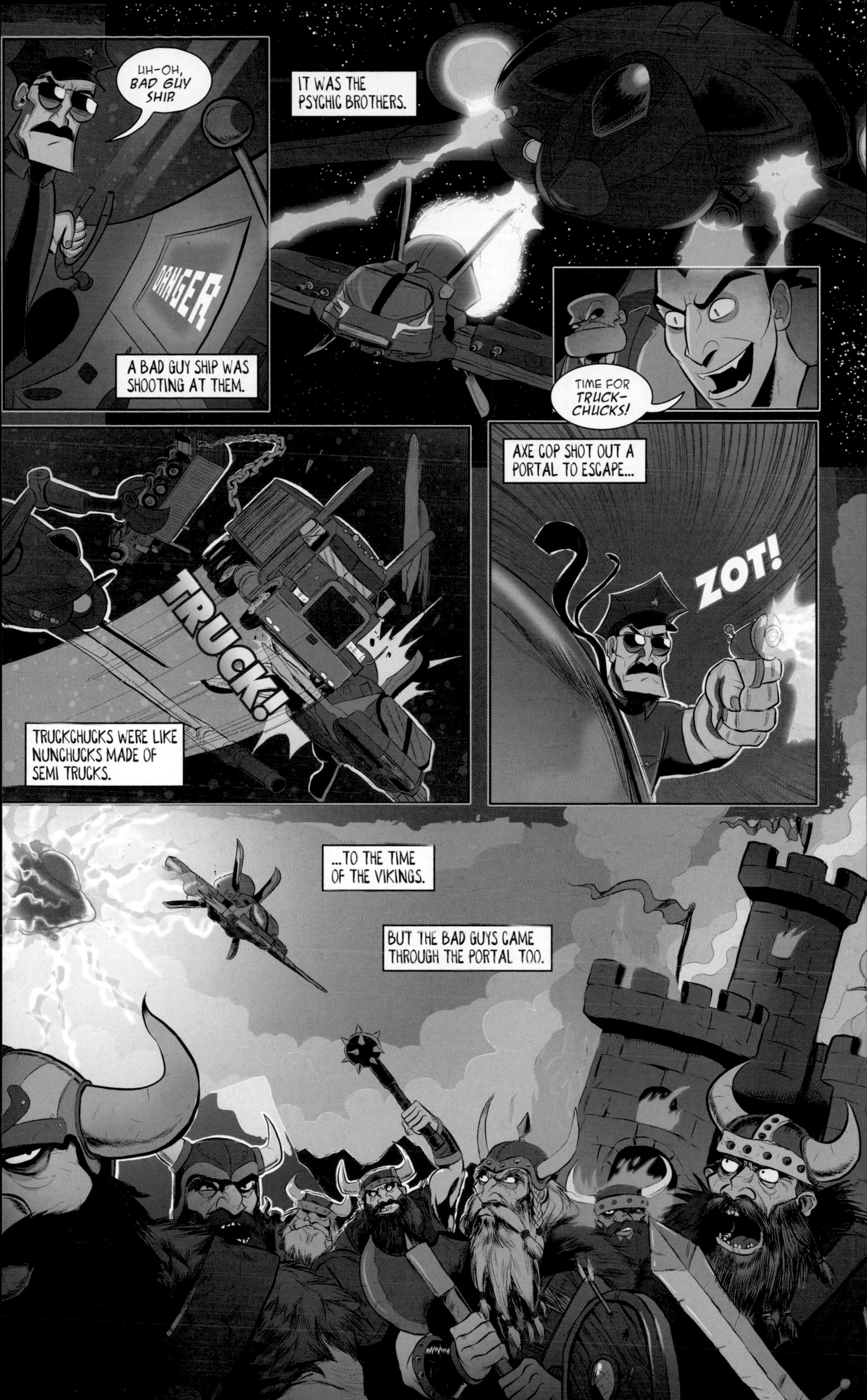
UH-OH, BAD GUY SHIP.
IT WAS THE PSYCHIC BROTHERS.
A BAD GUY SHIP WAS SHOOTING AT THEM.
DANGER
TIME FOR TRUCK-CHUCKS!
TRUCK!
TRUCKCHUCKS WERE LIKE NUNCHUCKS MADE OF SEMI TRUCKS.
AXE COP SHOT OUT A PORTAL TO ESCAPE...
ZOT!
...TO THE TIME OF THE VIKINGS.
BUT THE BAD GUYS CAME THROUGH THE PORTAL TOO.

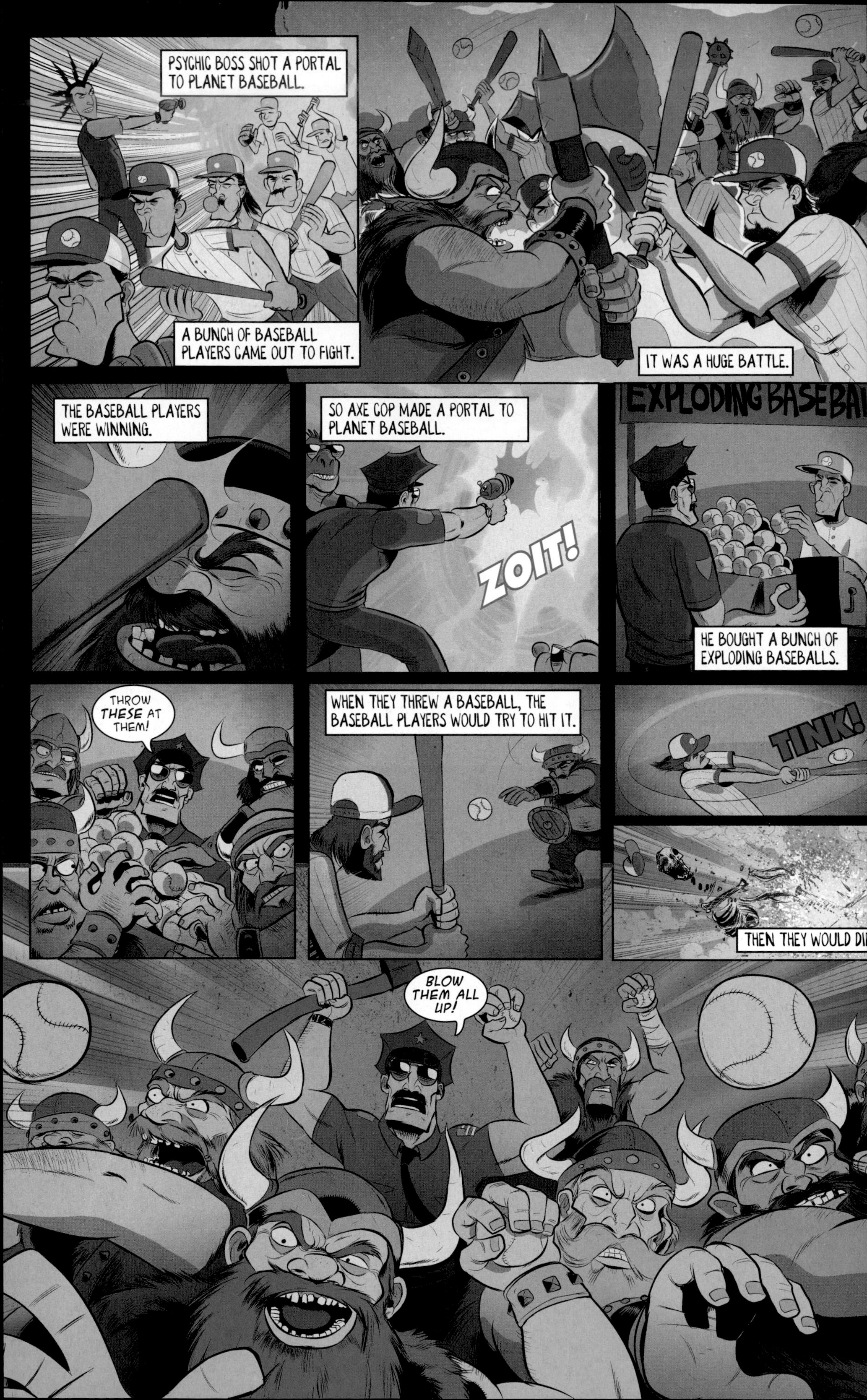
PSYCHIC BOSS SHOT A PORTAL TO PLANET BASEBALL.
A BUNCH OF BASEBALL PLAYERS CAME OUT TO FIGHT.
IT WAS A HUGE BATTLE.
THE BASEBALL PLAYERS WERE WINNING.
SO AXE COP MADE A PORTAL TO PLANET BASEBALL.
ZOIT!
EXPLODING BASEBA
HE BOUGHT A BUNCH OF EXPLODING BASEBALLS.
THROW THESE AT THEM!
WHEN THEY THREW A BASEBALL, THE BASEBALL PLAYERS WOULD TRY TO HIT IT.
TINK!
THEN THEY WOULD DI
BLOW THEM ALL UP!

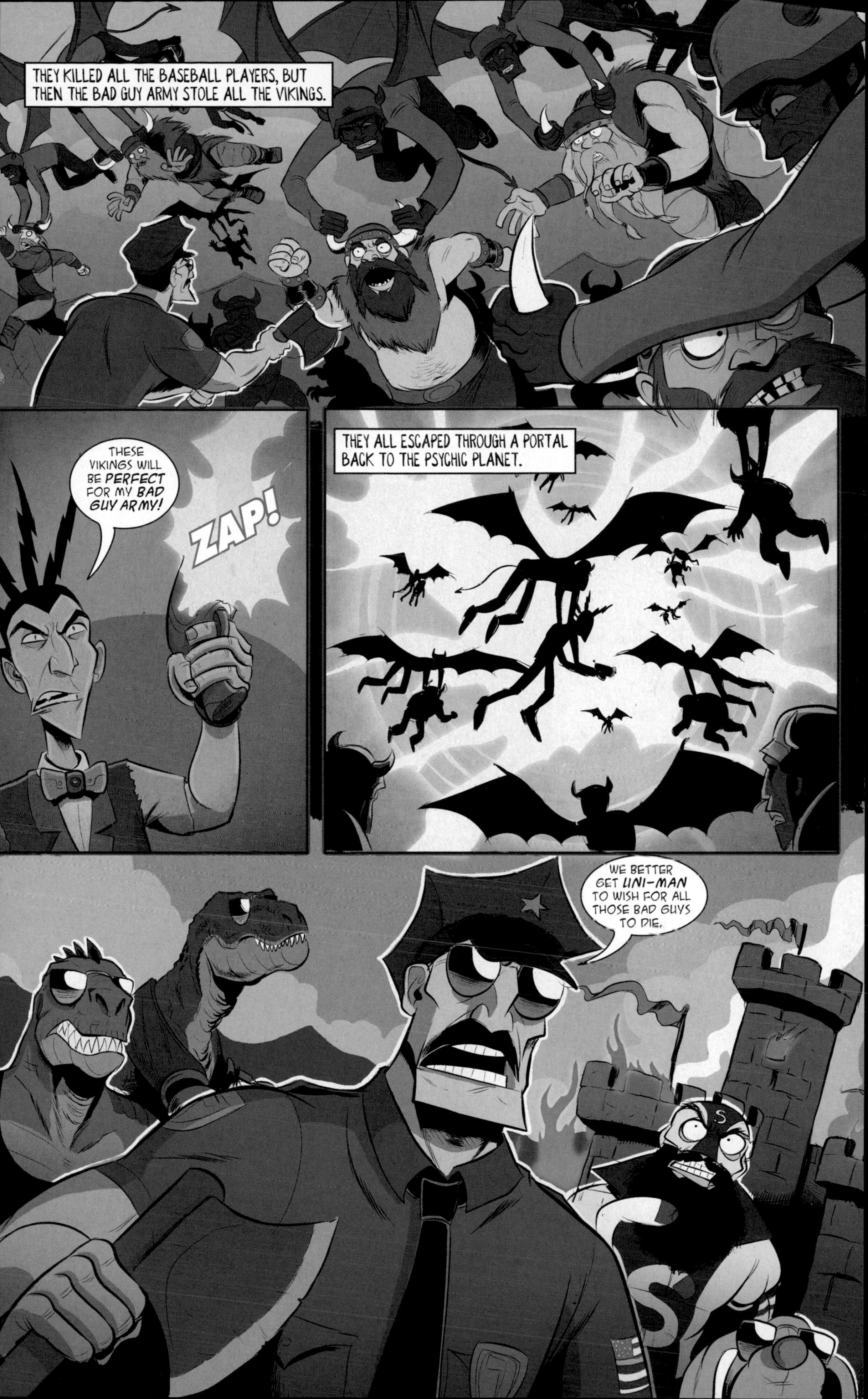
THEY KILLED ALL THE BASEBALL PLAYERS, BUT THEN THE BAD GUY ARMY STOLE ALL THE VIKINGS.
THESE VIKINGS WILL BE PERFECT FOR MY BAD GUY ARMY!
ZAP!
THEY ALL ESCAPED THROUGH A PORTAL BACK TO THE PSYCHIC PLANET.
WE BETTER GET UNI-MAN TO WISH FOR ALL THOSE BAD GUYS TO DIE.

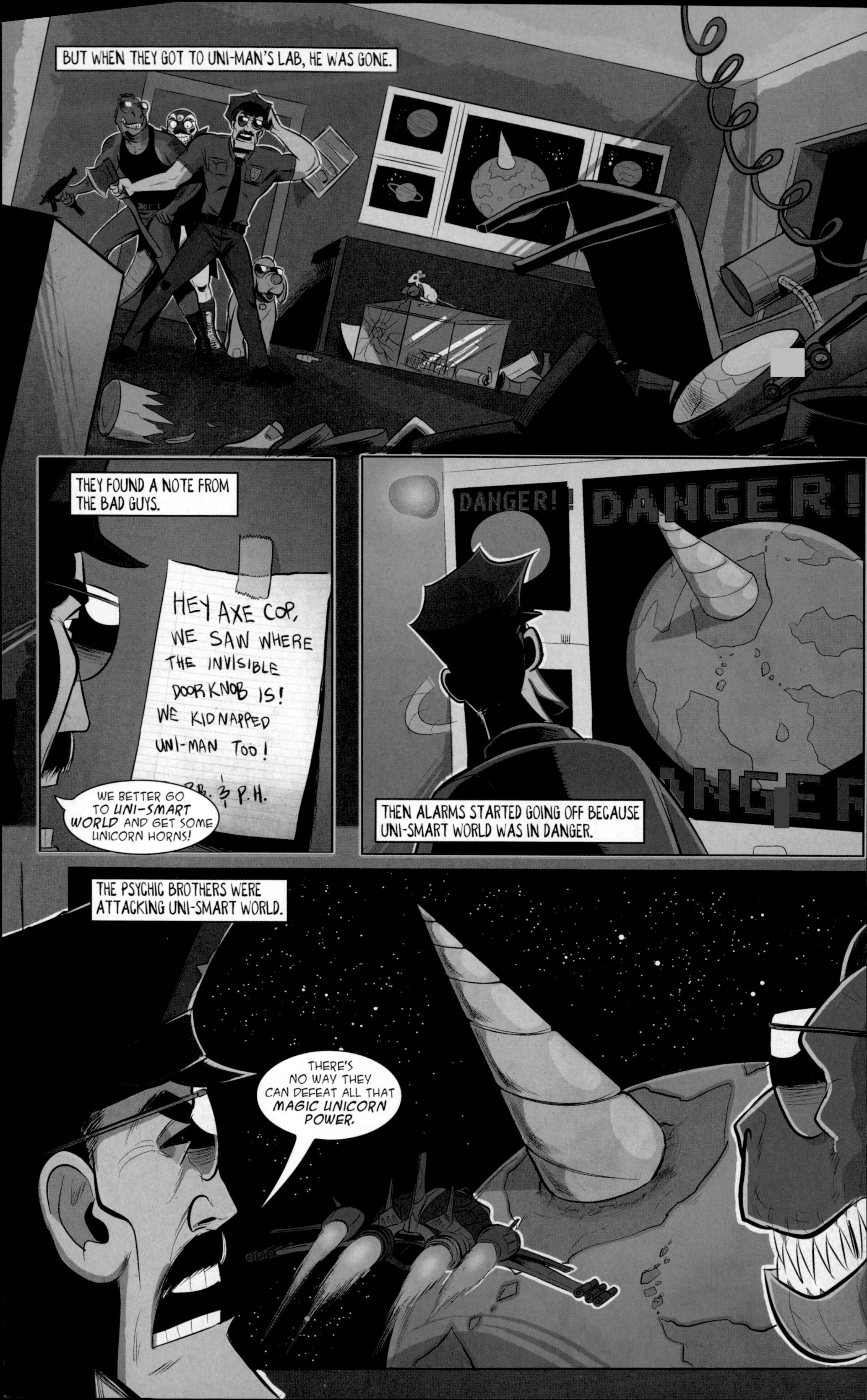

BUT WHEN THEY GOT TO UNI-MAN'S LAB, HE WAS GONE.
THEY FOUND A NOTE FROM THE BAD GUYS.
HEY AXE COP, WE SAW WHERE THE INVISIBLE DOOR KNOB IS! WE KIDNAPPED UNI-MAN TOO!
WE BETTER GO TO UNI-SMART WORLD AND GET SOME UNICORN HORNS!
DANGER!
DANGER!
THEN ALARMS STARTED GOING OFF BECAUSE UNI-SMART WORLD WAS IN DANGER.
THE PSYCHIC BROTHERS WERE ATTACKING UNI-SMART WORLD.
THERE'S NO WAY THEY CAN DEFEAT ALL THAT MAGIC UNICORN POWER.

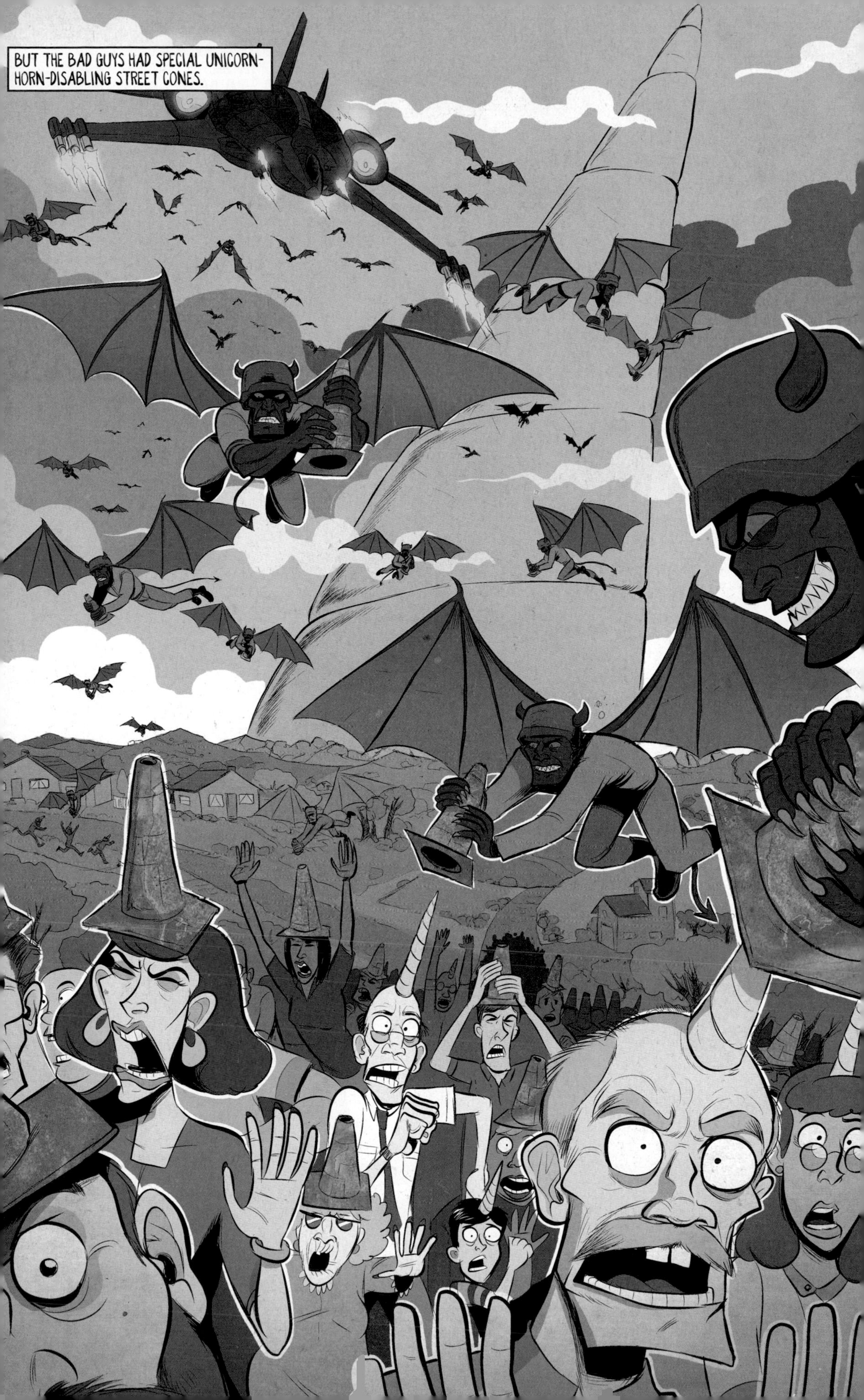
BUT THE BAD GUYS HAD SPECIAL UNICORN-HORN-DISABLING STREET CONES.

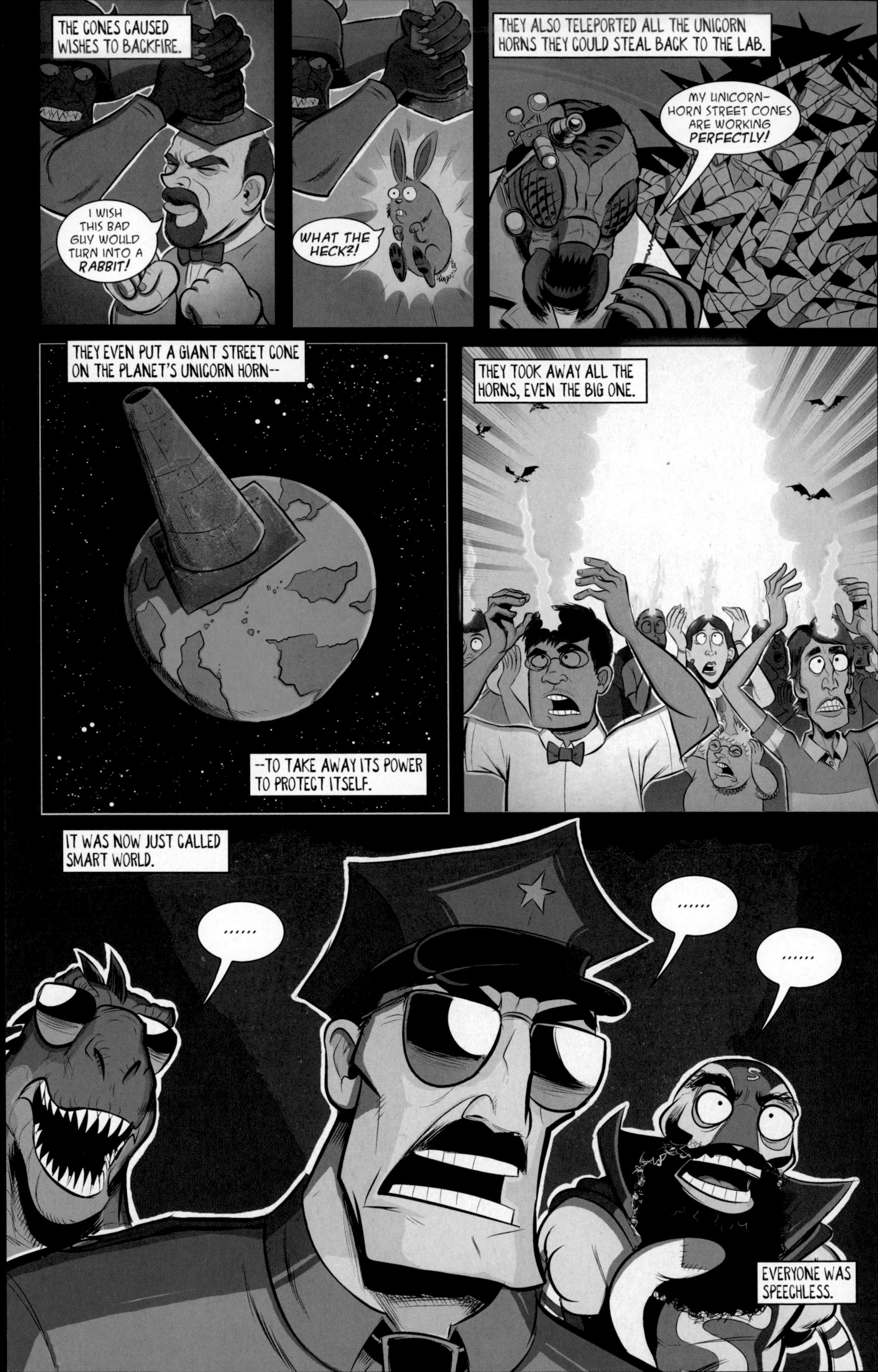
THE CONES CAUSED WISHES TO BACKFIRE.
I WISH THIS BAD GUY WOULD TURN INTO A RABBIT!
WHAT THE HECK?!
THEY ALSO TELEPORTED ALL THE UNICORN HORNS THEY COULD STEAL BACK TO THE LAB.
MY UNICORN-HORN STREET CONES ARE WORKING PERFECTLY!
THEY EVEN PUT A GIANT STREET CONE ON THE PLANET'S UNICORN HORN--
--TO TAKE AWAY ITS POWER TO PROTECT ITSELF.
THEY TOOK AWAY ALL THE HORNS, EVEN THE BIG ONE.
IT WAS NOW JUST CALLED SMART WORLD.
......
......
......
EVERYONE WAS SPEECHLESS.

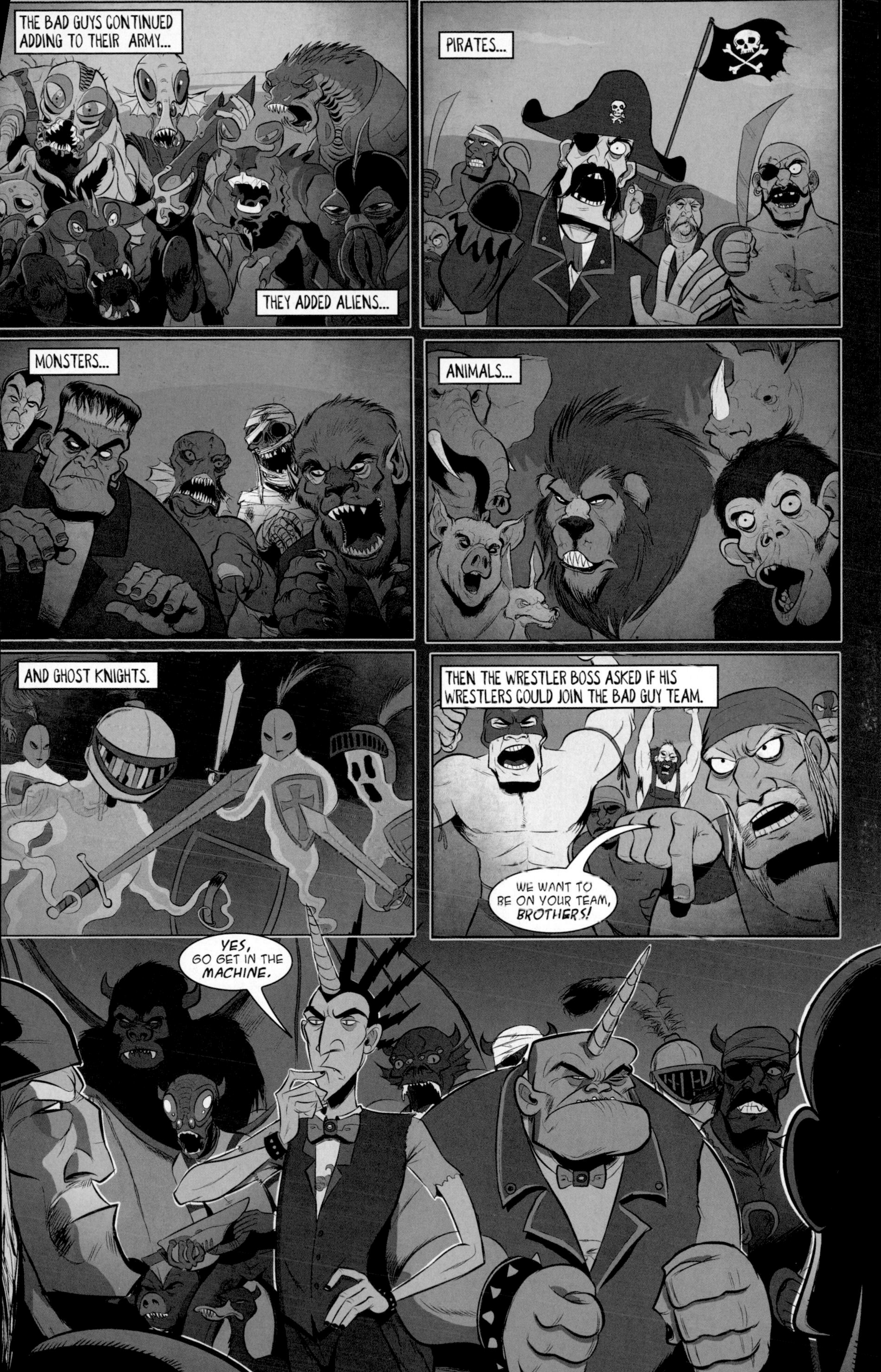
THE BAD GUYS CONTINUED ADDING TO THEIR ARMY...
THEY ADDED ALIENS...
PIRATES...
MONSTERS...
ANIMALS...
AND GHOST KNIGHTS.
THEN THE WRESTLER BOSS ASKED IF HIS WRESTLERS COULD JOIN THE BAD GUY TEAM.
WE WANT TO BE ON YOUR TEAM, BROTHERS!
YES, GO GET IN THE MACHINE.

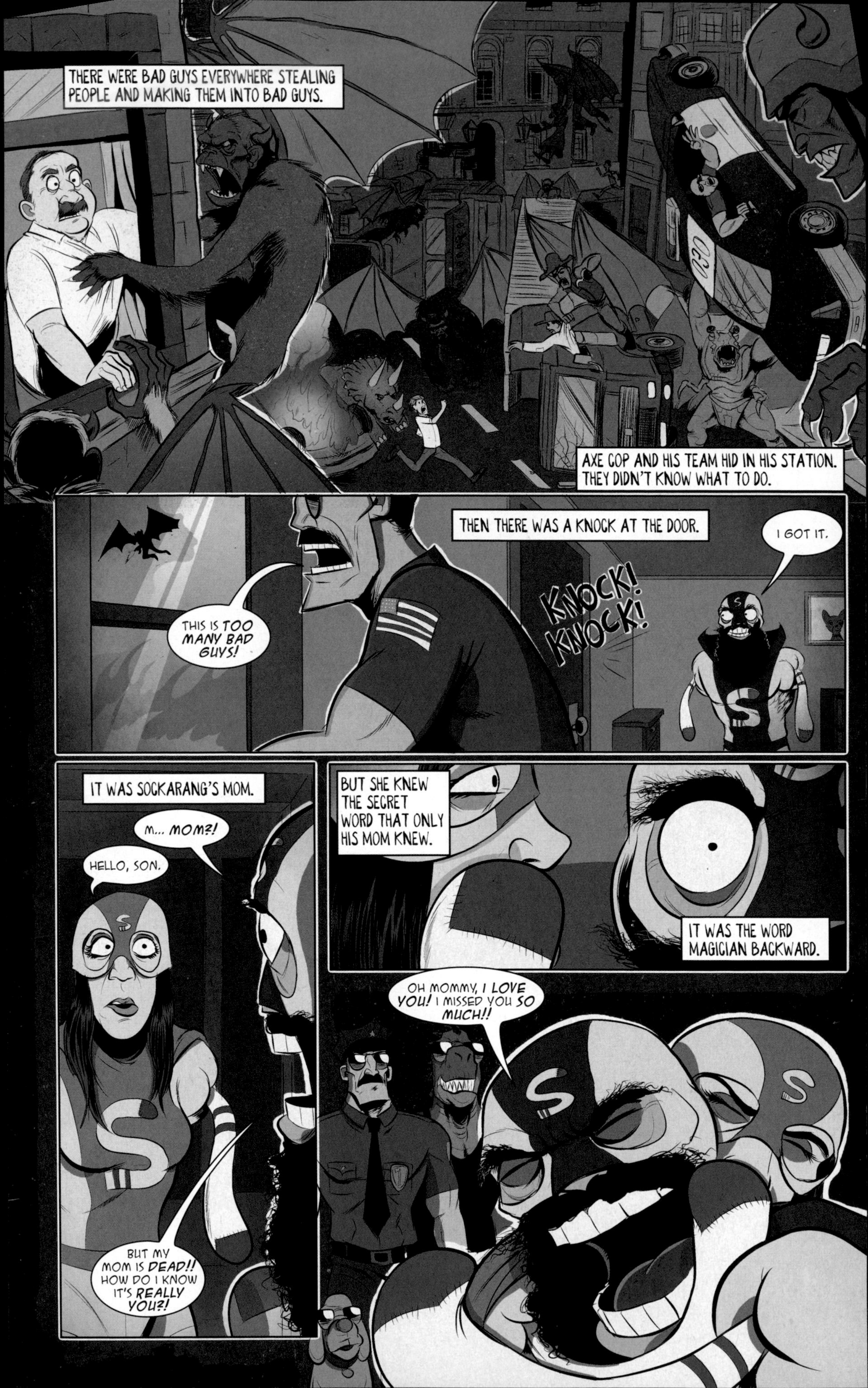
THERE WERE BAD GUYS EVERYWHERE STEALING PEOPLE AND MAKING THEM INTO BAD GUYS.
AXE COP AND HIS TEAM HID IN HIS STATION. THEY DIDN'T KNOW WHAT TO DO.
THEN THERE WAS A KNOCK AT THE DOOR.
THIS IS TOO MANY BAD GUYS!
KNOCK! KNOCK!
I GOT IT.
IT WAS SOCKARANG'S MOM.
M... MOM?!
HELLO, SON.
BUT MY MOM IS DEAD!! HOW DO I KNOW IT'S REALLY YOU?!
BUT SHE KNEW THE SECRET WORD THAT ONLY HIS MOM KNEW.
IT WAS THE WORD MAGICIAN BACKWARD.
OH MOMMY, I LOVE YOU! I MISSED YOU SO MUCH!!

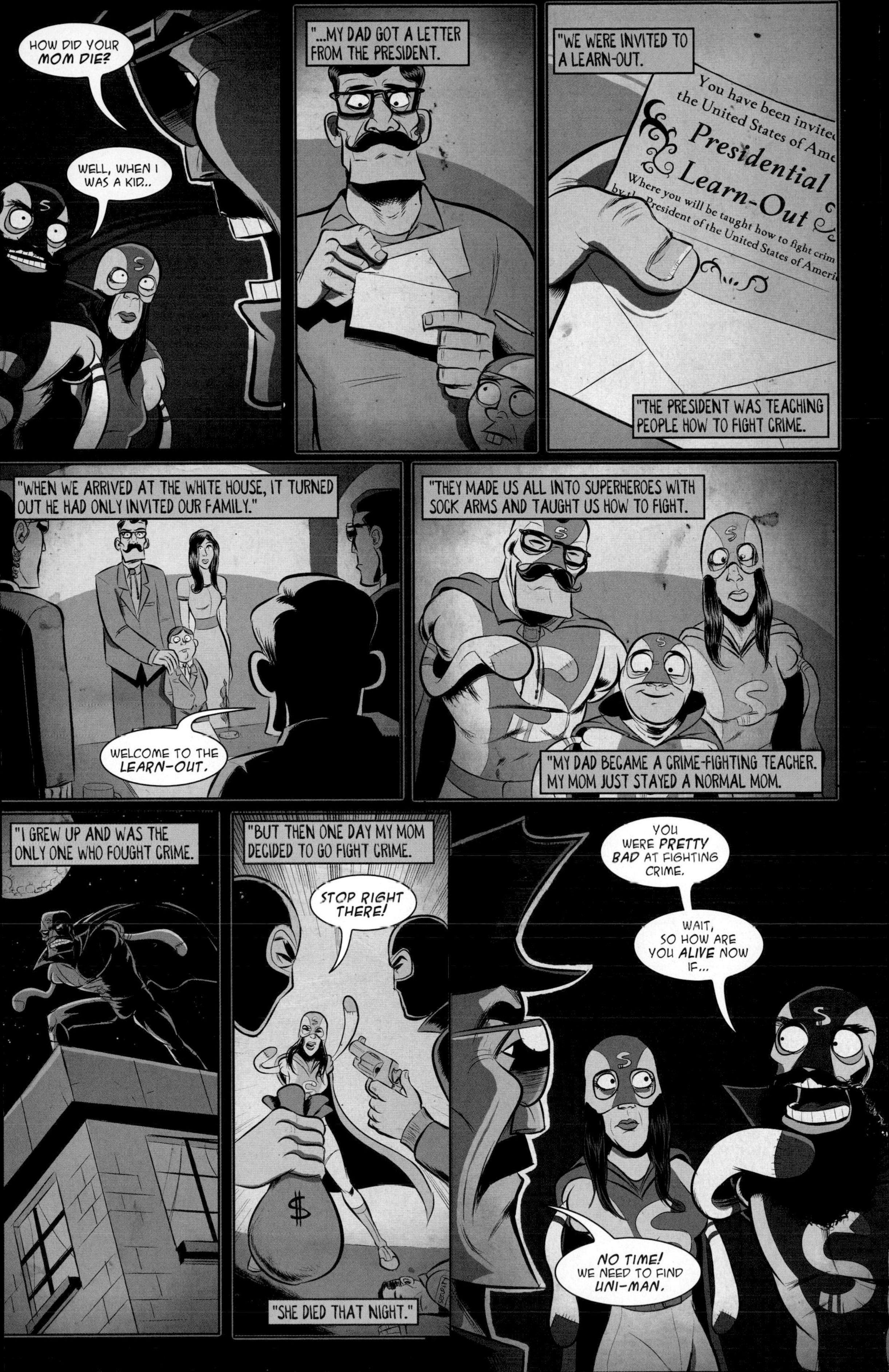
HOW DID YOUR MOM DIE?
WELL, WHEN I WAS A KID...
"...MY DAD GOT A LETTER FROM THE PRESIDENT.
"WE WERE INVITED TO A LEARN-OUT.
You have been invited ... the United States of Ame...
Presidential Learn-Out
Where you will be taught how to fight crim... by the President of the United States of Ameri...
"THE PRESIDENT WAS TEACHING PEOPLE HOW TO FIGHT CRIME.
"WHEN WE ARRIVED AT THE WHITE HOUSE, IT TURNED OUT HE HAD ONLY INVITED OUR FAMILY."
WELCOME TO THE LEARN-OUT.
"THEY MADE US ALL INTO SUPERHEROES WITH SOCK ARMS AND TAUGHT US HOW TO FIGHT.
"MY DAD BECAME A CRIME-FIGHTING TEACHER. MY MOM JUST STAYED A NORMAL MOM.
"I GREW UP AND WAS THE ONLY ONE WHO FOUGHT CRIME.
"BUT THEN ONE DAY MY MOM DECIDED TO GO FIGHT CRIME.
STOP RIGHT THERE!
$
"SHE DIED THAT NIGHT."
YOU WERE PRETTY BAD AT FIGHTING CRIME.
WAIT, SO HOW ARE YOU ALIVE NOW IF...
NO TIME! WE NEED TO FIND UNI-MAN.

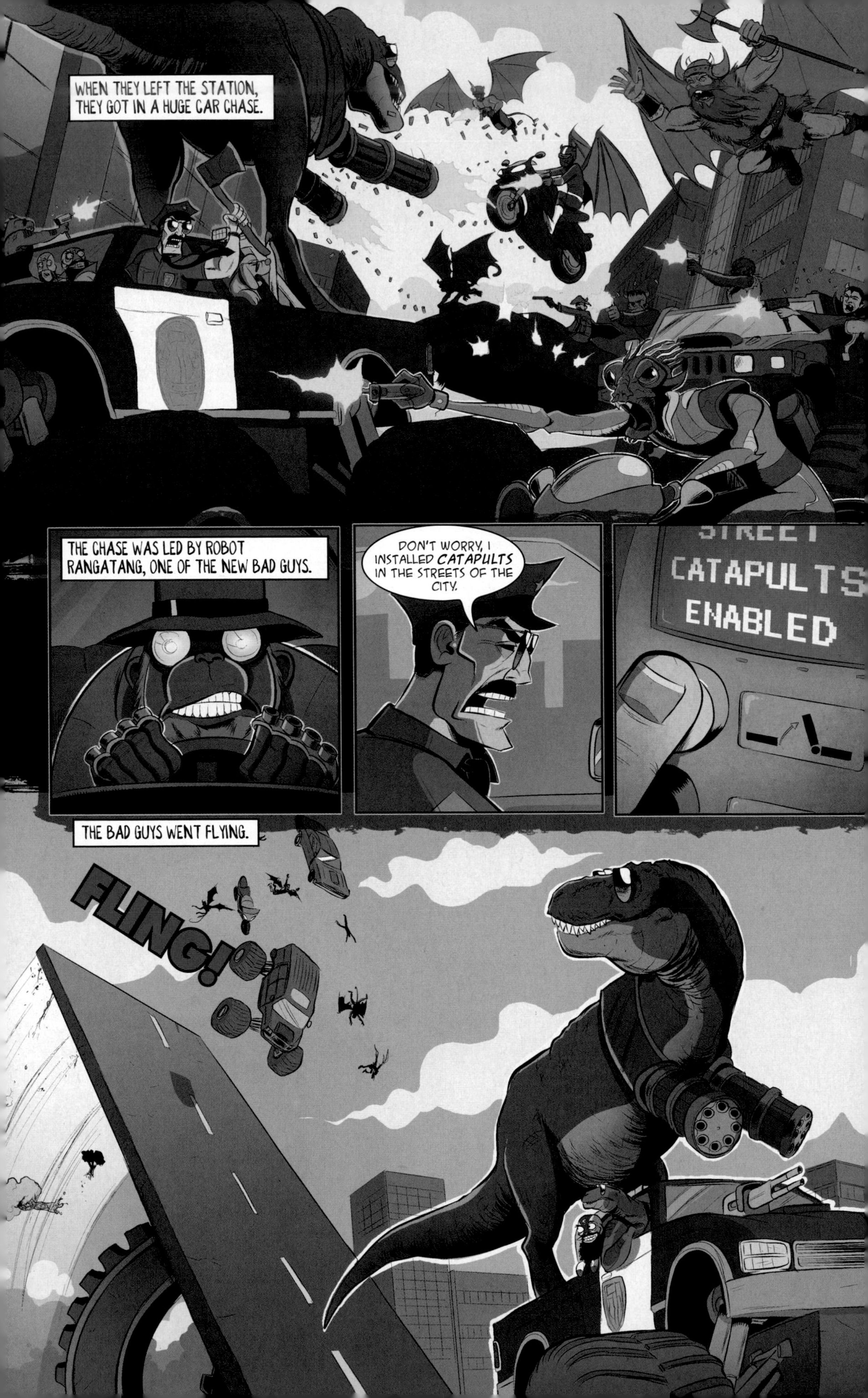

WHEN THEY LEFT THE STATION, THEY GOT IN A HUGE CAR CHASE.
THE CHASE WAS LED BY ROBOT RANGATANG, ONE OF THE NEW BAD GUYS.
DON'T WORRY, I INSTALLED CATAPULTS IN THE STREETS OF THE CITY.
STREET CATAPULTS ENABLED
THE BAD GUYS WENT FLYING.
FLING!

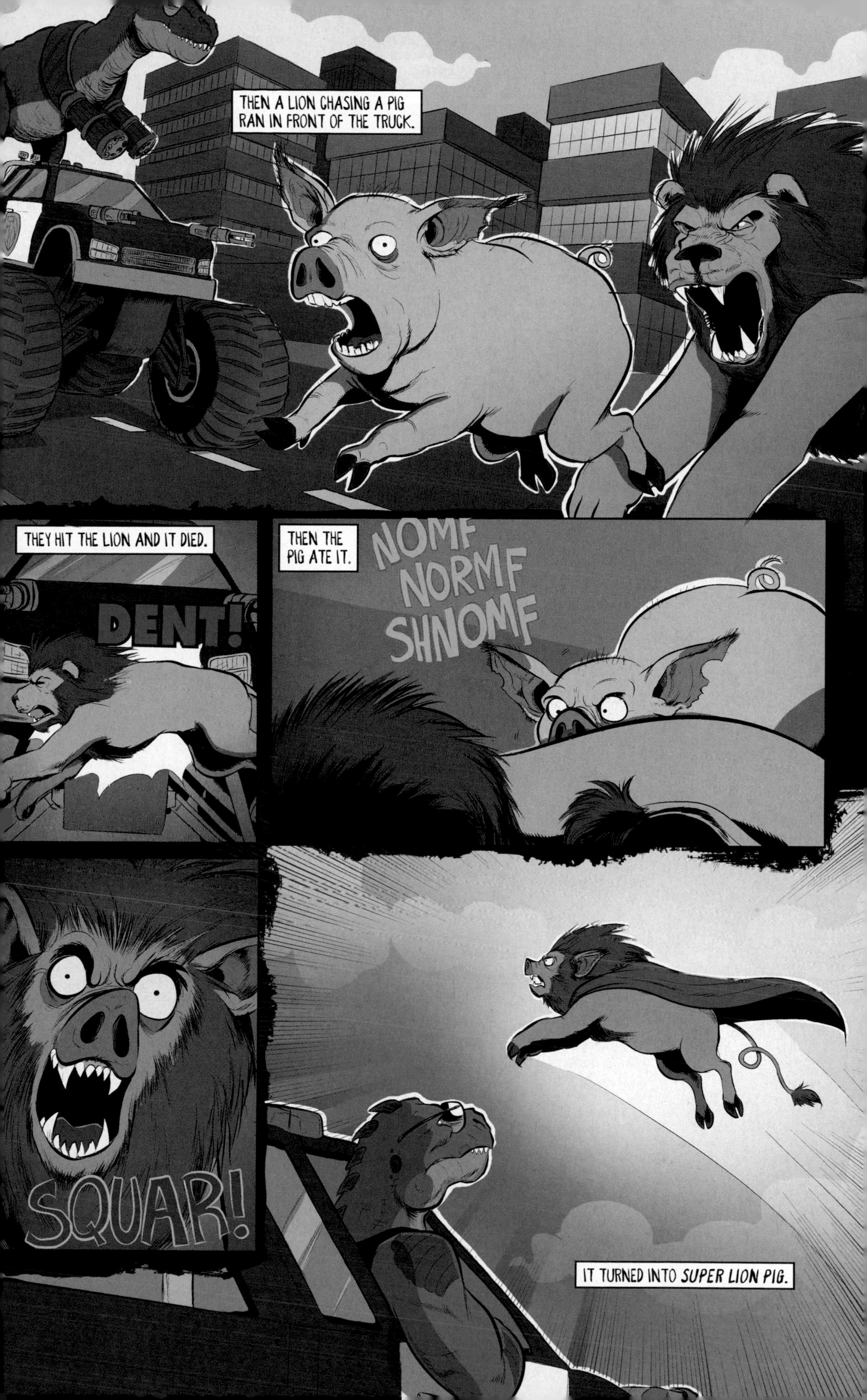
THEN A LION CHASING A PIG
RAN IN FRONT OF THE TRUCK.
THEY HIT THE LION AND IT DIED.
DENT!
THEN THE
PIG ATE IT.
NOMF
NORMF
SHNOMF
SQUAR!
IT TURNED INTO *SUPER LION PIG*.

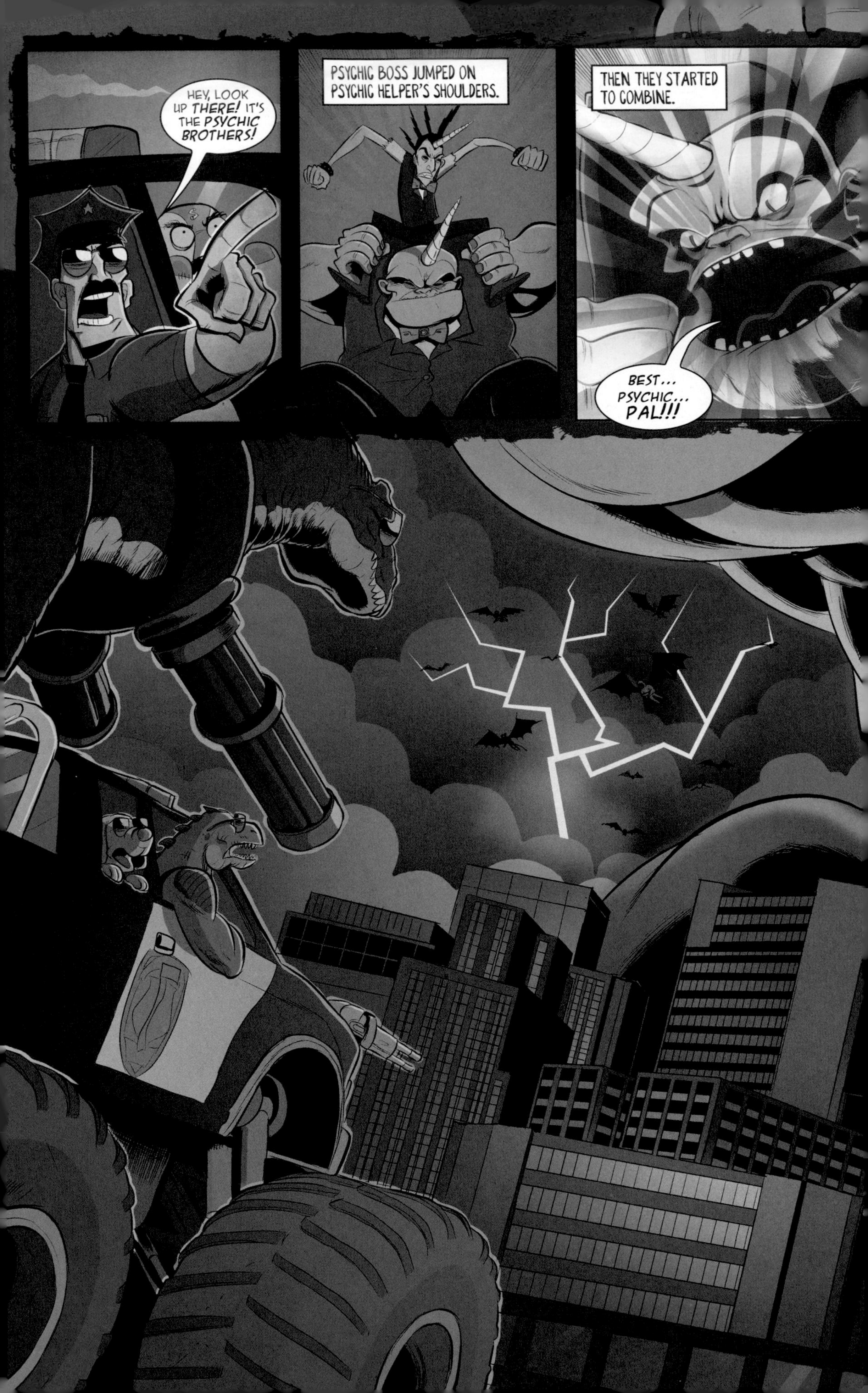
HEY, LOOK UP THERE! IT'S THE PSYCHIC BROTHERS!
PSYCHIC BOSS JUMPED ON PSYCHIC HELPER'S SHOULDERS.
THEN THEY STARTED TO COMBINE.
BEST... PSYCHIC... PAL!!!

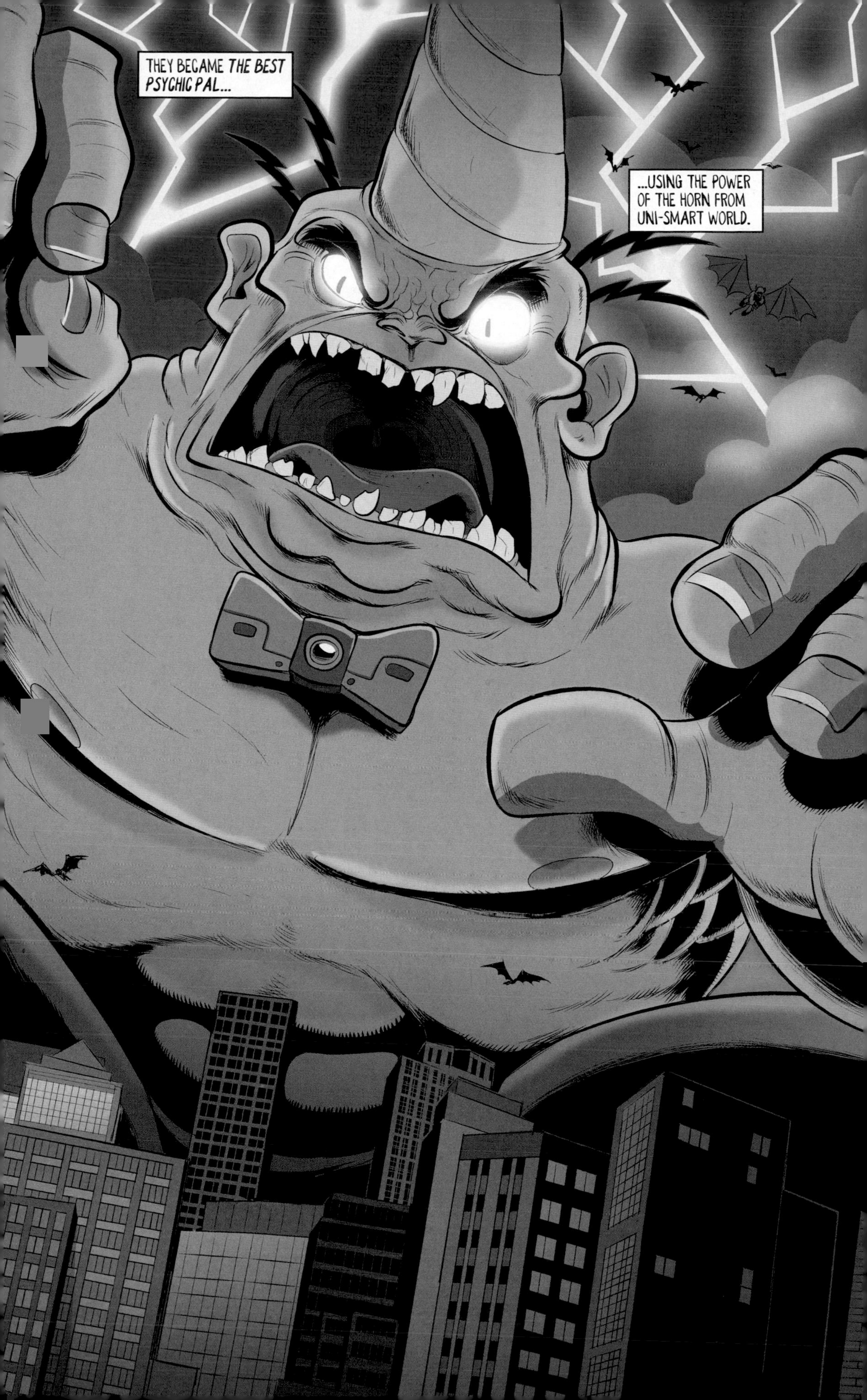
THEY BECAME *THE BEST PSYCHIC PAL*...
...USING THE POWER OF THE HORN FROM UNI-SMART WORLD.

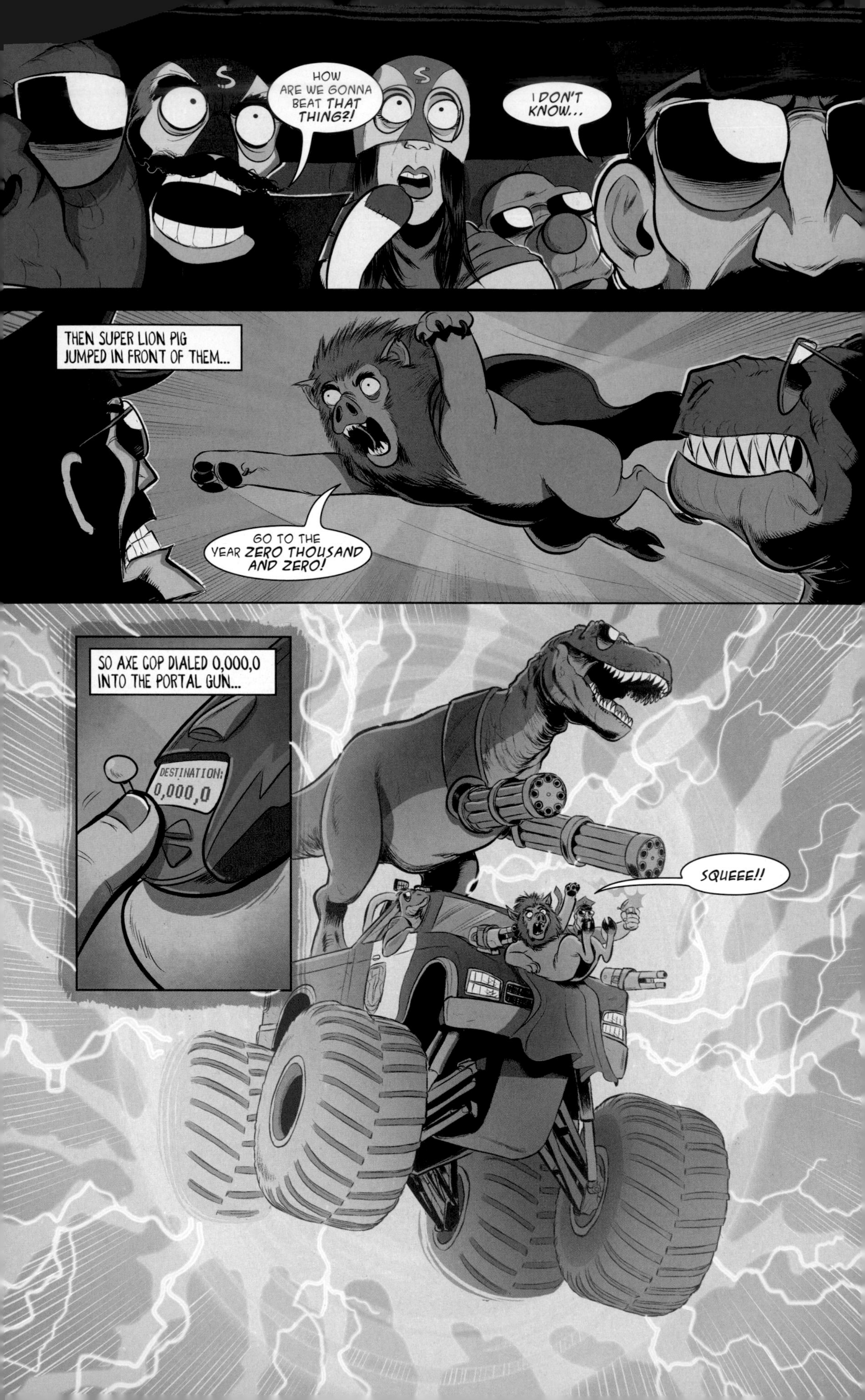
HOW ARE WE GONNA BEAT THAT THING?!
I DON'T KNOW...
THEN SUPER LION PIG JUMPED IN FRONT OF THEM...
GO TO THE YEAR ZERO THOUSAND AND ZERO!
SO AXE COP DIALED 0,000,0 INTO THE PORTAL GUN...
DESTINATION:
0,000,0
SQUEEE!!

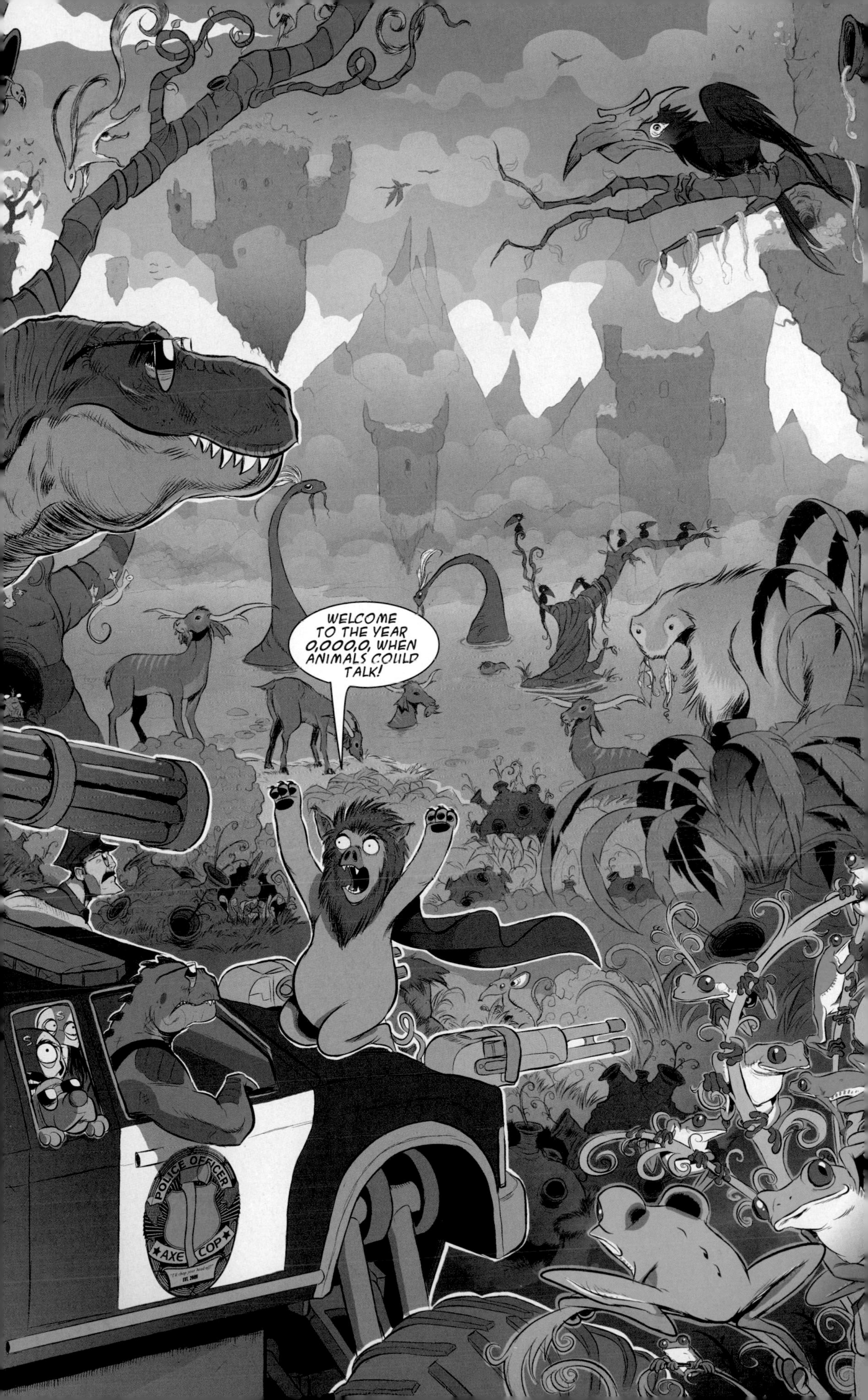
WELCOME TO THE YEAR 0,000,0, WHEN ANIMALS COULD TALK!
POLICE OFFICER
AXE COP

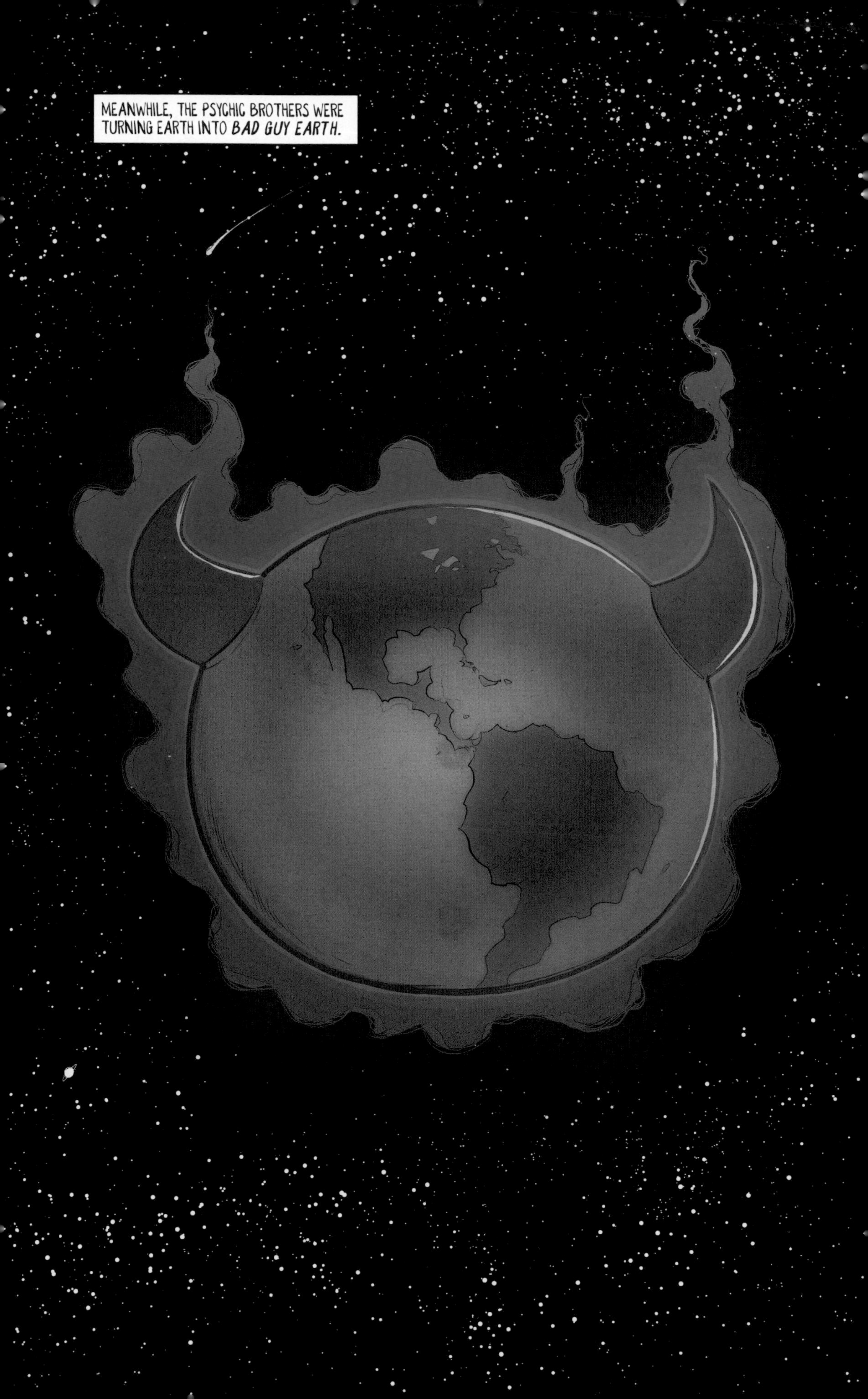
MEANWHILE, THE PSYCHIC BROTHERS WERE TURNING EARTH INTO *BAD GUY EARTH*.

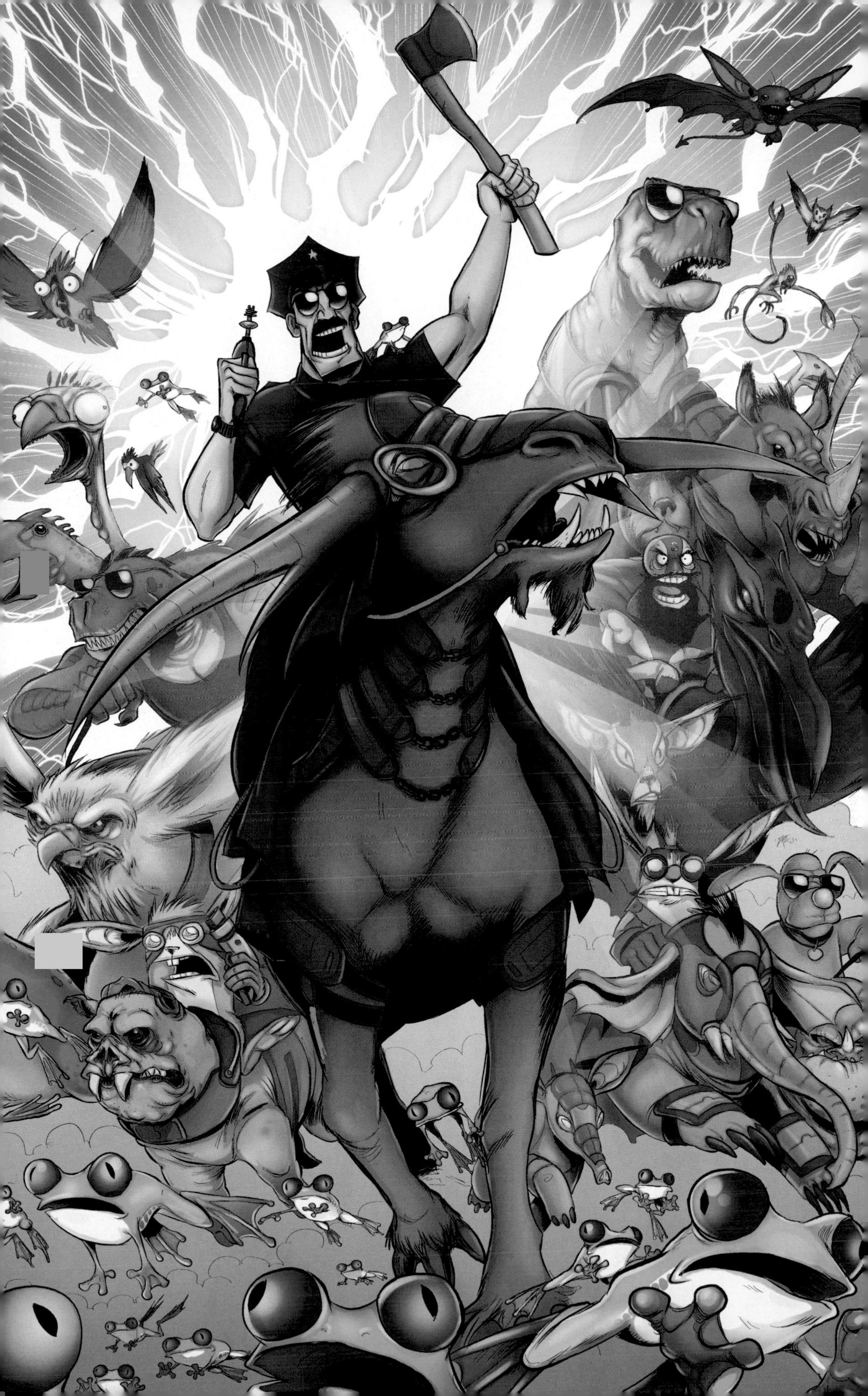

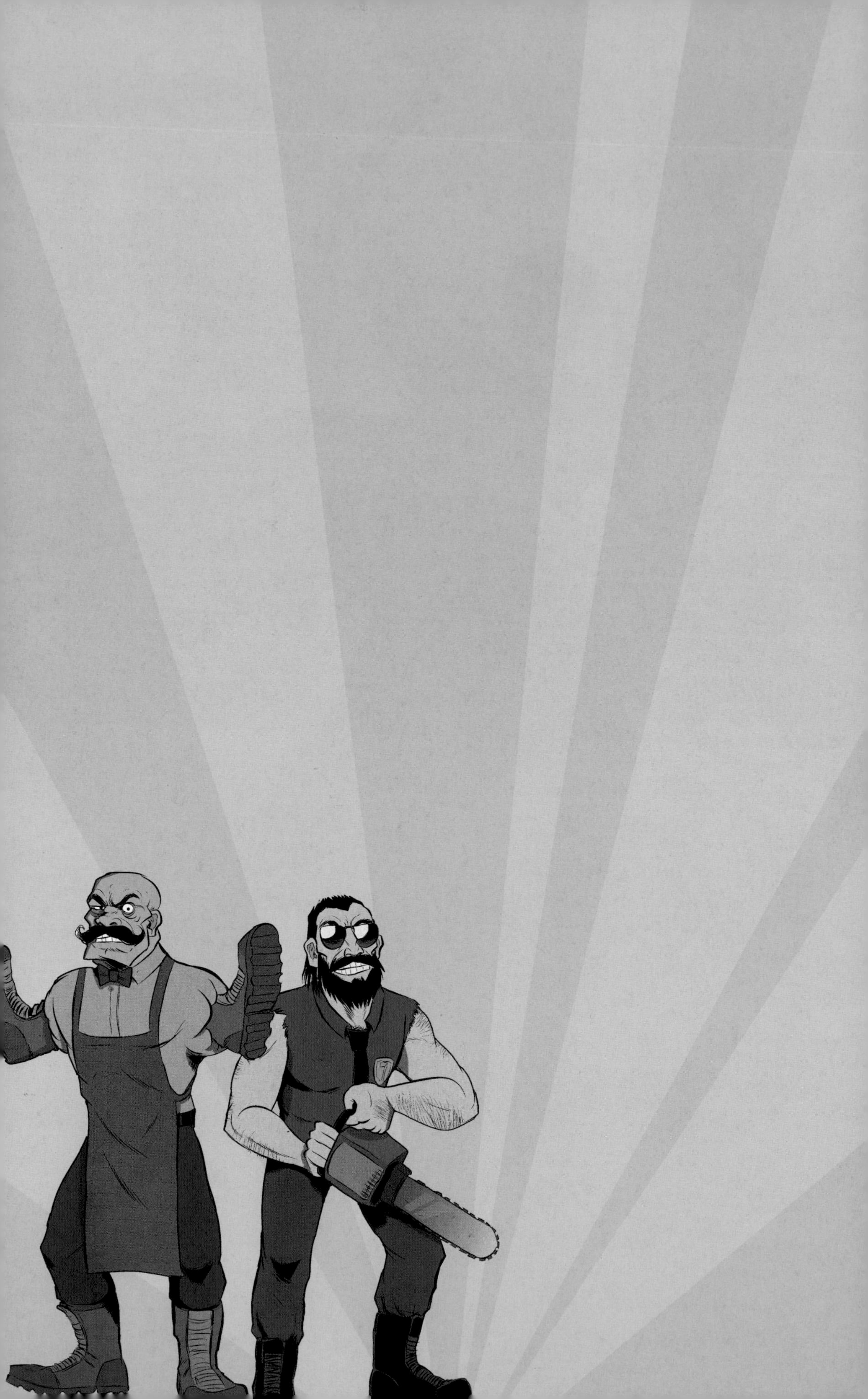

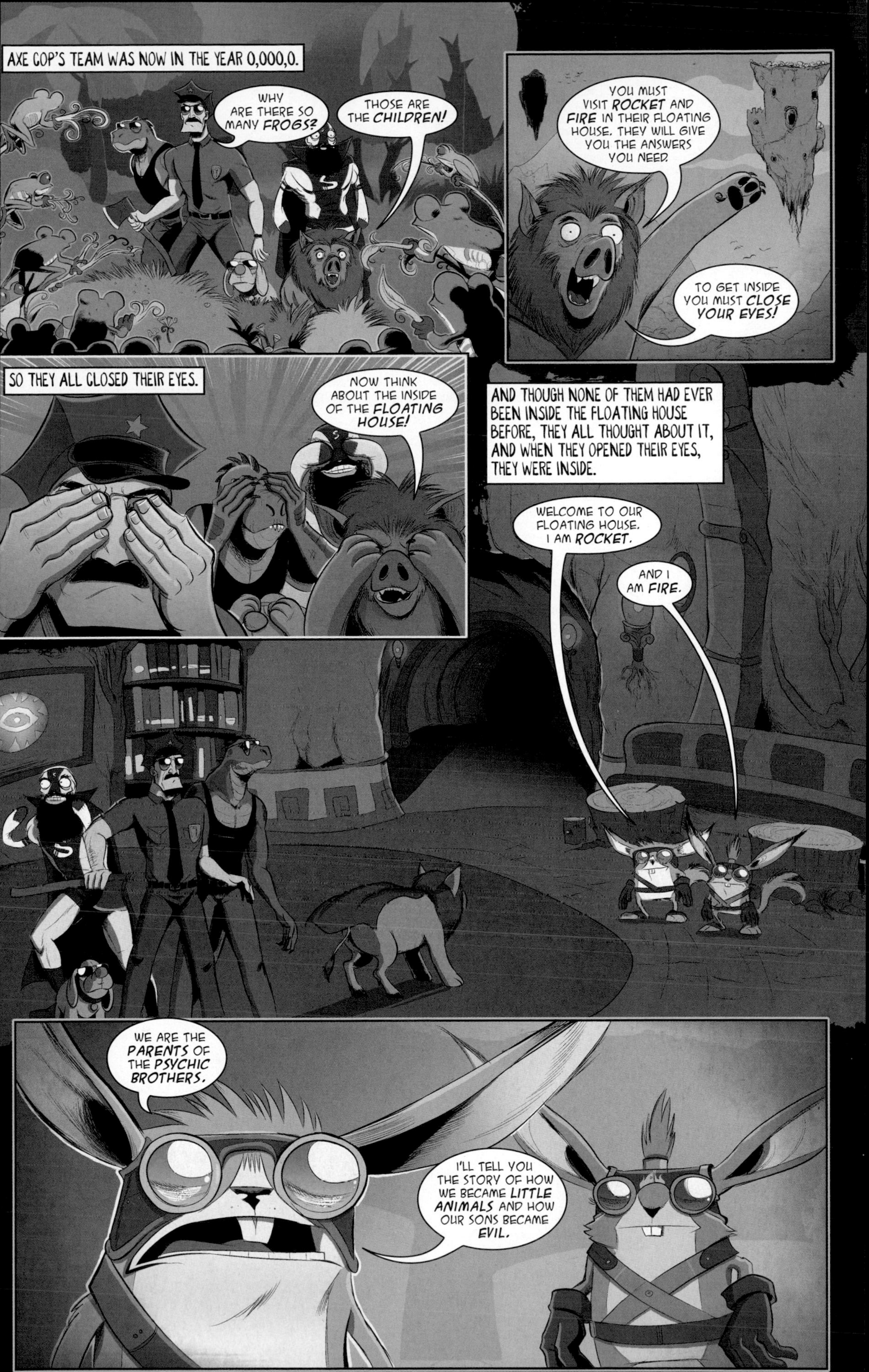
AXE COP'S TEAM WAS NOW IN THE YEAR 0,000,0.
WHY ARE THERE SO MANY FROGS?
THOSE ARE THE CHILDREN!
YOU MUST VISIT ROCKET AND FIRE IN THEIR FLOATING HOUSE. THEY WILL GIVE YOU THE ANSWERS YOU NEED.
TO GET INSIDE YOU MUST CLOSE YOUR EYES!
SO THEY ALL CLOSED THEIR EYES.
NOW THINK ABOUT THE INSIDE OF THE FLOATING HOUSE!
AND THOUGH NONE OF THEM HAD EVER BEEN INSIDE THE FLOATING HOUSE BEFORE, THEY ALL THOUGHT ABOUT IT, AND WHEN THEY OPENED THEIR EYES, THEY WERE INSIDE.
WELCOME TO OUR FLOATING HOUSE. I AM ROCKET.
AND I AM FIRE.
WE ARE THE PARENTS OF THE PSYCHIC BROTHERS.
I'LL TELL YOU THE STORY OF HOW WE BECAME LITTLE ANIMALS AND HOW OUR SONS BECAME EVIL.

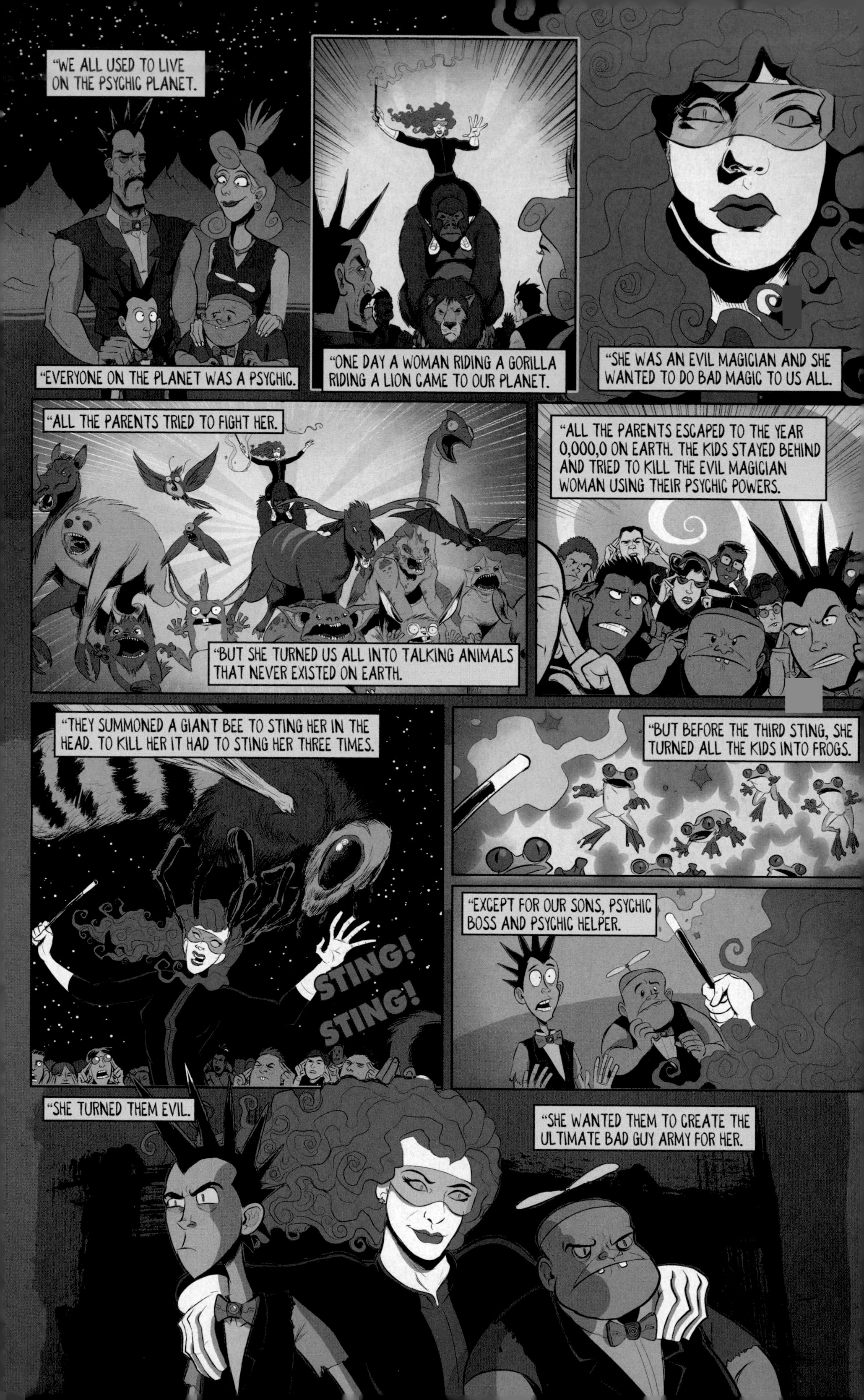
"WE ALL USED TO LIVE ON THE PSYCHIC PLANET.
"EVERYONE ON THE PLANET WAS A PSYCHIC.
"ONE DAY A WOMAN RIDING A GORILLA RIDING A LION CAME TO OUR PLANET.
"SHE WAS AN EVIL MAGICIAN AND SHE WANTED TO DO BAD MAGIC TO US ALL.
"ALL THE PARENTS TRIED TO FIGHT HER.
"BUT SHE TURNED US ALL INTO TALKING ANIMALS THAT NEVER EXISTED ON EARTH.
"ALL THE PARENTS ESCAPED TO THE YEAR 0,000,0 ON EARTH. THE KIDS STAYED BEHIND AND TRIED TO KILL THE EVIL MAGICIAN WOMAN USING THEIR PSYCHIC POWERS.
"THEY SUMMONED A GIANT BEE TO STING HER IN THE HEAD. TO KILL HER IT HAD TO STING HER THREE TIMES.
STING!
STING!
"BUT BEFORE THE THIRD STING, SHE TURNED ALL THE KIDS INTO FROGS.
"EXCEPT FOR OUR SONS, PSYCHIC BOSS AND PSYCHIC HELPER.
"SHE TURNED THEM EVIL.
"SHE WANTED THEM TO CREATE THE ULTIMATE BAD GUY ARMY FOR HER.

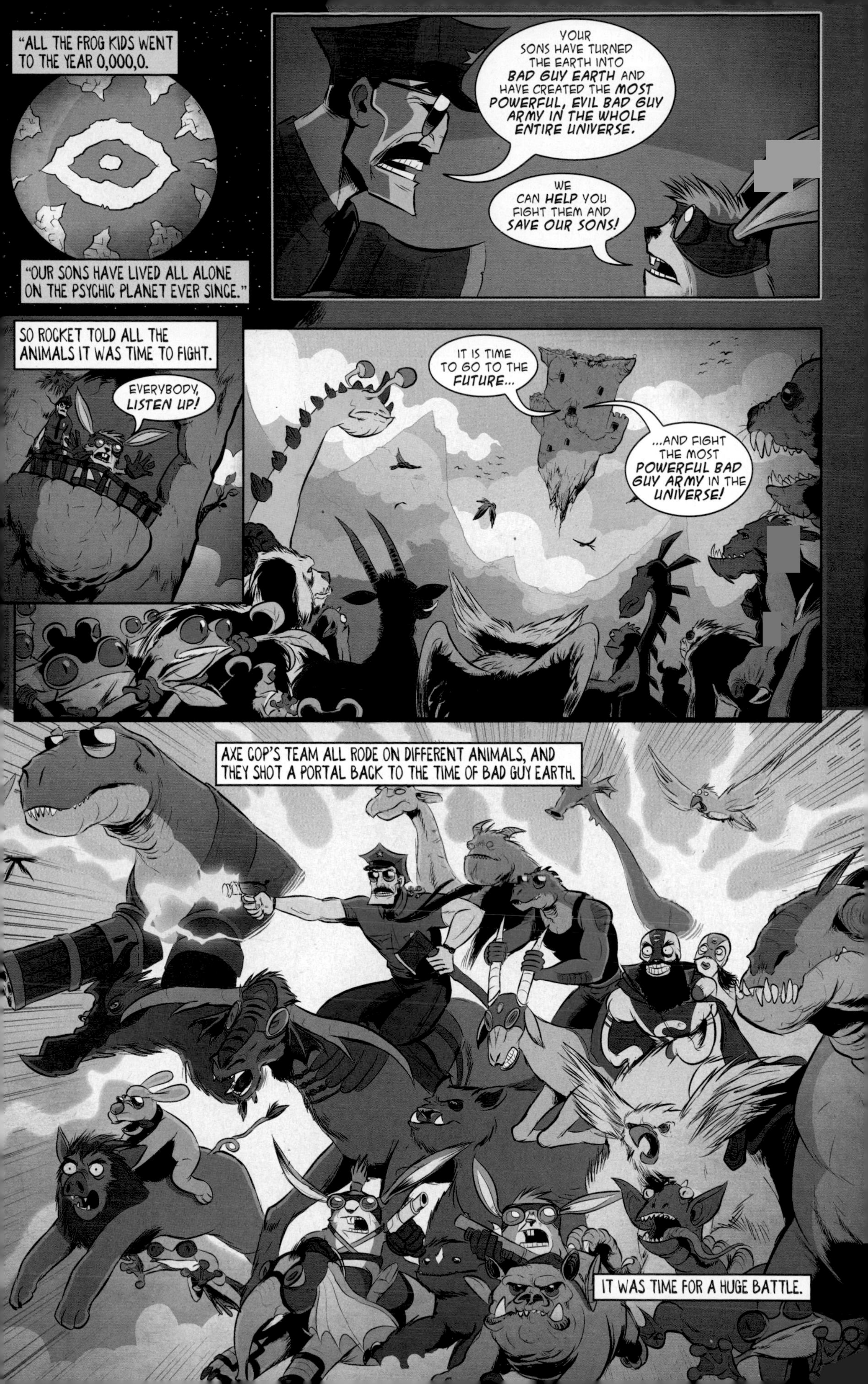
"ALL THE FROG KIDS WENT TO THE YEAR 0,000,0.
"OUR SONS HAVE LIVED ALL ALONE ON THE PSYCHIC PLANET EVER SINCE."
YOUR SONS HAVE TURNED THE EARTH INTO BAD GUY EARTH AND HAVE CREATED THE MOST POWERFUL, EVIL BAD GUY ARMY IN THE WHOLE ENTIRE UNIVERSE.
WE CAN HELP YOU FIGHT THEM AND SAVE OUR SONS!
SO ROCKET TOLD ALL THE ANIMALS IT WAS TIME TO FIGHT.
EVERYBODY, LISTEN UP!
IT IS TIME TO GO TO THE FUTURE...
...AND FIGHT THE MOST POWERFUL BAD GUY ARMY IN THE UNIVERSE!
AXE COP'S TEAM ALL RODE ON DIFFERENT ANIMALS, AND THEY SHOT A PORTAL BACK TO THE TIME OF BAD GUY EARTH.
IT WAS TIME FOR A HUGE BATTLE.

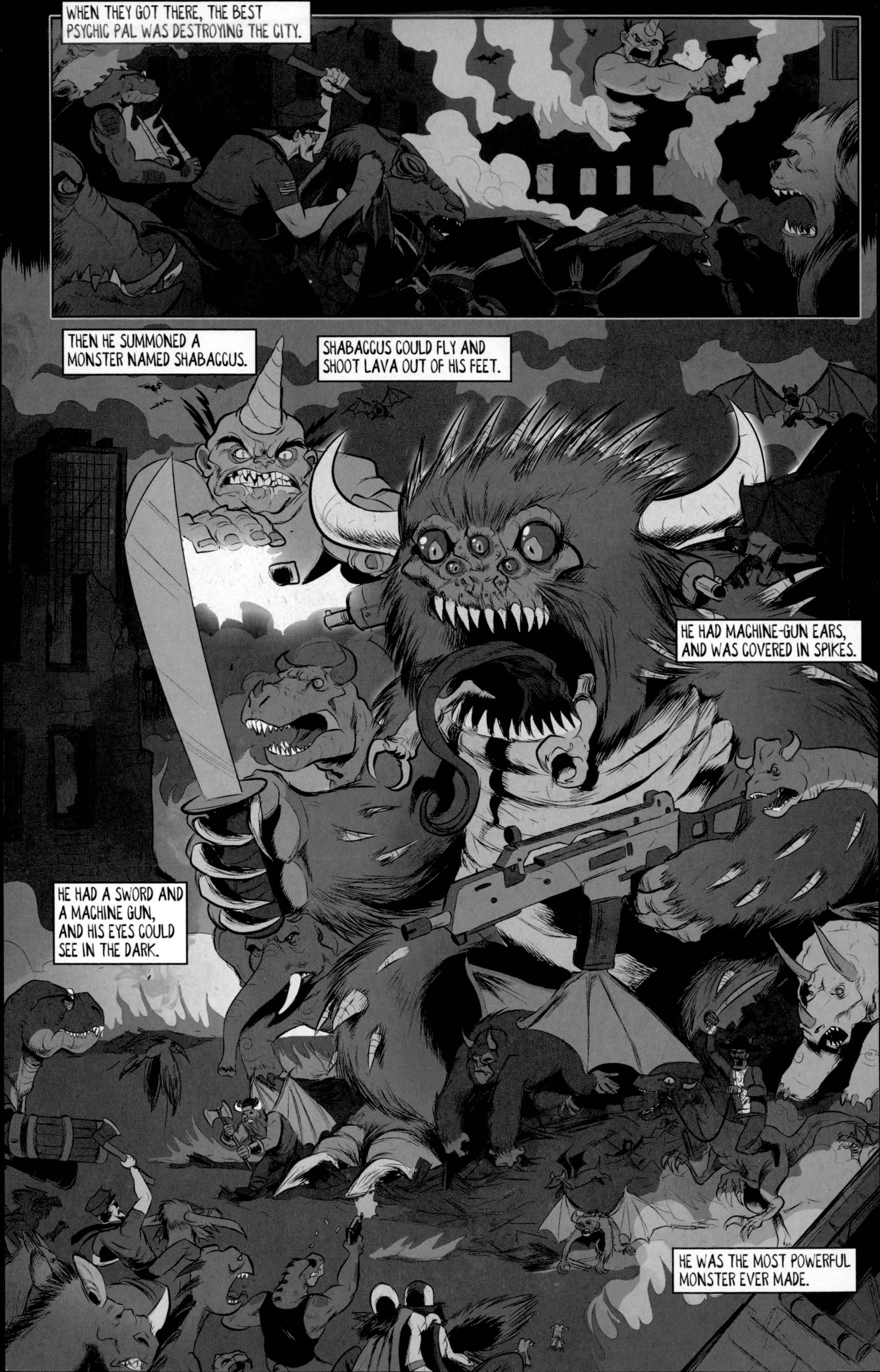
WHEN THEY GOT THERE, THE BEST PSYCHIC PAL WAS DESTROYING THE CITY.
THEN HE SUMMONED A MONSTER NAMED SHABACCUS.
SHABACCUS COULD FLY AND SHOOT LAVA OUT OF HIS FEET.
HE HAD MACHINE-GUN EARS, AND WAS COVERED IN SPIKES.
HE HAD A SWORD AND A MACHINE GUN, AND HIS EYES COULD SEE IN THE DARK.
HE WAS THE MOST POWERFUL MONSTER EVER MADE.

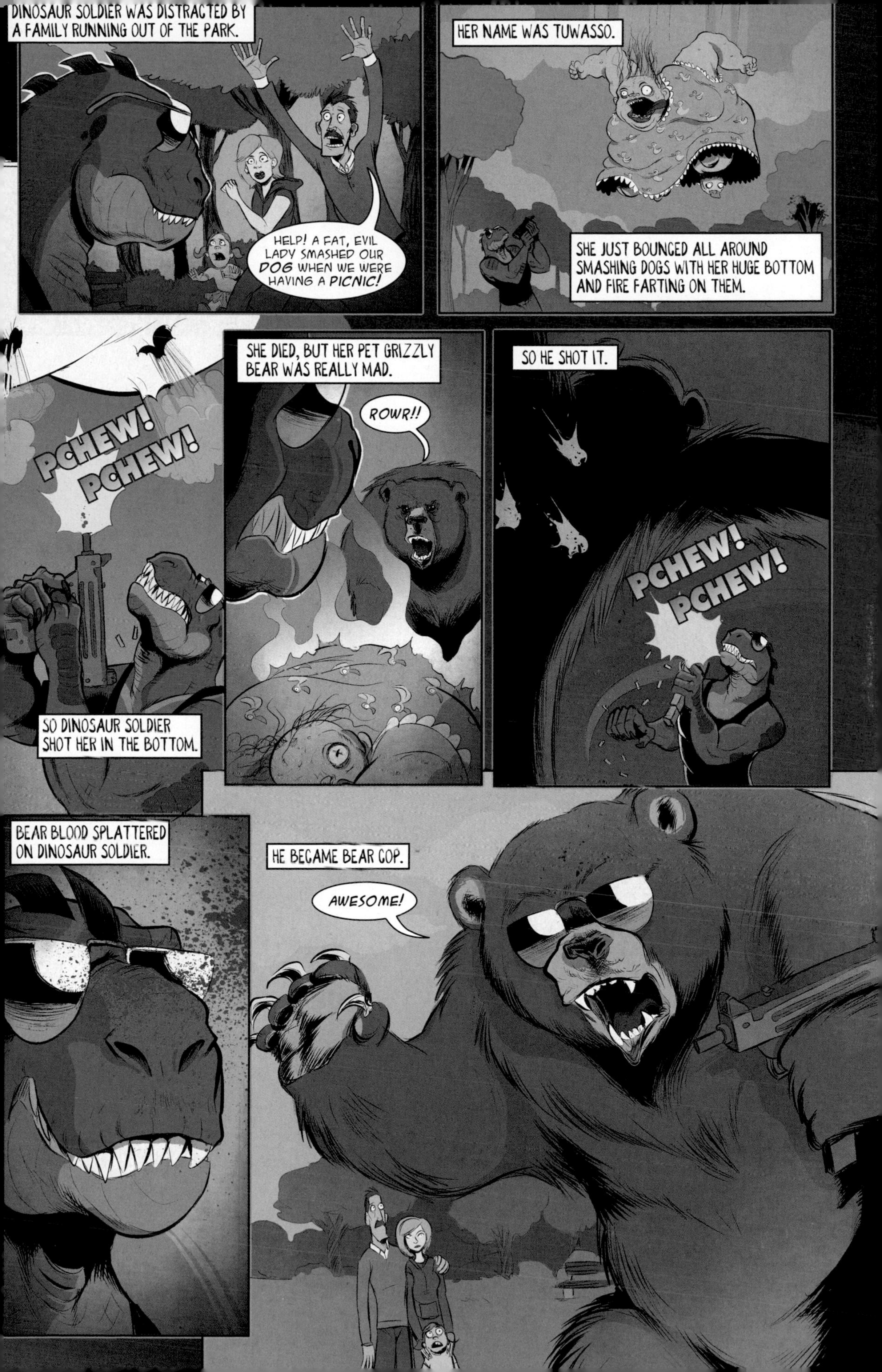
DINOSAUR SOLDIER WAS DISTRACTED BY A FAMILY RUNNING OUT OF THE PARK.
HELP! A FAT, EVIL LADY SMASHED OUR DOG WHEN WE WERE HAVING A PICNIC!
HER NAME WAS TUWASSO.
SHE JUST BOUNCED ALL AROUND SMASHING DOGS WITH HER HUGE BOTTOM AND FIRE FARTING ON THEM.
PCHEW! PCHEW!
SO DINOSAUR SOLDIER SHOT HER IN THE BOTTOM.
SHE DIED, BUT HER PET GRIZZLY BEAR WAS REALLY MAD.
ROWR!!
SO HE SHOT IT.
PCHEW! PCHEW!
BEAR BLOOD SPLATTERED ON DINOSAUR SOLDIER.
HE BECAME BEAR COP.
AWESOME!

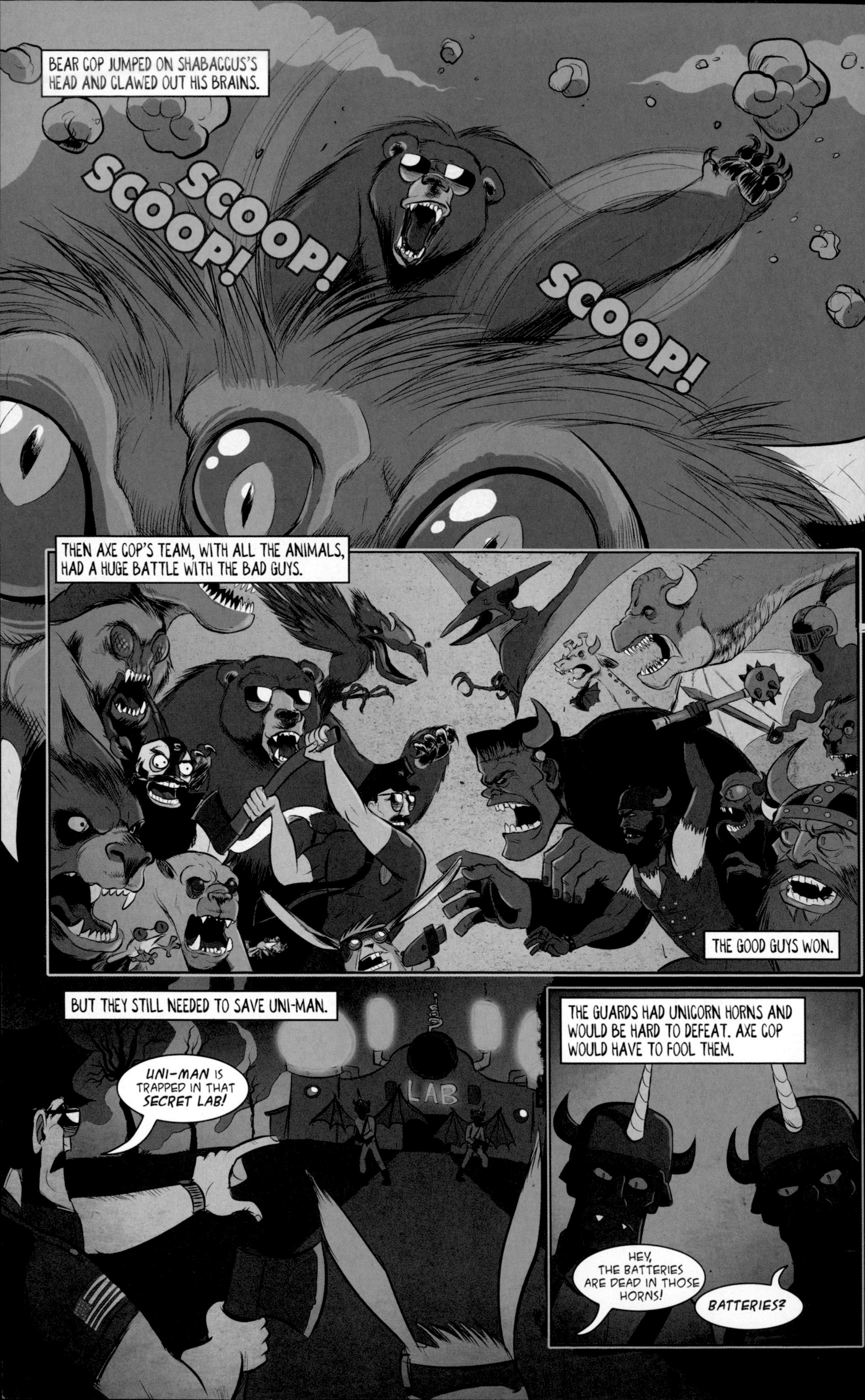
BEAR COP JUMPED ON SHABACCUS'S HEAD AND CLAWED OUT HIS BRAINS.
SCOOP! SCOOP!
SCOOP!
THEN AXE COP'S TEAM, WITH ALL THE ANIMALS, HAD A HUGE BATTLE WITH THE BAD GUYS.
THE GOOD GUYS WON.
BUT THEY STILL NEEDED TO SAVE UNI-MAN.
UNI-MAN IS TRAPPED IN THAT SECRET LAB!
LAB
THE GUARDS HAD UNICORN HORNS AND WOULD BE HARD TO DEFEAT. AXE COP WOULD HAVE TO FOOL THEM.
HEY, THE BATTERIES ARE DEAD IN THOSE HORNS!
BATTERIES?

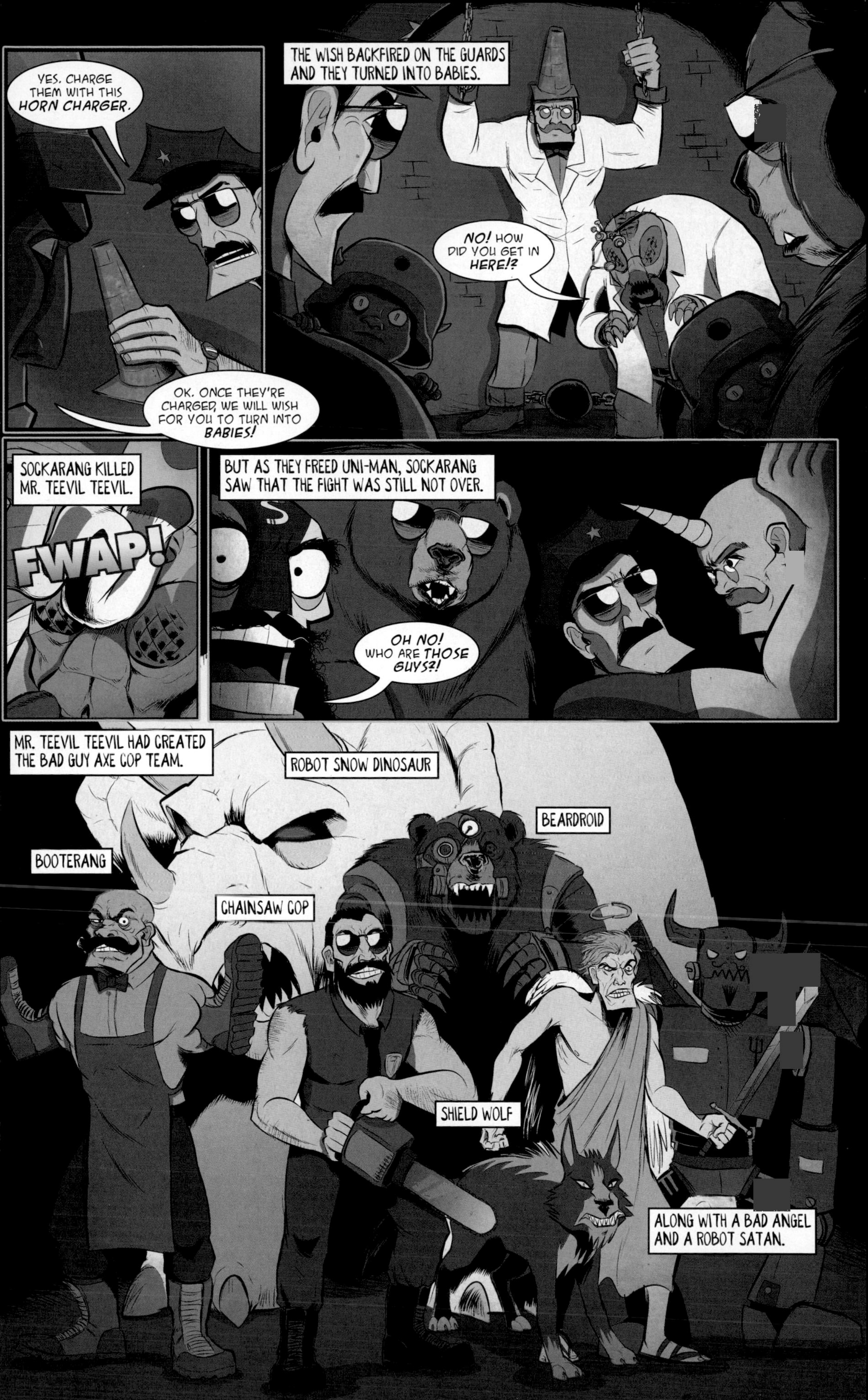
YES. CHARGE THEM WITH THIS HORN CHARGER.
OK. ONCE THEY'RE CHARGED, WE WILL WISH FOR YOU TO TURN INTO BABIES!
THE WISH BACKFIRED ON THE GUARDS AND THEY TURNED INTO BABIES.
NO! HOW DID YOU GET IN HERE!?
SOCKARANG KILLED MR. TEEVIL TEEVIL.
FWAP!
BUT AS THEY FREED UNI-MAN, SOCKARANG SAW THAT THE FIGHT WAS STILL NOT OVER.
OH NO! WHO ARE THOSE GUYS?!
MR. TEEVIL TEEVIL HAD CREATED THE BAD GUY AXE COP TEAM.
ROBOT SNOW DINOSAUR
BEARDROID
BOOTERANG
CHAINSAW COP
SHIELD WOLF
ALONG WITH A BAD ANGEL AND A ROBOT SATAN.

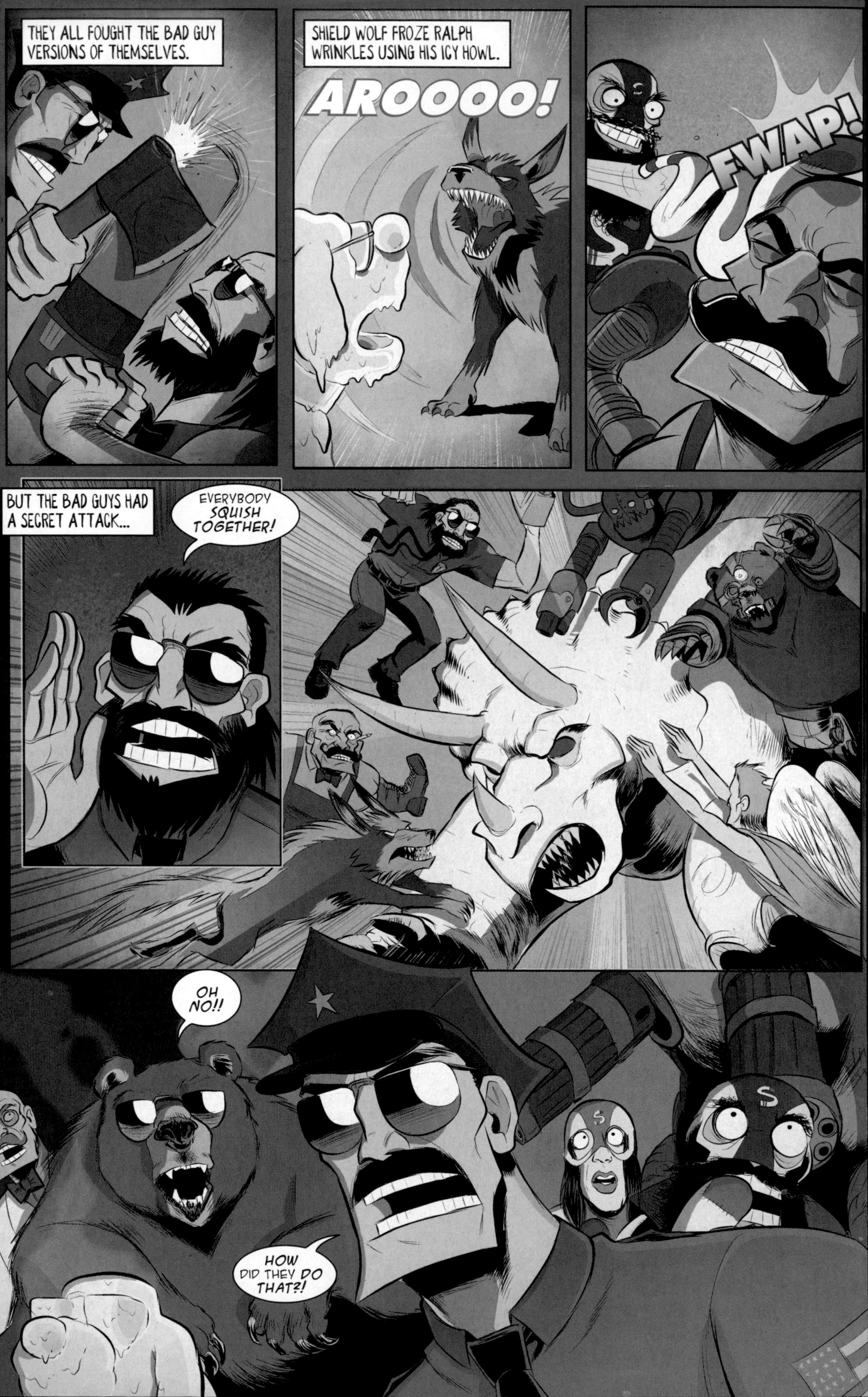
THEY ALL FOUGHT THE BAD GUY VERSIONS OF THEMSELVES.
SHIELD WOLF FROZE RALPH WRINKLES USING HIS ICY HOWL.
AROOOO!
FWAP!
BUT THE BAD GUYS HAD A SECRET ATTACK...
EVERYBODY SQUISH TOGETHER!
OH NO!!
HOW DID THEY DO THAT?!

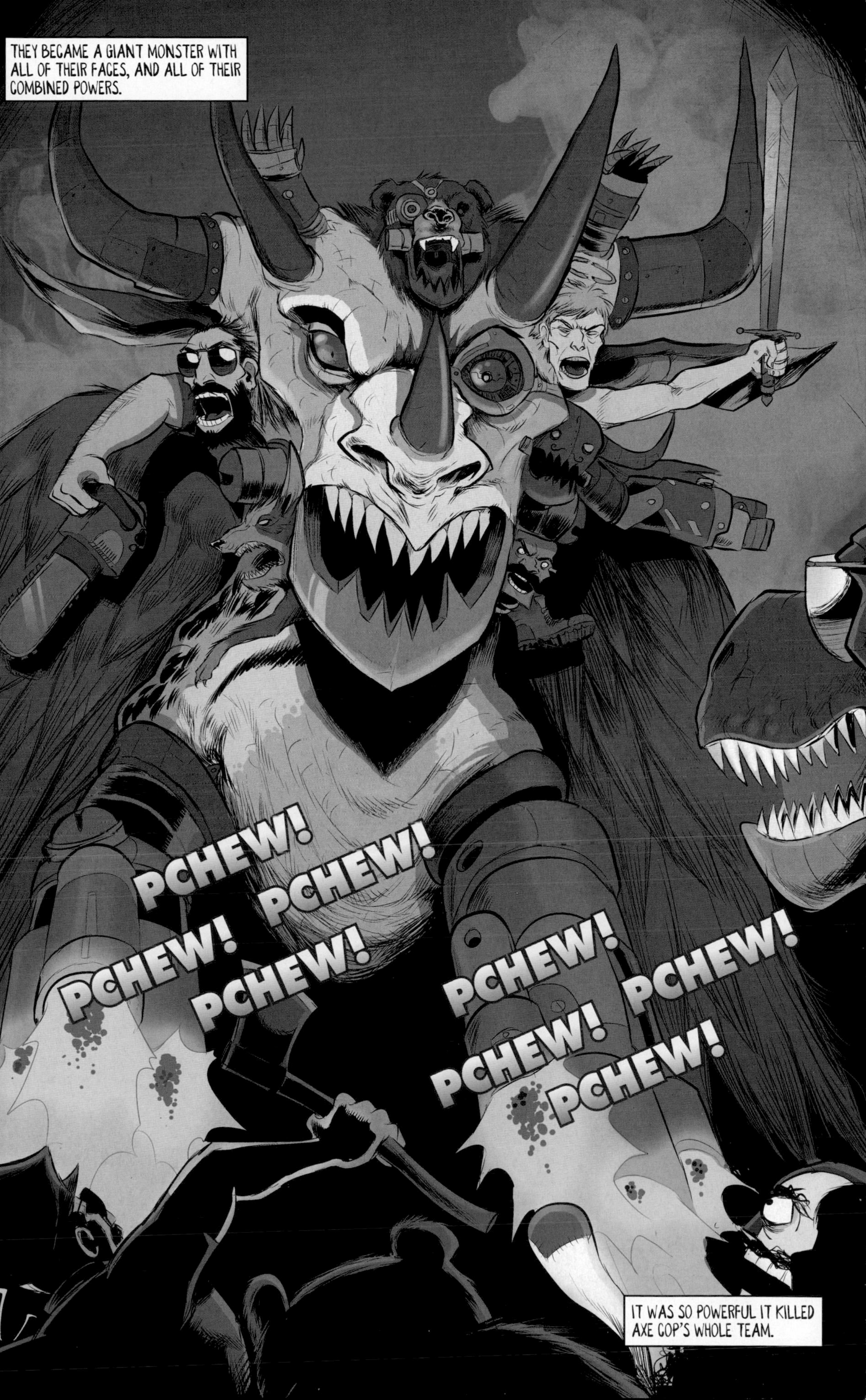
THEY BECAME A GIANT MONSTER WITH ALL OF THEIR FACES, AND ALL OF THEIR COMBINED POWERS.
PCHEW!
PCHEW!
PCHEW!
PCHEW!
PCHEW!
PCHEW!
PCHEW!
PCHEW!
IT WAS SO POWERFUL IT KILLED AXE COP'S WHOLE TEAM.

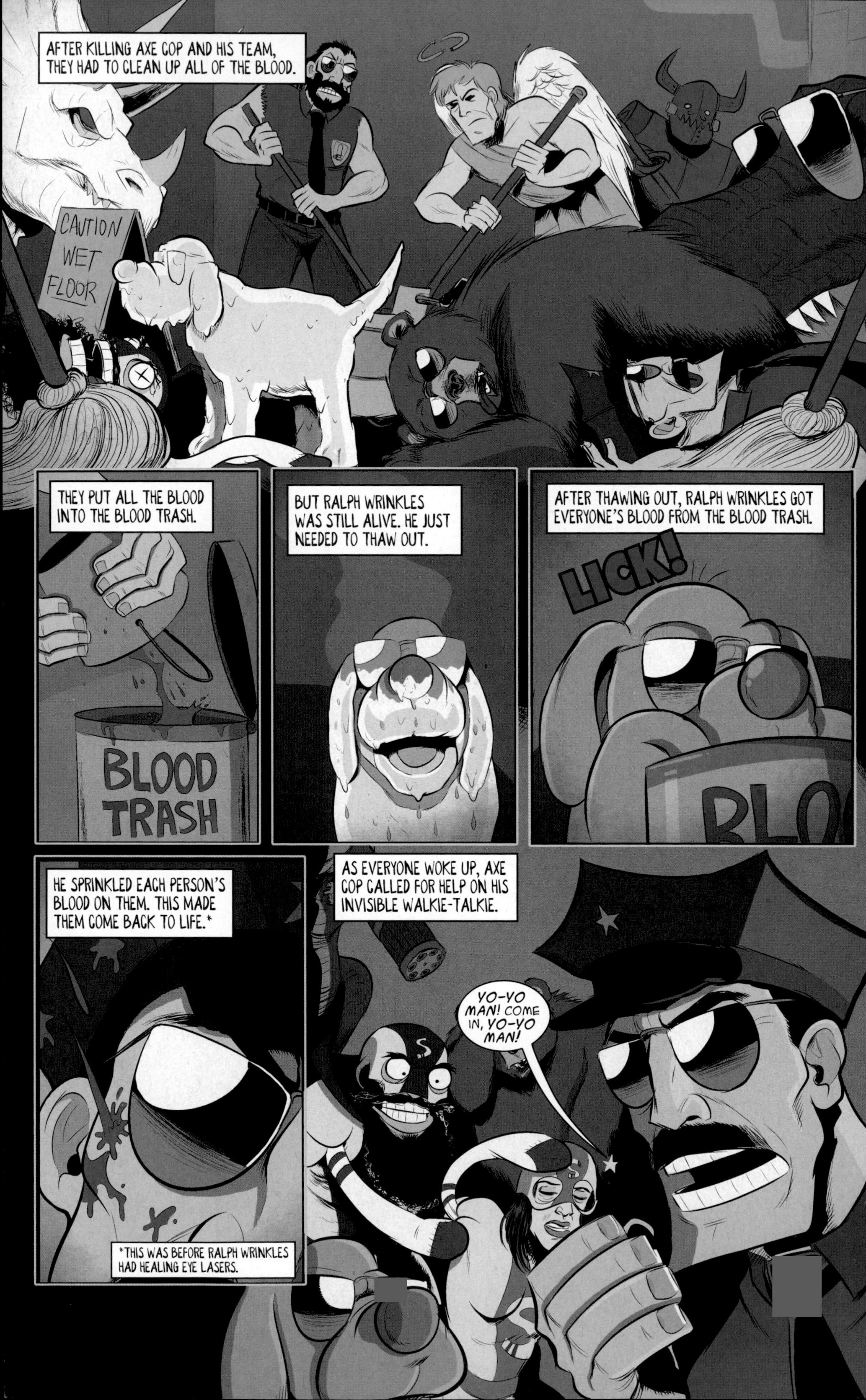
AFTER KILLING AXE COP AND HIS TEAM, THEY HAD TO CLEAN UP ALL OF THE BLOOD.
CAUTION WET FLOOR
THEY PUT ALL THE BLOOD INTO THE BLOOD TRASH.
BLOOD TRASH
BUT RALPH WRINKLES WAS STILL ALIVE. HE JUST NEEDED TO THAW OUT.
AFTER THAWING OUT, RALPH WRINKLES GOT EVERYONE'S BLOOD FROM THE BLOOD TRASH.
LICK!
HE SPRINKLED EACH PERSON'S BLOOD ON THEM. THIS MADE THEM COME BACK TO LIFE.*
*THIS WAS BEFORE RALPH WRINKLES HAD HEALING EYE LASERS.
AS EVERYONE WOKE UP, AXE COP CALLED FOR HELP ON HIS INVISIBLE WALKIE-TALKIE.
YO-YO MAN! COME IN, YO-YO MAN!

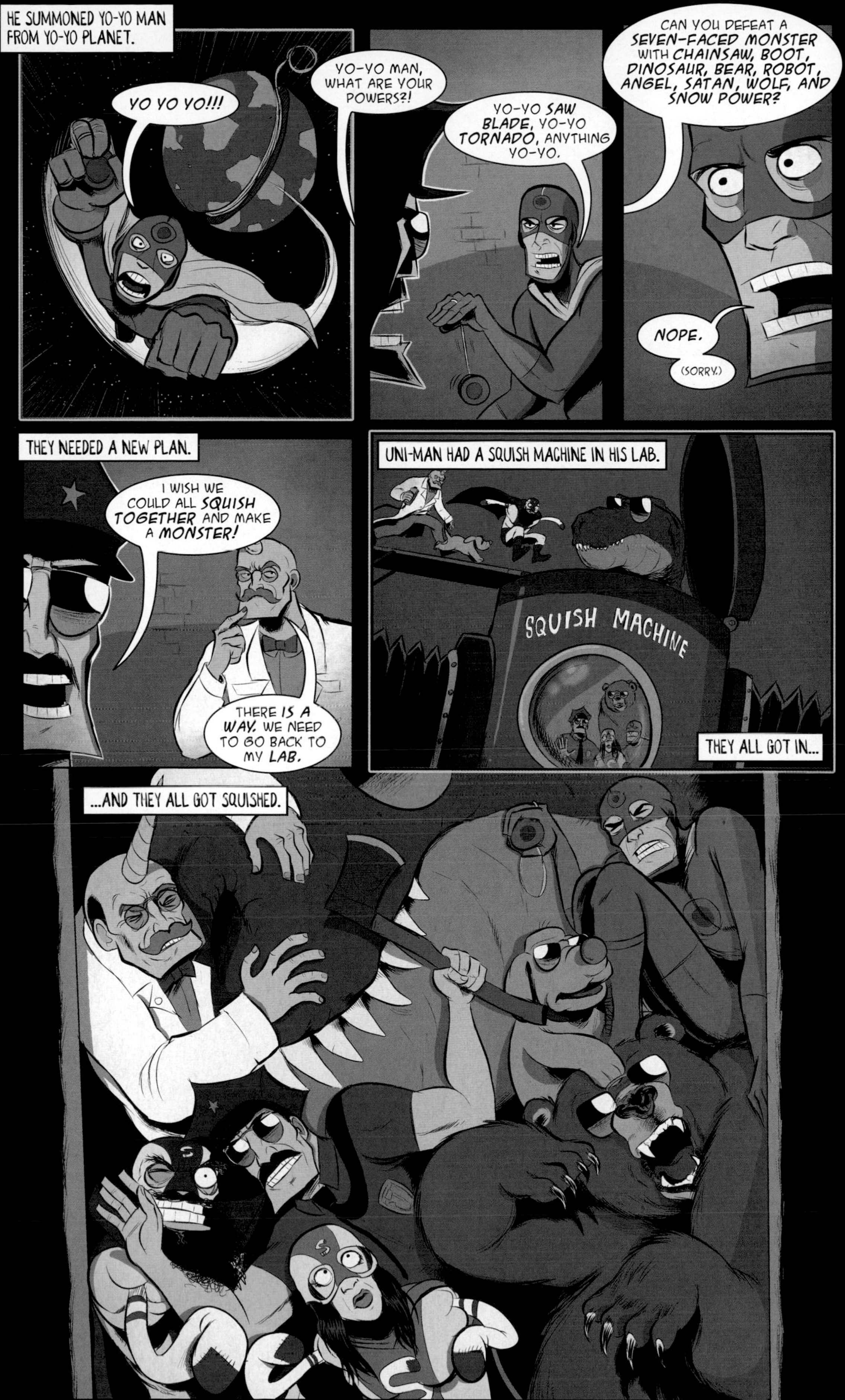
HE SUMMONED YO-YO MAN FROM YO-YO PLANET.
YO YO YO!!!
YO-YO MAN, WHAT ARE YOUR POWERS?!
YO-YO SAW BLADE, YO-YO TORNADO, ANYTHING YO-YO.
CAN YOU DEFEAT A SEVEN-FACED MONSTER WITH CHAINSAW, BOOT, DINOSAUR, BEAR, ROBOT, ANGEL, SATAN, WOLF, AND SNOW POWER?
NOPE.
(SORRY.)
THEY NEEDED A NEW PLAN.
I WISH WE COULD ALL SQUISH TOGETHER AND MAKE A MONSTER!
THERE IS A WAY. WE NEED TO GO BACK TO MY LAB.
UNI-MAN HAD A SQUISH MACHINE IN HIS LAB.
SQUISH MACHINE
THEY ALL GOT IN...
...AND THEY ALL GOT SQUISHED.

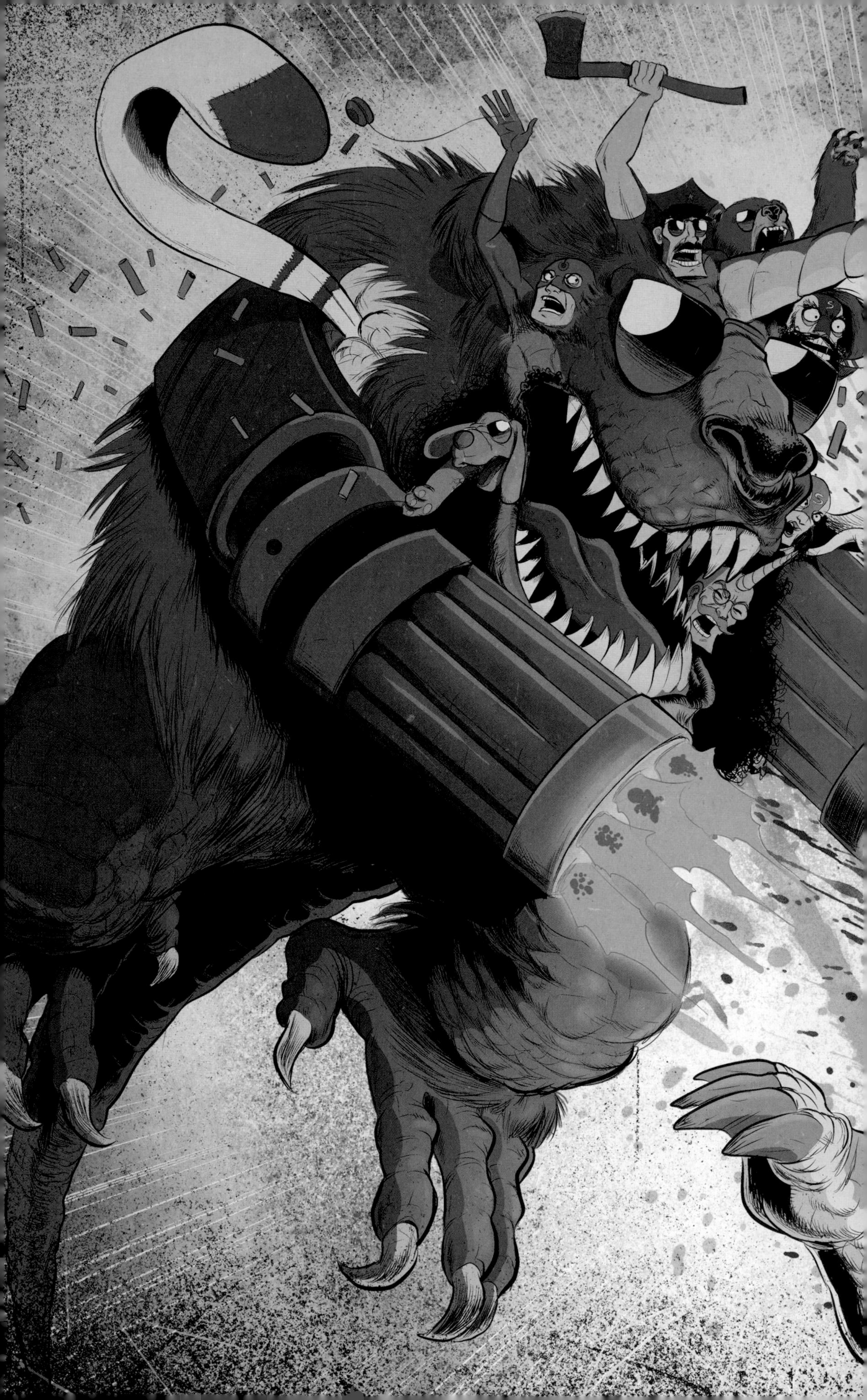

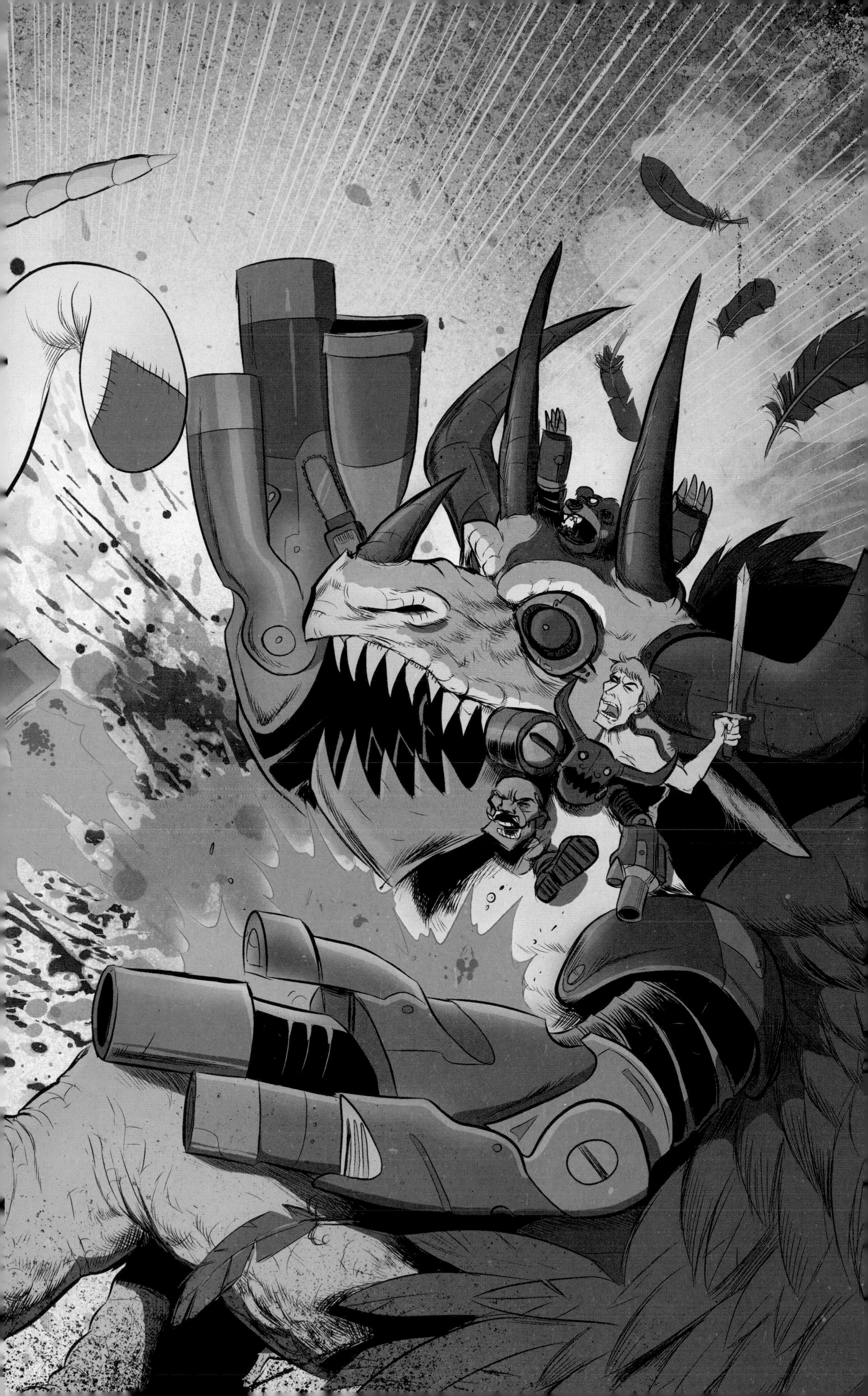

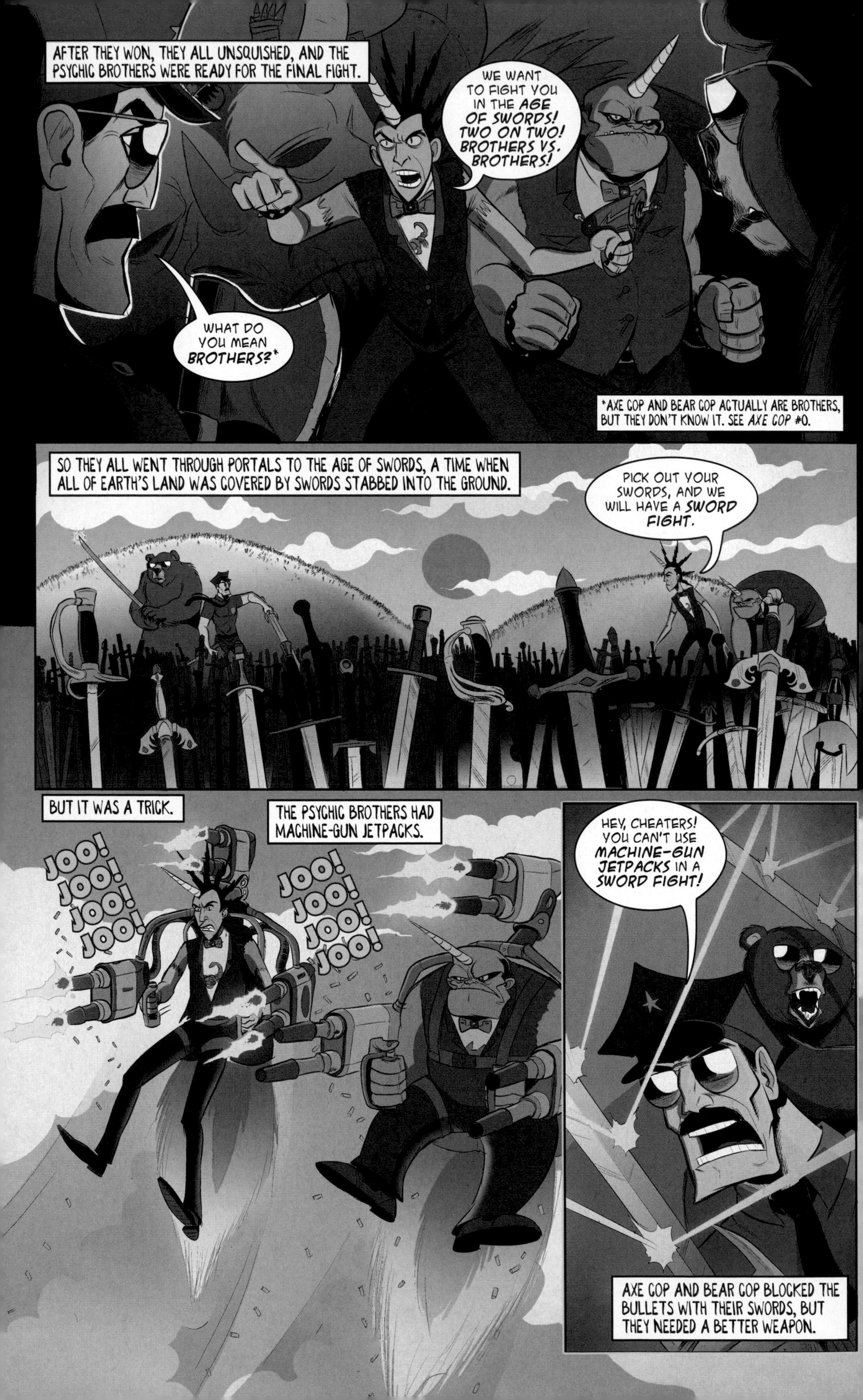
AFTER THEY WON, THEY ALL UNSQUISHED, AND THE PSYCHIC BROTHERS WERE READY FOR THE FINAL FIGHT.
WE WANT TO FIGHT YOU IN THE AGE OF SWORDS! TWO ON TWO! BROTHERS VS. BROTHERS!
WHAT DO YOU MEAN BROTHERS?*
*AXE COP AND BEAR COP ACTUALLY ARE BROTHERS, BUT THEY DON'T KNOW IT. SEE AXE COP #0.
SO THEY ALL WENT THROUGH PORTALS TO THE AGE OF SWORDS, A TIME WHEN ALL OF EARTH'S LAND WAS COVERED BY SWORDS STABBED INTO THE GROUND.
PICK OUT YOUR SWORDS, AND WE WILL HAVE A SWORD FIGHT.
BUT IT WAS A TRICK.
THE PSYCHIC BROTHERS HAD MACHINE-GUN JETPACKS.
JOO! JOO! JOO! JOO!
JOO! JOO! JOO! JOO!
HEY, CHEATERS! YOU CAN'T USE MACHINE-GUN JETPACKS IN A SWORD FIGHT!
AXE COP AND BEAR COP BLOCKED THE BULLETS WITH THEIR SWORDS, BUT THEY NEEDED A BETTER WEAPON.

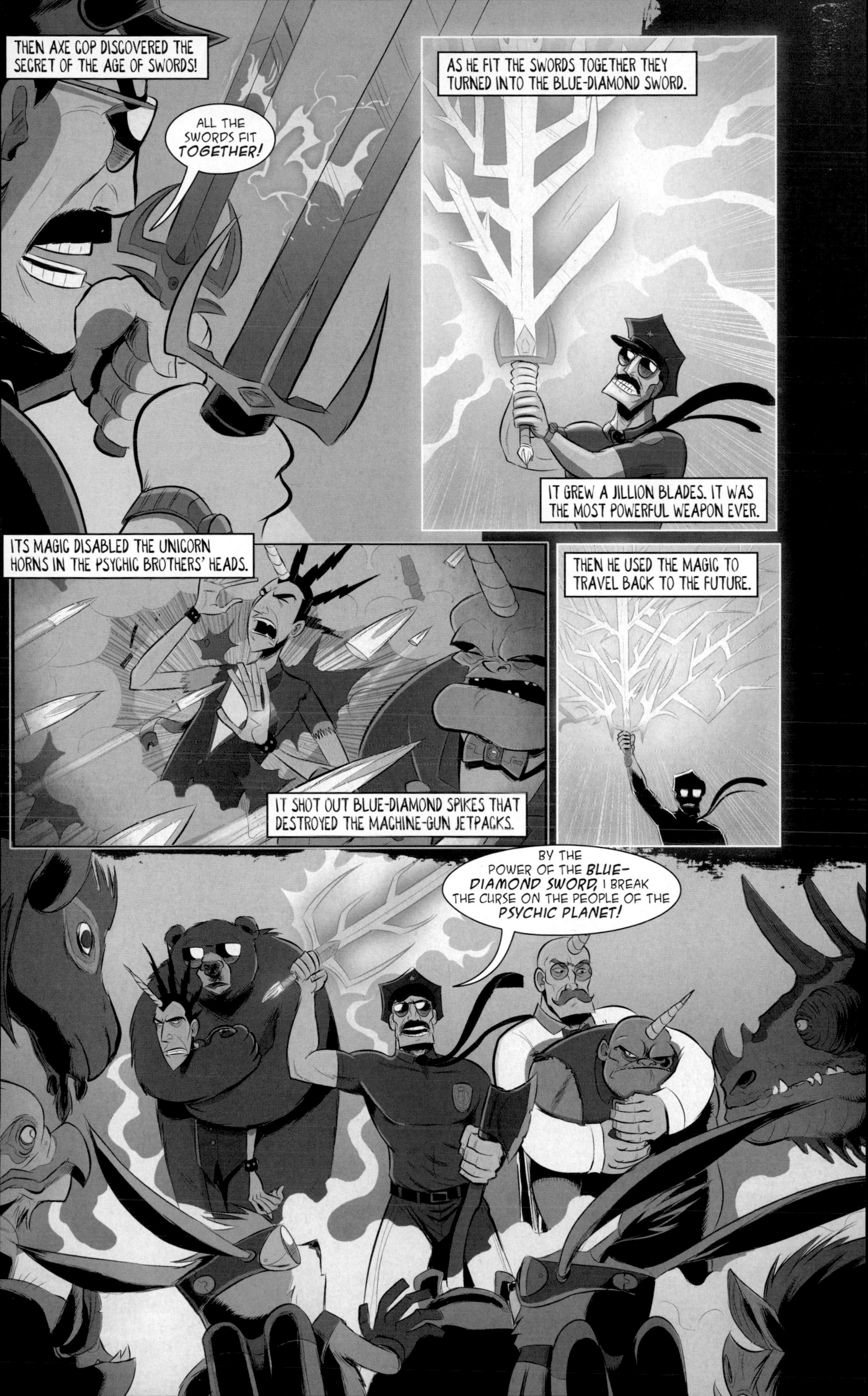

THEN AXE COP DISCOVERED THE SECRET OF THE AGE OF SWORDS!
ALL THE SWORDS FIT TOGETHER!
AS HE FIT THE SWORDS TOGETHER THEY TURNED INTO THE BLUE-DIAMOND SWORD.
IT GREW A JILLION BLADES. IT WAS THE MOST POWERFUL WEAPON EVER.
ITS MAGIC DISABLED THE UNICORN HORNS IN THE PSYCHIC BROTHERS' HEADS.
IT SHOT OUT BLUE-DIAMOND SPIKES THAT DESTROYED THE MACHINE-GUN JETPACKS.
THEN HE USED THE MAGIC TO TRAVEL BACK TO THE FUTURE.
BY THE POWER OF THE BLUE-DIAMOND SWORD, I BREAK THE CURSE ON THE PEOPLE OF THE PSYCHIC PLANET!

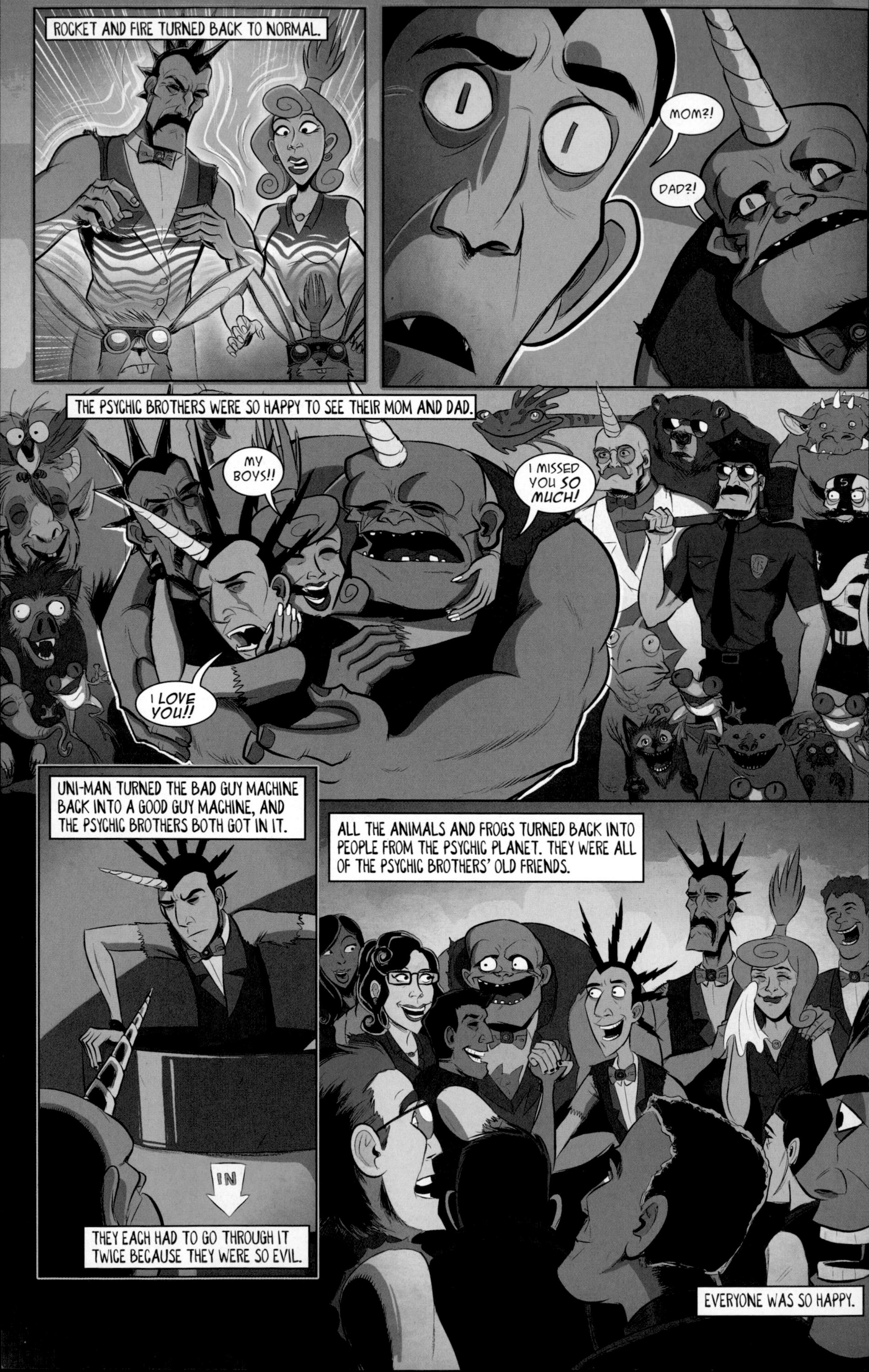

ROCKET AND FIRE TURNED BACK TO NORMAL.
MOM?!
DAD?!
THE PSYCHIC BROTHERS WERE SO HAPPY TO SEE THEIR MOM AND DAD.
MY BOYS!!
I MISSED YOU SO MUCH!
I LOVE YOU!!
UNI-MAN TURNED THE BAD GUY MACHINE BACK INTO A GOOD GUY MACHINE, AND THE PSYCHIC BROTHERS BOTH GOT IN IT.
IN
THEY EACH HAD TO GO THROUGH IT TWICE BECAUSE THEY WERE SO EVIL.
ALL THE ANIMALS AND FROGS TURNED BACK INTO PEOPLE FROM THE PSYCHIC PLANET. THEY WERE ALL OF THE PSYCHIC BROTHERS' OLD FRIENDS.
EVERYONE WAS SO HAPPY.

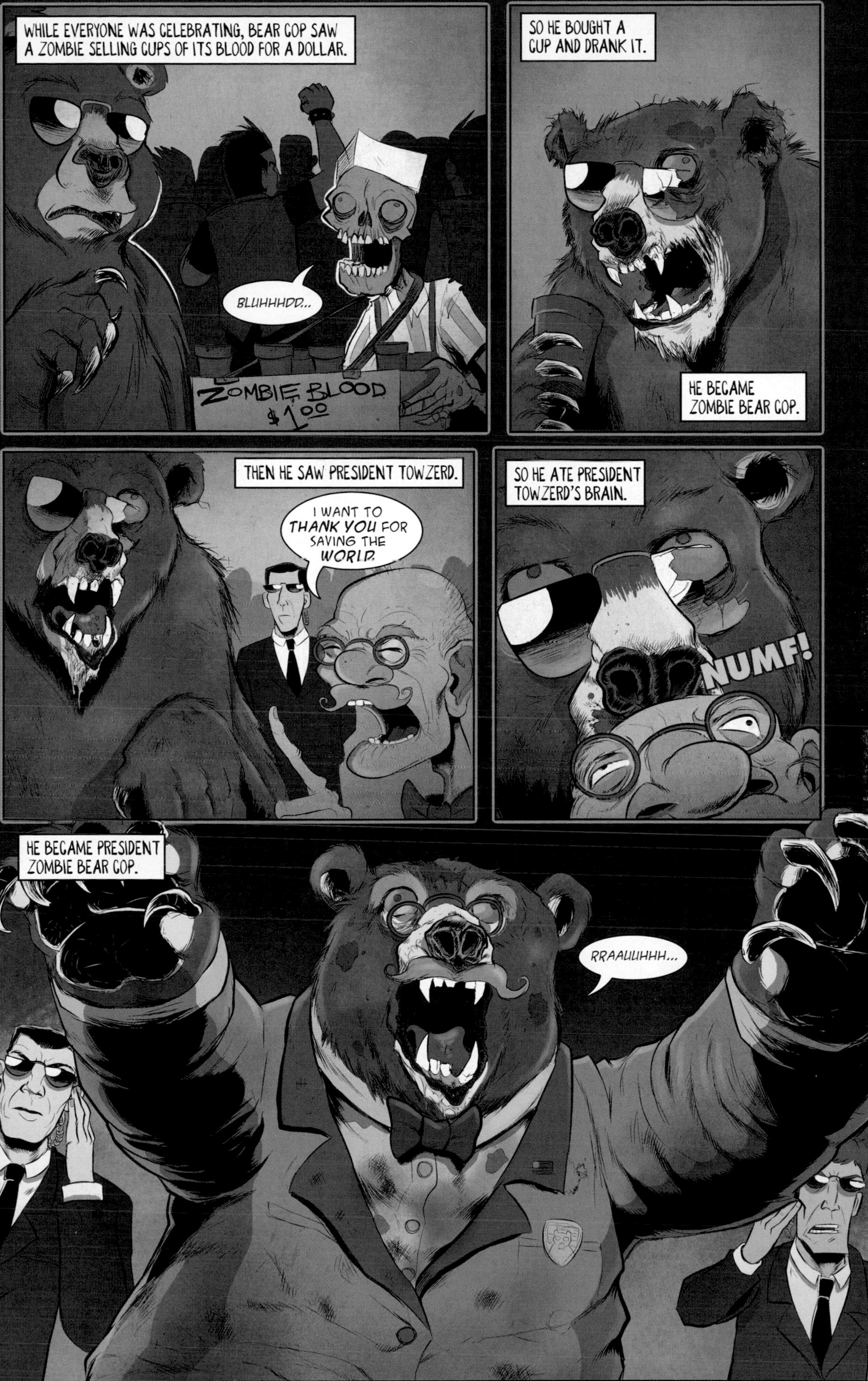
WHILE EVERYONE WAS CELEBRATING, BEAR COP SAW A ZOMBIE SELLING CUPS OF ITS BLOOD FOR A DOLLAR.
BLUHHHDD...
ZOMBIE BLOOD $1.00
SO HE BOUGHT A CUP AND DRANK IT.
HE BECAME ZOMBIE BEAR COP.
THEN HE SAW PRESIDENT TOWZERD.
I WANT TO THANK YOU FOR SAVING THE WORLD.
SO HE ATE PRESIDENT TOWZERD'S BRAIN.
NUMF!
HE BECAME PRESIDENT ZOMBIE BEAR COP.
RRAAUUHHH...

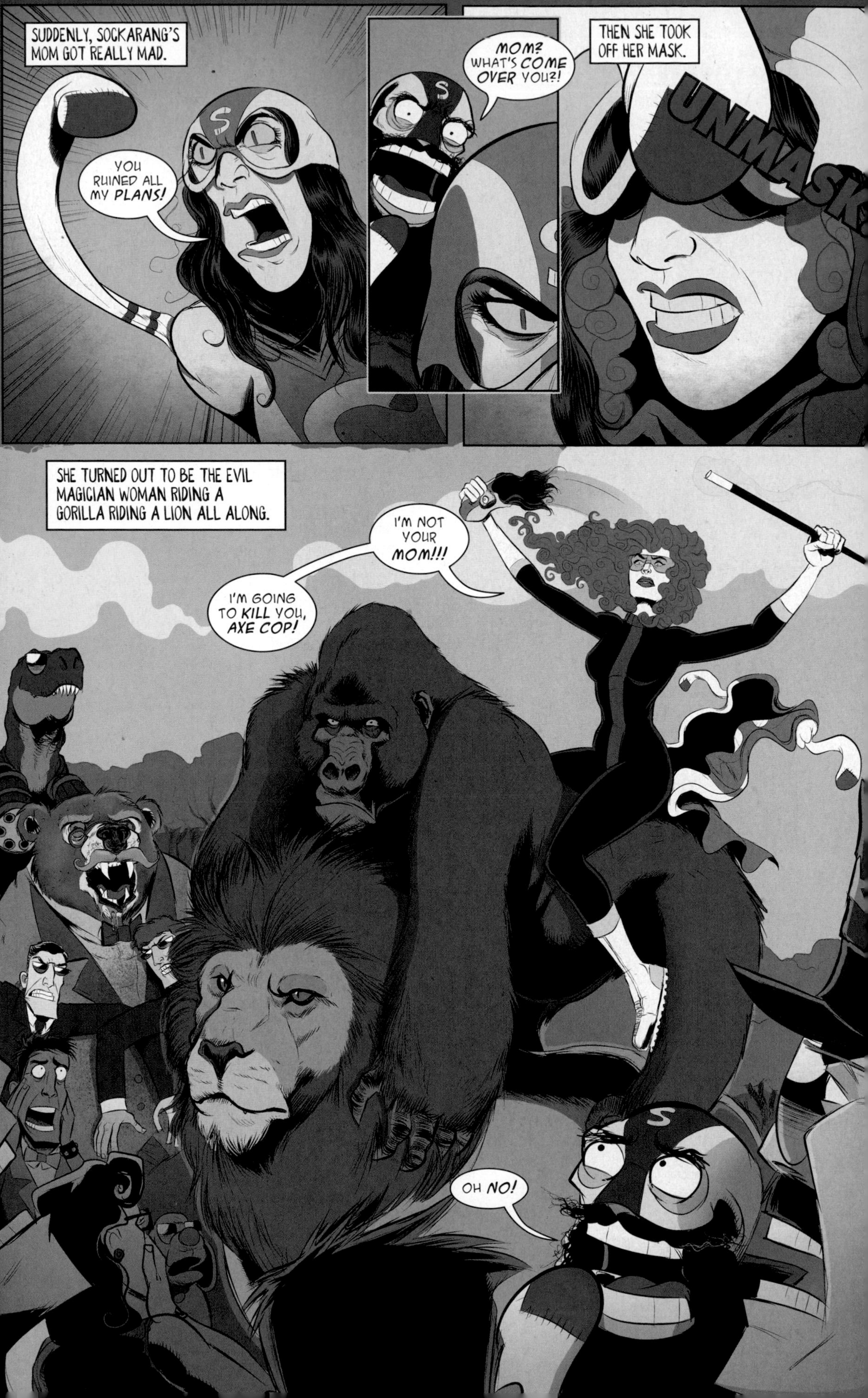
SUDDENLY, SOCKARANG'S MOM GOT REALLY MAD.
YOU RUINED ALL MY PLANS!
MOM? WHAT'S COME OVER YOU?!
THEN SHE TOOK OFF HER MASK.
UNMASK!
SHE TURNED OUT TO BE THE EVIL MAGICIAN WOMAN RIDING A GORILLA RIDING A LION ALL ALONG.
I'M NOT YOUR MOM!!!
I'M GOING TO KILL YOU, AXE COP!
OH NO!

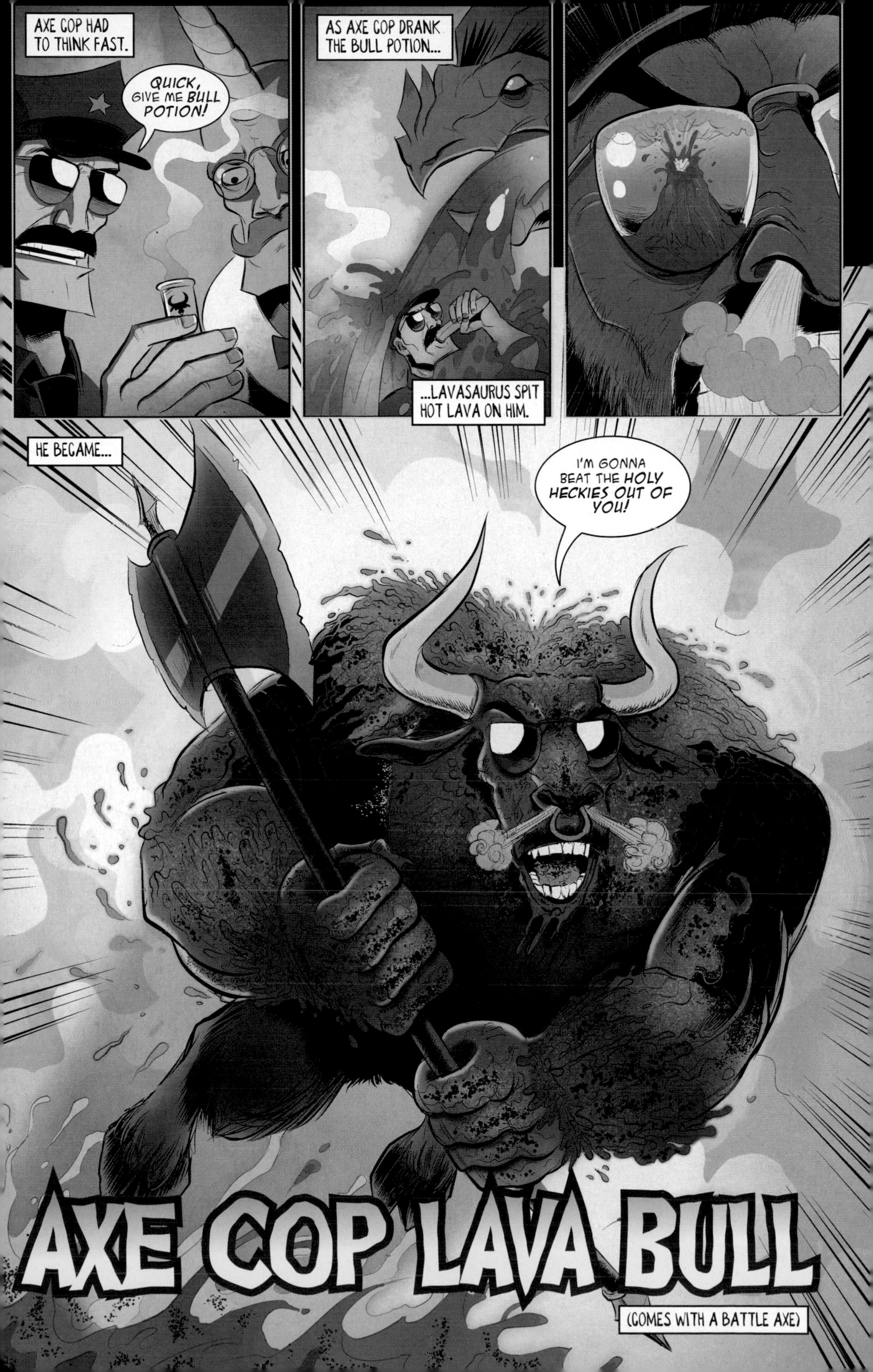
AXE COP HAD TO THINK FAST.
QUICK, GIVE ME BULL POTION!
AS AXE COP DRANK THE BULL POTION...
...LAVASAURUS SPIT HOT LAVA ON HIM.
HE BECAME...
I'M GONNA BEAT THE HOLY HECKIES OUT OF YOU!
AXE COP LAVA BULL
(COMES WITH A BATTLE AXE)

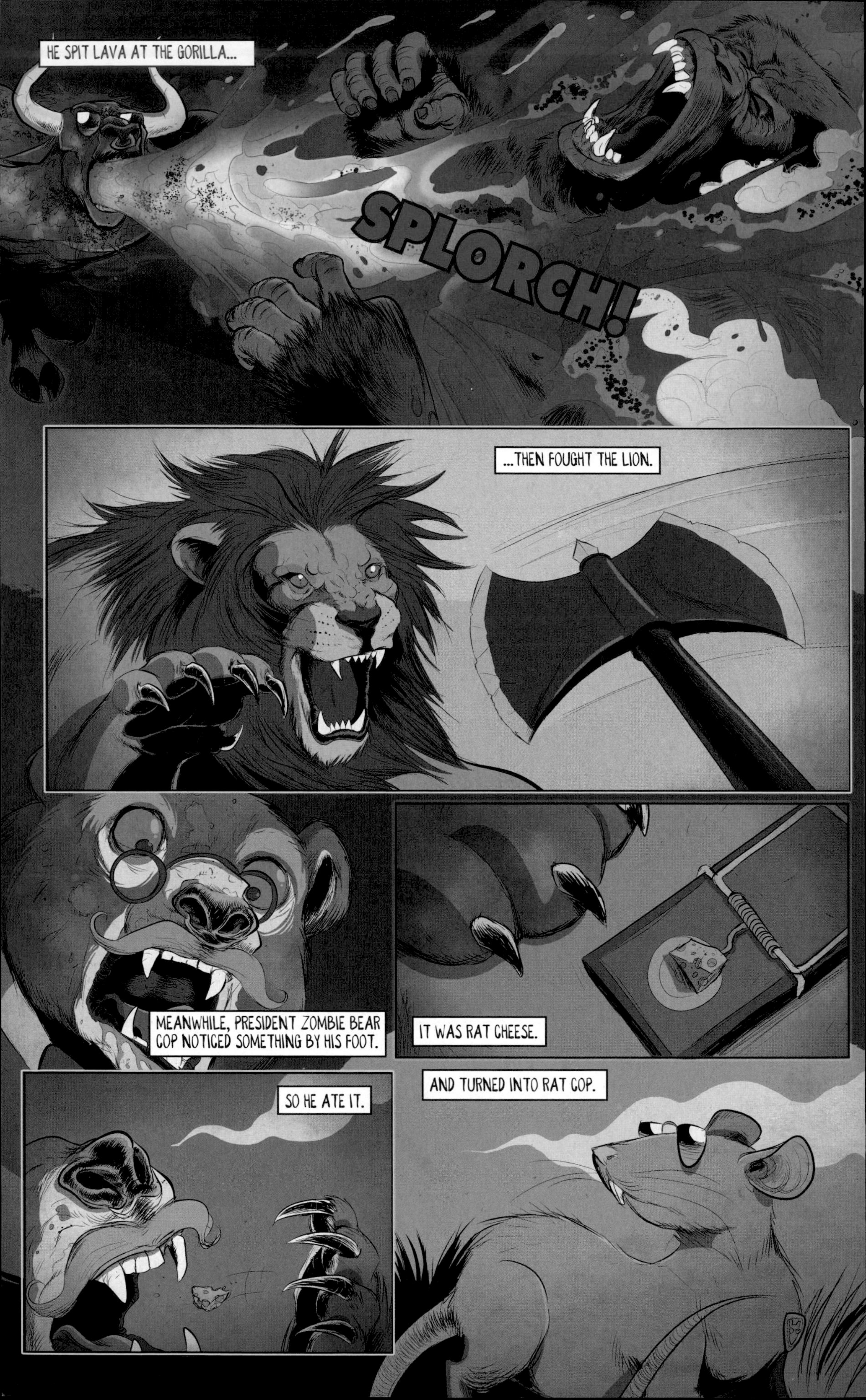
HE SPIT LAVA AT THE GORILLA...
SPLORCH!
...THEN FOUGHT THE LION.
MEANWHILE, PRESIDENT ZOMBIE BEAR COP NOTICED SOMETHING BY HIS FOOT.
IT WAS RAT CHEESE.
SO HE ATE IT.
AND TURNED INTO RAT COP.

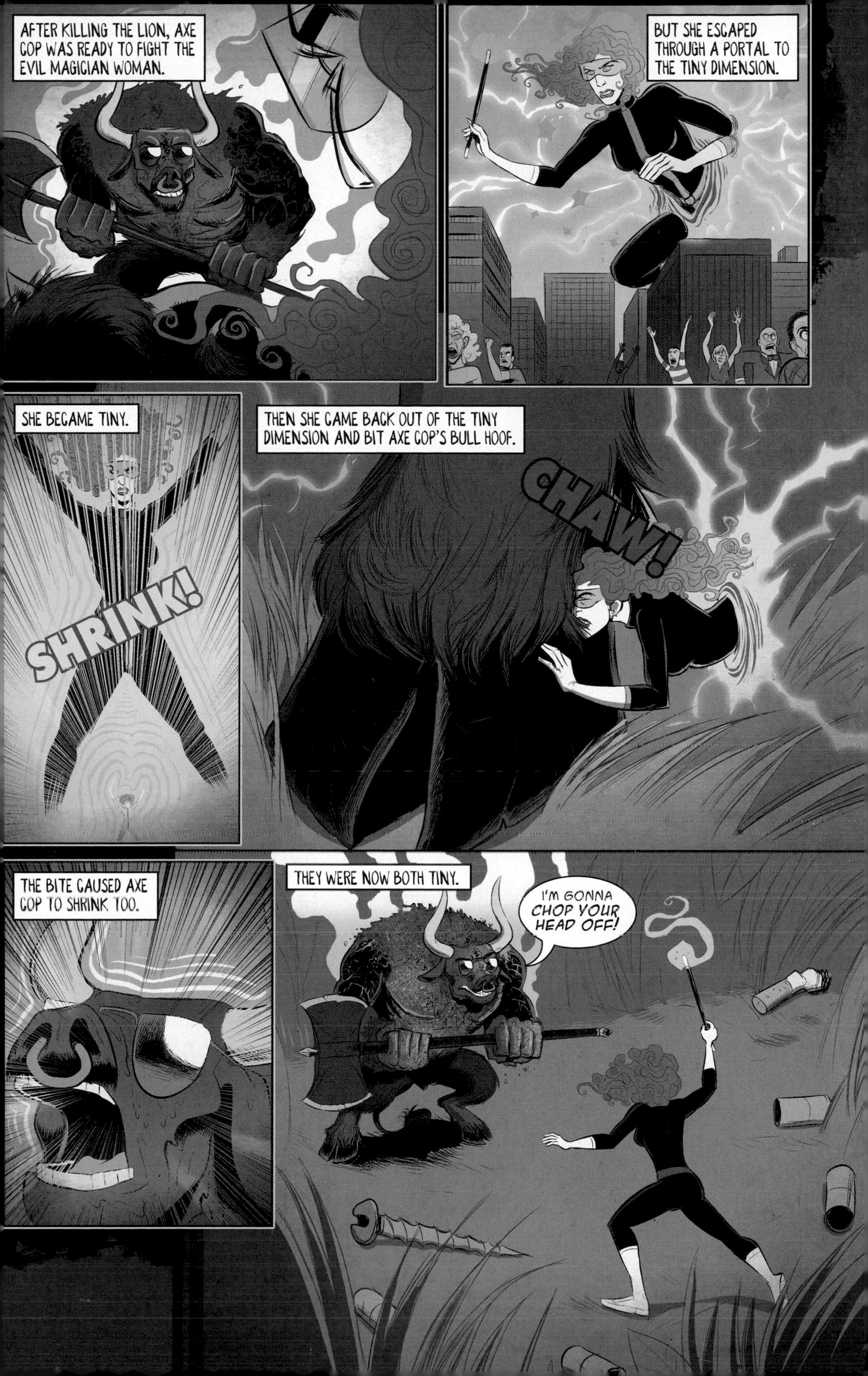
AFTER KILLING THE LION, AXE COP WAS READY TO FIGHT THE EVIL MAGICIAN WOMAN.
BUT SHE ESCAPED THROUGH A PORTAL TO THE TINY DIMENSION.
SHE BECAME TINY.
SHRINK!
THEN SHE CAME BACK OUT OF THE TINY DIMENSION AND BIT AXE COP'S BULL HOOF.
CHAW!
THE BITE CAUSED AXE COP TO SHRINK TOO.
THEY WERE NOW BOTH TINY.
I'M GONNA CHOP YOUR HEAD OFF!

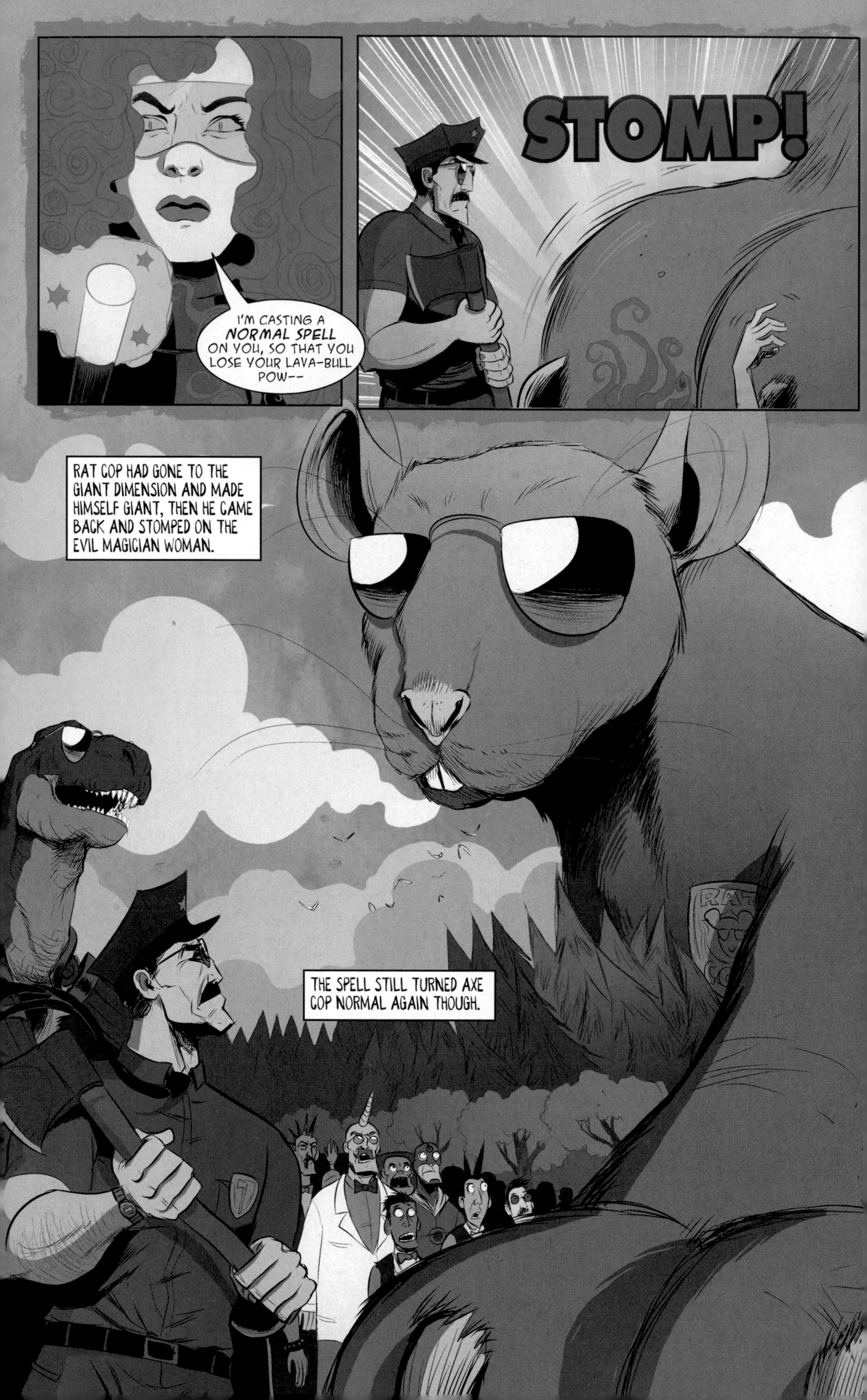
I'M CASTING A NORMAL SPELL ON YOU, SO THAT YOU LOSE YOUR LAVA-BULL POW--
STOMP!
RAT COP HAD GONE TO THE GIANT DIMENSION AND MADE HIMSELF GIANT, THEN HE CAME BACK AND STOMPED ON THE EVIL MAGICIAN WOMAN.
THE SPELL STILL TURNED AXE COP NORMAL AGAIN THOUGH.

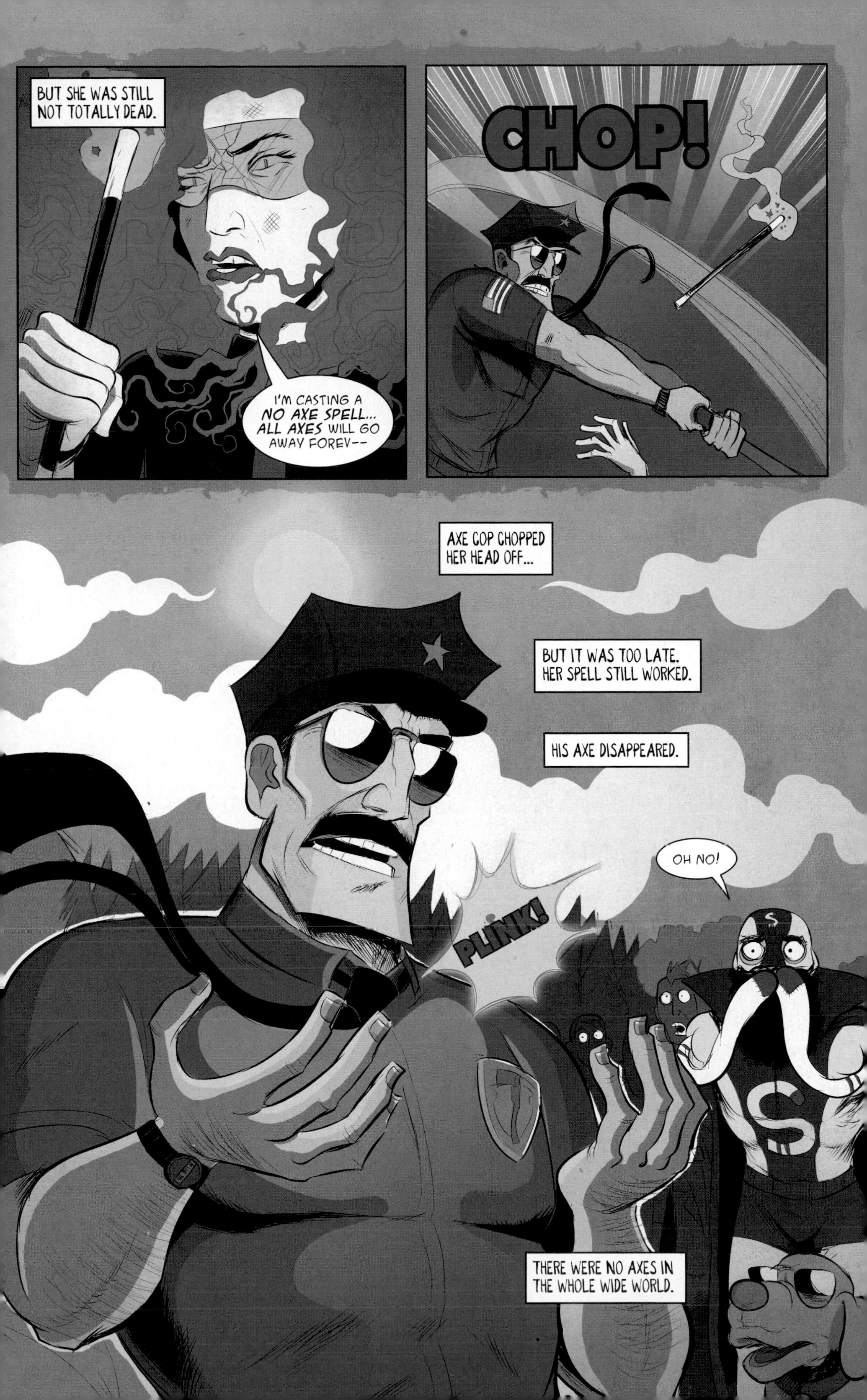
BUT SHE WAS STILL NOT TOTALLY DEAD.
I'M CASTING A NO AXE SPELL... ALL AXES WILL GO AWAY FOREV--
CHOP!
AXE COP CHOPPED HER HEAD OFF...
BUT IT WAS TOO LATE. HER SPELL STILL WORKED.
HIS AXE DISAPPEARED.
OH NO!
PLINK!
THERE WERE NO AXES IN THE WHOLE WIDE WORLD.

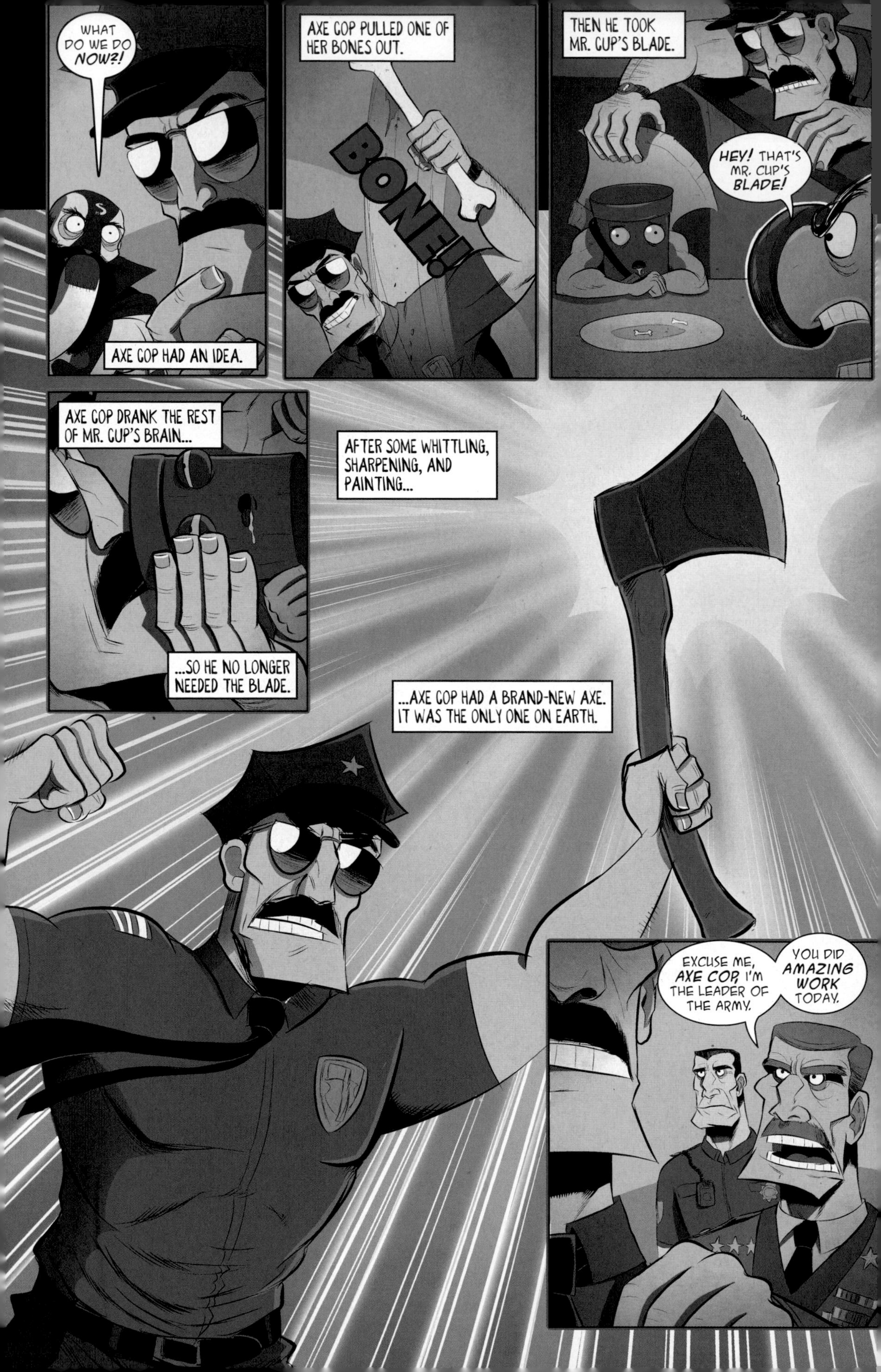

WHAT DO WE DO NOW?!
AXE COP HAD AN IDEA.
AXE COP PULLED ONE OF HER BONES OUT.
BONE!
THEN HE TOOK MR. CUP'S BLADE.
HEY! THAT'S MR. CUP'S BLADE!
AXE COP DRANK THE REST OF MR. CUP'S BRAIN...
...SO HE NO LONGER NEEDED THE BLADE.
AFTER SOME WHITTLING, SHARPENING, AND PAINTING...
...AXE COP HAD A BRAND-NEW AXE. IT WAS THE ONLY ONE ON EARTH.
EXCUSE ME, AXE COP, I'M THE LEADER OF THE ARMY.
YOU DID AMAZING WORK TODAY.

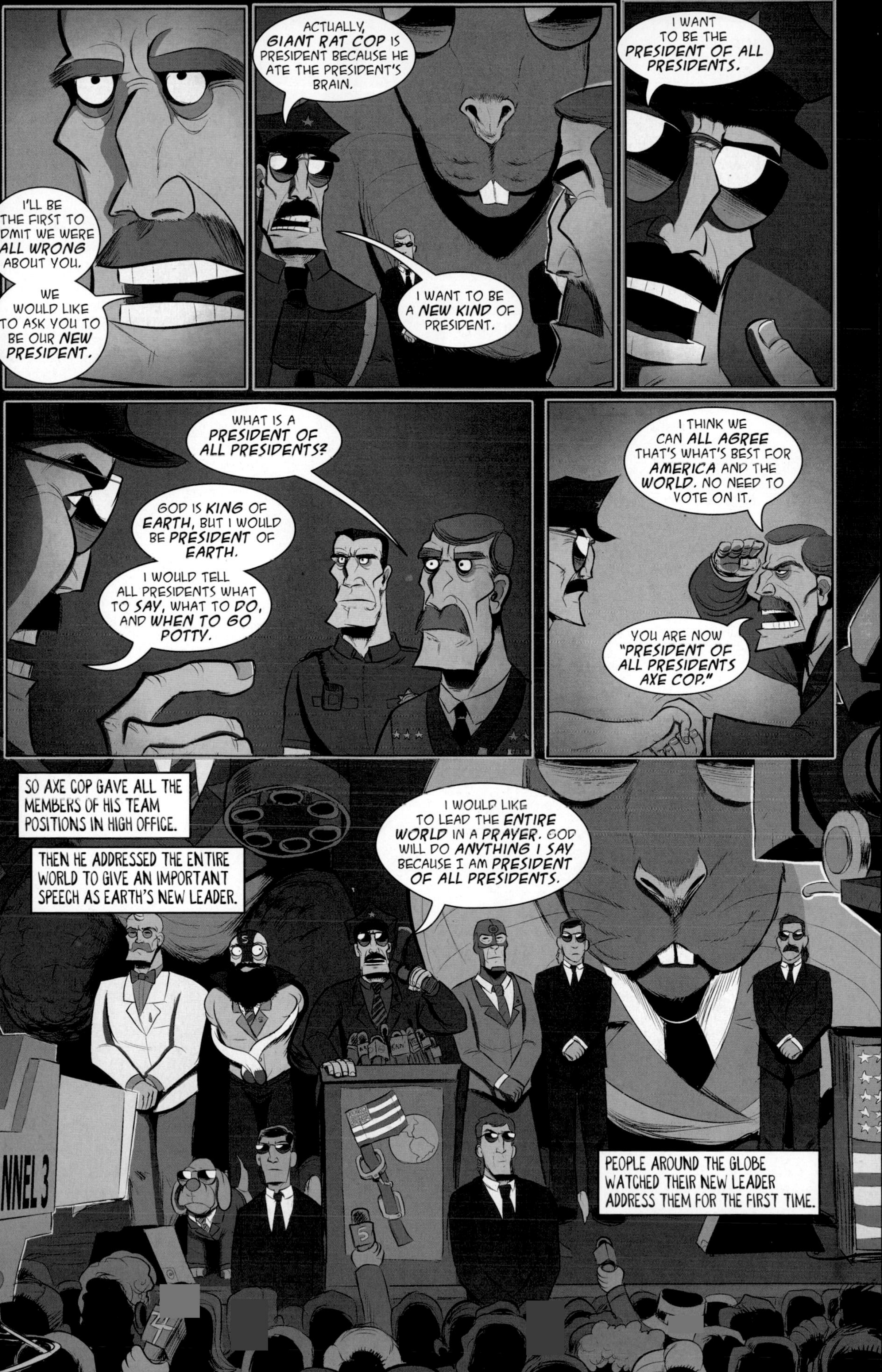
I'LL BE THE FIRST TO ADMIT WE WERE ALL WRONG ABOUT YOU.
WE WOULD LIKE TO ASK YOU TO BE OUR NEW PRESIDENT.
ACTUALLY, GIANT RAT COP IS PRESIDENT BECAUSE HE ATE THE PRESIDENT'S BRAIN.
I WANT TO BE A NEW KIND OF PRESIDENT.
I WANT TO BE THE PRESIDENT OF ALL PRESIDENTS.
WHAT IS A PRESIDENT OF ALL PRESIDENTS?
GOD IS KING OF EARTH, BUT I WOULD BE PRESIDENT OF EARTH.
I WOULD TELL ALL PRESIDENTS WHAT TO SAY, WHAT TO DO, AND WHEN TO GO POTTY.
I THINK WE CAN ALL AGREE THAT'S WHAT'S BEST FOR AMERICA AND THE WORLD. NO NEED TO VOTE ON IT.
YOU ARE NOW "PRESIDENT OF ALL PRESIDENTS AXE COP."
SO AXE COP GAVE ALL THE MEMBERS OF HIS TEAM POSITIONS IN HIGH OFFICE.
THEN HE ADDRESSED THE ENTIRE WORLD TO GIVE AN IMPORTANT SPEECH AS EARTH'S NEW LEADER.
I WOULD LIKE TO LEAD THE ENTIRE WORLD IN A PRAYER. GOD WILL DO ANYTHING I SAY BECAUSE I AM PRESIDENT OF ALL PRESIDENTS.
PEOPLE AROUND THE GLOBE WATCHED THEIR NEW LEADER ADDRESS THEM FOR THE FIRST TIME.

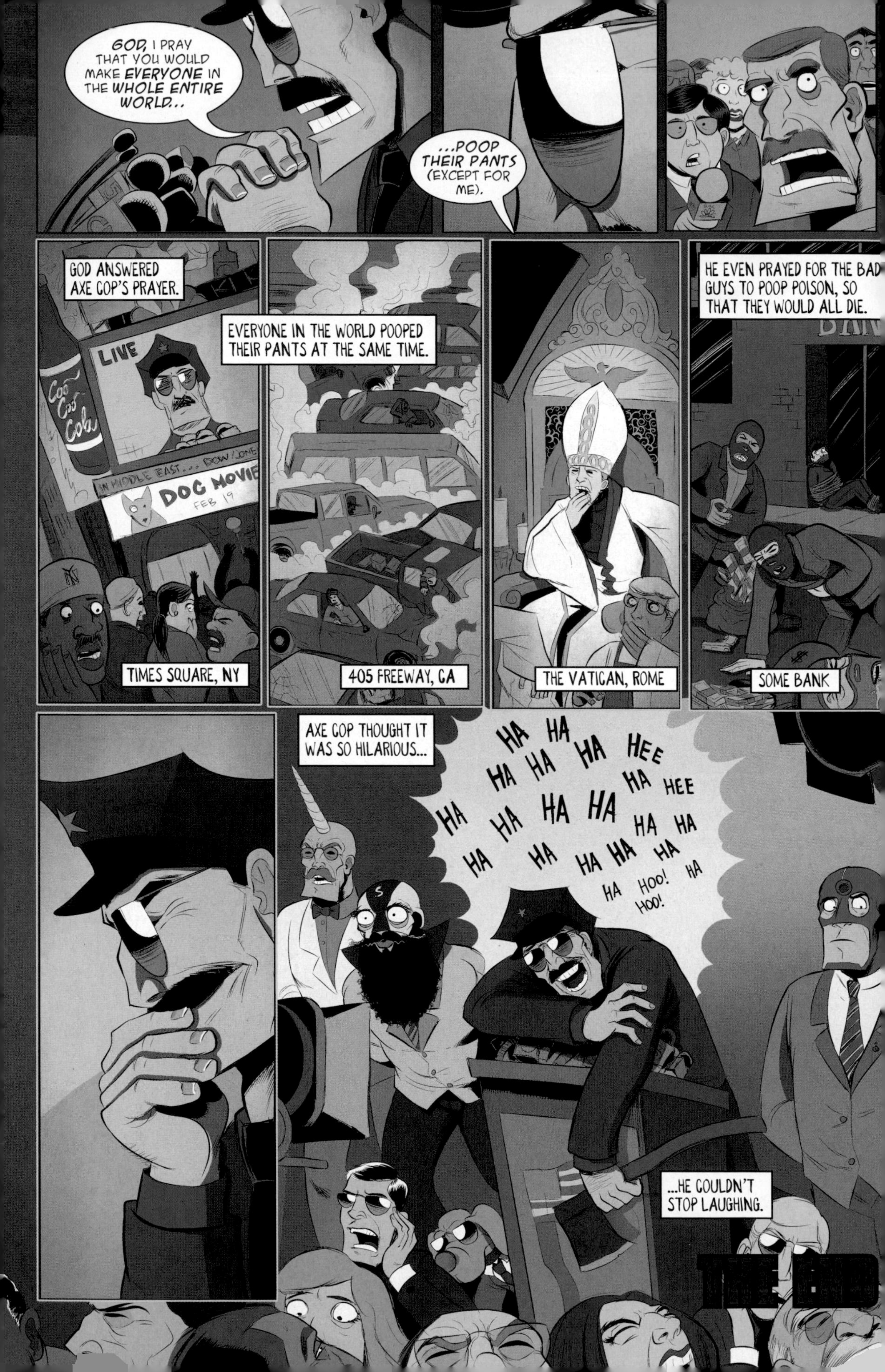
GOD, I PRAY THAT YOU WOULD MAKE EVERYONE IN THE WHOLE ENTIRE WORLD...
...POOP THEIR PANTS (EXCEPT FOR ME).
GOD ANSWERED AXE COP'S PRAYER.
LIVE
DOG MOVIE FEB 19
TIMES SQUARE, NY
EVERYONE IN THE WORLD POOPED THEIR PANTS AT THE SAME TIME.
405 FREEWAY, CA
THE VATICAN, ROME
HE EVEN PRAYED FOR THE BAD GUYS TO POOP POISON, SO THAT THEY WOULD ALL DIE.
SOME BANK
AXE COP THOUGHT IT WAS SO HILARIOUS...
HA HA HA HA HEE HA HA HA HEE HA HA HA HA HA HA HA HA HA HA HA HA HA HA HOO! HOO! HA
...HE COULDN'T STOP LAUGHING.
THE END

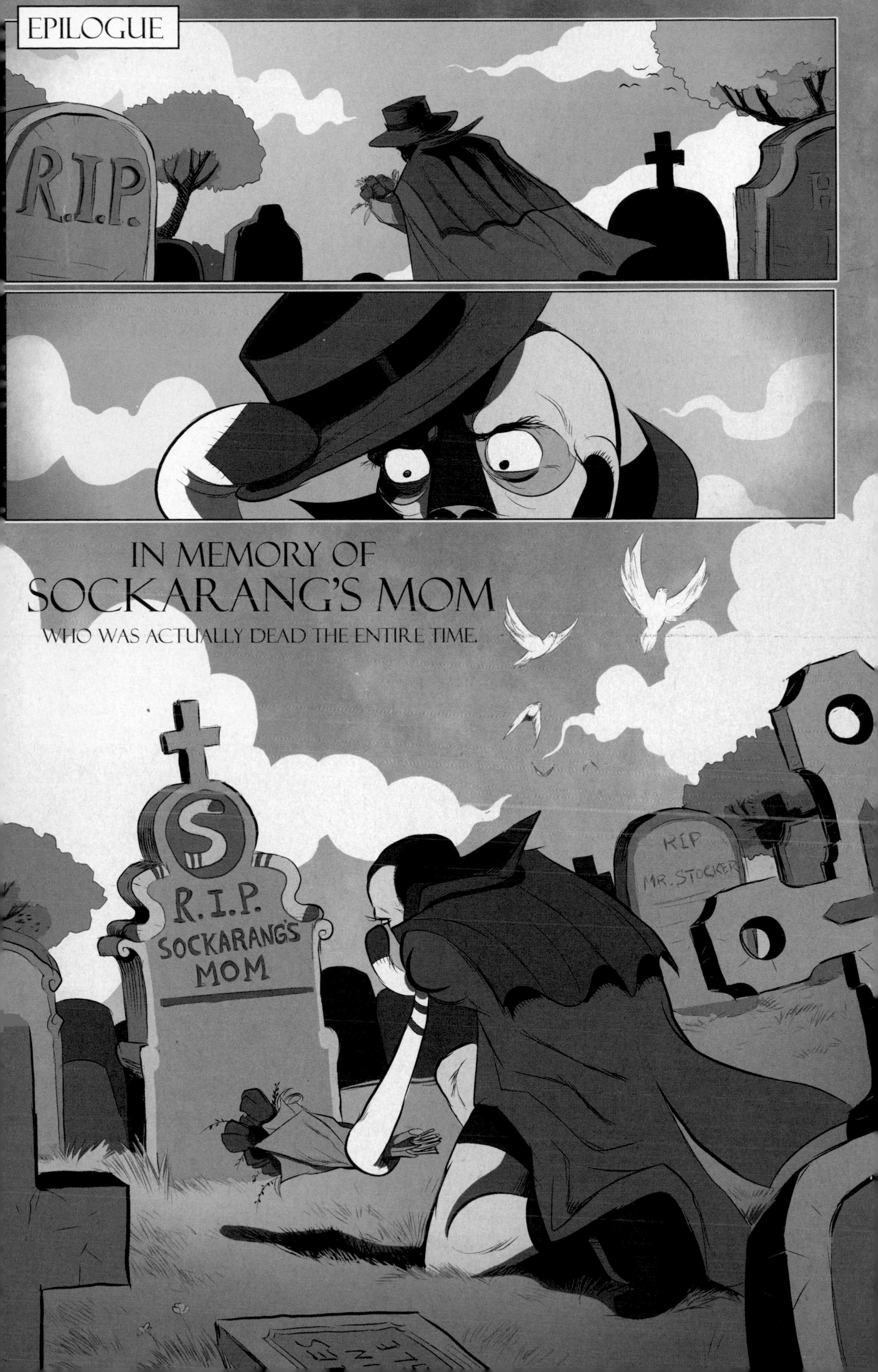
EPILOGUE
R.I.P.
IN MEMORY OF
SOCKARANG'S MOM
WHO WAS ACTUALLY DEAD THE ENTIRE TIME.
R.I.P.
SOCKARANG'S
MOM
RIP
MR. STOCKER

THE MAKING OF BAD GUY EARTH

WHAT YOU JUST READ HAS BEEN ONE OF THE MOST INTENSE CREATIVE ENDEAVORS I HAVE EVER UNDERTAKEN. I AM NOT SAYING MORE-CREATIVE WORKS HAVE NOT BEEN DONE, ONLY THAT IN THE SCOPE OF MY OWN WORK, *AXE COP: BAD GUY EARTH* PUSHED ME INTO NEW REALMS OF CREATIVITY I WOULD NEVER HAVE DARED TO ENTER HAD IT NOT BEEN FOR THE FACT THAT THIS BOOK CAME OUT OF A MONTH-LONG VISIT WITH MY (THEN) SIX-YEAR-OLD BROTHER, MALACHAI.

WHAT MAKES *BAD GUY EARTH* UNIQUE AS A COMIC AND AS AN *AXE COP* ADVENTURE IS HOW IT WAS MADE. WHILE MOST OF THE PREVIOUS *AXE COP* STORIES HAVE BEEN WRITTEN OVER THE PHONE, MAINLY IN THE FORMS OF QUESTIONS AND ANSWERS, *BAD GUY EARTH* WAS DONE 90 PERCENT IN PERSON, PLAYING WITH TOYS, RUNNING AROUND THE HOUSE WITH TOY AXES AND GUNS, ROLE-PLAYING, AND BRINGING TO LIFE THE STORY YOU NOW HOLD IN YOUR HANDS.

SOME MAY SAY IT IS A DEPARTURE FROM THE ORIGINAL AXE COP EPISODE, WHERE HE FINDS THE PERFECT FIREMAN AXE AND DISCOVERS HIS OWN FATE AS AN AXE COP, BUT THE TRUTH IS THAT IT IS A RETURN. THAT FIRST EPISODE, MORE THAN ANY OTHER, CAME DIRECTLY FROM A REAL PLAY TIME BETWEEN MALACHAI AND ME. MUCH OF WHAT CAME AFTER THAT WAS WRITTEN IN PLAYFUL CONVERSATION, BUT IT WAS THROUGH THE SUCCESS OF THOSE COMICS THAT I WAS ABLE TO TAKE A MONTH OUT OF MY LIFE, DRIVE OVER 1,000 MILES NORTH, AND SPEND TIME WITH MALACHAI IN PERSON TO SEE JUST WHAT WE COULD COME UP WITH.

OF COURSE THERE WAS A DIFFERENCE, AND THAT DIFFERENCE IS I KNEW THE ENTIRE TIME THAT I WAS WORKING ON THE BIGGEST PROJECT OF MY LIFE UP TO THEN, WHEREAS WHEN WE MADE THE FIRST EPISODE OF *AXE COP* I THOUGHT ITS ONLY REAL DESTINY WAS HANGING ON MY PARENTS' REFRIGERATOR AND ON MY PERSONAL ART BLOG, WHERE I GET AN AVERAGE OF TWELVE VISITS A MONTH. WITH THIS PROJECT I WAS TRYING TO ANSWER A QUESTION I DIDN'T REALLY HAVE AN ANSWER TO: CAN A SIX-YEAR-OLD WRITE AN EPIC?

THE QUESTION REALLY CAME UP WHEN *AXE COP* HAD GONE VIRAL, AND I WAS IN THE MIDDLE OF NEGOTIATING A PUBLISHING CONTRACT WITH DARK HORSE COMICS. THEY PROPOSED DOING A THREE-PART MINISERIES, ONE CONTINUING STORY ARC THAT WOULD SPAN THREE COMICS AND TELL A COMPLETE STORY. IN NORMAL COMICS TERMS THAT'S ABOUT SEVENTY-FIVE PAGES, AND IN TERMS OF GRAPHIC NOVELS THAT'S PRETTY SHORT, BUT JUST ENOUGH TO TELL A FULL-LENGTH STORY. BUT IN THE WORLD OF *AXE COP* SEVENTY-FIVE PAGES IS *THE LORD OF THE RINGS*. THE IDEA OVERWHELMED ME AT FIRST. I HAD ONLY DONE ABOUT TEN PAGES OF *AXE COP* AT THAT POINT, AFTER ALL. I HAD NO IDEA IF MALACHAI WOULD TIRE OF THE CHARACTER OR JUST START COMING UP WITH IDEAS SO REPETITIVE THEY WOULDN'T BE WORTH PUBLISHING. ALSO, SINCE I HAD GONE AROUND TO A FEW FILM STUDIOS AND HAD SOME CONVERSATIONS ABOUT THE POSSIBILITIES OF AN AXE COP FILM, ONE COMMON THING I HEARD WAS THAT AN ENTIRE MOVIE WRITTEN IN THE CRAZY FORM OF AN AXE COP STRIP WOULD NOT WORK. AT FIRST I AGREED, BUT I STARTED TO WONDER . . . WHY NOT? HAS ANYONE REALLY EVER TRIED IT?

I REMAINED HESITANT, BUT AS THE NEGOTIATIONS WITH DARK HORSE WENT BACK AND FORTH, I BEGAN TO REALIZE THAT MALACHAI WAS NOT SEEMING TO BE ANYWHERE NEAR RUNNING OUT OF GREAT IDEAS, AND I WAS ONTO SOMETHING VERY SPECIAL WITH THIS PROJECT. I WAS UNLOCKING MY LITTLE BROTHER'S IMAGINATION IN A WAY I HAD NEVER SEEN DONE BEFORE, AND IT WAS EXCITING TO SEE IT UNFOLD. IT BECAME TRULY FASCINATING, AND I FOUND MYSELF WONDERING IF THIS COULD REALLY BE DONE . . . COULD I REALLY KEEP MALACHAI IN ONE STORY LINE FOR LONG ENOUGH TO GET A FULL EPIC TALE OUT OF HIM? HE SEEMED READY TO TRY IT. I WAS READY TO TRY IT. AND BESIDES, AFTER ALL OF THE SURREAL ONLINE SUCCESS, PHONE CALLS, AND SKYPE CONVERSATIONS SINCE THE CHRISTMAS WE CREATED THE FATEFUL CHARACTER, WE HAD REALLY BEGUN TO MISS EACH OTHER. I WAS READY TO TAKE *AXE COP* TO THE NEXT LEVEL AND HAVE THE MOST EPIC PLAY TIME EVER.

YOU MAY OR MAY NOT THINK I SUCCEEDED, AND THAT IS UP TO EACH READER TO DECIDE. I CAN'T SAY WHAT CAME OUT OF THAT MONTH TURNED OUT AS I EXPECTED, BECAUSE I HAD NO IDEA WHAT TO EXPECT. ALL I CAN SAY IS THAT IT WAS A FUN AND EXHAUSTING RIDE. NOT ONLY DID I DO ALL I COULD TO INSPIRE MALACHAI TO LET HIS IMAGINATION GO TOTALLY WILD, BUT HIS IDEAS PUSHED ME CREATIVELY AS HE CAME UP WITH INSANE CONCEPTS THAT I WOULD NOW HAVE TO IMAGINE FOR MYSELF, AND THEN FLESH OUT ON PAPER.

I CAN SAY WITH CONFIDENCE THAT THIS IS SOME OF THE BEST AXE COP MATERIAL WE HAVE EVER DONE, AND I'M VERY PROUD OF IT. IT'S A WILD RIDE THROUGH MY LITTLE BROTHER'S BRAIN AS VISUALIZED BY ME. MAKING IT WAS A BLAST. I HOPE READING IT WAS TOO.

'11

ETHAN NICOLLE
MAY 5, 2011

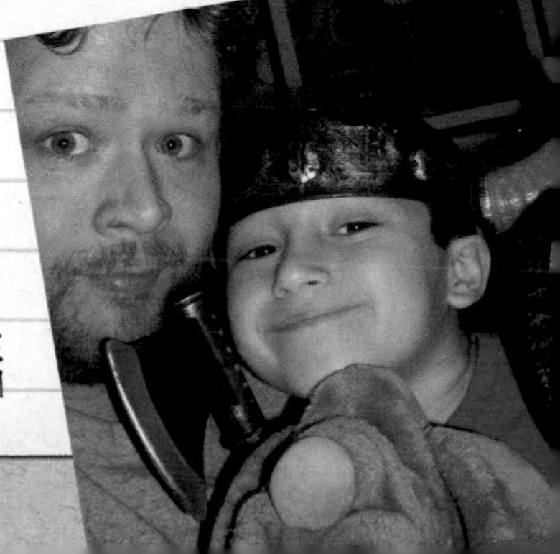

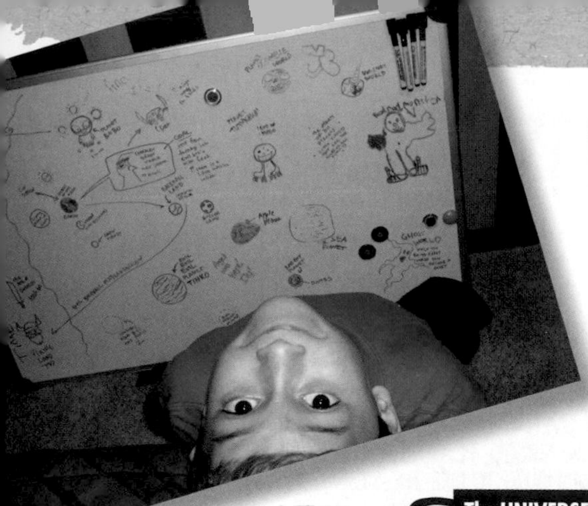

PLAY TIME

CREATING THE UNIVERSE

TO GET STARTED, LIKE ANY WRITER, WE JUST NEEDED TO START BRAINSTORMING. ONE OF OUR FAVORITE THINGS TO DO WAS ADD A PLANET OR TWO TO THE WHITEBOARD BEFORE WE GOT OUT THE TOYS. OVER OUR MONTH TOGETHER WE KEPT ADDING TO THE BOARD UNTIL WE HAD ONE CRAZY SOLAR SYSTEM. MANY OF THESE PLACES CAME WITH DIFFERENT MISSIONS WE WOULD GO ON, AND EXPANDED OUTSIDE OF JUST THE *BAD GUY EARTH* STORY LINE.

The UNIVERSE: An illustration based on our whiteboard of the Axe Cop universe (so far).

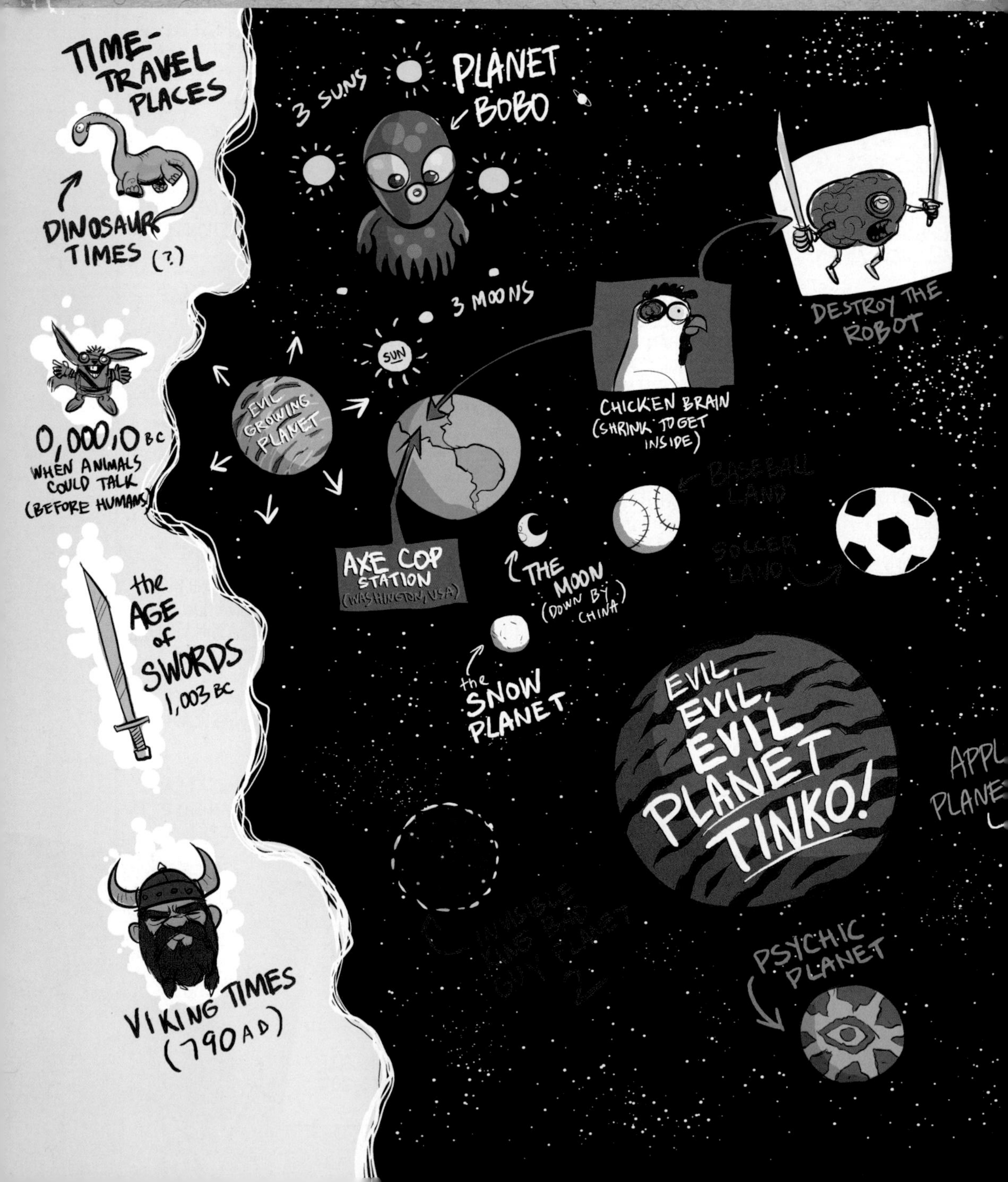

TIME-TRAVEL PLACES
DINOSAUR TIMES (?)
0,000,0 BC WHEN ANIMALS COULD TALK (BEFORE HUMANS)
the AGE of SWORDS 1,003 BC
VIKING TIMES (790 AD)
3 SUNS
PLANET BOBO
3 MOONS
SUN
EVIL GROWING PLANET
AXE COP STATION (WASHINGTON, USA)
CHICKEN BRAIN (SHRINK TO GET INSIDE)
DESTROY THE ROBOT
BASEBALL LAND
SOCCER LAND
THE MOON (DOWN BY CHINA)
the SNOW PLANET
EVIL, EVIL, EVIL PLANET TINKO!
APPL PLANE
PSYCHIC PLANET

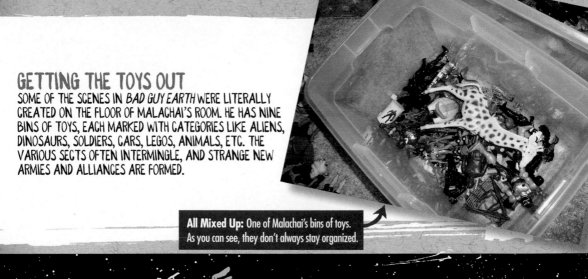

GETTING THE TOYS OUT

SOME OF THE SCENES IN *BAD GUY EARTH* WERE LITERALLY CREATED ON THE FLOOR OF MALACHAI'S ROOM. HE HAS NINE BINS OF TOYS, EACH MARKED WITH CATEGORIES LIKE ALIENS, DINOSAURS, SOLDIERS, CARS, LEGOS, ANIMALS, ETC. THE VARIOUS SECTS OFTEN INTERMINGLE, AND STRANGE NEW ARMIES AND ALLIANCES ARE FORMED.

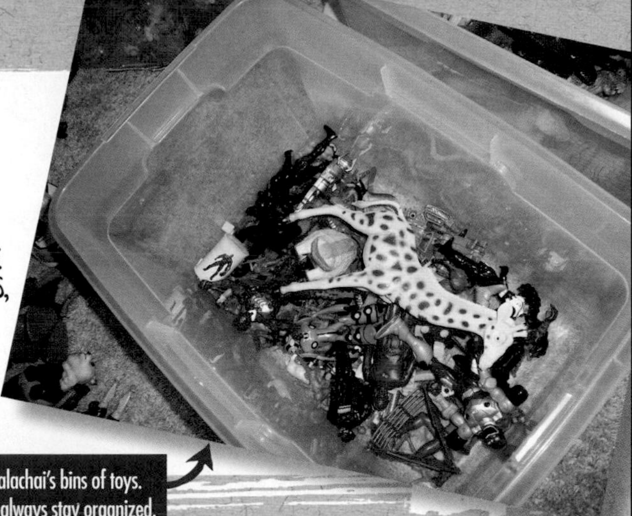

All Mixed Up: One of Malachai's bins of toys. As you can see, they don't always stay organized.

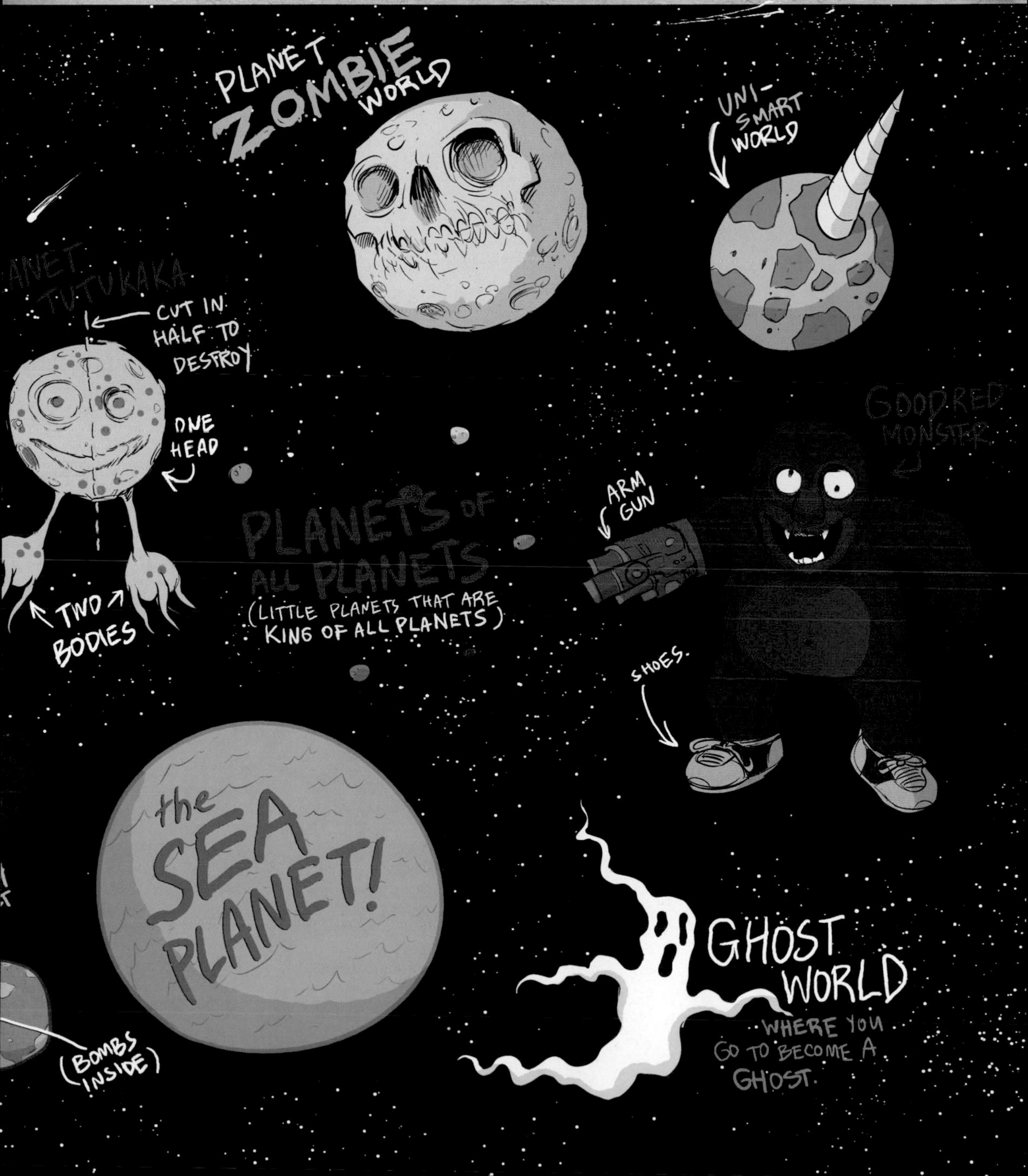
PLANET ZOMBIE WORLD
UNI-SMART WORLD
ANET TUTUKAKA
CUT IN HALF TO DESTROY
ONE HEAD
TWO BODIES
PLANETS OF ALL PLANETS
(LITTLE PLANETS THAT ARE KING OF ALL PLANETS)
GOODRED MONSTER
ARM GUN
SHOES.
the SEA PLANET!
(BOMBS INSIDE)
GHOST WORLD
WHERE YOU GO TO BECOME A GHOST.

MAKING A MESS

IT'S EASY TO SEE HOW THE STORY OF *BAD GUY EARTH* BECAME SO APOCALYPTIC WHEN YOU TAKE A QUICK LOOK AT MALACHAI'S ROOM AFTER ABOUT FIVE MINUTES OF PLAY TIME.

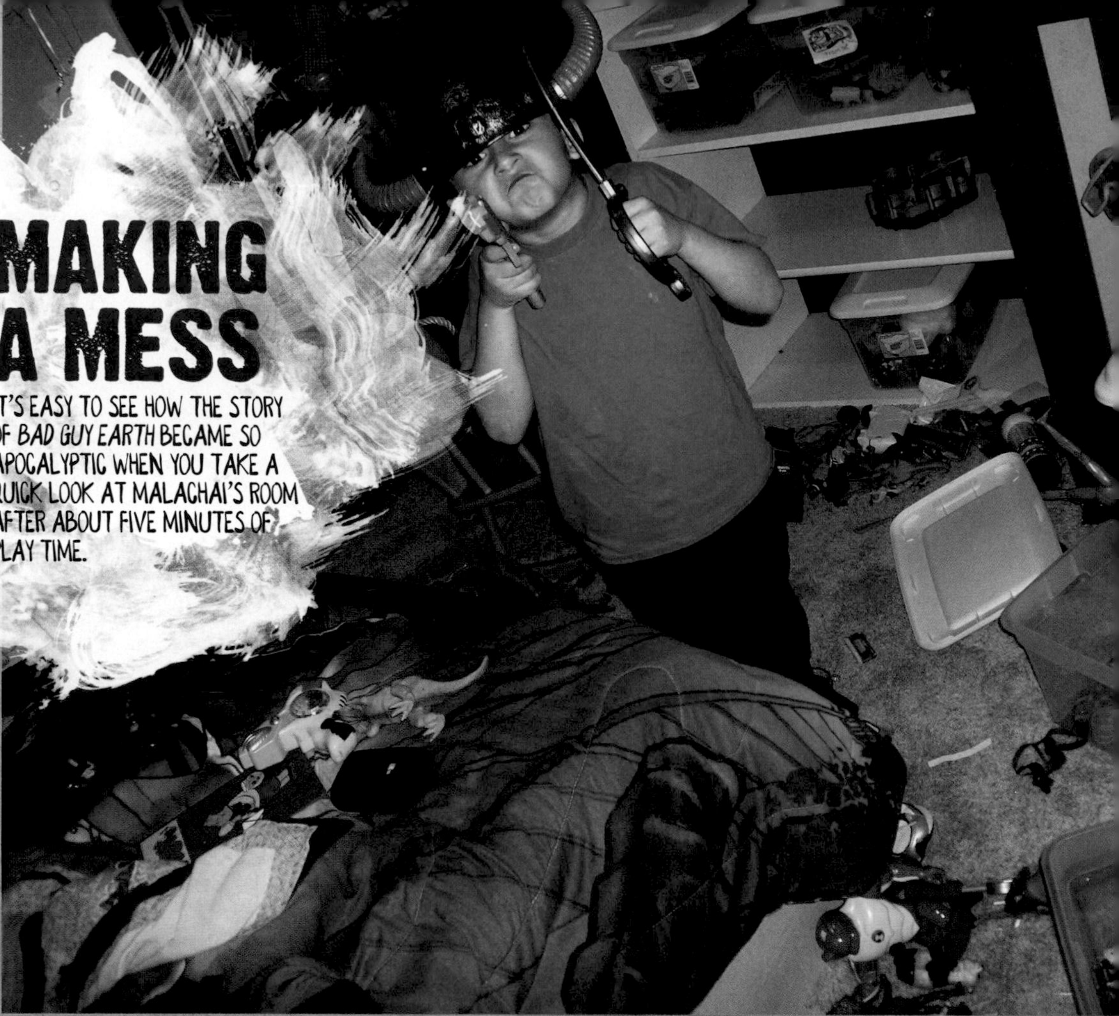

Uni-Smart World: We made a foam replica of Uni-Smart World because we knew it was going to get attacked.

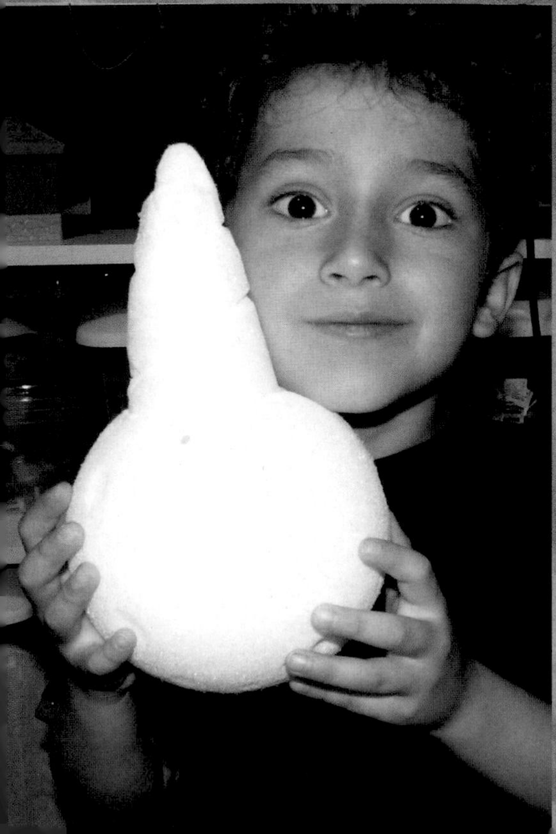

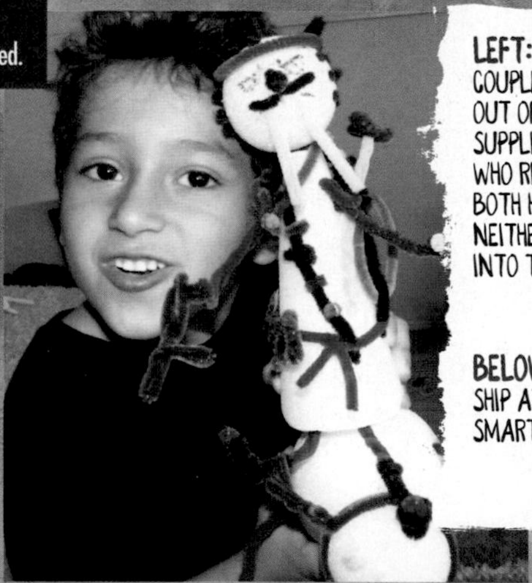

LEFT: WE MADE A COUPLE OF CHARACTERS OUT OF VARIOUS CRAFT SUPPLIES. A WOLF GUY WHO RIDES A TURTLE GUY, BOTH HEAVILY ARMED. NEITHER EVER MADE IT INTO THE NARRATIVE.

BELOW: THE BAD GUY SHIP ATTACKS UNI-SMART WORLD!

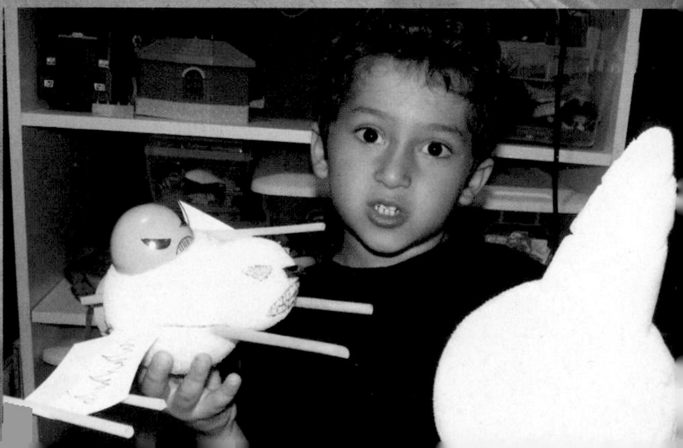

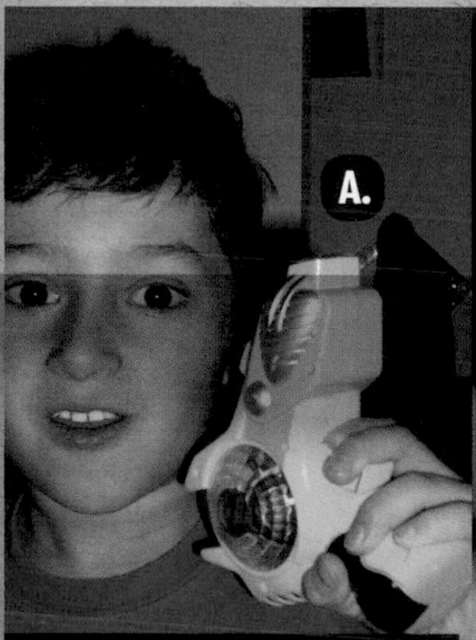
A.

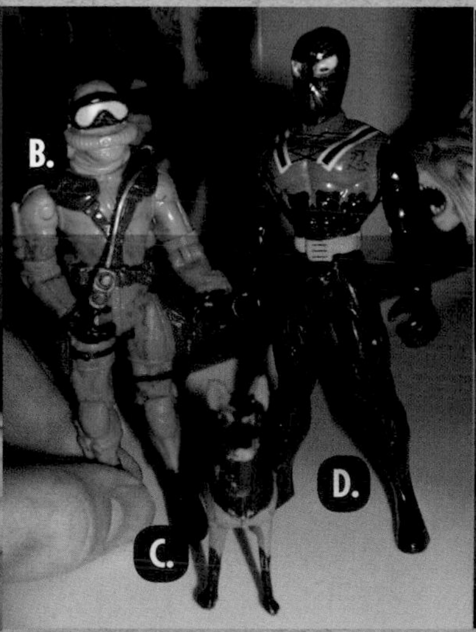
B.
C.
D.

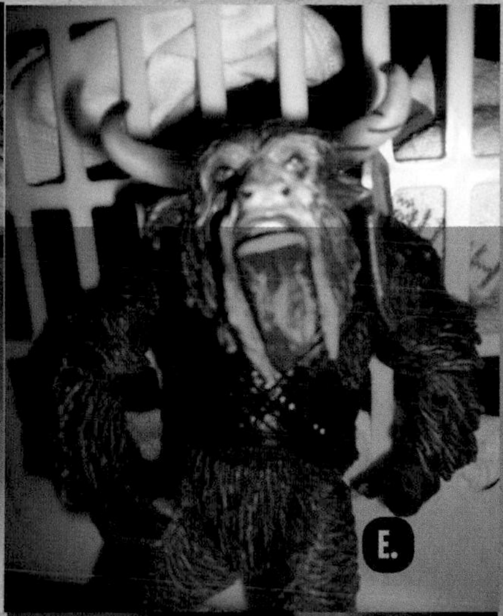
E.

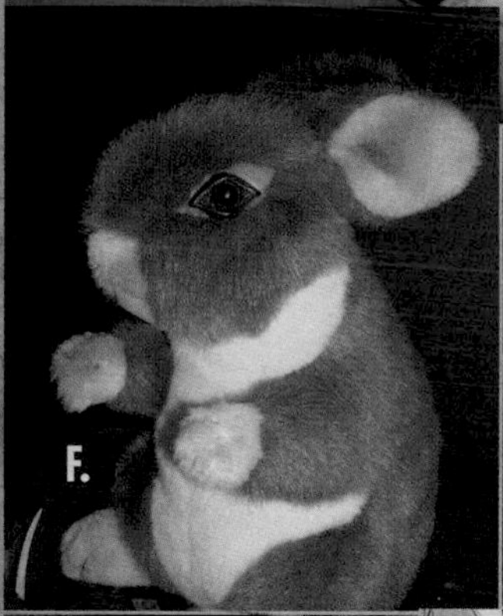
F.

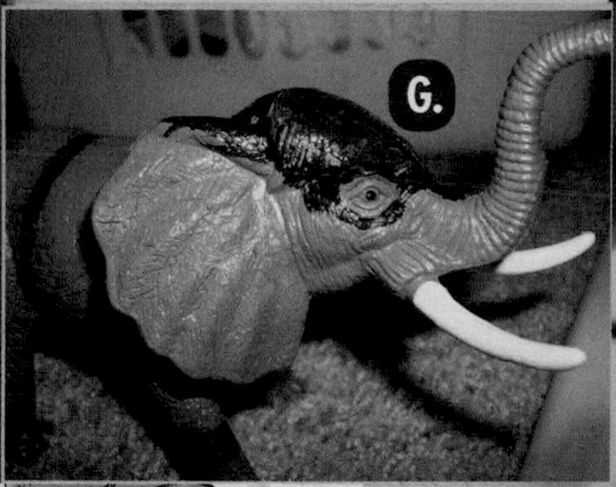
G.

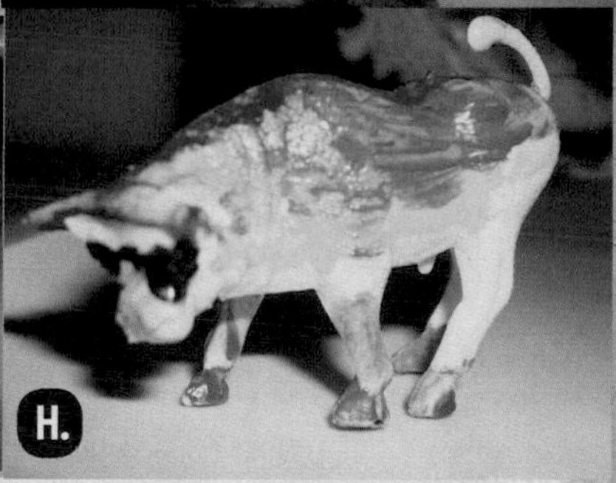
H.

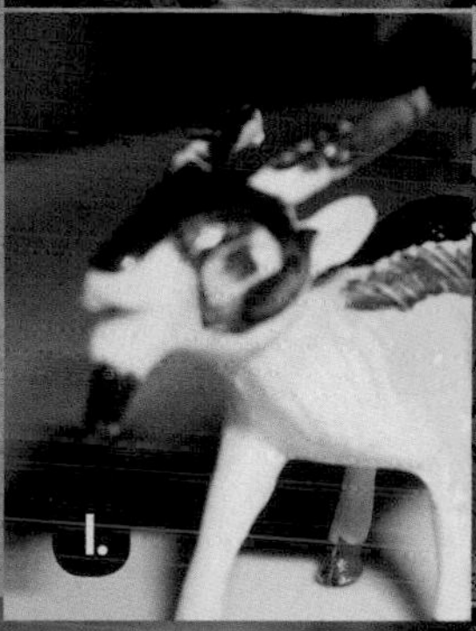
I.

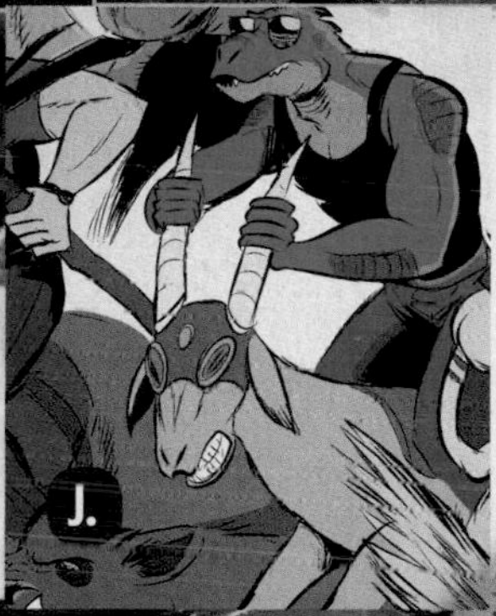
J.

A.) Laser-portal gun
B.) Generic bad guy soldier
C.) Dog with ninja costume
D.) Moon Warrior's new costume
E.) Narnia minotaur/Axe Cop bull
F.) The rabbit on the beach
G.) Ninja elephant
H.) Axe Cop Lava Bull
I.) Ibex with battle armor
J.) Ibex as drawn in the comic
K.) Wrestler riding a bear
L.) A giant fly
M.) The real cops
N.) The Chinese (Mexican) wrestler
O.) Aviators and a toy axe
P.) Handcuffs

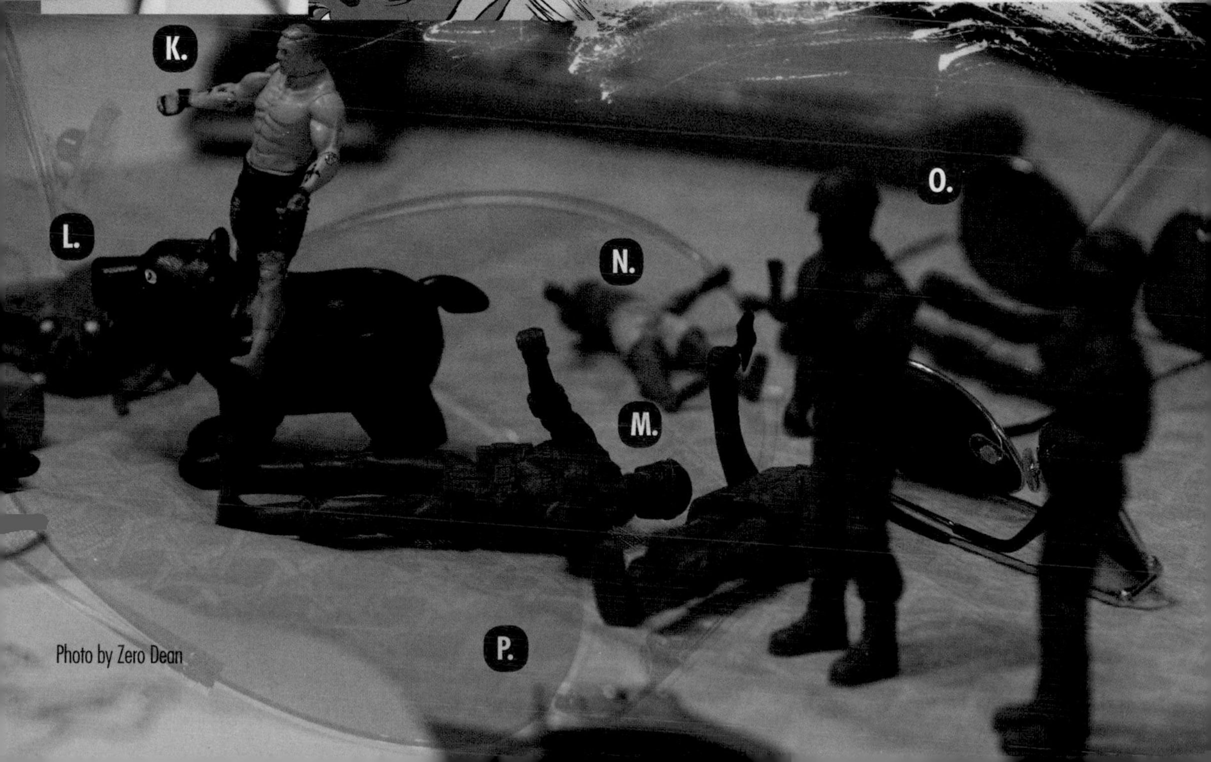
K.
L.
N.
O.
M.
P.

Photo by Zero Dean

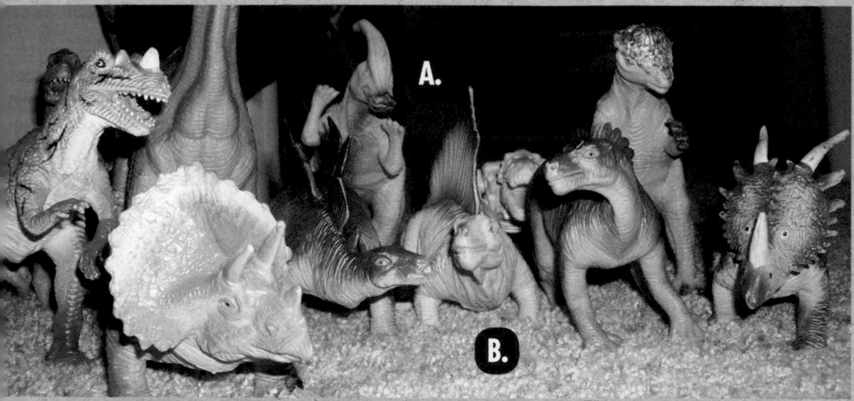
A.
B.

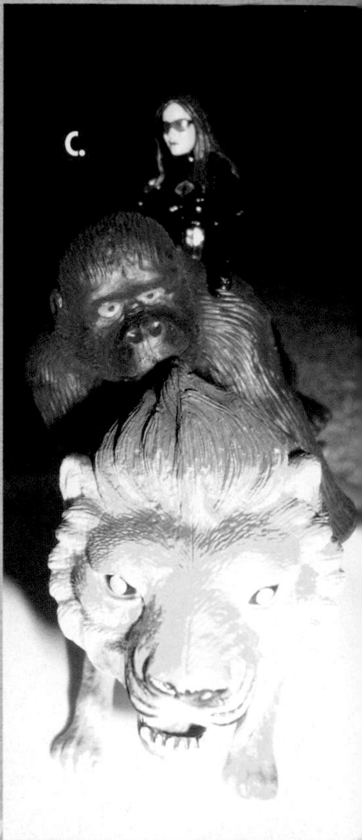
C.

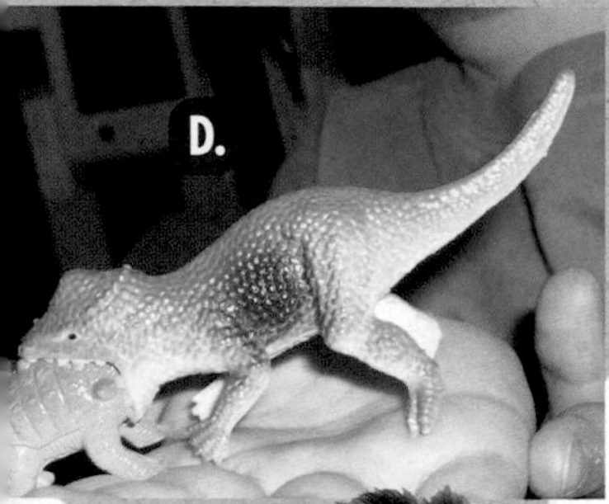
D.

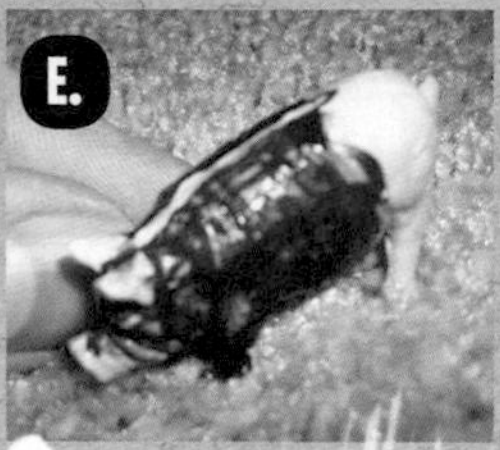
E.

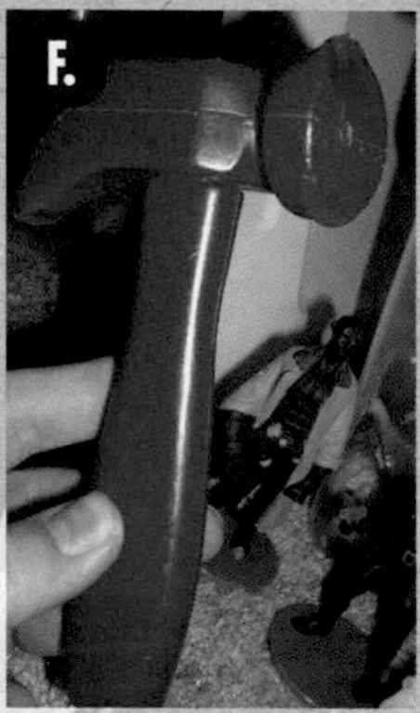
F.

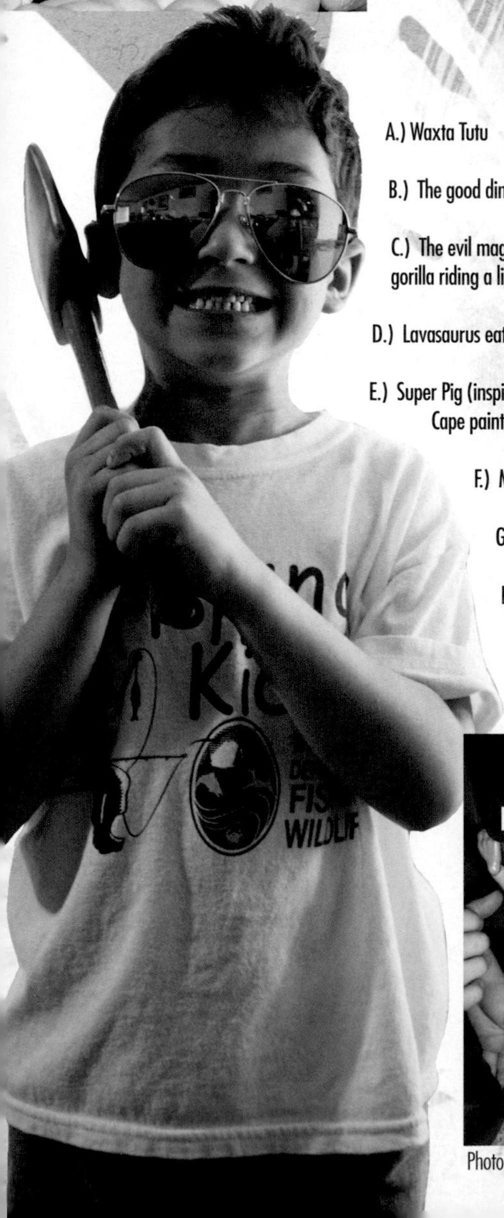

A.) Waxta Tutu

B.) The good dinosaurs

C.) The evil magician woman who rides a gorilla riding a lion

D.) Lavasaurus eating a baby dinosaur

E.) Super Pig (inspiration for Super Lion Pig). Cape painted on by Malachai.

F.) Mr. Hammer

G.) Ralph Wrinkles

H.) Various aliens

I.) Naked soldier with butt in front (Malachai insisted this be included)

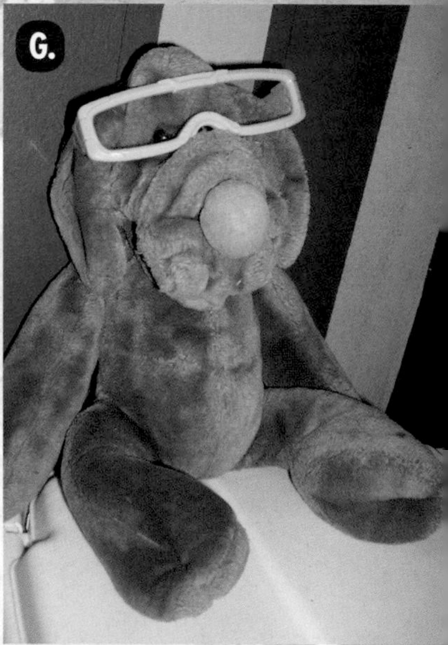
G.

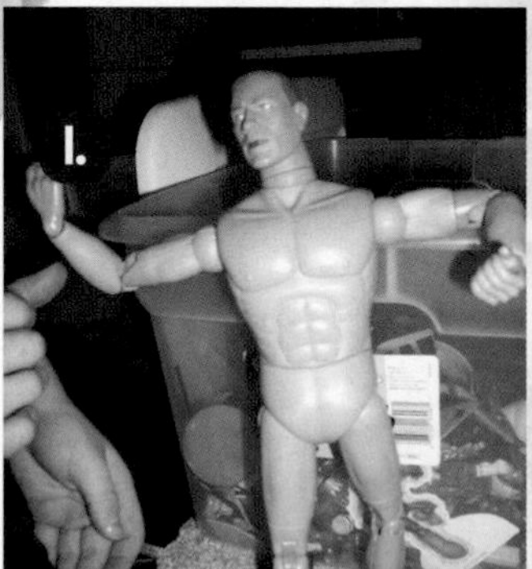
I.

Photo by Zero Dean

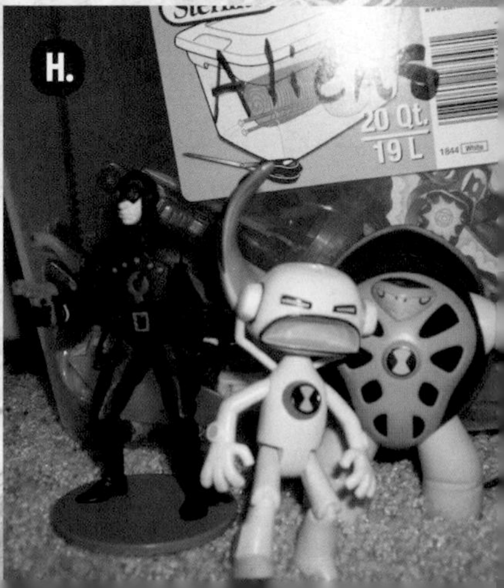
H.
Aliens
20 Qt.
19 L

TAKING NOTES

DURING PLAY TIME A NOTEBOOK OR SKETCHBOOK WAS ALWAYS OUT. SOMETIMES MALACHAI WOULD TELL ME WHAT TO DRAW. SOMETIMES I WOULD DRAW AS HE TALKED. SOMETIMES HE WOULD ERASE WHAT I WAS DRAWING AS I DREW IT. EVERY ONCE IN A WHILE, MALACHAI WOULD DRAW. BUT MOSTLY, I WOULD JUST TAKE FRANTIC NOTES AND DO LITTLE DOODLES TO REMIND ME WHAT WE CAME UP WITH.

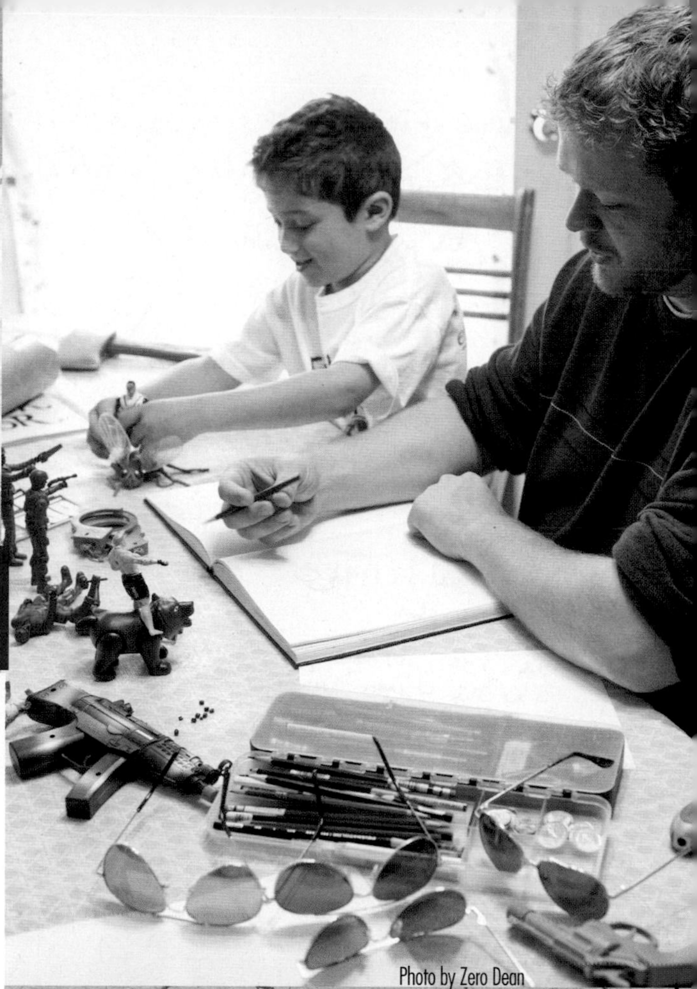

Photo by Zero Dean

Robot Snail Scientist: This character was made up before Axe Cop. Malachai sat and explained him and I drew him according to his specifications. He later created "Drill Helicopter Shooting Snake Snail" below.

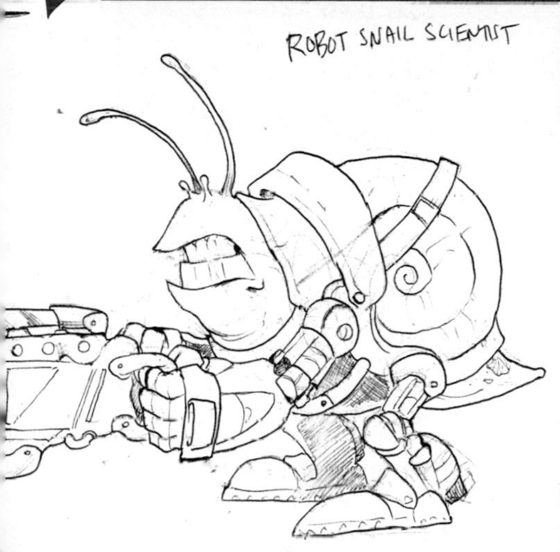
ROBOT SNAIL SCIENTIST

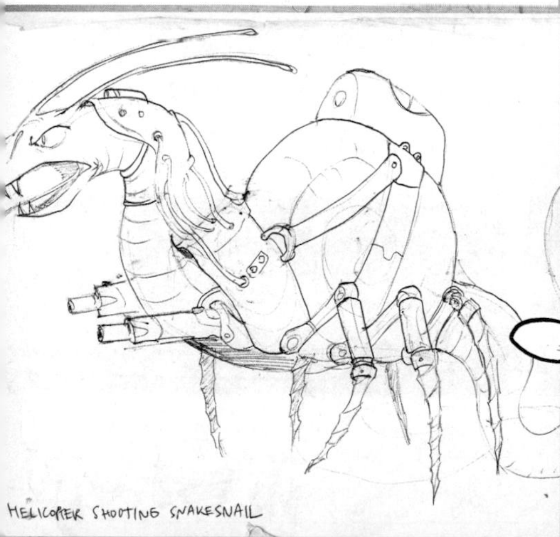
HELICOPTER SHOOTING SNAKESNAIL

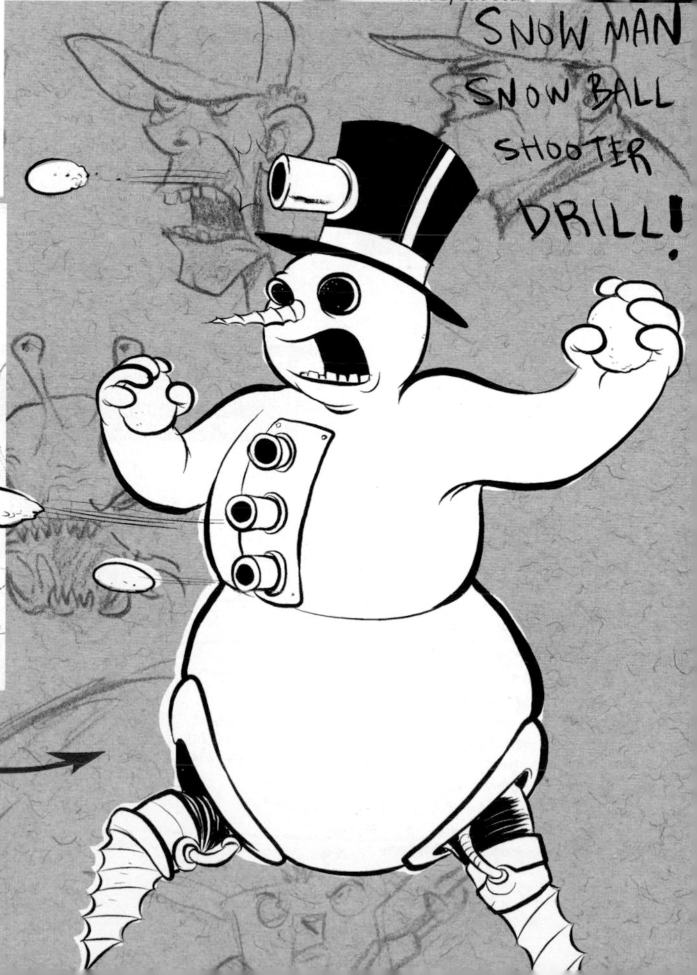
SNOW MAN
SNOW BALL
SHOOTER
DRILL!

Snowman Snowball Shooter Drill: Another character Malachai made up just a day or two before we made Axe Cop up during my 2009 Christmas visit.

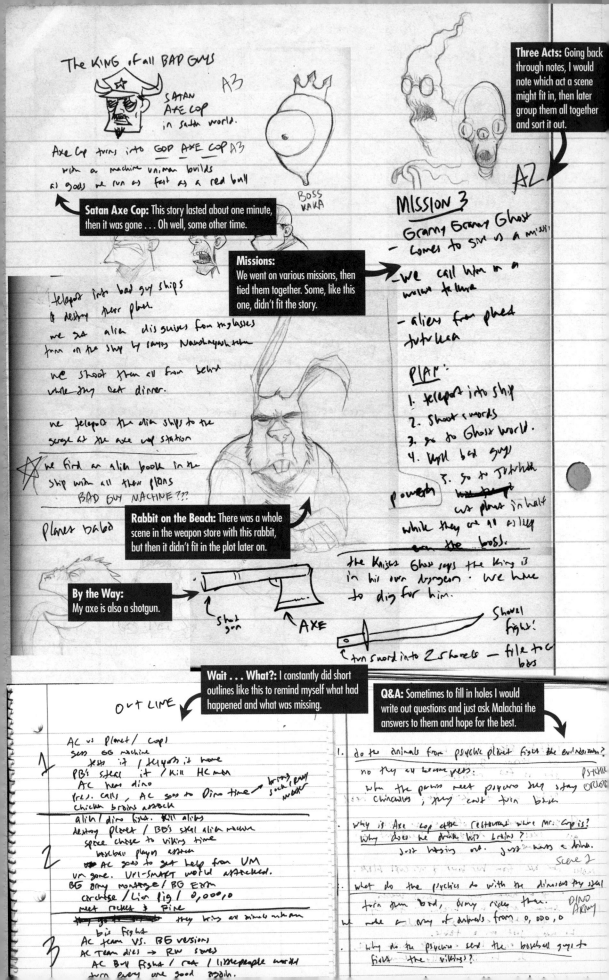

The KING of all BAD GUYS

A3

SATAN
AXE COP
in satan world.

Axe Cop turns into GOD AXE COP A3

with a machine uniman builds
as gods he run as fast as a red bull

BOSS
KAKA

Satan Axe Cop: This story lasted about one minute, then it was gone . . . Oh well, some other time.

teleport into bad guy ships
to destroy their plans.

we see alien disguises from sunglasses
found on the ship by James Nardhayonstein

we shoot them all from behind
while they eat dinner.

we teleport the alien ships to the
scrap at the axe cop station

we find an alien book in the
ship with all their plans
BAD GUY MACHINE???

Planet blood

Missions:
We went on various missions, then tied them together. Some, like this one, didn't fit the story.

Three Acts: Going back through notes, I would note which act a scene might fit in, then later group them all together and sort it out.

A2

MISSION 3
Granny Granny Ghost
- comes to save us a mission
- we call him in a
worse failure
- aliens from phed future lea

PLAN:
1. teleport into ship
2. shoot swords
3. go to Ghost World.
4. kill bad guy
5. go to Jababah
powers   cut plans in half
while they are all asleep
the boss.

the Knives Ghost says the King is
in his own dungeon. We have
to dig for him.

Rabbit on the Beach: There was a whole scene in the weapon store with this rabbit, but then it didn't fit in the plot later on.

By the Way:
My axe is also a shotgun.

Shot gun   AXE

Shovel fight!

turn sword into 2 shovels — file to boss

OUTLINE

Wait . . . What?: I constantly did short outlines like this to remind myself what had happened and what was missing.

1
AC vs planet / cops
sees BG machine
tests it / teleports it home
PB's steal it / kill HC man
AC hears dino
pres. calls, AC goes to Dino time
chicken brains attack

2
alien / dino fight. kill aliens
destroy planet / BB's steal alien machine
space chase to viking time
baseball players attack
AC goes to get help from UM
UM gone. Uni-smart world attacked.
BG army montage / BG Earth
car chase / lion pig / 0,000,0
meet rocket & fire
they bring all dinos when
big fight

3
AC team vs. BG version
AC team dies → RW saves
AC BG fight / rest / little people world
turn everyone good again.

Q&A: Sometimes to fill in holes I would write out questions and just ask Malachai the answers to them and hope for the best.

1. do the animals from psychic planet fight the evil dinosaur?
no they all become pets.   PSYCHIC
when the powers meet psyches they stay ORIGINAL
chircules; they can't turn bad

· why is Axe Cop at the restaurant where Mr. Cop is?
Why does he drink his brains?
Just having out. Just wants a drink.
Scene 2

· what do the psychics do with the dinosaurs they steal
turn them bad, army rides them.   DINO ARMY
we make an army of dinosaurs from 0,000,0

· why do the psychics send the baseball guys to
fight the vikings?

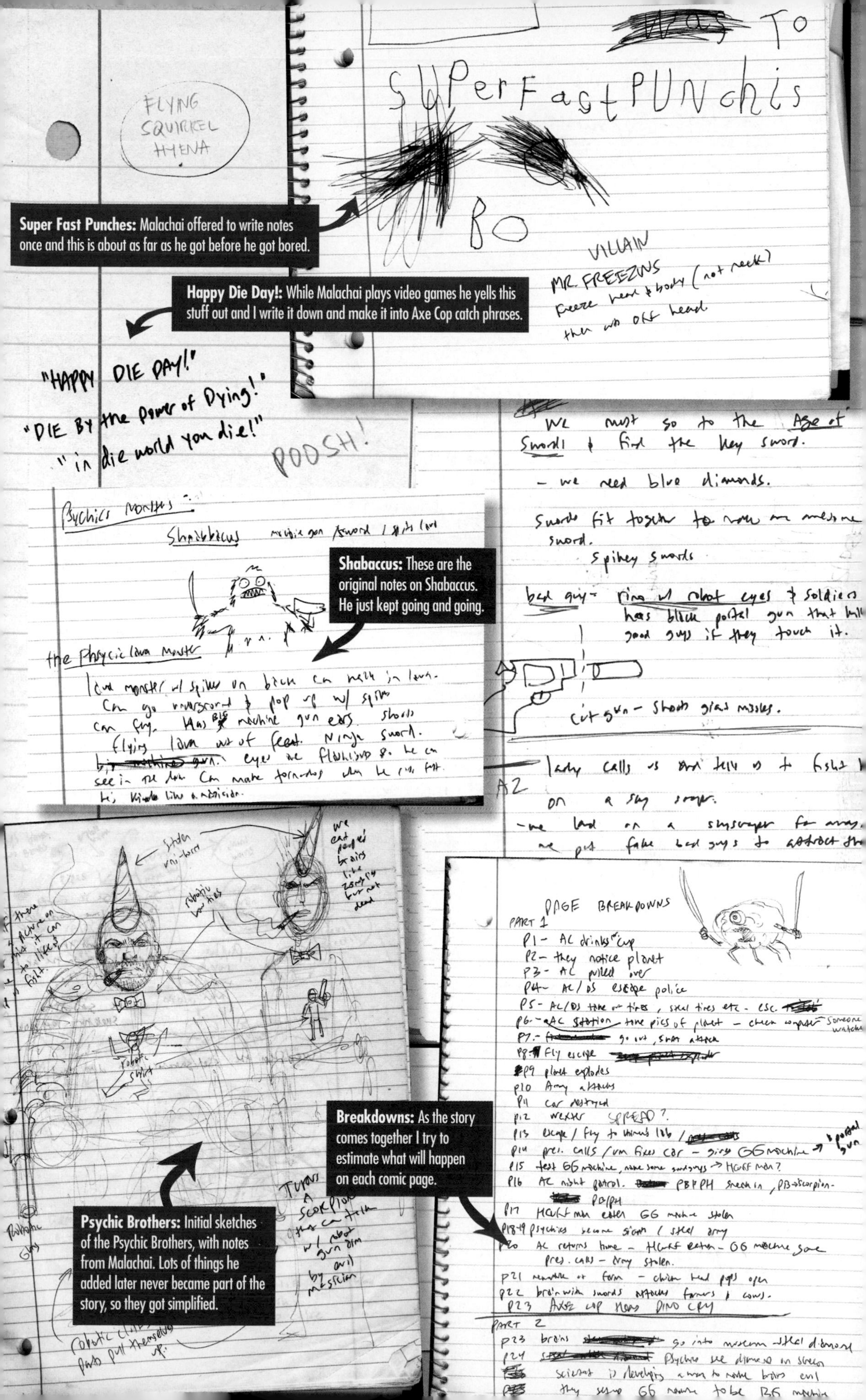

FLYING
SQUIRREL
HYENA

SUPERFASTPUNCHES

BO

VILLAIN

MR. FREEZUNS
Freeze head & body (not neck)
then whO OFF head

Super Fast Punches: Malachai offered to write notes once and this is about as far as he got before he got bored.

Happy Die Day!: While Malachai plays video games he yells this stuff out and I write it down and make it into Axe Cop catch phrases.

"HAPPY DIE DAY!"
"DIE BY the Power of Dying!"
"in die world you die!"

POOSH!

Psychics Monsters

Shabbacus

Shabaccus: These are the original notes on Shabaccus. He just kept going and going.

the Phsyci lava Monster

lava monster w/ spikes on back can melt in lava.
Can go underwater & pop up w/ spikes
can fly. Has BIG machine gun ears. shoots
flying lava out of feet. Ninja sword.
big ___ gun. eyes are flashlights & he can
see in the dark. Can make tornados when he can fart.
He's kinda like a ___.

We must go to the Age of
Sword & find the key sword.

- We need blue diamonds.

Swords fit together to make one awesome
sword.
Spikey swords

bad guy - ring w/ robot eyes & soldiers
has black portal gun that kill
good guys if they touch it.

Cut gun - Shoots glass missiles.

lady calls us and tell us to fight
on a sky scraper.
- we land on a skyscraper far away
we put fake bad guys to distract

Psychic Brothers: Initial sketches of the Psychic Brothers, with notes from Malachai. Lots of things he added later never became part of the story, so they got simplified.

Breakdowns: As the story comes together I try to estimate what will happen on each comic page.

PAGE BREAKDOWNS
PART 1
P1 - AC drinks "cup"
P2 - they notice planet
P3 - AC pulled over
P4 - AC/DS escape police
P5 - AC/DS take out tires, steal tires etc - esc.
P6 - AC station - time pics of planet - check computer someone watches
P7 - go out, start attack
P8 - Fly escape
P9 planet explodes
P10 Army attacks
P11 car destroyed
P12 WEAPON SPREAD?
P13 escape / fly to worm 186 /
P14 pres. calls / um fixes car - give GG machine → portal gun
P15 test GG machine, make some badguys → HCUFF man?
P16 AC night patrol. PB/PH sneak in, PB → scorpion
RALPH
P17 HCUFF man eaten GG machine stolen
P18+9 Psychics become giant (steal army)
P20 AC returns home - HCUFF eaten - GG machine gone
pres. calls - army stolen.
P21 member of farm - chicken head pops open
P22 brain with swords attacks farmer & cows.
P23 Axe cop hears DINO CRY
PART 2
P23 brains go into museum steal dinosaur
P24 Psychic use dinosaur on steroids
scientist is developing a way to make brains evil
they using GG machine to be BIG machine

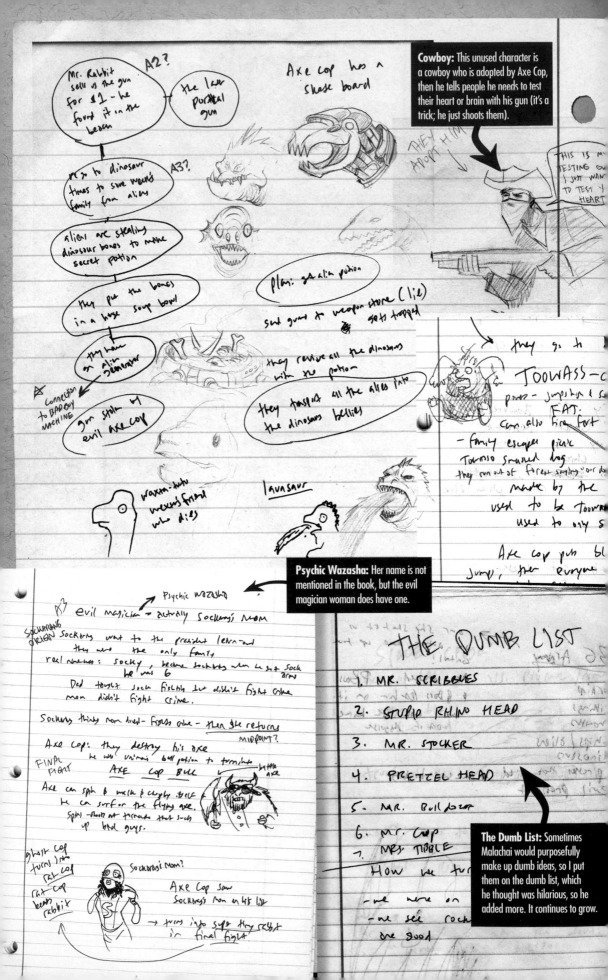

Mr. Rabbit sells us the gun for $1 - he found it in the beach

A2?

the laser portal gun

Axe Cop has a skate board

go to dinosaur times to save world's family from alien

A3?

aliens are stealing dinosaur bones to make secret potion

they put the bones in a huge soup bowl

they have an alien generator

connection to BAD GUY machine

gun stolen by evil Axe Cop

plan: steal potion

send guns to weapon store (lie) sets trapped

they revive all the dinosaurs with the potion

they trapped all the aliens into the dinosaurs bellies

waxasha-witch weasas friend who dies

lavasaur

Cowboy: This unused character is a cowboy who is adopted by Axe Cop, then he tells people he needs to test their heart or brain with his gun (it's a trick; he just shoots them).

THEY ADOPT HIM

THIS IS MY TESTING GUN I JUST WANT TO TEST YOUR HEART

they go to

TOOWASS-O

power - jumping & s FAT. can also fire fart

- family escaped picnic Toowaso snared dog they ran out of forest saying "our do

made by the

used to be Toowr used to only s

Axe Cop puts bl jump, then everyone

Psychic Wazasha: Her name is not mentioned in the book, but the evil magician woman does have one.

Psychic WAZASHA

evil magician → actually Sockarang's Mom

SOCKARANG ORIGIN Sockarang went to the president Lenn—and they were the only family

real names: Socky, became Sockarang when he lost Sock arm he was 6

Dad taught Sock fighting but didn't fight crime. mom didn't fight crime.

Sockarang thinks mom died—fights crime — then she returns

MIDPOINT?

Axe Cop: they destroy his axe he was unimal bull potion to terminate

FINAL FIGHT AXE COP BULL

battle axe

Axe can split & multiply & clearly itself he can surf on the flying axe. Split - shoots out tornado that sucks up bad guys.

ghost cop turns into RAT COP

RAT COP bears Rabbit

Sockarang's Mom?

Axe Cop saw Sockarang's mom in 45 list

→ turns into supe they reset in final fight

THE DUMB LIST

1. MR. SCRIBBLES
2. STUPID RHINO HEAD
3. MR. STOCKER
4. PRETZEL HEAD
5. MR. BULLDOZER
6. MR. COP
7. MRS. TIBBLE

How we tur

- we were on

- we see rock

are good

The Dumb List: Sometimes Malachai would purposefully make up dumb ideas, so I put them on the dumb list, which he thought was hilarious, so he added more. It continues to grow.

Mr. Chicken Chicken Slice: One of my favorite characters who never made it into the actual story line was "Mr. Chicken Chicken Slice." When he covers his eyes, a chicken shoots out of his brain. Some day I will get Malachai to put this character in a story.

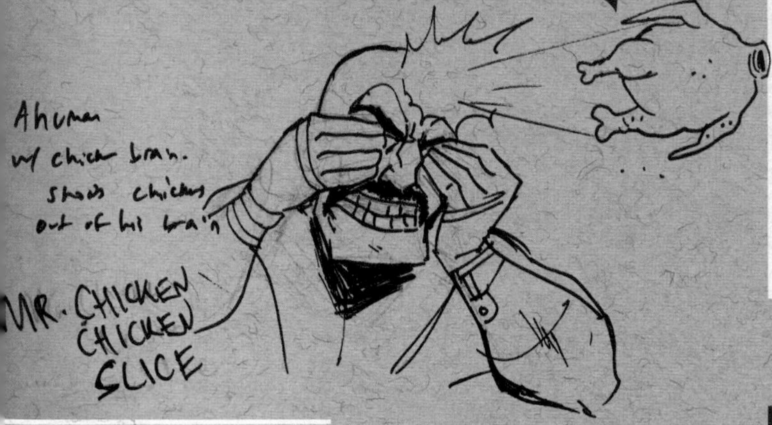
MR. CHICKEN CHICKEN SLICE

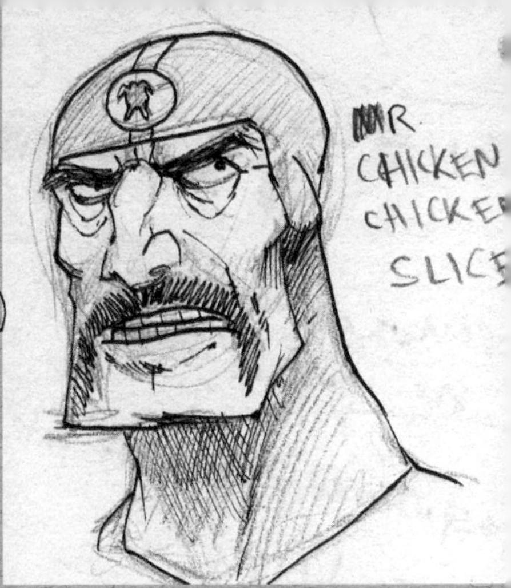
MR. CHICKEN CHICKEN SLICE

Bombs: Bad guys have two kinds of bombs. Red bombs explode the universe, black bombs explode history. Very thorough.

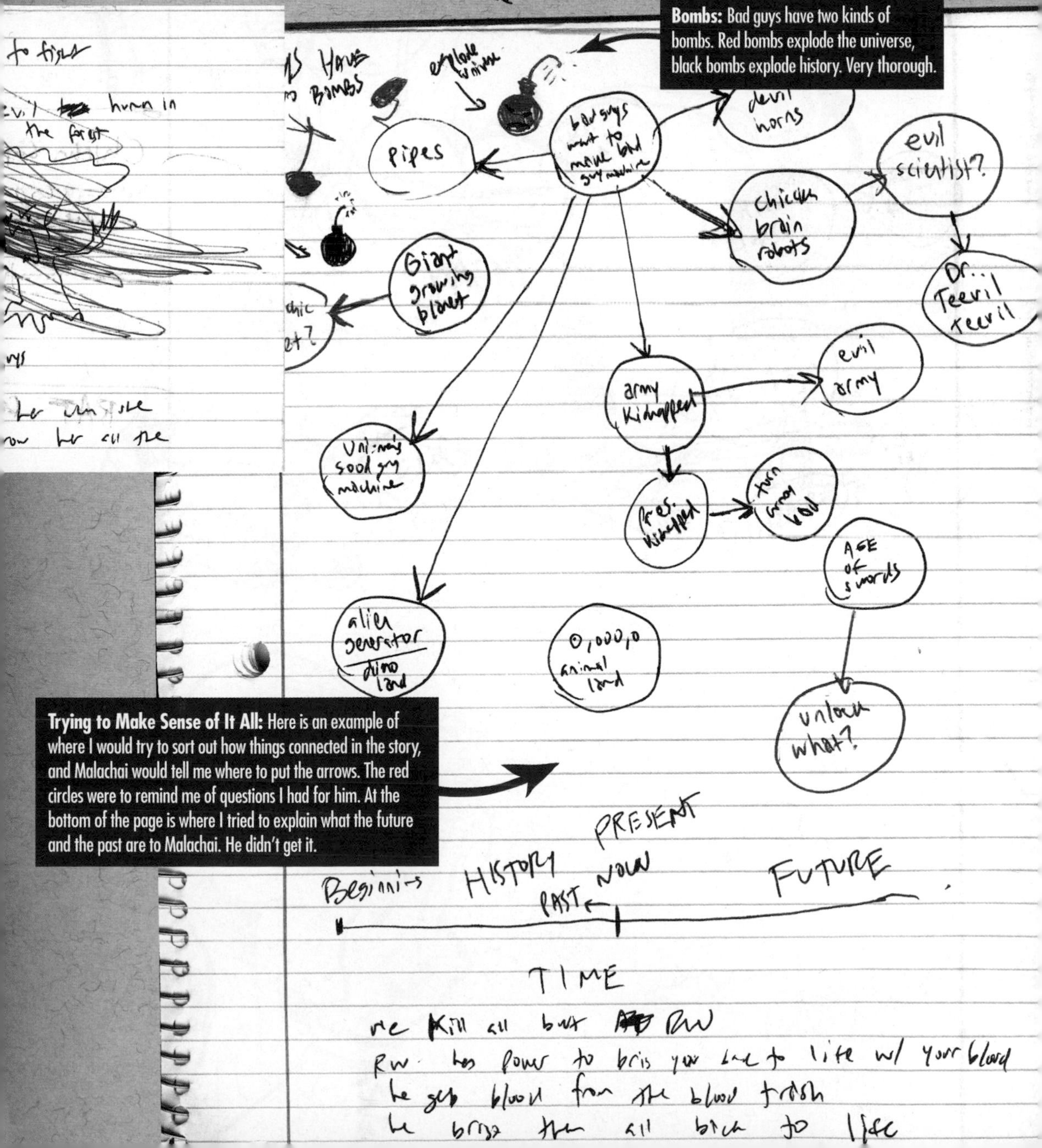
pipes
devil horns
chicken brain robots
evil scientist?
Dr. Teevil Teevil
Giant growing planet
army kidnapped
evil army
AGE of swords
alien generator
dino land
animal land
unlock what?
PRESENT
HISTORY
PAST
NOW
FUTURE
TIME

Trying to Make Sense of It All: Here is an example of where I would try to sort out how things connected in the story, and Malachai would tell me where to put the arrows. The red circles were to remind me of questions I had for him. At the bottom of the page is where I tried to explain what the future and the past are to Malachai. He didn't get it.

SKETCHBOOK

THE TRUTH IS THAT I DON'T DO A LOT OF PREPARATORY SKETCHES FOR *AXE COP* CHARACTERS BECAUSE SO MANY OF THEM COME AND GO SO FAST. I TRY TO COME UP WITH AS MUCH OF IT ON THE FLY AS I CAN TO KEEP IT IN THE SPIRIT OF HOW MALACHAI WRITES . . . HIS IMAGINATION IS A MACHINE GUN, SO I TRY TO AT LEAST KEEP MINE ON SEMIAUTOMATIC. A LOT OF THESE SKETCHES WERE DONE JUST TO GET A GRASP ON WHAT MALACHAI WAS TRYING TO SAY. OTHERS WERE DONE TO ESTABLISH CHARACTERS WHO WOULD BE MORE CONSISTENT (LIKE THE PSYCHIC BROTHERS).

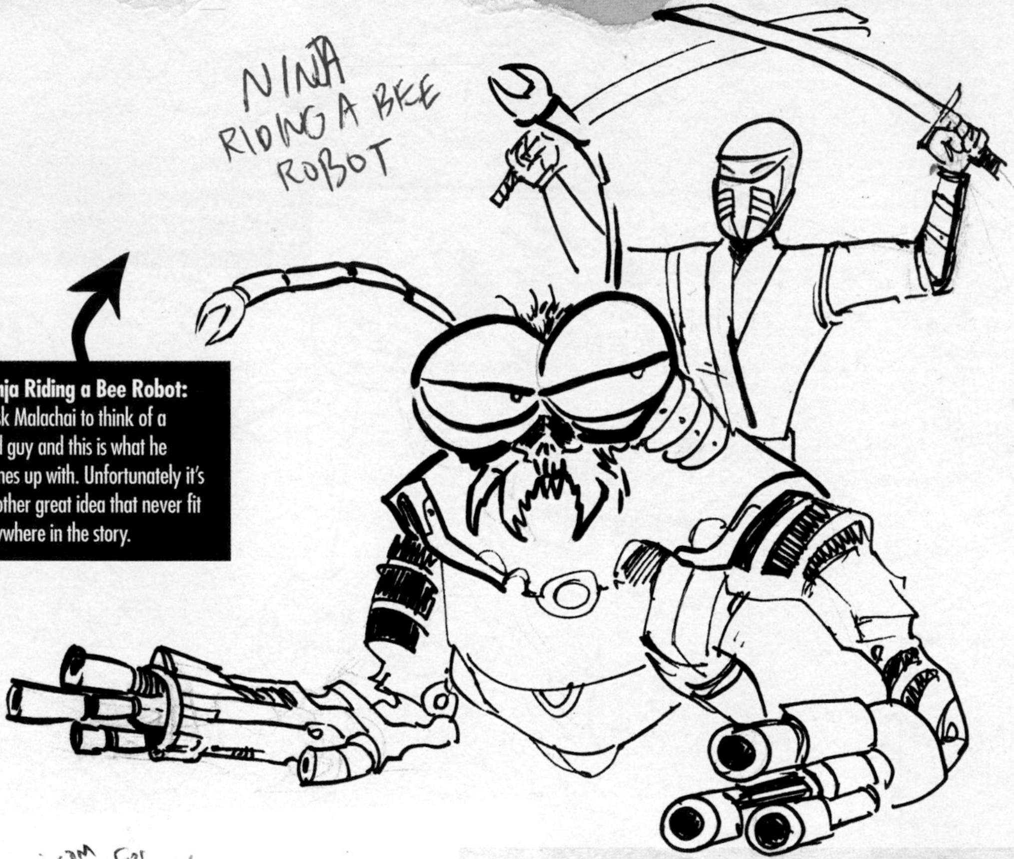
NINJA
RIDING A BEE
ROBOT

Ninja Riding a Bee Robot: I ask Malachai to think of a bad guy and this is what he comes up with. Unfortunately it's another great idea that never fit anywhere in the story.

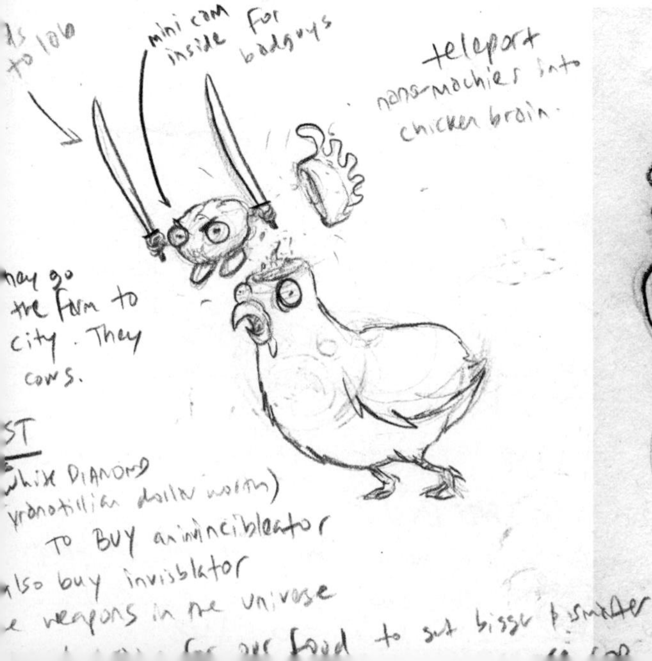
mini cam inside
for badguys
teleport nano-machies into chicken brain

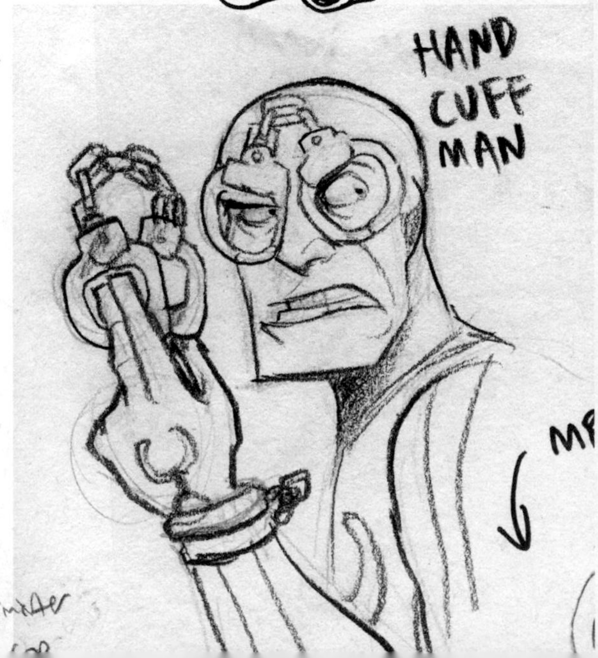
HAND
CUFF
MAN

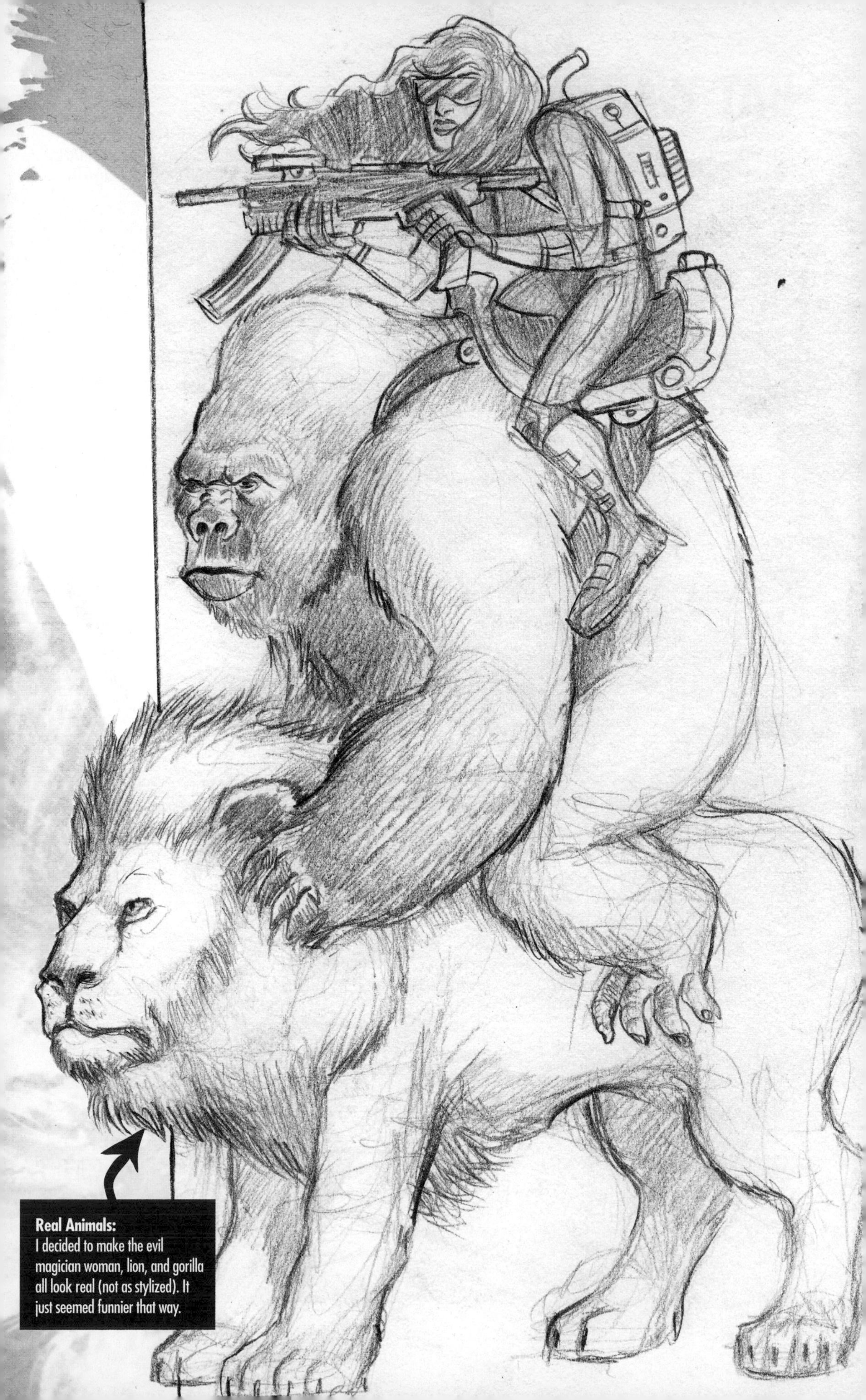

Real Animals:
I decided to make the evil magician woman, lion, and gorilla all look real (not as stylized). It just seemed funnier that way.

BAT WARTHOGS

THE BAT WARTHOG NEVER MADE IT INTO *BAD GUY EARTH*, BUT IF YOU HAVE KEPT UP WITH THE *AXE COP* WEB SERIES YOU KNOW THAT THE CREATURE BECAME THE INSPIRATION FOR MALACHAI'S BATMAN UPGRADE: BAT WARTHOG MAN. THE DRAWING AT THE BOTTOM WAS THE ORIGINAL DRAWING WITH HIS NOTES. I THINK HE WAS SO FASCINATED WITH WARTHOGS BECAUSE HE THOUGHT THEY WERE CALLED "WAR HOGS."

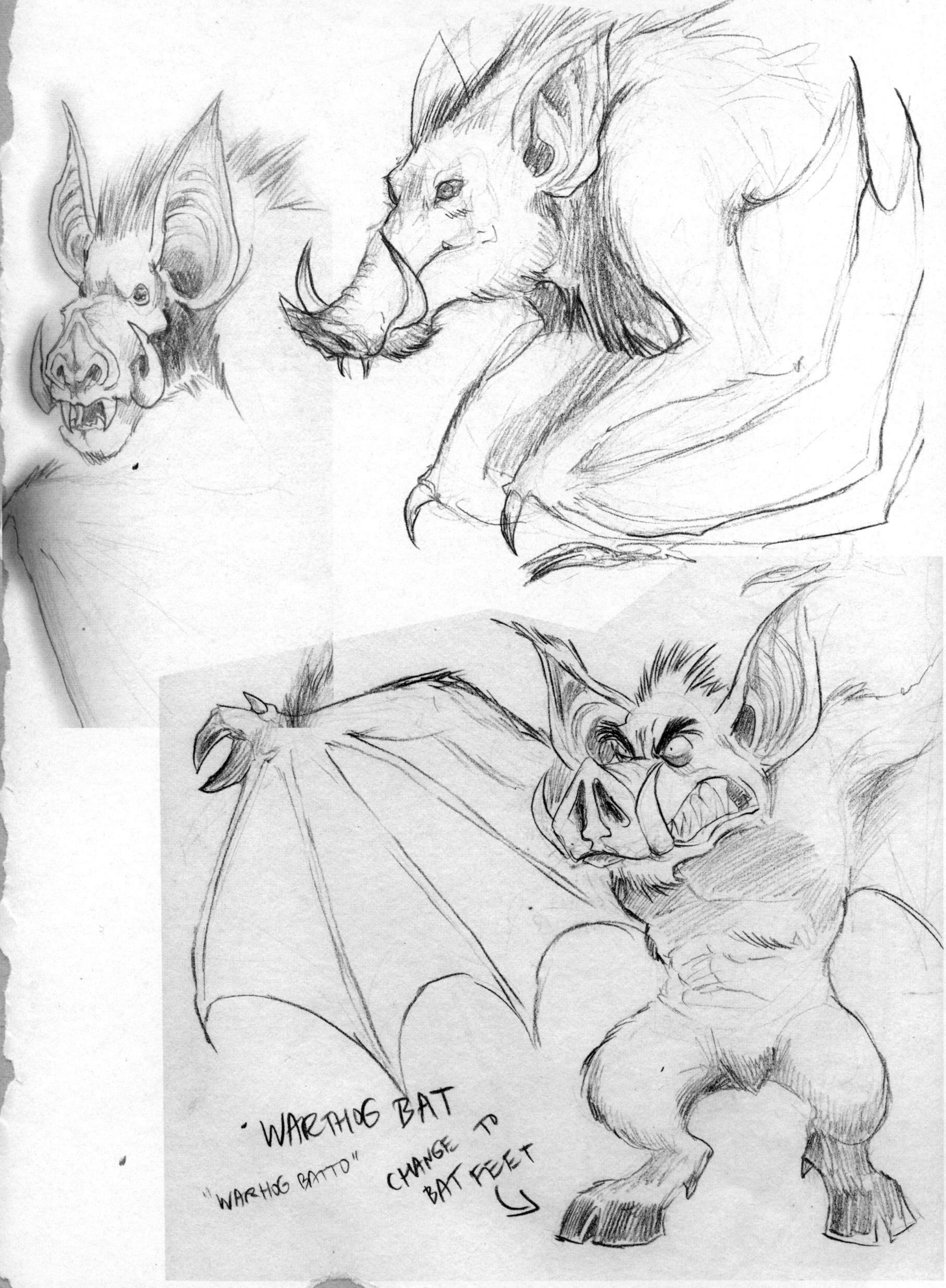

WARTHOG BAT
"WARHOG BATTO"
CHANGE TO BAT FEET

MAKING MONSTERS

MALACHAI RARELY WANTS TO DO ANY DRAWINGS. BUT HERE ARE A COUPLE OF MONSTERS HE DID HIS OWN VERSIONS OF, AND THEN WHAT THEY BECAME IN THE COMIC.

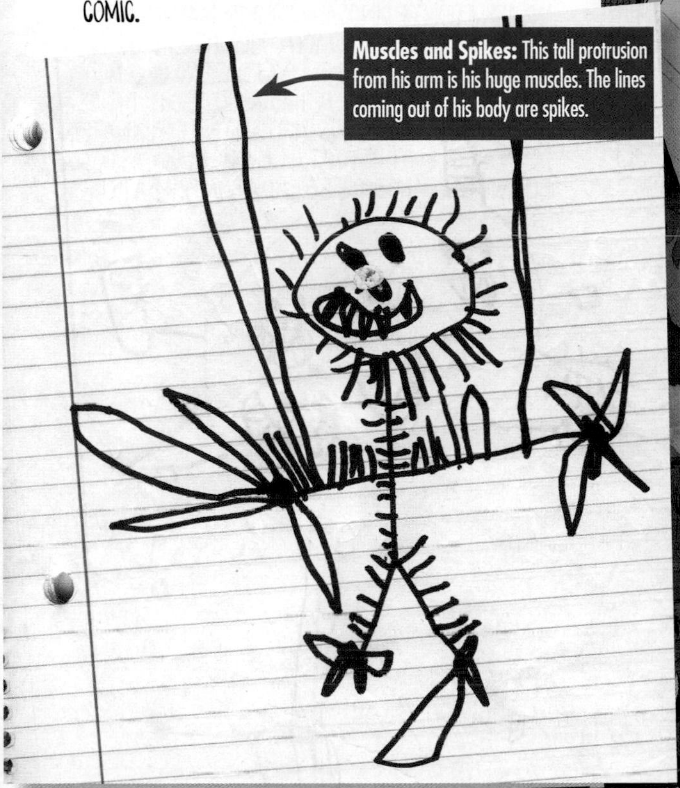

Muscles and Spikes: This tall protrusion from his arm is his huge muscles. The lines coming out of his body are spikes.

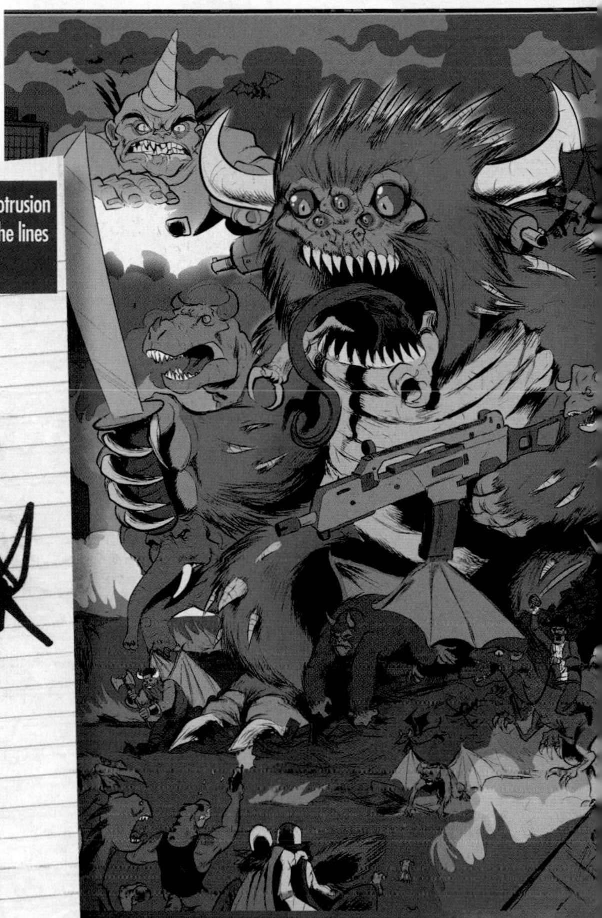

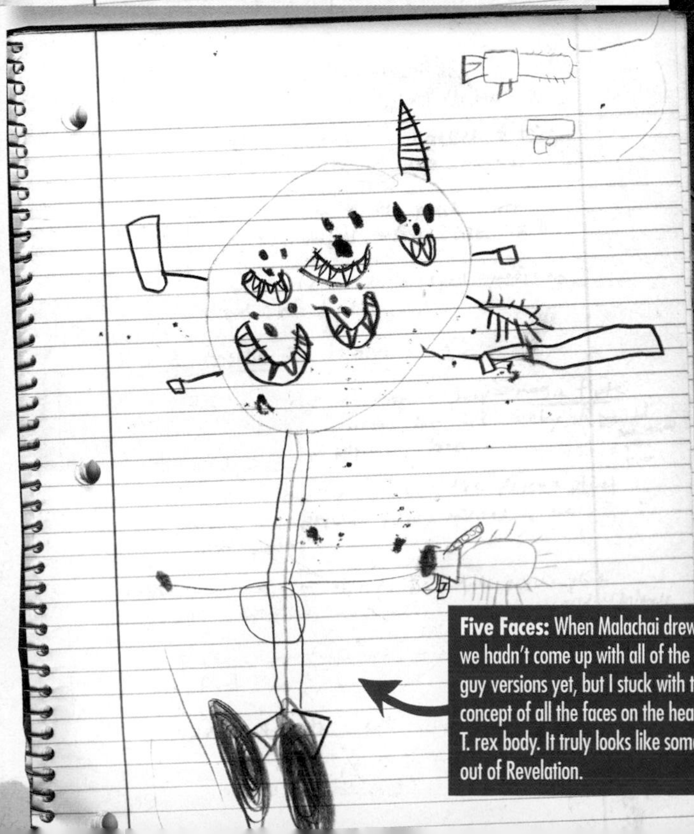

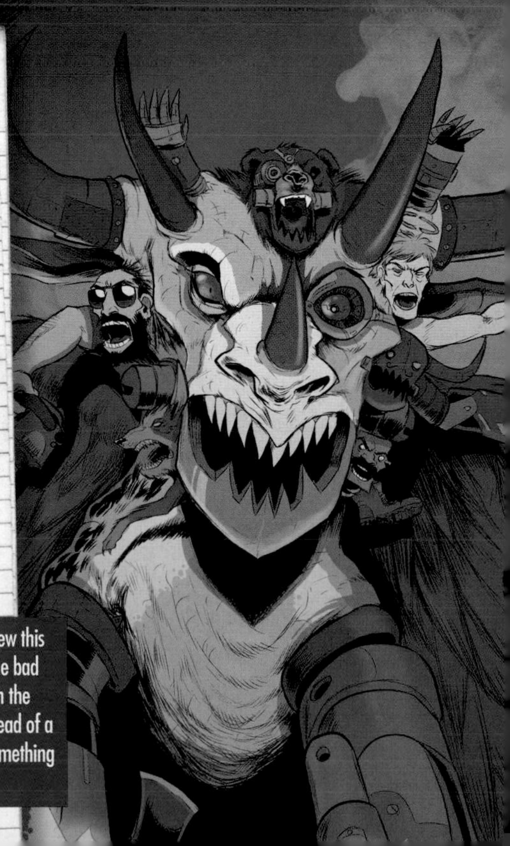

Five Faces: When Malachai drew this we hadn't come up with all of the bad guy versions yet, but I stuck with the concept of all the faces on the head of a T. rex body. It truly looks like something out of Revelation.

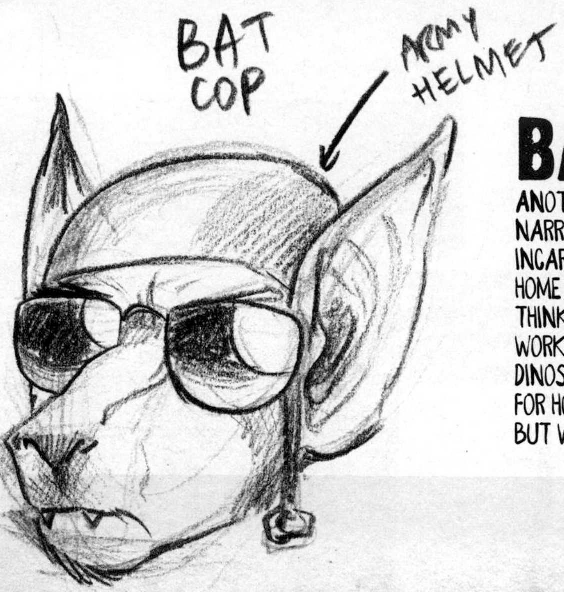

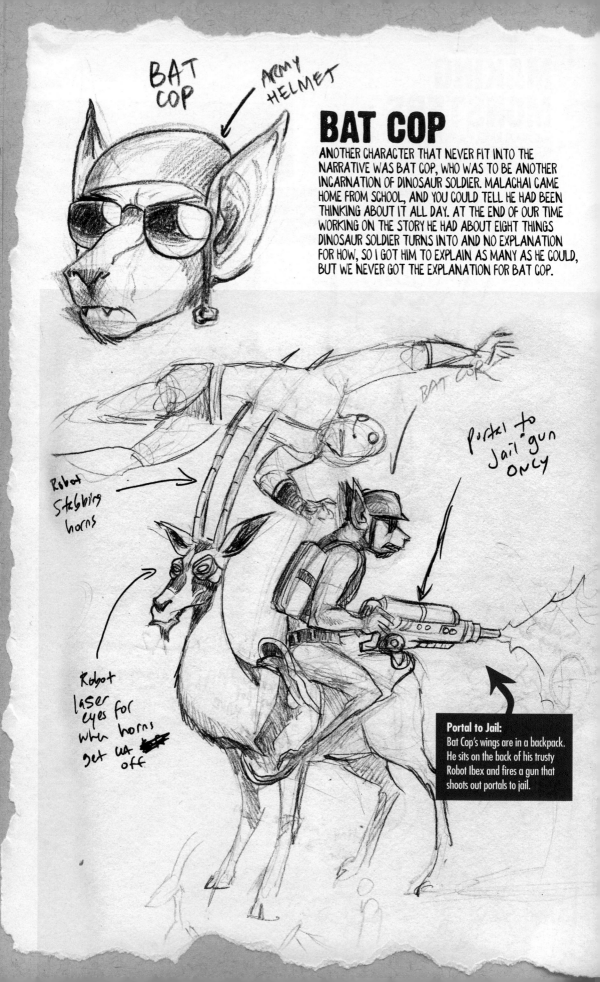

BAT COP
ARMY HELMET

BAT COP

ANOTHER CHARACTER THAT NEVER FIT INTO THE NARRATIVE WAS BAT COP, WHO WAS TO BE ANOTHER INCARNATION OF DINOSAUR SOLDIER. MALACHAI CAME HOME FROM SCHOOL, AND YOU COULD TELL HE HAD BEEN THINKING ABOUT IT ALL DAY. AT THE END OF OUR TIME WORKING ON THE STORY HE HAD ABOUT EIGHT THINGS DINOSAUR SOLDIER TURNS INTO AND NO EXPLANATION FOR HOW, SO I GOT HIM TO EXPLAIN AS MANY AS HE COULD, BUT WE NEVER GOT THE EXPLANATION FOR BAT COP.

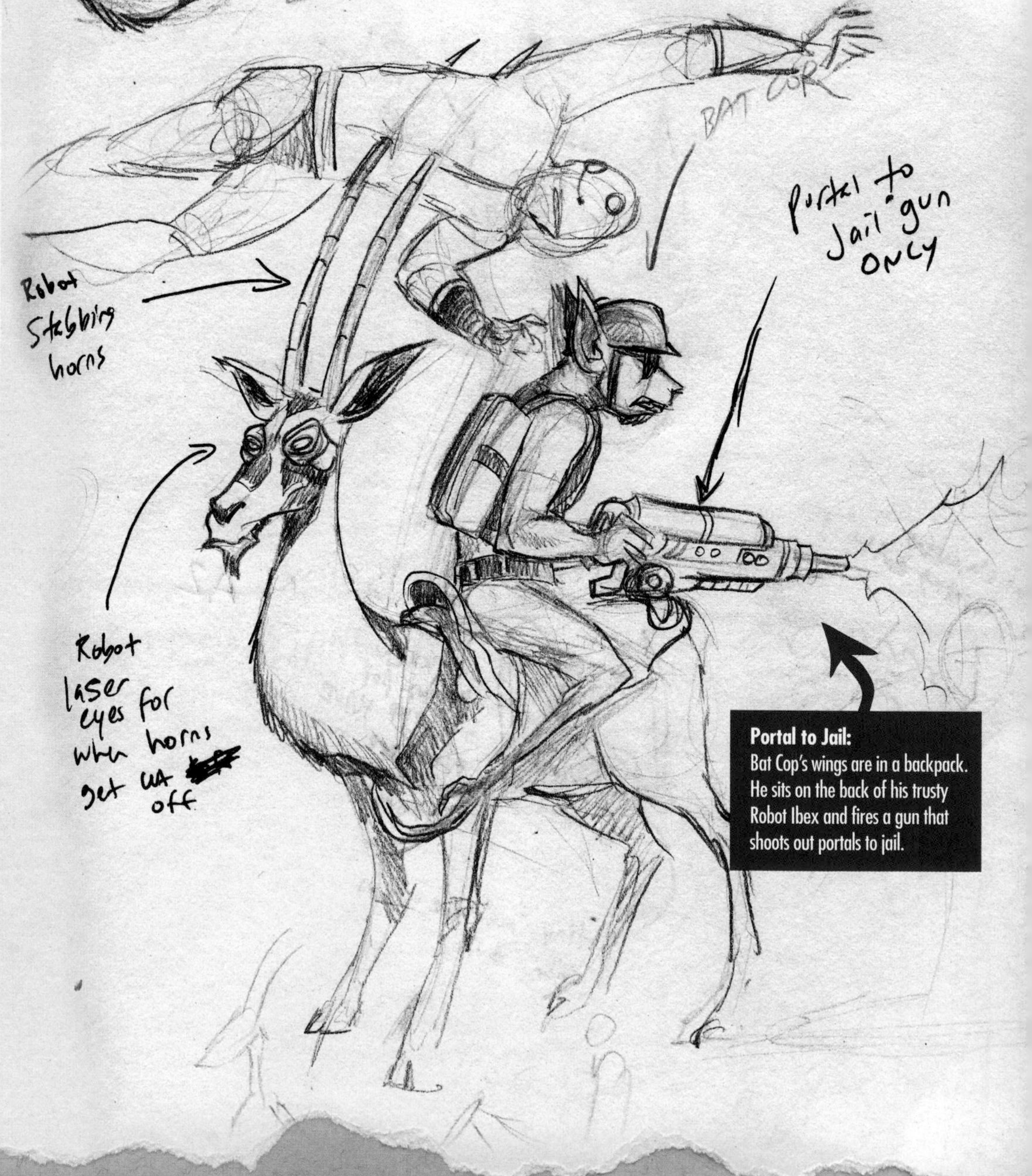

BAT COP
portal to jail gun ONLY
Robot Stabbing horns
Robot laser eyes for when horns get off

Portal to Jail:
Bat Cop's wings are in a backpack. He sits on the back of his trusty Robot Ibex and fires a gun that shoots out portals to jail.

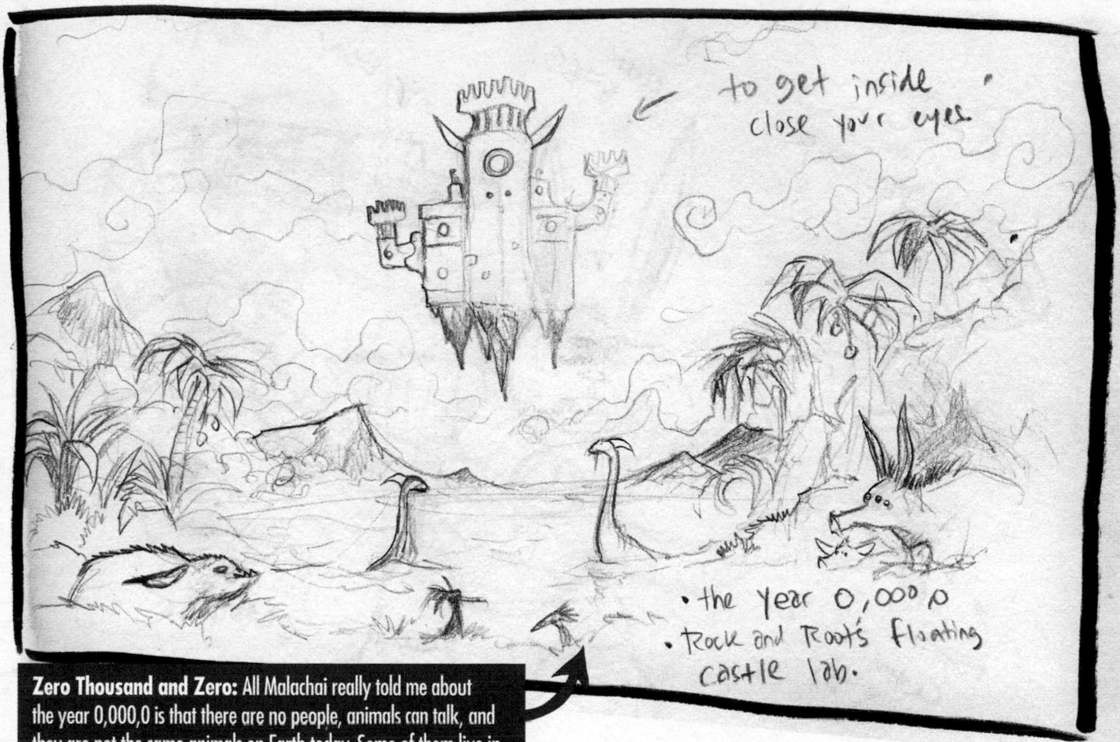
to get inside
close your eyes.
• the year 0,000,0
• Rock and Root's floating
castle lab.

Zero Thousand and Zero: All Malachai really told me about the year 0,000,0 is that there are no people, animals can talk, and they are not the same animals on Earth today. Some of them live in floating castles. This was my first concept.

ROBOTRANGATANG

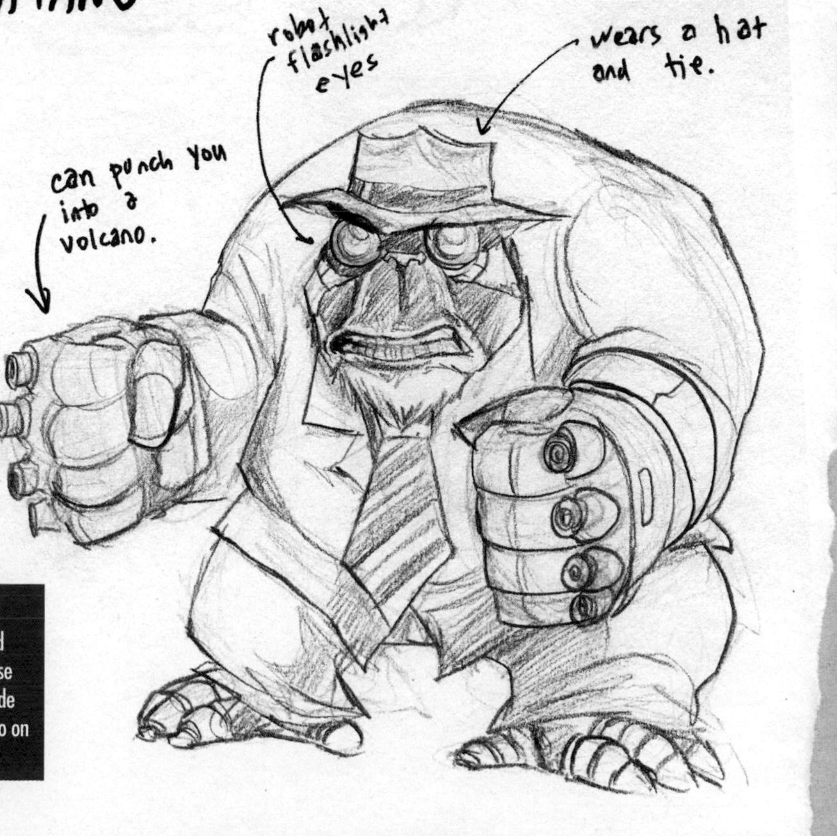
robot
flashlight
eyes
wears a hat
and tie.
can punch you
into a
volcano.

Robotrangatang:
Another great character. I squeezed him into the car-chase scene because that is where he fit in when we made him up, but we never got much info on where he came from.

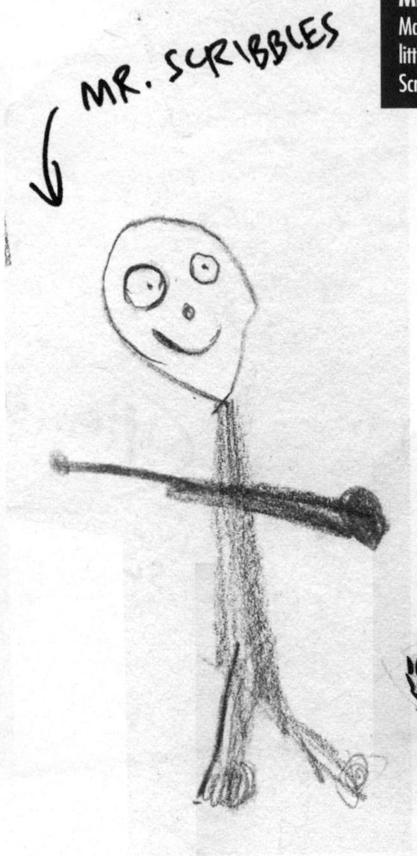
MR. SCRIBBLES

Mr. Scribbles:
Malachai's creation. Very little is known about Mr. Scribbles.

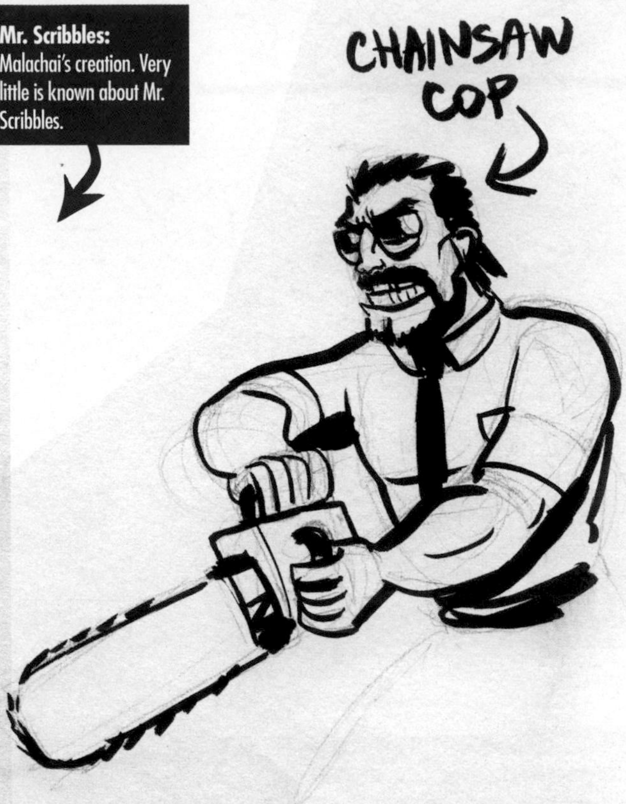
CHAINSAW COP

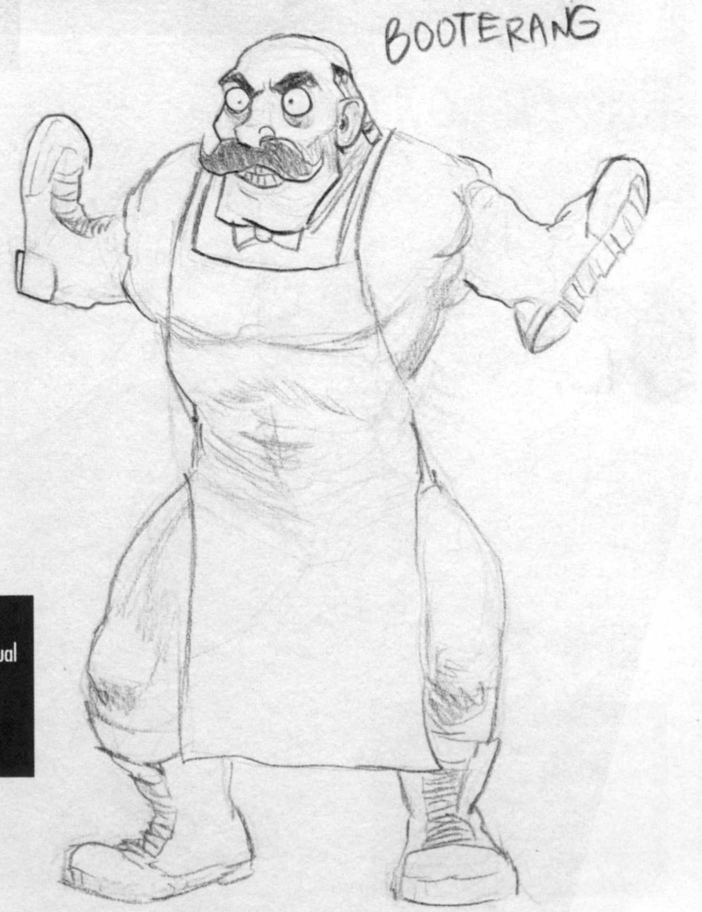
BOOTERANG

Booterang:
Malachai gave me no visual direction on Booterang. I just imagined a German boot-maker-looking guy.

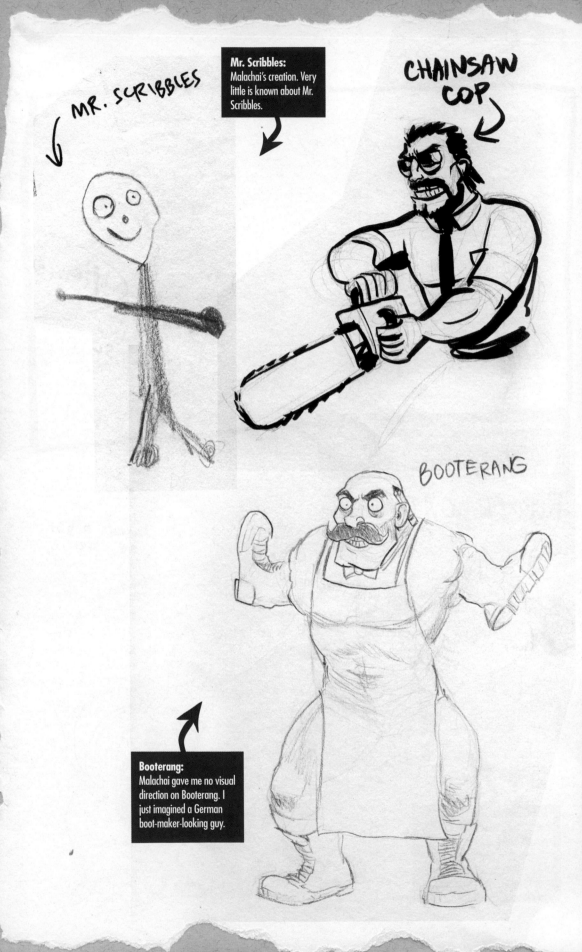

ALIENS
MALACHAI WAS ALWAYS VERY CRITICAL OF MY ALIEN DESIGNS. HE THOUGHT THESE WERE ALL WRONG AND NOT AT ALL WHAT ALIENS ARE SUPPOSED TO LOOK LIKE. HE DID GIVE ME SOME NOTES ON THEM, BUT I NEVER ENDED UP USING ANY OF THESE DESIGNS. THE ALIENS IN *BAD GUY EARTH* NEVER REALLY NEED TO TALK, SO I WENT WITH LESS INTELLIGENT-LOOKING ALIENS IN THE END.

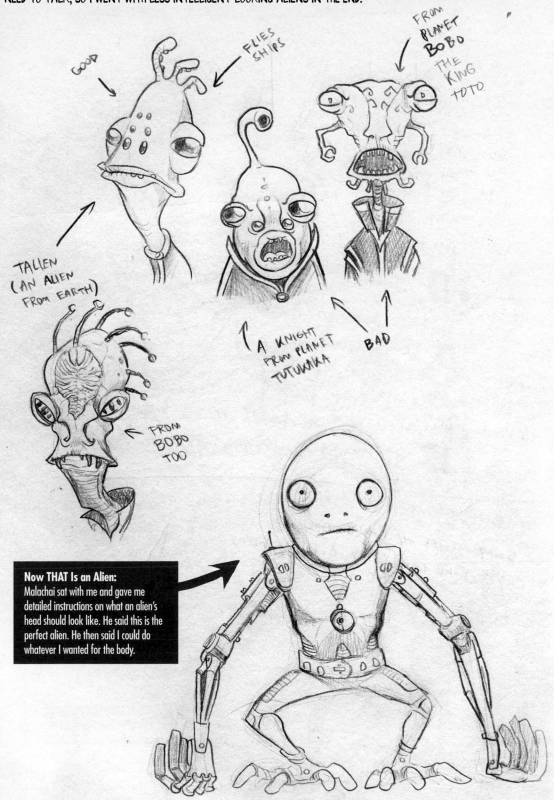

GOOD

FLIES SHIPS

FROM PLANET BOBO THE KING TOTO

TALIEN (AN ALIEN FROM EARTH)

A KNIGHT FROM PLANET TUTUWAKA

BAD

FROM BOBO TOO

Now THAT Is an Alien:
Malachai sat with me and gave me detailed instructions on what an alien's head should look like. He said this is the perfect alien. He then said I could do whatever I wanted for the body.

Side Project: When Malachai was not in the mood to play Axe Cop we played this other story with these little characters with tails that can punch. They became the inspiration for Rocket and Fire.

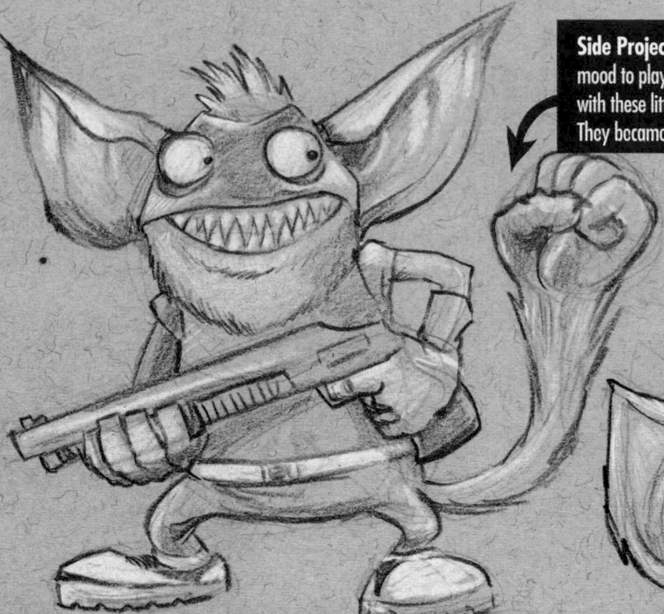

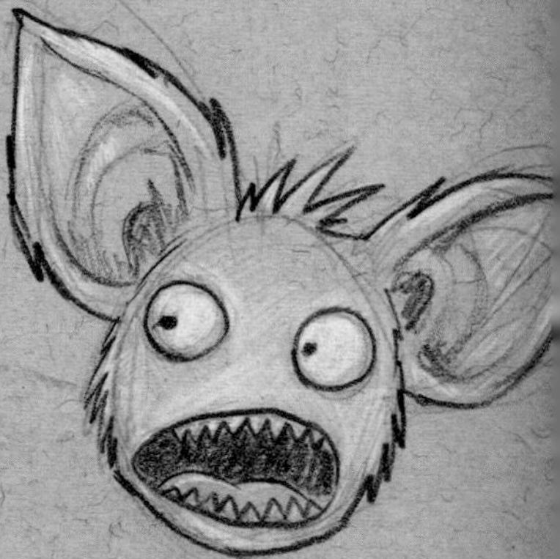

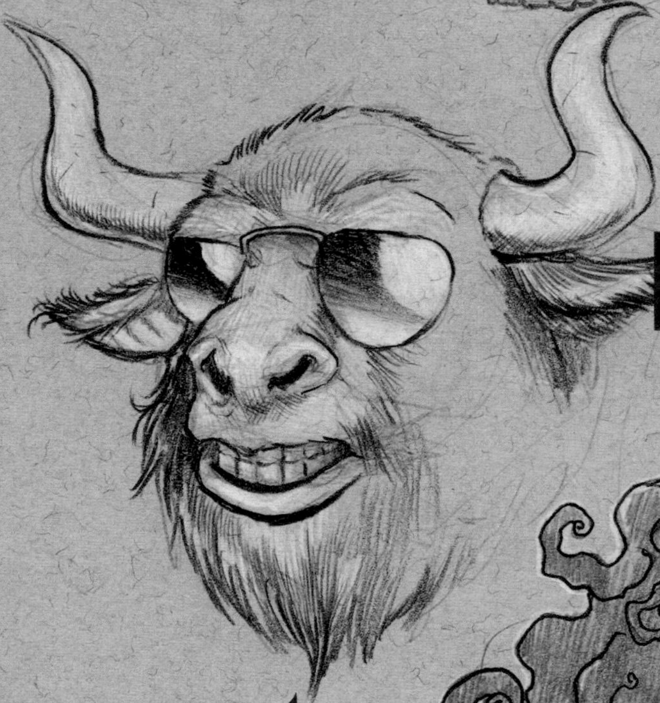

Evil Magician Woman: This is where I decided to give her the funky hair. Sort of like genie-smoke hair.

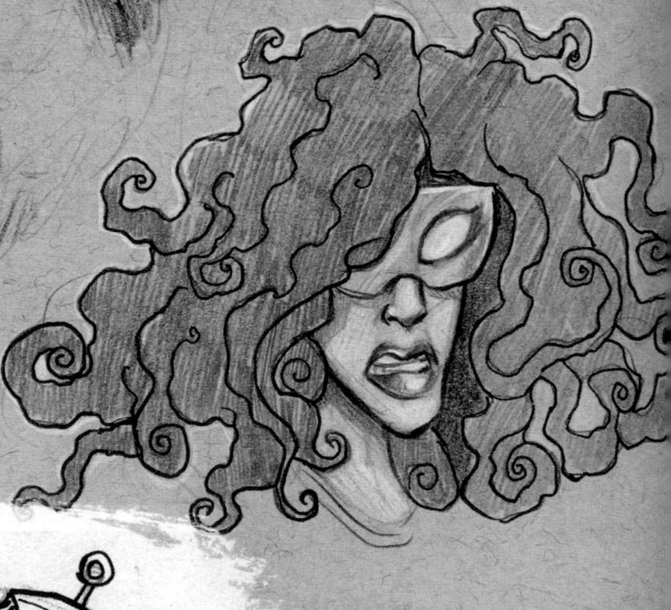

Bull Cop: Originally he would have been Bull Cop, then Axe Cop Lava Bull, but things got condensed.

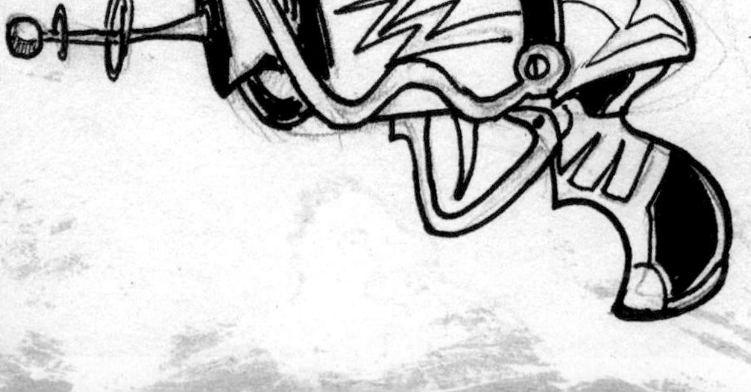

Laser-Portal Gun: Original design based on Malachai's toy gun.

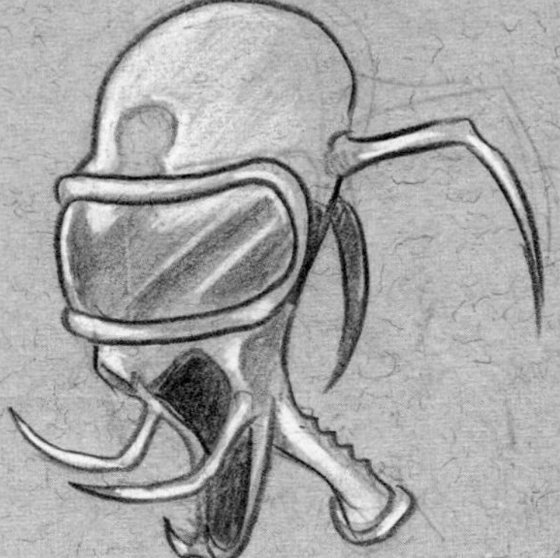

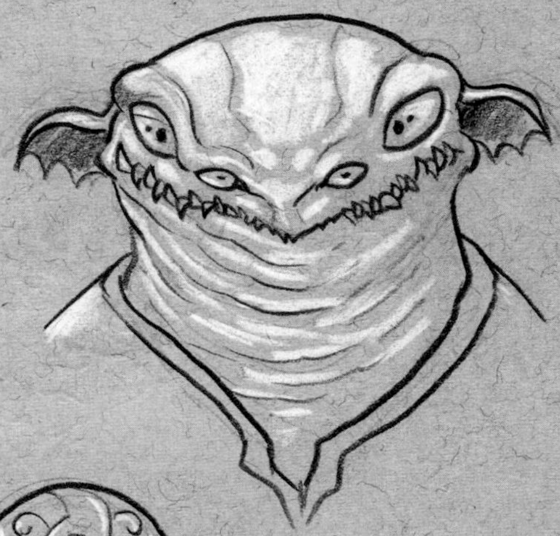

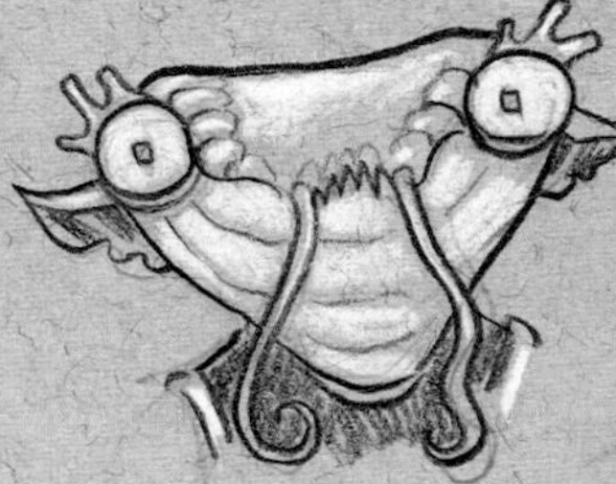

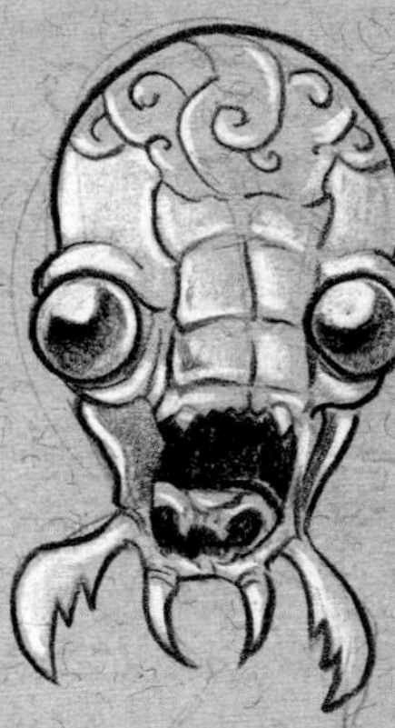

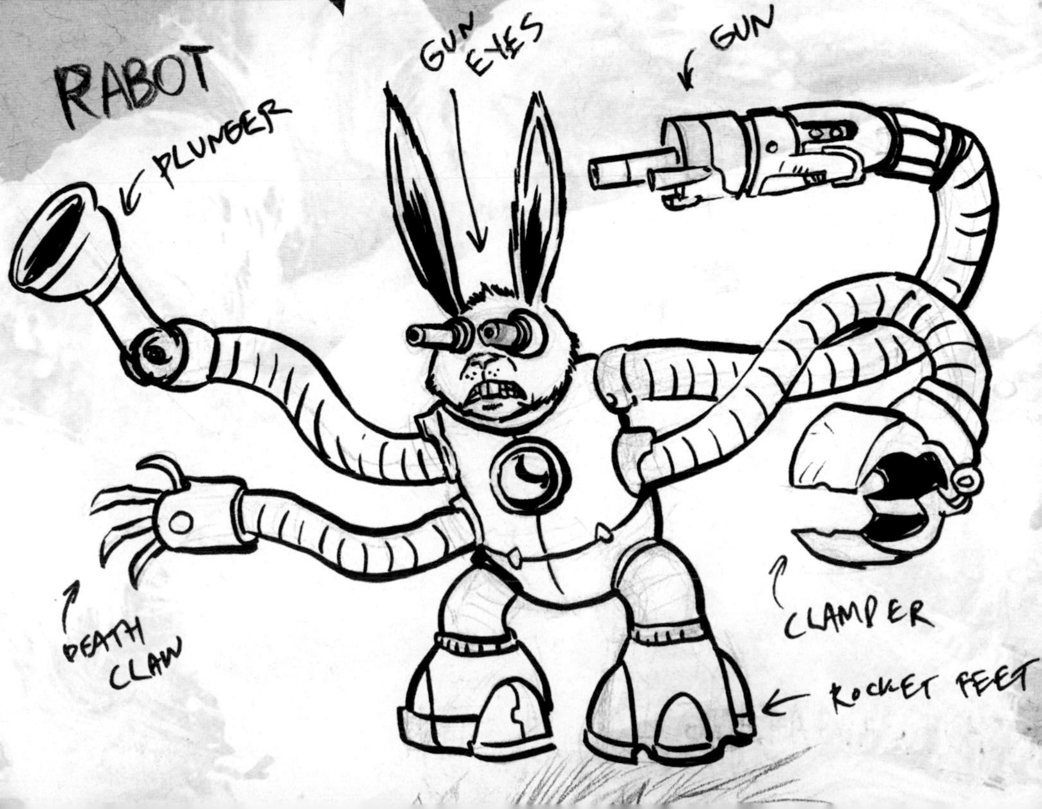
RABOT
GUN EYES
GUN
PLUNGER
DEATH CLAW
CLAMPER
ROCKET FEET

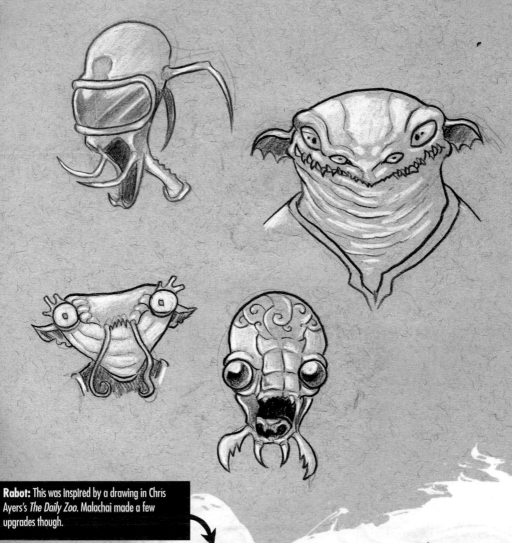

Rabot: This was inspired by a drawing in Chris Ayers's *The Daily Zoo*. Malachai made a few upgrades though.

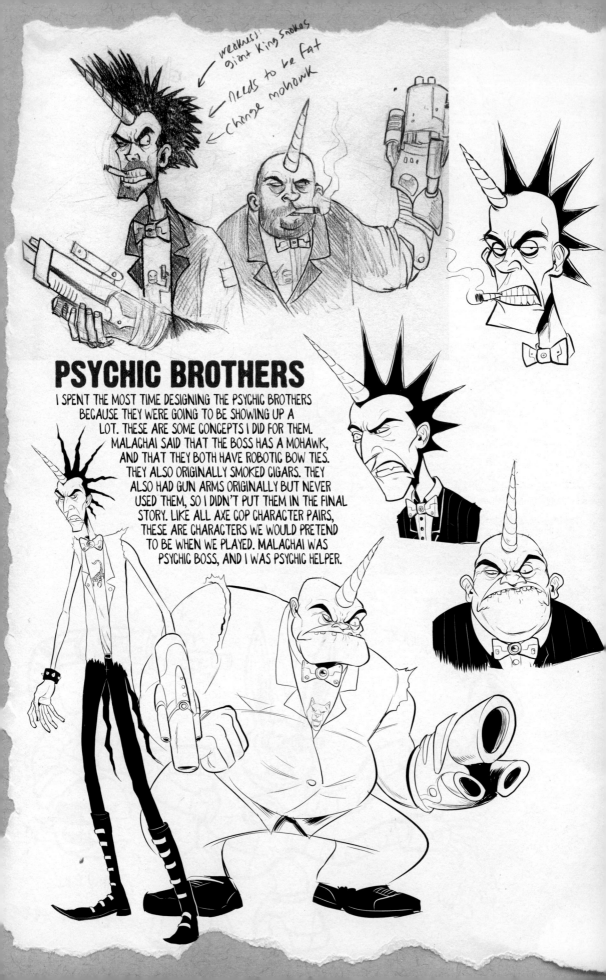

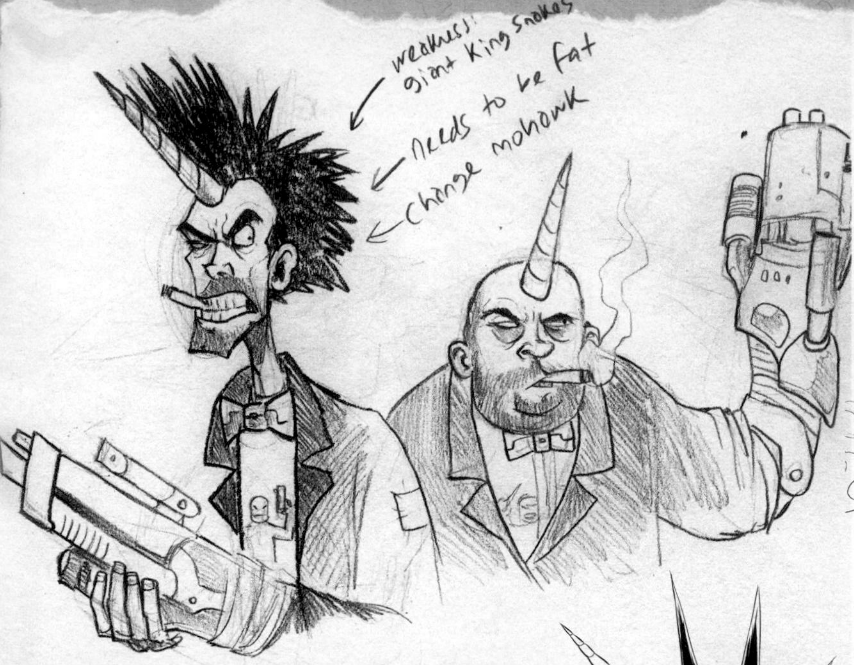
weakness! giant King Snakes
needs to be fat
change mohowk

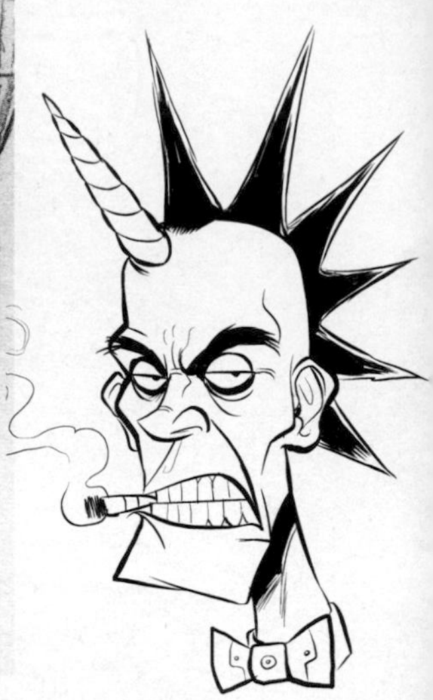

PSYCHIC BROTHERS

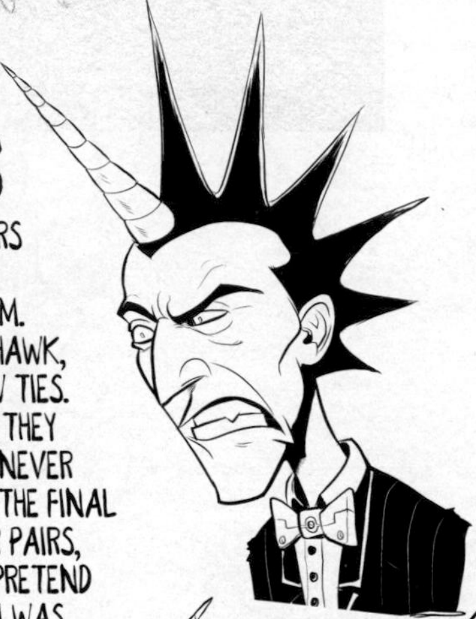

I SPENT THE MOST TIME DESIGNING THE PSYCHIC BROTHERS BECAUSE THEY WERE GOING TO BE SHOWING UP A LOT. THESE ARE SOME CONCEPTS I DID FOR THEM. MALACHAI SAID THAT THE BOSS HAS A MOHAWK, AND THAT THEY BOTH HAVE ROBOTIC BOW TIES. THEY ALSO ORIGINALLY SMOKED CIGARS. THEY ALSO HAD GUN ARMS ORIGINALLY BUT NEVER USED THEM, SO I DIDN'T PUT THEM IN THE FINAL STORY. LIKE ALL AXE COP CHARACTER PAIRS, THESE ARE CHARACTERS WE WOULD PRETEND TO BE WHEN WE PLAYED. MALACHAI WAS PSYCHIC BOSS, AND I WAS PSYCHIC HELPER.

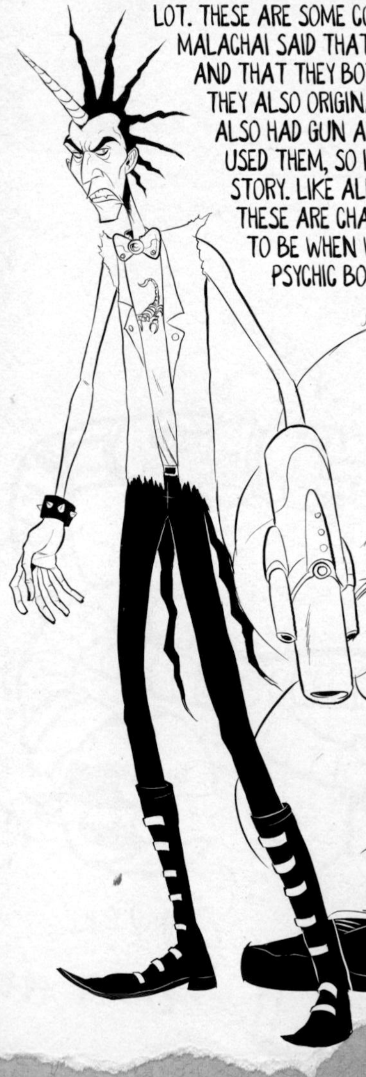

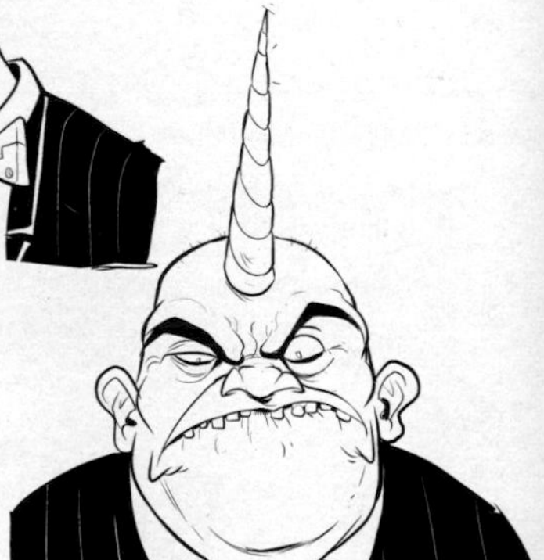

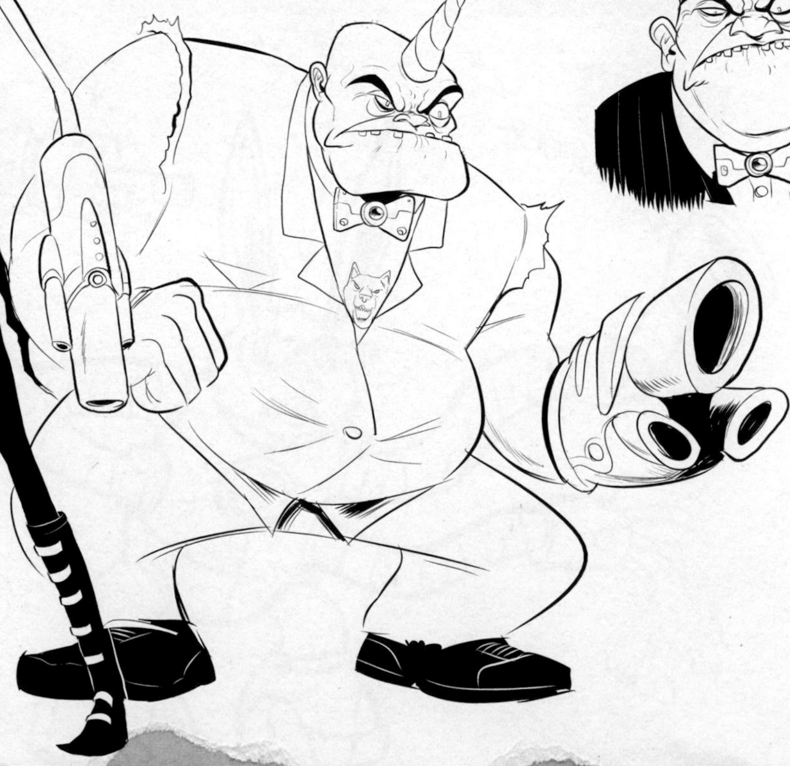

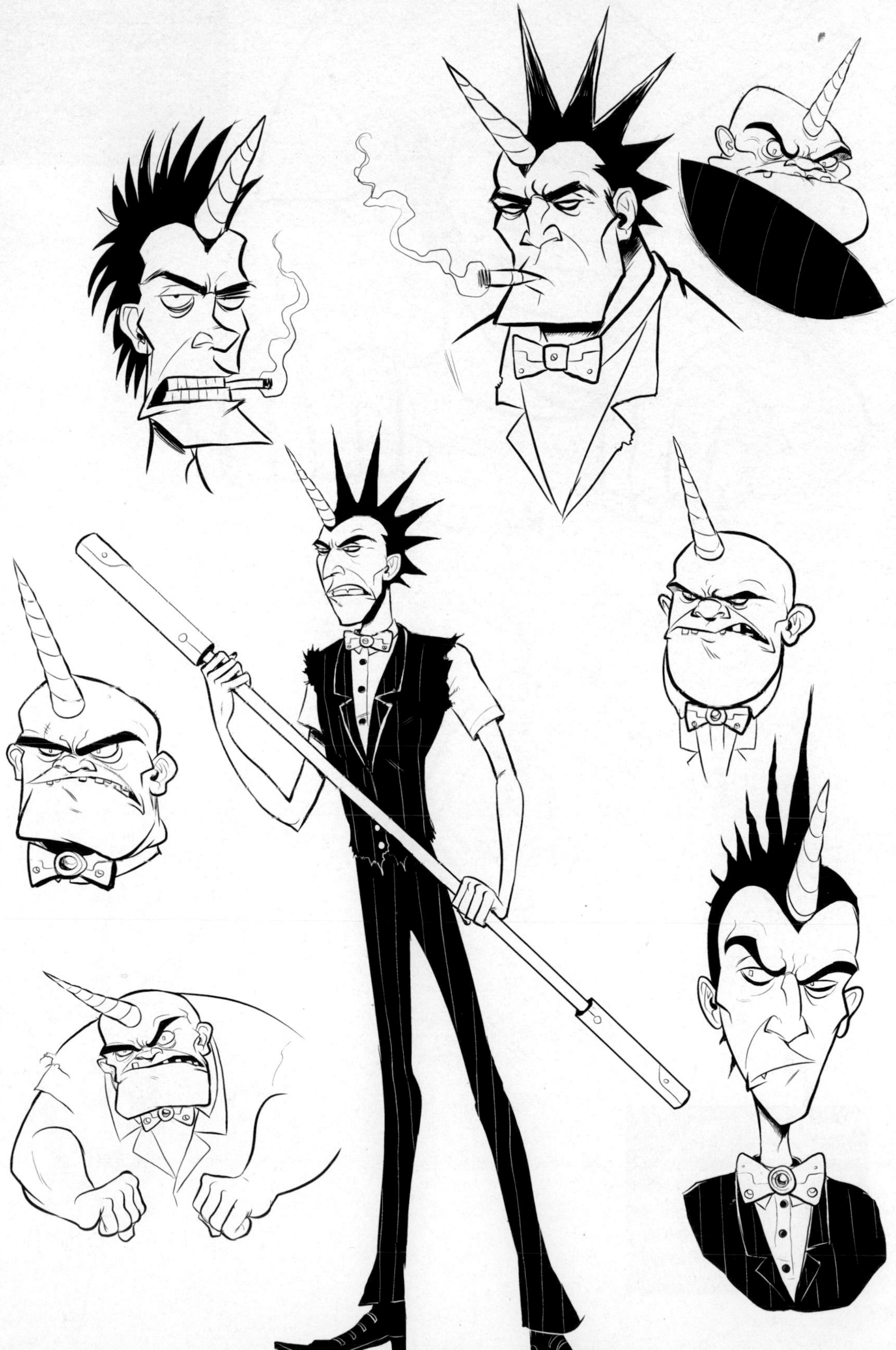

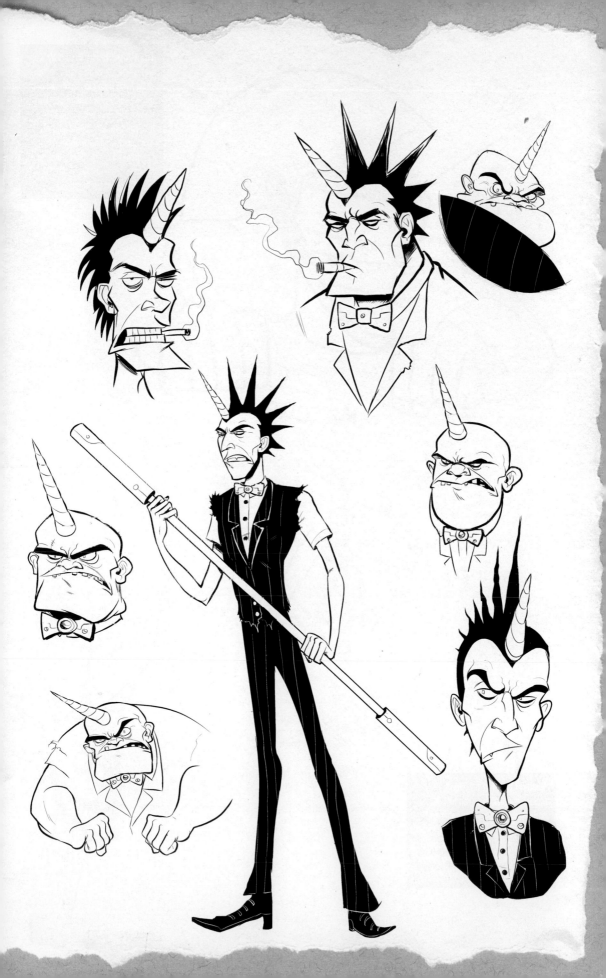

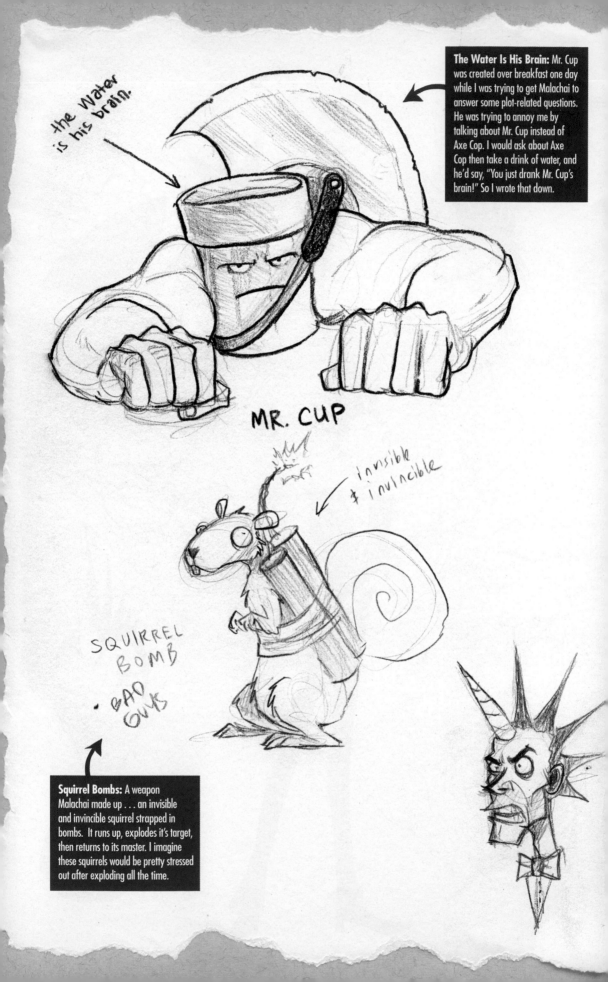

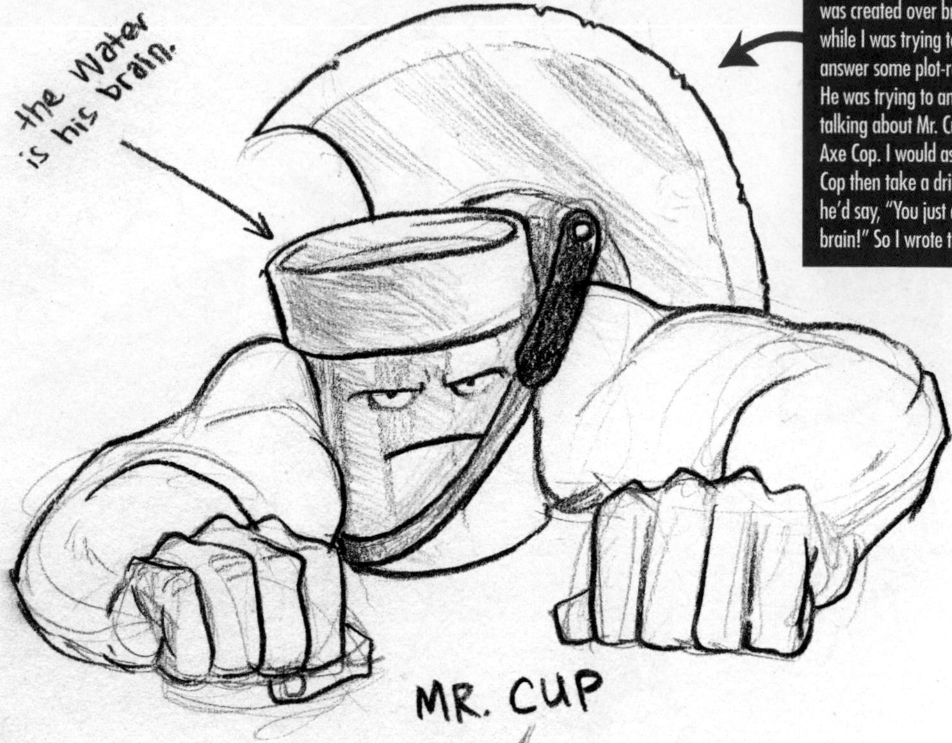
the water is his brain.
MR. CUP

The Water Is His Brain: Mr. Cup was created over breakfast one day while I was trying to get Malachai to answer some plot-related questions. He was trying to annoy me by talking about Mr. Cup instead of Axe Cop. I would ask about Axe Cop then take a drink of water, and he'd say, "You just drank Mr. Cup's brain!" So I wrote that down.

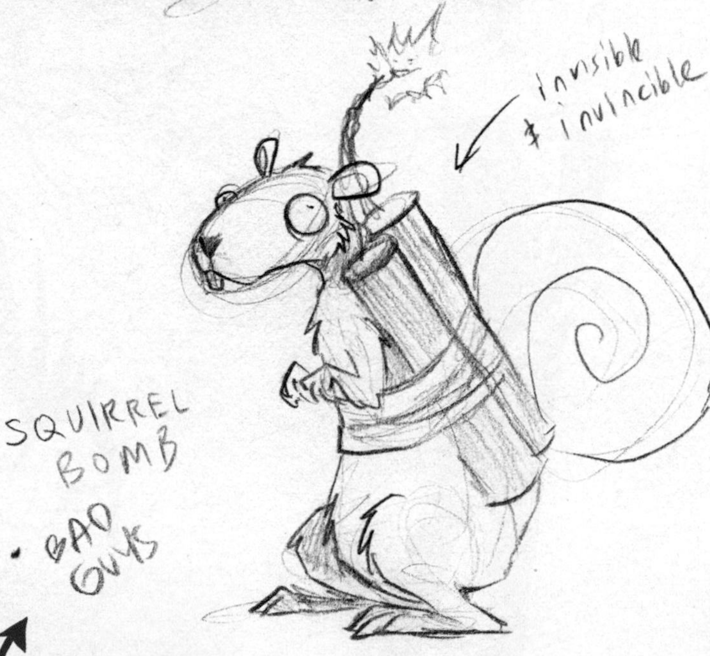
invisible
& invincible
SQUIRREL
BOMB
• BAD
GUYS

Squirrel Bombs: A weapon Malachai made up . . . an invisible and invincible squirrel strapped in bombs. It runs up, explodes it's target, then returns to its master. I imagine these squirrels would be pretty stressed out after exploding all the time.

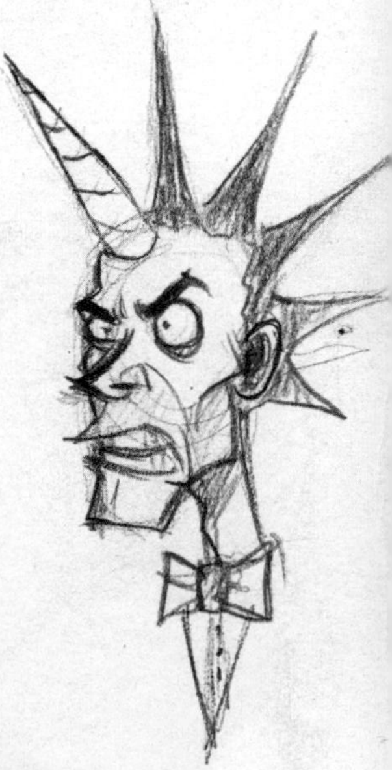

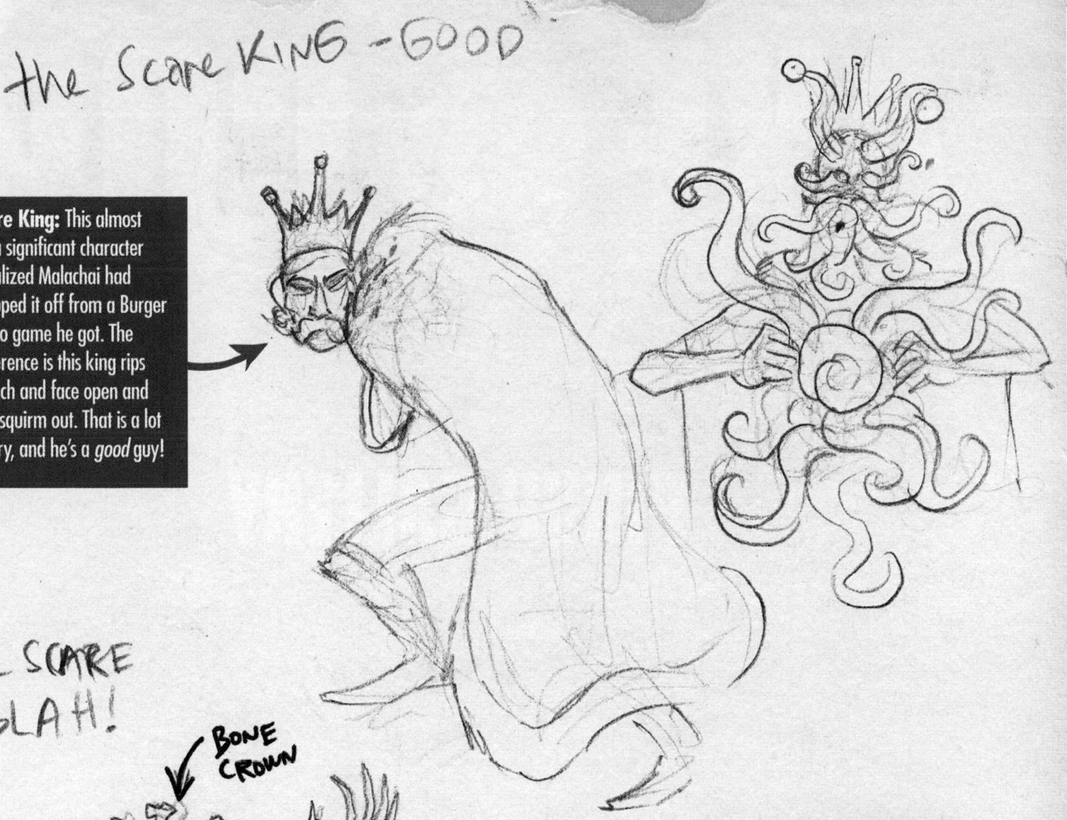
the Scare KING -GOOD

The Scare King: This almost became a significant character until I realized Malachai had totally ripped it off from a Burger King video game he got. The only difference is this king rips his stomach and face open and tentacles squirm out. That is a lot more scary, and he's a *good* guy!

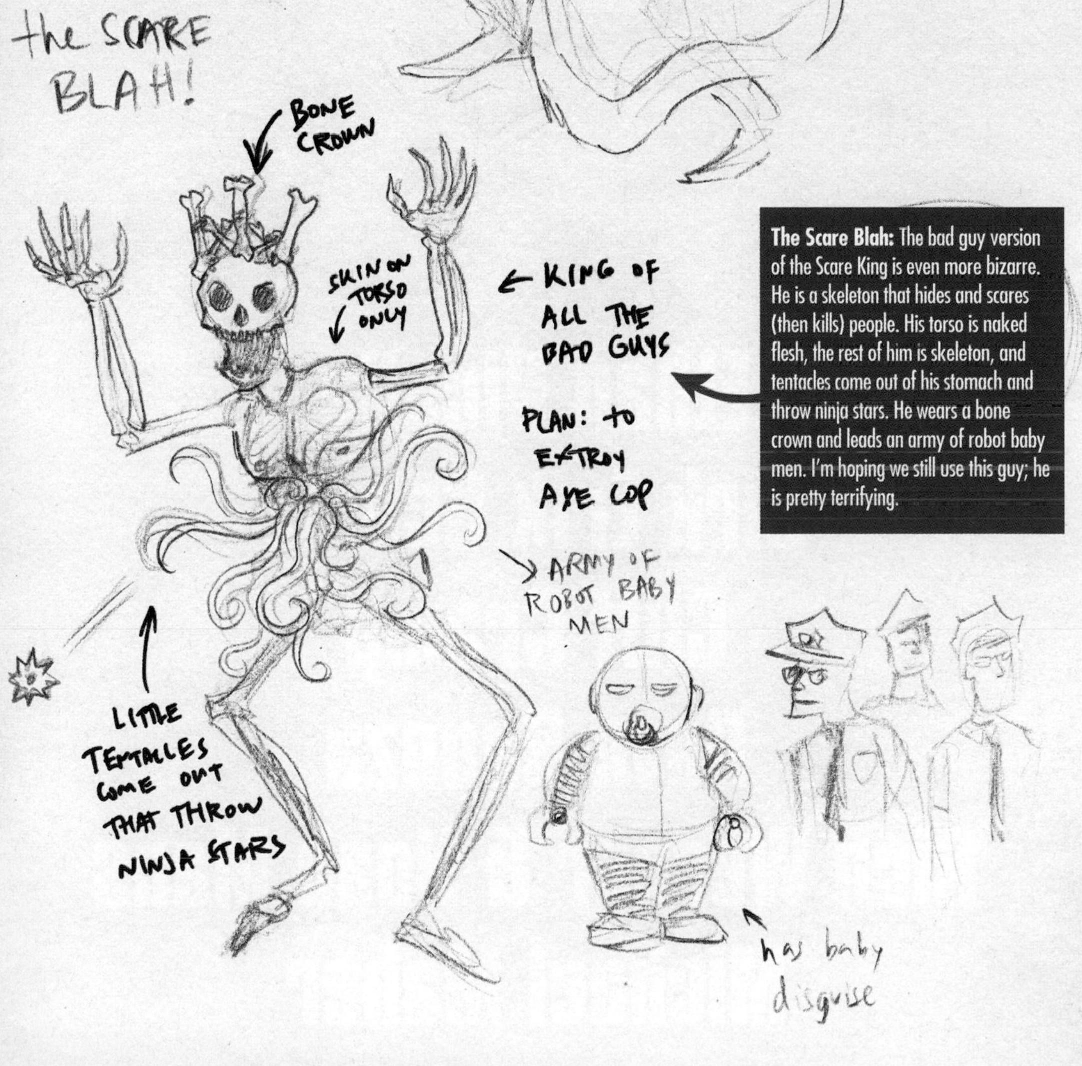
the SCARE BLAH!
BONE CROWN
SKIN ON TORSO ONLY
KING OF ALL THE BAD GUYS
PLAN: to EXTROY AYE COP
ARMY OF ROBOT BABY MEN
LITTLE TENTACLES COME OUT THAT THROW NINJA STARS
has baby disguise

The Scare Blah: The bad guy version of the Scare King is even more bizarre. He is a skeleton that hides and scares (then kills) people. His torso is naked flesh, the rest of him is skeleton, and tentacles come out of his stomach and throw ninja stars. He wears a bone crown and leads an army of robot baby men. I'm hoping we still use this guy; he is pretty terrifying.

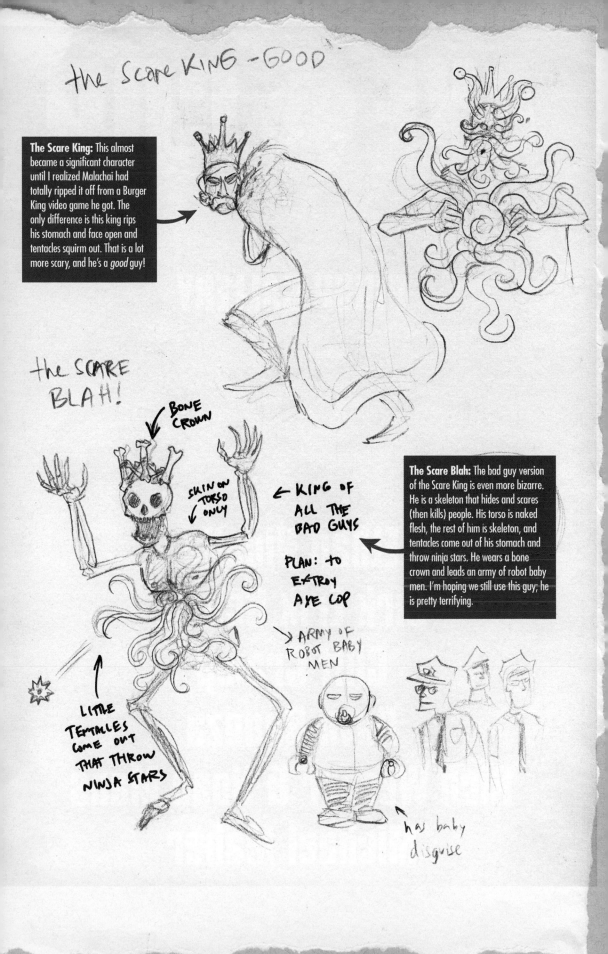

AXE COP

BAD GUY EARTH

PINUP GALLERY

PINUPS BY

Ethan Nicolle
Dirk Erik Schulz
Cliff Cramp
Dave Rapoza
Rich Werner & Noah Maas
Michael Maher

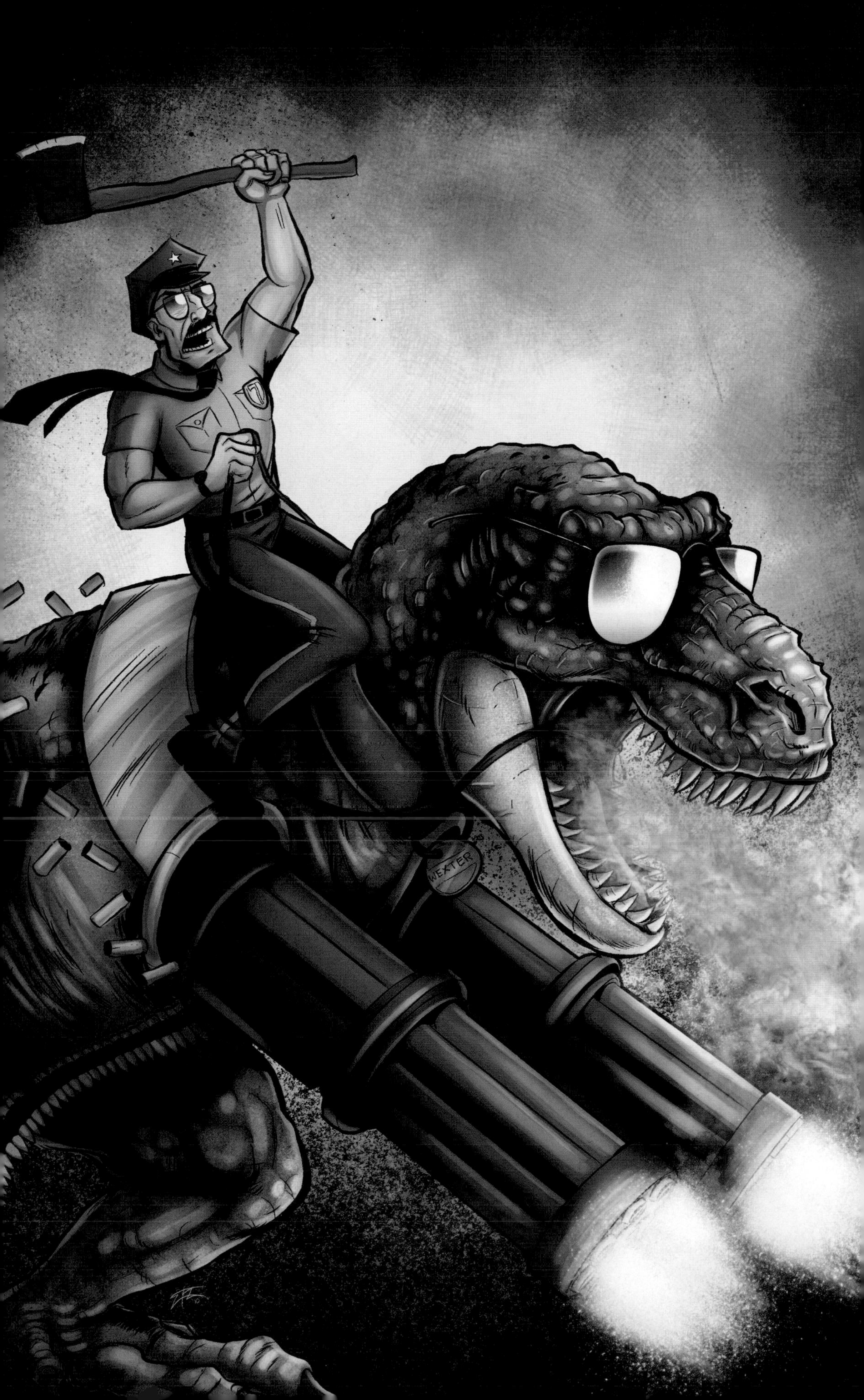
WEXTER

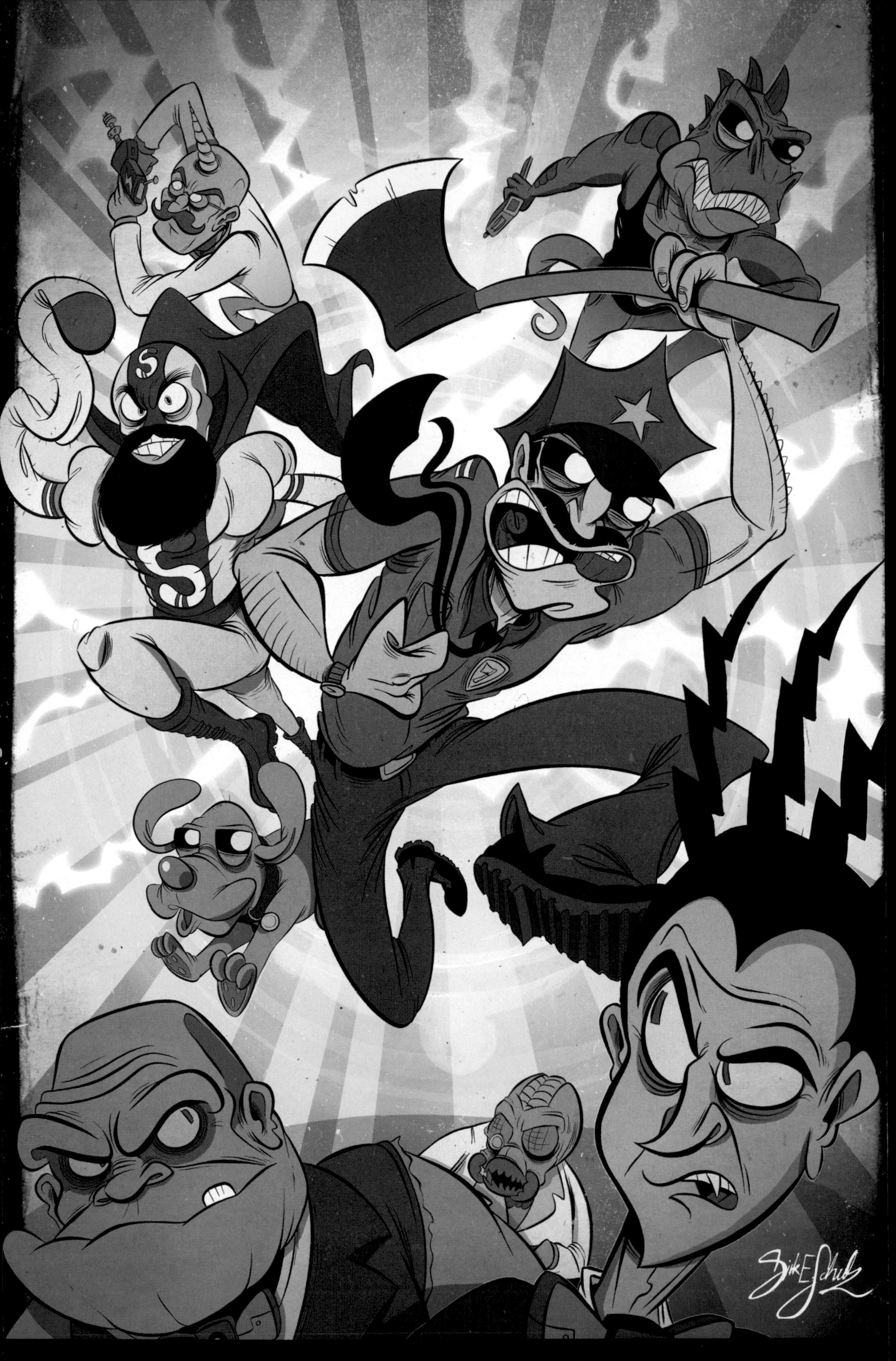

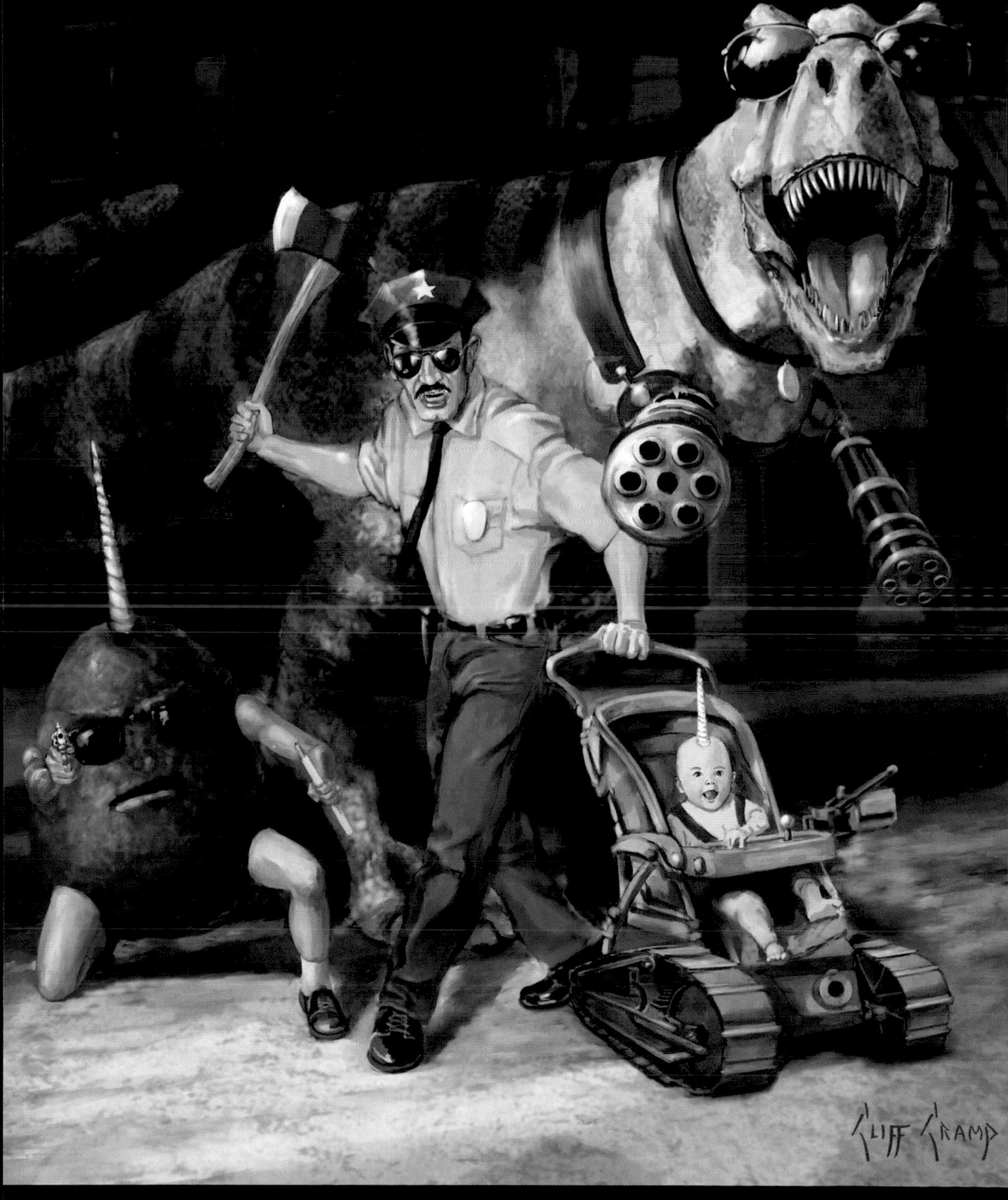

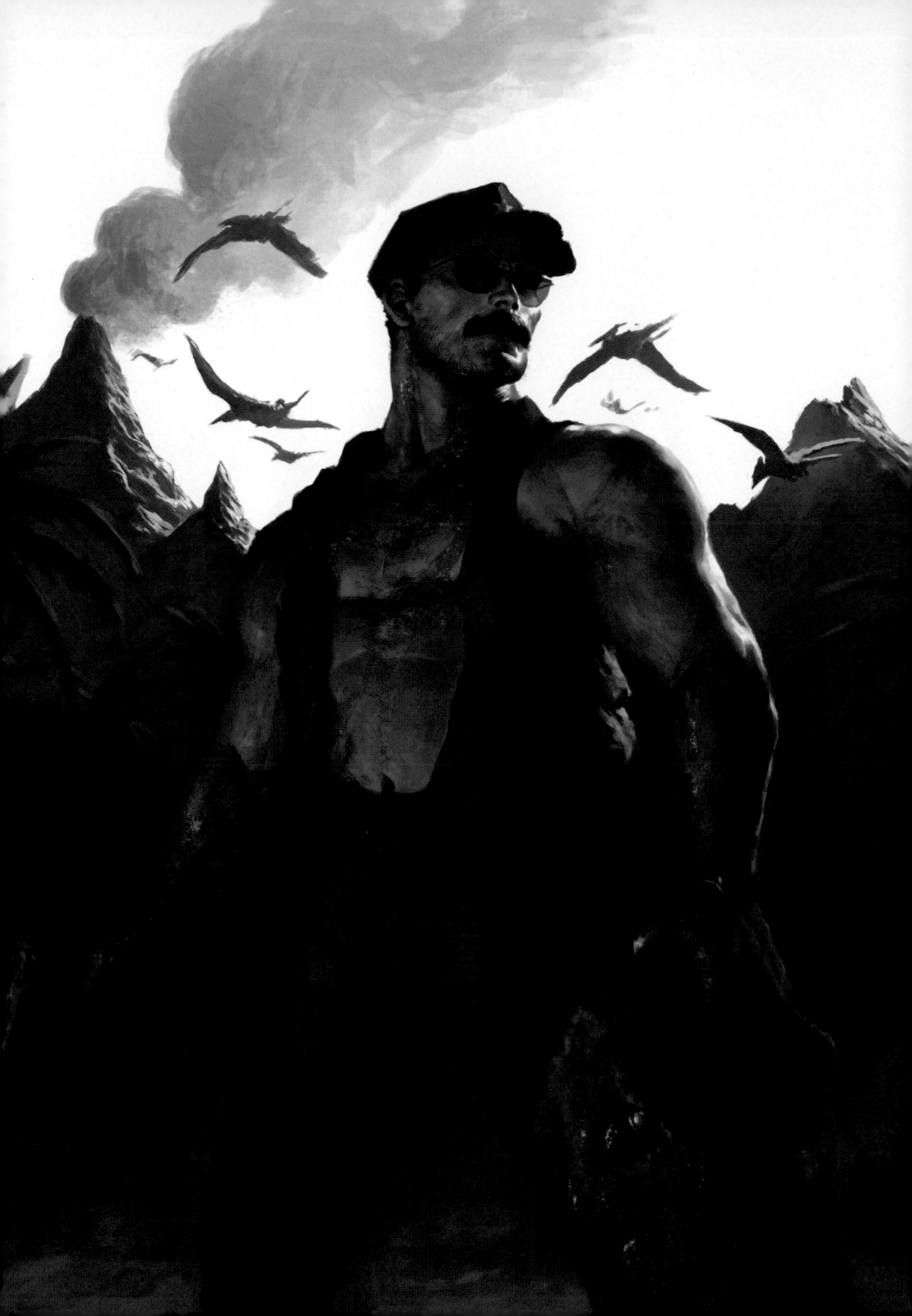

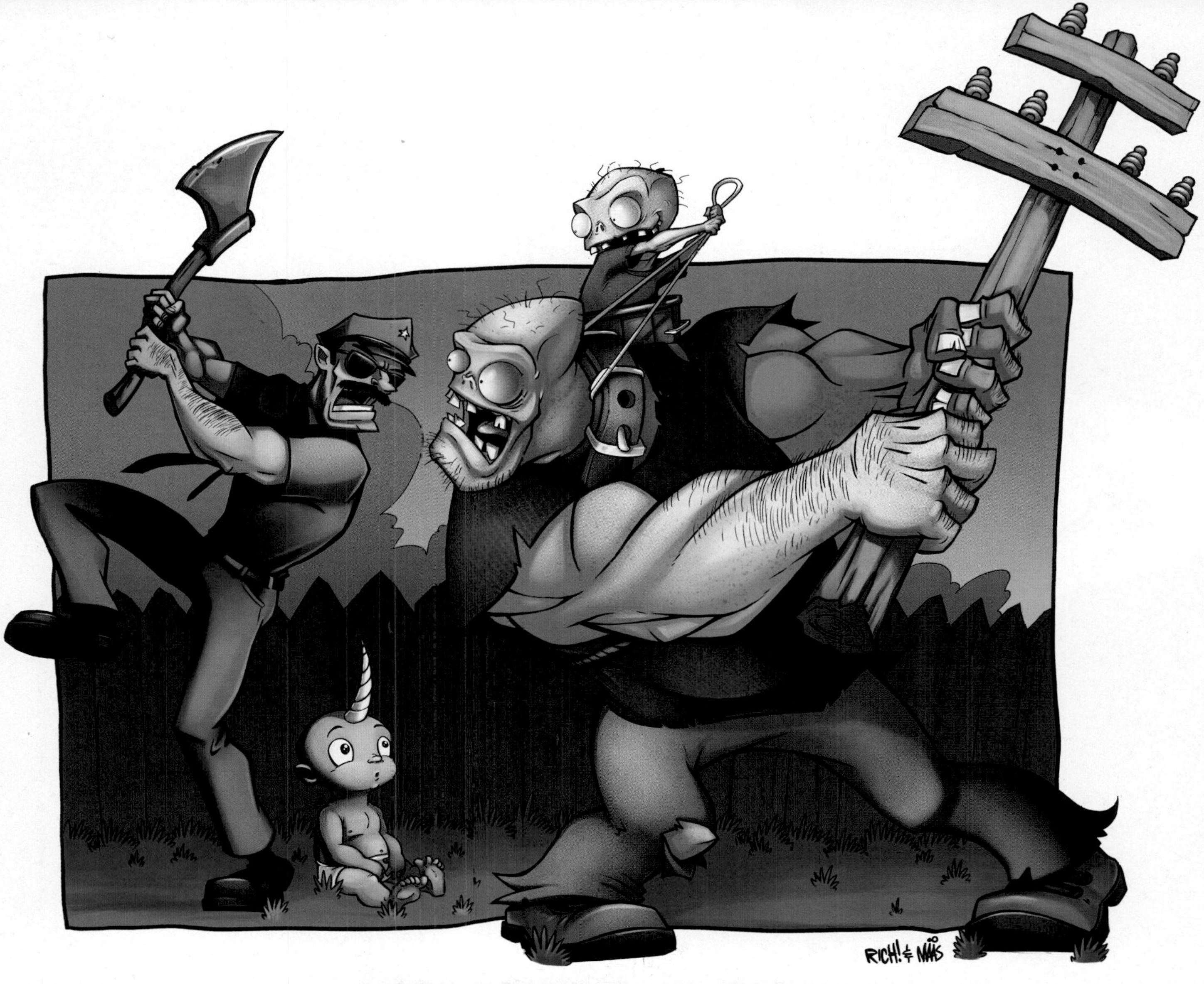
RICH! & MAS

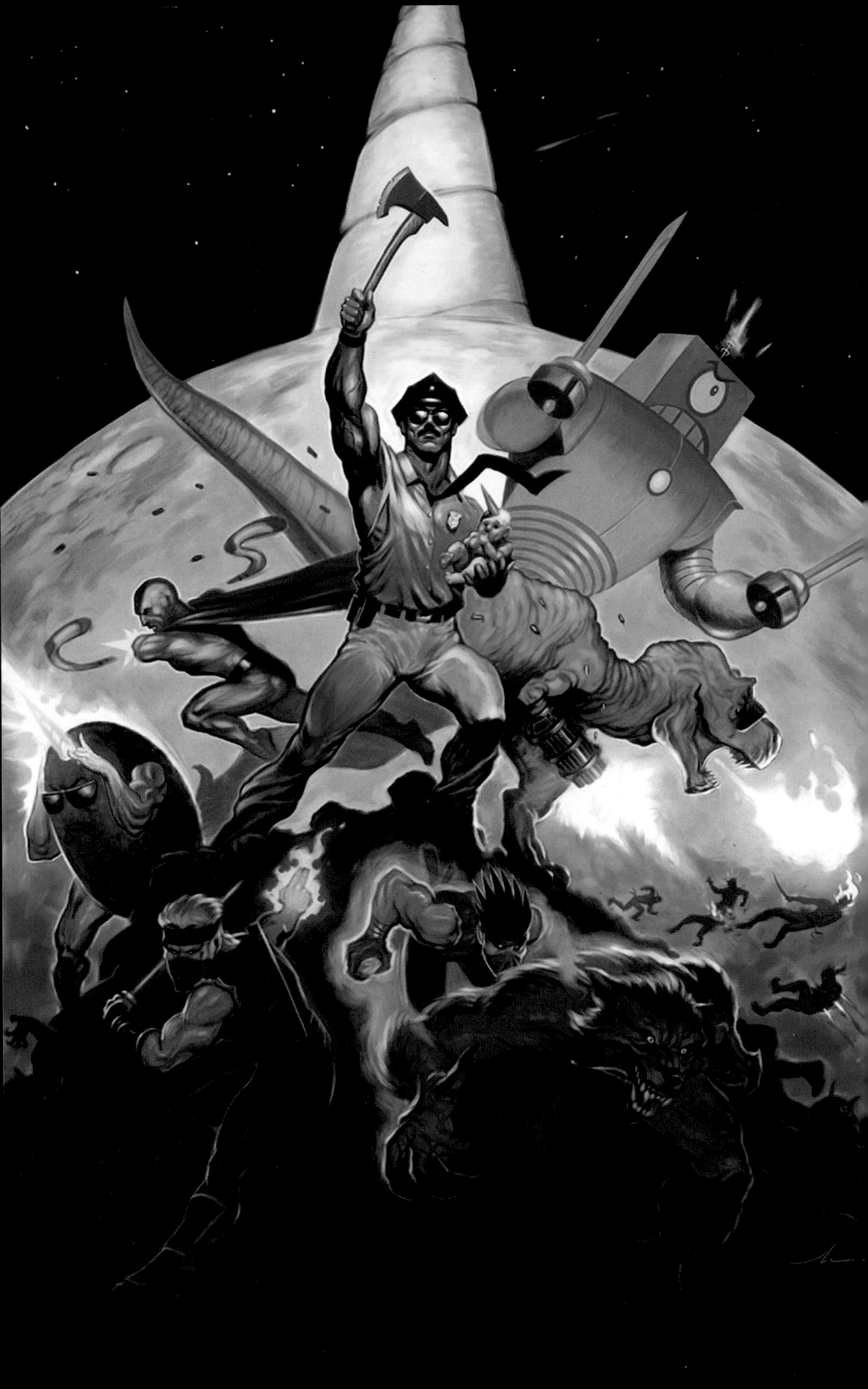

Ethan and Malachai Nicolle are brothers born twenty-four years apart. Ethan was twenty-nine and already an accomplished (and Eisner Award-nominated!) humor artist when he started drawing comic strips based on then-five-year-old Malachai's newly invented character, a hard-nosed cop with a fireman's axe and a talent for dispatching bad guys. After the online debut of their collaborative comic strip *Axe Cop*, the brothers gained a massive media following and began publishing *Axe Cop* adventures in print with Dark Horse Comics. Now ages thirty and seven, respectively, Ethan and Malachai are currently at work on their second *Axe Cop* miniseries for Dark Horse, a second print collection of the online archives of the webcomic, and various games and other projects based on the mustachioed crime fighter and his insane exploits battling the forces of evil. Ethan currently lives in Los Angeles, while Malachai lives in eastern Washington with his family.

Photo by Molly McIsaac

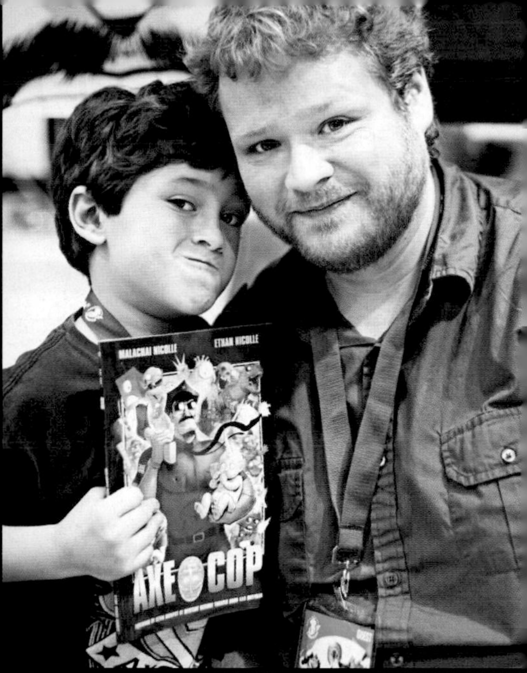
MALACHAI NICOLLE
ETHAN NICOLLE
AXE COP

Dirk Erik Schulz is from Berlin, Germany. With no training in art, he first published art and comics in school and later in local newspapers. In 2002 after earning his high-school diploma he decided to start a career in the field of art and entered art school in 2004. He graduated in 2007 with the best results of his class. His thesis was a sixty-page comic called *The Mossgod,* which he published in a small run. After school he worked in studios including Hahn Film, Laika Films, and Stenarts as a character designer and colorist for animation and big comic projects. Since 2009 he has worked as a freelancer and started a webcomic called *The SWEFS* which is successful on the Net and has received positive reviews.

He began coloring *Axe Cop* in 2010.

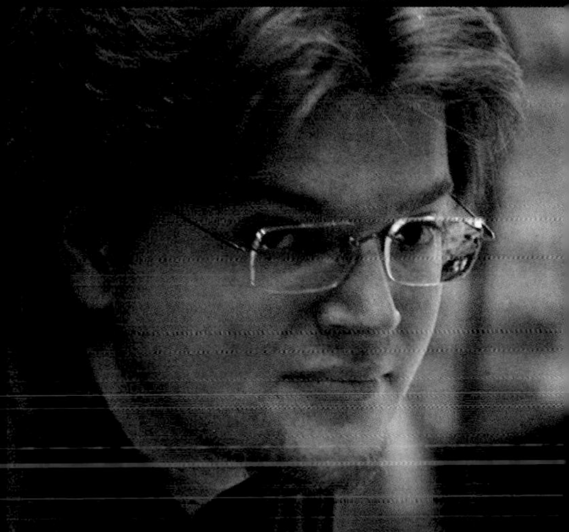

Ethan and Malachai would like to thank . . .

OUR DAD, TOM, AND OUR MOMS, DEELA AND DIANE. OUR SISTERS, MEGAN AND KAITLYN, AND OUR BROTHERS, NOAH AND ISAIAH. DOUG AND ANGIE TENNAPEL, ANTHONY AND AMY MUNOZ, CARYN AND LOU WALTER, PETER MCHUGH, EDDIE GAMARRA, NATE MATTESON, MARK AND ELAN FREEDMAN, SHAWNA GORE, MIKE RICHARDSON, RACHEL EDIDIN AND EVERYONE AT DARK HORSE COMICS, DAVE DEANDREA, BOB SOUER, JAY M. JOHAR, DYLAN MARVIN, TONY LAUGHTON, DONALD LIM, GLEN COONEY, MAURICE LAMARCHE, LEE GORDON, MARCUS IRVINE, COLLEGEHUMOR.COM, STEPDAD, CARL SONDROL, NANCY OEY, DYLAN O'BRIEN, JAMES KENNISON, DAVE RAPOZA, KAILEY FRIZZELL, CHRISTOPHER BRAHM, JOHN STEINKLAUBER, KEVIN MURPHY, BILL CORBETT, MIKE NELSON, JOSH GEMMA AND EVERYONE ELSE AT RIFF TRAX, SEAN MCGOWAN, ERIC BRANSCUM, KATHERINE GARNER, JEFFREY ROWLAND AND EVERYONE AT TOPATOCO, ERIC PETERSON AND EPIC DIGITAL MEDIA, CHRIS HASTINGS, DAN VADO AND EVERYONE AT SLG, DOUG JONES, RYAN AGADONI, JOSH KENFIELD, CLIFF CRAMP, WILL CRAWFORD, PAUL AND STORM, GRAHAM LINEHAN, PETER SERAFINOWICZ, KIM HOLCOMB, JENNY NAPIER, STEVE JACKSON, BRIDGE CITY COMICS, MELTDOWN COMICS, EMERALD CITY COMICON, STUMPTOWN COMICS FEST, CALGARY EXPO, COMIC-CON INTERNATIONAL, ALL OUR GUEST-EPISODE CONTRIBUTORS, EVERYONE IN THE FORUM, ON FACEBOOK, AND ON TWITTER, AND PRETTY MUCH EVERYONE WHO READS *AXE COP*!

AXE COP™

MALACHAI NICOLLE
ETHAN NICOLLE
AXE COP
FOREWORD BY KEVIN MURPHY OF MYSTERY SCIENCE THEATER 3000 AND RIFFTRAX

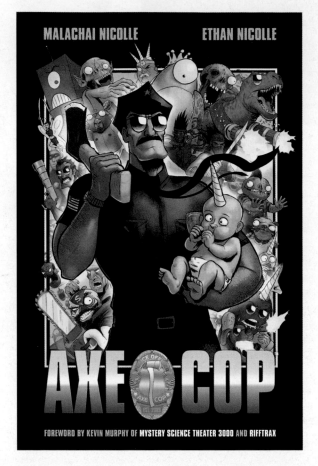

Bad guys, beware! Evil aliens, run for your lives! Axe Cop is here, and he's going to chop your head off! We live in a strange world, and our strange problems call for strange heroes.

Axe Cop Volume 1 collects the entire original run of the hit webcomic that has captured the world's attention with its insanely imaginative adventures, including his insightful advice column, Ask Axe Cop!

ISBN 978-1-59582-681-7 | $14.99

DARK HORSE BOOKS
DarkHorse.com

AVAILABLE AT YOUR LOCAL COMICS SHOP OR BOOKSTORE

To find a comics shop in your area, call 1-888-266-4226. For more information or to order direct, visit DarkHorse.com or call 1-800-862-0052 • Mon.–Fri. 9 a.m. to 5 p.m. Pacific Time. Prices and availability subject to change without notice.